Our Lovely Virginia Lady and Our Handsome Vermont Cavalier Love Story

Book Three: Alexandria, Sunshine Hills, Carnifex Ferry, Ball's Bluff, and Elk Garden, Virginia

Davidé Mario Romano and Pamela Bella

Permission granted to the authors from the Ratcliffe Foundation to use the photograph of the Governor's Mansion on the front cover located at 1951 Elk Garden Road in Lebanon, Virginia, the use of the photo of the Ellenbrook Mansion inside Book Three as the residence of the Davis Family, and the use of the photo of the General Robert E. Lee Portrait in our story.

Special credits for artistic services and cover designs by Sammy's Sign Shop.

Photographic services by Davidé Mario Romano. Illustrator and photographic assistance by Tomazin Scanning Services and Howling Computer Services.

ISBN: 978-1-959700-16-6
Hoot Books Publishing

Victoria Fletcher
hootbookspublishing.biz
vfletcher56@gmail.com

Description

An adventurous, casual, fictional, military, multi-lingual, personal, and realistic account of a very romantic couple who grow up and live in Antebellum America. In 1861, our Army Officers see one another in a distance and know in their hearts that their dreams are coming true. Consequently, Captain Pamela Mae Brewer and Captain Mario LaGrande are predestined to fall passionately in love during the early battles of the United States Civil War. In Book Three of our Trilogy, the very intense amorous and physical desire for each other continues and is described in detail from July through December of the year 1861. Pamela Mae and Mario experience independently and together the bellicose, exciting, and tumultuous events of the United States Civil War in Alexandria, Sunshine Hills, Carnifex Ferry, Ball's Bluff, and finally in Elk Garden, Virginia.

Dedication

Pamela Bella wants to personally dedicate Book Three to "My Family of Lovely Virginia Ladies" to include my mother Lois Ann Booth and Maternal Grandmothers, Virginia Viola Booth, Anna Maria Young, Elizabeth Garrett, Elizabeth Hendricks, and Sarah (Van Hook) Hendricks. In addition, this historical novel is dedicated to Thomas Aaron Hendricks, my 5th Great Grandfather Patriot, who is the basis of my Daughters of the American Revolution (DAR) ancestry. Furthermore, Pamela Bella wishes to dedicate this book to her father, Leo Franklin Young, a World War II U.S. Army Veteran, "who inspired me to have a love for reading, especially the Holy Bible. Amen."

Also, the authors want to dedicate our books to all of our physical and spiritual families of Virginia and Vermont. The authors want to uniquely honor their memory emotionally and historically. We intend to give thanks to all of the people of the United States: military and civilian; slave and free; black and white; immigrants; indentured servants; native born; those who fought, worked, and sacrificed everything to include their health, existence, and livelihood during the "War Between the States."

Davidé Mario Romano and Pamela Bella

Furthermore, the authors wish to dedicate this "Romantic Military Novel" to all of our fellow authors who thoroughly researched the events and personalities of the "Antebellum Period and United States Civil War" while emphasizing the historiography aspects in their published works.

Acknowledgments

The authors, Davidé Mario Romano and Pamela Bella, wish to acknowledge the influence and inspiration of all of our family members who have served in the American Colonial Militia, United States Armed Forces, Confederate States of America, and the Italian Military Services for their dedication and devotion to their countries, fellow service members, and their friends and neighbors. We are very blessed to have received advice, communications, inspiration, support, and recommendations from our dear fellow authors: Sam Varney (Wife-Martha) and Helen Owens in the completion of our books.

In addition, the writers are very grateful to Victoria Fletcher and Hoot Books Publishing for her extensive cover, editing, proofreading, and publication services.

Furthermore, we wish to especially acknowledge the contributions of Wikipedia and the American Battlefield Trust. These excellent academic and historical organizations have provided the authors with very pertinent and valuable military, mapping, photographic information, and images that were necessary to complete Book Three and our entire Trilogy. Also, we acknowledge the Mount Vernon Ladies

Association for the use of their photo in Book Three.

Finally, the authors express appreciation to artist Larry Bragg, *in Memoriam,* for his friendship, the use of his paintings, and his teachings in the completion of our trilogy of books.

Book Two Summary

Book Two of four tells chronologically the exhilarating love story of "Our Handsome Vermont Cavalier," Captain Mario Patrizio LaGrande, from January through July 1861, in the states of Vermont, New York, Pennsylvania, Maryland and Virginia.

In addition, Book Two tells the thrilling narrative of "Our Lovely Virginia Lady," Captain Pamela Mae Brewer, from May through July 1861, in the Commonwealth of Virginia.

Pamela Mae and Mario's love-filled and prayerful dreams begin to come to fruition when they see one another for the first time during the Battle of Philippi, Virginia (now West Virginia), on June 3rd, 1861.

One month later, during the Battle of Manassas/Bull Run Creek, on July 21st, 1861, our leading lady and gentleman finally meet and subsequently fall completely and passionately in love. The reader will greatly enjoy the many amorous scenes at the home of Pamela Mae, called the "Sunshine Hills" plantation and later in Alexandria, Virginia.

Book Two culminates with the daring rescue of Captain Brewer's father, Confederate Lieutenant Colonel John Brewer, from a temporary prison in Arlington, Virginia. The authors, Davidé Mario Romano and Pamela Bella, have spent many years of academic and personal research of the "Antebellum and Civil War" period. Their work will provide the reader with a very compelling, detailed, military, and riveting literary romantic experience.

Contents

Our Lovely Virginia Lady and Our Handsome Vermont Cavalier Love Story Book 3

Chapter 1
Pamela Mae and Gloria Faye after Rescue
Alexandria, Virginia, July 26th, 1861

"Our Lovely Virginia Lady" and Virginia Army Captain, Pamela Mae Brewer, breathes a grateful sigh of relief and thankfulness. Her bold movement of the wagon into the road causes the "Union Army" pursuers to stop. She looks upwards, with her very luminous brown eyes, to the dark rainy skies. Quietly and prayerfully, she says, "I praise You Lord of Heaven, that we were able to rescue Papa (Confederate Lieutenant Colonel John Brewer) and he has a head start in his volatile escape and trip back home. You freed him from his 'Yankee Captors,' from the 'Custis-Lee Arlington House Estate,' and may he arrive safely back to our 'Sunshine Hills' plantation home, near Manassas, Virginia. Hopefully, by your mercy, Papa will be with his wife and my mother Sarah Anne. Amen!"

Our very brave and clever Pamela Mae decides to take her bonnet off, which reveals her long luxurious pitch black hair. This of course, gives her the most attractive look, as a "Provost Marshal Sergeant," gets off his horse. He initially appears to be irate and ready to admonish the two women in the wagon, who are occupying the middle of the muddy "Potomac River Road" in Alexandria, Virginia.

Gloria Faye Brewer is a "Freedwoman" and former servant of the Brewer family. She is also a close childhood friend and is very apprehensive, nervous, and firmly holds onto Pamela Mae's arm.

Gloria Faye says softly to her former mistress, "I do not have total knowledge or understanding of what will happen next, so Lord have mercy on us, and help me sister. Amen!" Our courageous Captain Brewer answers back in Virginia style, "Gloria Faye, the 'Good Lord' willing, and the creeks don't rise, we will be back and safe with 'Our Vermont Officers,' by midnight!"

Pamela Mae starts to feel less tense and vulnerable when she looks at the entire group of blue-coated soldiers and recognizes the unmistakable face and stature of someone familiar who is still on his horse. She thinks to herself, *Oh my goodness, by the grace of God, it appears that the ranking Officer-in-charge is Captain Workman!*

Fortunately, Pamela Mae was correct, as she remembers his name and promptly blurts out in an Irish complimentary fashion saying, "May the

Saints be praised, if it isn't the handsome Captain Horace Workman from the 'Provost Marshal's Office' to come to our assistance." Well, the very attractive face, hair, and charming voice of Pamela Mae completely disarms the hard-charging Captain Workman. He recognizes Pamela Mae and Gloria Faye from a couple of days ago and says seriously, "Mrs. LaGrande, you and your companion should not be out this late at night. There is an escaped Confederate Officer on the run. Listen, I will have my good Sergeant Snyder escort you two women to the Vermont (Green Mountain) Brigade area to be with your husbands."

Pamela Mae smiles and thinks, *Even-though I am not married to my man, Captain Mario LaGrande, and neither is Gloria Faye married to her man, Captain Maurice Flambeau, Captain Workman and other Union personnel believe that we are married young ladies. Therefore, it is vital for us to maintain this ruse in order to stay with "Our Vermont Officers." God have mercy on us!*

The rest of the "Federal Troops" depart in their inquiry and pursuit of the escaped Virginia Lieutenant Colonel John Brewer. Sergeant Luke Snyder, who knows this area extremely well, greets the young women nicely.

Sergeant Snyder states sincerely, "Ladies, follow me to the 'Vermont Camp,' and I will get you out of the rain to a safe and warm location. I am sure your husbands are anxious for your return." Sergeant Luke Snyder fondly remembers *that the two officers of the Saint Albans' Mountaineer Regiment, Captain Mario LaGrande and Captain Maurice Flambeau, are so very lucky enough to be with the adorable Pamela Mae and the beautiful Gloria Faye.*

Pamela Mae is currently feeling much better as she contemplates her unsettled situation and fondly thinks of her very "Handsome Vermont Cavalier" who has Italian and French ancestry. *I am so excited and long to be in his warm embrace and receive the welcoming Italian flavored kisses of Mio Mario Bello (My Handsome Mario).*

It is now close to 11:00 p.m. on that Friday, July 26th, 1861, with a single candle burning in a sturdy tent. Captain Mario LaGrande of the Saint Albans' Mountaineer Regiment is still wearing his uniform and is hoping and praying for a safe and sound return of his Pamela Mae Brewer, who he calls Pamela Bella, his Italian term of endearment, meaning Pretty Pamela. The light steady rain continues to fall on his tent and the beat of the drops can be heard softly on the heavy canvas material above. Captain LaGrande is fluent in Italian, English, and French as he supplicates to the "Master of Creation" praying in all three languages, saying, *"Nostro Signore Gesu' e la Benedetta Madre Maria* (Our Lord Jesus and the Blessed Mother Mary), I humbly ask that you protect my Pamela Mae while I promise to You, by Your grace, that we will be married by the end of this calendar year. *Prego questo nel nome del Padre, del Figlio, e lo Spirito Santo, Cosi sia* (I pray this in the name of the Father, of the Son, and the Holy Ghost. Amen). *De plus, Mon Dieu* (In addition, My God), bless and safeguard her friend Gloria Faye.

Within fifteen minutes, Mario's prayers were answered as he could hear the very sweet dulcet voice of his Pamela Bella (Pretty Pamela) who is trilingual say in German, Spanish, and English, *"Mein Traummann wird wahr* (My Dream man come true), *Donde estas mi amor?* (Where are you my love?) and Handsome Mario, come quickly, I have so much to tell you."

Well, Captain LaGrande responded rapidly as he emerged from his tent and saw his "Adorable Virginia Woman" wearing men's clothing with her long-wet hair. He was obviously elated to see his gorgeous girl. Mario ran to her in the rain, while admiring the incredible elegance of her beautiful face. He grabbed her very strongly and held on tight as they both cried "tears of joy." They then French kissed for a long time, until Pamela Mae said, "Sweetheart, let's go inside the tent so I can take these rain-soaked clothes off and dry my hair."

Captain Mario LaGrande happened to be very prepared for the arrival of his most fetching and bountiful young lady as he helped take off her soaked clothing and dried her off with two large cotton bath towels. Pamela Mae responded affectionately saying in Spanish and English, "*Muchas gracias mi amor maravillosa* (Thank you so much my wonderful love). Gloria Faye and I were very successful in the rescue of Papa, and by the 'Grace of God,' and his guardian angels, I pray that he makes it back to our 'Sunshine Hills' home by tomorrow. "

Pamela Mae continued to describe the escape of her father, Lieutenant Colonel John Brewer, who was the Executive Officer of the 1st Manassas (Virginia) Infantry Regiment. He had been a prisoner since "The Battle of Manassas/ Bull Run Creek" and was held captive by the "Federals" in the rear of the "Arlington House" property. Captain LaGrande was amazed at the details of the operation and the bravery of Pamela Mae and Gloria Faye. He is also glad that his good friend and fellow officer, Captain

Maurice Flambeau, will be in the tent next door, with Gloria Faye to keep him warm.

However, Mario's manly attributes and feelings were intensified as he looked at the dry naked superb form of his "heart's desire" and told her in French and English, "*Magnifique Pamela Belle, ma charmante jeune demoiselle* (Magnificent Pretty Pamela, my lovely young miss) come lay down with me on this soft comforter, and let's celebrate and make love until we fall asleep." Both of our lead characters had the most amatory expressions on their faces and exchanged suggestive winks as they prepared for another exciting session of ardent love-making.

Pamela Mae was feeling very happy, giddy, and lays down on her appealing and contoured back and looks up to her sensual man and says lovingly and poetically, "Mario Bello (Handsome Mario), come to me Darling and let me kiss your 'Luscious Lips,' over and over again, My Gallant Cavalier Man!"

Mario considered Pamela Mae to be the most alluring woman in the world as he holds her close, and humorously responds, "Yes, let me kiss your ruby red delectable lips, too."

It is now after midnight and, "Our Lovely Virginia Lady and Our Handsome Vermont Cavalier" began to physically engage romantically and vigorously for the next hour. Pamela Mae soon gasped for air, sighed affectionately, and told Mario in German and in English, "*Liebling, du bist die Freude Meines Herzens* (Darling man, you are my hearts' delight) and I dream about our precious love, day and night!" Mario responded, "Sweetheart, you are the woman I was looking for." Pamela Mae answered accordingly, "Yes, Honey, and you are the man that I found!"

Pamela Mae and Mario continued to embrace, kiss, and mate for the next thirty minutes "Missionary Style" with our "Virginia Lady" in the supine position as she looked up adoringly to her "Italian Lover." Our "Vermont Officer" is in the dominant, prone position and thinks in English and Italian in a very confident manner, *I am the luckiest man in the universe, to have such a fantastic emotional and physical relationship with my most beautiful and captivating young, Mia Cara Pamela Bella (My Dear Pretty Pamela).* Mario then said in Italian to his irresistible Pamela Mae, "*Bambina, baciami di più con le tue dolci labbra rosse* (Baby, kiss me more with your sweet red lips)!"

Captain LaGrande, being a military man by nature, also thinks amusingly and literally. "This is the very best and most satisfying method to "Storm the Breastworks," as he continues to be intimate with his "Voluptuous Pamela Mae." Mario is overwhelmed with pleasure as he maintains his rapid rhythmic activities upon his seductive woman and compliments her in his mother's native language saying, *"Mia Cara Signorinella, tu sei piu favolosa, fantastica, e splendida raggio di sole, di tutte le donne del mondo* (My dear little Miss, you are the most gorgeous, fantastic, and splendid ray of sunshine of all the ladies in the world)!"

Our very acrobatic, athletic, and strong Captain Brewer was deriving an extra amount of pleasure with her lover above, when she decided to "turn the tables,' and held on firmly, with both hands to Captain LaGrande's back and performed a superb roll-over movement. Pamela Mae was in a naughty and mischievous mood, and comically stated "I am, after all, a Virginia Cavalier, riding my own personal 'Italian Stallion,' and I Love Him." After more loving exercises, Pamela Mae reverts back to her "Southern Heritage" and says, "I do declare Mario, you are 100%, all-man, and I love your muscular strength, Oh my goodness, gracious."

Mario, of course, smiled broadly and was amazingly pleased with Pamela Mae's courageous, carnal, daring, and verbal response and replied to her in English and in French, "Darling, you are all of my desires, dreams, fantasies, and wishes come true, *et merci beaucoup ma merveilleuse Mademoiselle* (and thank you very much my marvelous young Lady)! "

Even though, yesterday had been a long and challenging day, Pamela Mae was in such a celebratory and jovial mood after midnight. Her father, John Brewer was traveling towards his Prince William County Virginia Home, and she is fully connected to the "Man of Her Dreams."

In her uniquely charming "Southern Belle" accent and voice, Pamela Mae exclaimed poetically to Mario, "Honey, you drive me wild with desire, and my soul is on fire." Indeed, Mario and Pamela Mae had been generating a tremendous amount of impassioned heat within one another.

Shortly thereafter, "Our Romantic Vermont Cavalier" sweetly said to his "Irresistible Virginia Lady" in a soft endearing Italian way, "*Buona notte e* buon riposo, mia Pamela Bella (Good night and good rest, my Pretty Pamela)." She answered in a very sleepy and tender way, "Good night and sweet dreams, Mario my love."

The amorous couple eventually fell fast asleep in a very affectionate and comforting embrace. Pamela Mae did have a wonderful loving dream that night in which she remembered saying to her extremely handsome Vermont Cavalier, "Mario, Your Pamela Bella (Pretty Pamela) adores, loves, and desires you, so much, always and forevermore!" It continued to rain and finally stopped before sunrise on that Saturday, July 27th, 1861, in the camp of the Saint Albans' Mountaineer Regiment.

At exactly 5:00 a.m., the Vermont (Green Mountain) Brigade Bugler sounded the "Morning Reveille" song. Consequently, Captain Mario LaGrande and Captain Maurice Flambeau had to awaken and depart from their devoted "Virginia Young Ladies," Pamela Mae and Gloria Faye, respectively.

By 5:30 a.m., the Saint Albans' Mountaineer Regiment was in a muster formation and prepared for the morning inspection by the Commanding Officer, Colonel Donald Simpson and his subordinate officers. Lieutenant Colonel (LTC) Jonathan Wilson, the Executive Officer of the regiment looked intently towards his

Company Commanders. His thoughts went back to Vermont when he was an instructor at the Military Academy, *I have very vivid memories of Cadets LaGrande and Flambeau and now take great pride in seeing them lead A Company and B Company, respectively!*

Meanwhile, back in Captain LaGrande's canvas tent, Pamela Mae is tidying things up in Mario's quarters and is very hungry and in dire need of some strong tasty coffee. She remembers her "Italian-American Vermont Officer's" phrase recited before drinking coffee together, "*Che buon caffè, a la salute, a mia Pamela Bella e Mario, e viva Italia* (What good coffee, to the health, to my Pretty Pamela and Mario, and long live Italy)!"

Pamela Mae is now dressed in a tight casual beige dress, with her full-length luxurious hair hanging down over her back and shoulders. As they say down South, "She is looking pretty as a peach." Her bright brown eyes are glowing with joy, as she approached Captain Flambeau's tent. She calls out asking, "Gloria Faye are you ready to go to the mess tent and get some vittles and drink?" She waited for a moment and faithfully contemplated the situation at hand, *There are sure to be many possibilities and uncertainties ahead and I need to be reasonable in my actions.*

However, I do believe that "Our Good Lord" in heaven is watching over me, my family, friends, and my Dearest Mario LaGrande. Amen!

Moments later, Gloria Faye emerges from the dew and rain covered tent, looking very nice in a matching tight casual beige dress. She looks at her former mistress and friend and says in an amusing "Irish and Southern Manner" in a clear voice, "Top of the morning to you sister, and land sakes alive, I'm hungry and let's skedaddle to where the food and coffee are being served!"

Pamela Mae gives Gloria Faye a big hug and asks, "Girl, are you ready for another one of our adventures? Let's endear ourselves to the cooks and servers right away." Gloria Faye was always amazed in the techniques used by Pamela Mae to get her way into and out of many different difficulties and situations.

Our Pamela Mae sizes up all of the negro and white field kitchen personnel and evaluates the preparation of the aromatic food and the serving of hot coffee during breakfast. She approached one of the laborers and inquires, "Brother, where is the head cook and what is his name? Do you need any assistance?" The young man pointed to the heavier, older man and replied, "Ma'am his name is Willie Glass, and he could sure use some help this morning."

Well, that was just the opening Pamela Mae needed when she got close by Mister Glass. Gloria Faye happened to be standing to her right. Then, in a very respectful manner, Pamela Mae interjected, "Excuse me, Sir, and good morning, my friend and I are hungry and in need of coffee and are willing to help cook, prepare, and serve breakfast to 'Our Union Soldiers' if that would be alright with You." Pamela Mae introduced herself as a Virginia Lady and Gloria Faye, as a close friend, to the obvious delight of the "Head Cook."

Of course, Willie Glass is surprised at seeing the two very attractive, well-built women: one white and one colored. The females are wearing matching light cotton dresses; while he looks them both over from top to bottom. He thinks in an inquisitive manner, *Is it possible to have in my presence two very pretty sparkling young women here to help me feed hundreds of soldiers?* He begins to smile and said, "Yes Ma'am, You may share in our breakfast and coffee and we would appreciate your help."

Pamela Mae and Gloria Faye thanked the "Head Cook" and proceeded to partake in the scrumptious breakfast meal and imbibe the very flavorful coffee. Shortly thereafter, Pamela Mae joined in the cutting and frying of potatoes and onions in bacon grease; while Gloria Faye helped mix and cook the "Hominy grits" made with corn, salt, black pepper, and fresh butter."

Approximately thirty minutes passed and both Pamela Mae and Gloria Faye were very pleased to see their men, Captain Mario LaGrande and Captain Maurice Flambeau, walk through their "Army Chow Line." They were accompanied by their friend and Quartermaster Officer, Captain Joseph Wei. Pamela Mae fondly remembered Mario telling her stories about himself, Maurice, and Joseph. The young men have known each other since their childhood years back in Burlington, Vermont.

Willie Glass was very impressed by the culinary and kitchen skills of his two lovely volunteers. Consequently, just before the young ladies were going to join their Captains in the Officer tent, Mister Glass ambled toward the young negro woman and took Gloria Faye to the side. He asked her directly, "My dear, if you are available, I might be able to procure you a job working for and with me." He paused momentarily, and then continued to talk to Gloria Faye.

"The 'Mess Folks,' here provide our 'Union Troops' in the garrison three hot meals a day, plus coffee and water. You would be paid one dollar per day in 'Greenbacks.' If you agree, I will just need the approval of Our Food Service Officer, Captain Wei."

Gloria Faye was so very happy to hear about the job offer and tells her best friend, Pamela Mae, about the position opening. Gloria Faye then joins her Captain Flambeau for breakfast and discusses the work of being a "Mess Hall Orderly and Cook." Maurice fully supports her interest in employment, which is immediately approved by Captain Wei, who is sitting right next to Captain Flambeau. She will start to work officially next month in August 1861. Later on, Gloria Faye gleefully tells Willie Glass, "Sir, thank you for the job offer, as I am pleased to tell you that Captain Flambeau agrees with my working here for you and Captain Wei approved my employment. Hallelujah!"

Pamela Mae was so elated to hear about the good fortune of her good friend Gloria Faye. However, a few moments later, she thought prayerfully about her father, Lieutenant Colonel John Brewer, who was hopefully on his way safely to her family home near Manassas, Virginia. *Dearest Lord in Heaven, please take care of Papa, who escaped the prison area in Arlington, and who is, I pray, securely on the road home to "Sunshine Hills." Amen!*

Pamela Mae's next thought was about her mother, Sarah Anne, who must be worried about the status of her devoted husband, John. She also remembered her mother telling her about her own English, Scottish, and Dutch ancestry. Sarah Anne emphasized that her family was related to the "British Monarchy" through Elizabeth of York, who married King Henry VII. That meant Pamela Mae was related to Queen Victoria, who is currently on the throne in England, and she warmly thought, "I *do feel very blessed to have a royal heritage and I know my Mario LaGrande makes me feel like a queen.*

Chapter 2
Downtown Alexandria: Shopping and Residing
Afternoon of July 27th, 1861

Gloria Faye Brewer was driving the wagon, pulled by a single workhorse, while her former mistress and best friend, Pamela Mae Brewer, was riding in the passenger seat. The two intrepid young "Virginia Ladies, "from Prince William County" are leaving the Saint Albans' Mountaineer Regiment camp area and are ready to face many possibilities that afternoon, Saturday, July 27th, 1861, at approximately 12:30 p.m.

Each woman is armed with a small five shot percussion revolver, hidden in their respective purses. Also, there is a shotgun, in a concealed compartment, under the wooden seats. They arrive on the outskirts of "Downtown Alexandria, Virginia" soon thereafter.

Pamela Mae was carrying a modest amount of cash and bank notes in her tan purse. She was looking to buy dresses, undergarments, and possibly some seductive night outfits for herself and her companion. She looks at her friend, who has an off-white draw-string bag with a few dollars inside, and candidly says, with a sly grin in a typical southern manner, "Sister, I reckon we are ready for another one of our Pamela Mae and Gloria Faye adventures."

After a substantial breakfast, Pamela Mae and Gloria Faye are not currently feeling hungry. Therefore, they decide to go shopping first and to ask someone for recommendations and advice.

Fortunately, they see a couple of well-dressed young women who appear to be in their late teenage years. The gregarious and outgoing Pamela Mae said to them, "Good afternoon ladies, my friend and I are looking to buy elegant dresses and other feminine apparel in order to please our 'Italian and French husbands.' What do you recommend?" Well, one of the pretty young ladies looked over the finely formed strangers, Pamela Mae and Gloria Faye. They giggled and responded, "I would say with your beautiful and graceful shapes and 'European husbands,' go over and see Madame Brigitte Moreau. She lives really close to here on 17 Letart Lane. The Madame will provide you, everything you need to please your men, *comme les dames françaises ont* (as the French Ladies have), if you know what I mean?"

Pamela Mae and Gloria Faye expressed their appreciation to the helpful young women and then rode their wagon through an unfamiliar neighborhood for couple of blocks east and up a slight hill.

After only a few minutes ride, both of our young women looked up and were totally amazed to see the very elegant, magnificent three-story structure. The impressive mansion's outside façade surfaces were expertly painted with a brilliant color combination of beige, fawn, soft ivory, and taupe hues with bone white trim. It was a very large, new "Victorian Home" with two prominent towers, and architecturally topped off with slate grey and "Union Blue" gables and roof tiles. All of these qualities highlighted the most grandeur features of the house. Pamela Mae exclaimed to her best friend, "Gloria Faye, I really do love this majestic mansion and would love to go inside and even live here one day!" See photo of the *Mansion du Moreau* (Moreau Mansion).

Mansion du Moreau, Alexandria, Virginia

They were able to park the wagon under the "Carriage Porch" on the side of the mansion. There was an attendant who spoke French and English to Pamela Mae and Gloria Faye. The negro man, wearing a horse groom outfit, approached our two lovely ladies, smiled and politely stated *"Bonjour demoiselles et Bienvenue au Mansion du Moreau* (Good day young ladies and welcome to the Moreau Mansion) and if you are shopping, please walk around to the front and knock on the large doors."

Pamela Mae and Gloria Faye found out that the man's name was Henri, and he took care of all the outside duties, to include the horses, carriages, and wagons for the Moreau household. It only took a couple of minutes for our two prospective dress and undergarment shoppers to make their way to the front of the house. They both admired the imposing home, as they looked up to the top and marveled at the intricacies of the mansion. Pamela Mae, who had a keen eye for exterior design features and a brilliant mind, was able to scan and survey the number of frontal windows. She was great with figures and calculated that there were over twenty of them.

While her dearest friend was analyzing the *Mansion du Moreau*, Gloria Faye became the first to ascend the four front steps and set foot on the oak wooden landing. Even though she was feeling a slight bit awkward, Gloria Faye knocked three times. Within a few seconds, an attractive slender woman opened both of the approximate eight-foot-tall mahogany doors. She was wearing a formal black and white "French Maid" knee-length dress/skirt outfit. She was presumptively in her thirties. She smiled and did a slight curtsy. The woman formally greeted them in French and English, "*Bonjour mes chers et bienvenue, entrez s'il vous plait* (Good day my dears, and welcome, come in please) and I will tell Madame Moreau that you are here."

The maid's name was Camille and she was borne in Haiti and performed numerous duties to maintain the inside of the home and to serve the owners and guests. Her friendly and tranquil personality did much to relax both Pamela Mae and Gloria Faye.

While they were waiting, Pamela Mae was astonished at the very embellished interior furnishings of the home. In the vestibule, she was impressed by the ornate candelabra which currently contained six unlit candles with glimmering glass, silver, and bronze ornaments dangling on the bottom section of the light fixture.

Within a few minutes, a sophisticated European-looking middle-aged woman who was dressed very fashionably walked towards her potential lady clients. Her name was Madame Brigitte Moreau who was born in Paris, France.

She greeted Pamela Mae and Gloria Faye in her three fluent languages saying in French, German, and English, "*Bonjour mademoiselles, bienvenue* (Good day young ladies, welcome) *und bitte* (and please), how may I assist you today?" Her husband, Julian Moreau, was a very successful international businessman and he was currently out of the country.

Well, Pamela Mae recognized the words that Madame Moreau spoke and felt good that she had used two of Pamela Mae's most fluent languages, English and German. She decided to utilize her German and English knowledge and responded to Madame Moreau saying, in a polite and respective manner, "*Schönen Nachmittag Madame* (Good afternoon Madam), my name is Pamela Mae Brewer. My friend, Gloria Faye, and I are interested in seeing your collection of dresses, undergarments, and other feminine accessories, please."

Madame Moreau decided to have her potential clients follow her into the highly furnished parlor on the west side of the home that was adjacent to the large elaborate dining room. The young lady guests were seated on the crimson red velvet *Rococo* sofa that had a high back on each end and was lower in the middle. The rich color of the large piece of elaborate furniture reminded Pamela Mae of her Christmas party last year. *Oh my, if I were seated here, wearing my crimson red Christmas dress, there would be a perfect match of the colors.* Furthermore, Pamela Mae noticed additional mohair and horsehair covered pillows and a matching red ottoman in the highly decorated parlor.

Within a few minutes, Camille brought in a tray full of a very pleasant aromatic simmering kettle, with small sandwiches and cakes, a "Proper French Tea." Madame Moreau was facing the doorway and seated on a matching red ruby chair, with a tall, padded backrest and vertical stitching and button tufting. Pamela Mae had a big interest and love of interior design and thought, *It would be nice in the future to be able to work professionally with expensive furniture, draperies, and other home décor pieces for wealthy clients and customers.*

Immediately after the first sip of tea, Pamela Mae carefully initiated the conversation with the business proprietor saying, "Madame Moreau, I would like to see and try on a few of your best formal dresses. In addition, my friend Gloria Faye is looking to try on and wear some beautiful outfits, too. We are both engaged and I will probably be married sometime this year and want to be looking very elegant and stunning for our future Vermont Army Captain Husbands."

After about thirty minutes of lady-friendly conversations and exchange of pleasantries, the consumption of two cups of spicy French Tea, and delicious pastries, Madame Moreau escorted Pamela Mae and Gloria Faye to her dress shop which was on the opposite (east) side of the *Mansion du Moreau.*

Pamela Mae was so very pleasantly surprised to see the many styles and variety of beauteous dresses, skirts, and naughty/saucy under-garments. There were several glamorous women's fashion items that were on display. Some additional clothing items were apparently stored in numerous fancy boxes that were stacked appropriately in the expansive dress shop. Gloria Faye was, of course, astonished at the possibility of her wearing such lovely lady apparel. She thought about her previous life of anxious servitude and her current life of freedom, *Hallelujah, Praise the Lord Jesus, can I really now be free? You have blessed me so much with a generous friend, to be wearing luxurious clothes, and to have my Dearest Captain Maurice Flambeau to love!*

Camille, who had a lively sense of humor, joined her Mistress in the ladies shop and was directed to bring out the tape and first measured Gloria Faye, when she thought, *This young woman is curvaceous like myself when I was in my late teens.* Camille soon thereafter announced that , "*Toi, ma fille bien faite* (You, my shapely girl) are a busty 40"x 24"x 40"and your Vermont Officer Maurice is a 'Lucky Man,' for sure!"

Pamela Mae disrobed next, and was standing before Camille, it was now her turn to be measured.   Again   Camille   made   the announcement to all of the women in the room to hear, "*Et tu Mademoiselle* (And you Young Madam) are a buxom 38"x 22"x 38"and your Captain Mario is a very 'Lucky Man' to have such a well-proportioned lover indeed!" At that instant, all of the ladies began to giggle and smile, as the shopping environment became more light and relaxed.

Madame Moreau looked at Pamela Mae in regard to her loveliness and vivaciousness and thought to herself in a nostalgic manner, *Miss Pamela Mae does remind me of when I was her age. I was modernly dressed in the latest Paris fashions, sauntering down along the Seine River. Many of the younger and older men smiled at me, flirted, and said "Bonjour Mademoiselle, et*

*comment vas-tu (Good day Young Lady, and how
are you)?"*

The next hour was spent selecting and trying
on formal ball gowns and elegant dresses.
Furthermore, Camille took a few of the more
risqué nighttime outfits out of the storage boxes.
Pamela Mae and Gloria Faye then blushed with
delight at the site of the exceedingly revealing
bustiers and lacy corsets. Pamela Mae thought to
herself and then went ahead and said out loud, "I
do believe that Gloria Faye and I, with our
abundant firm cleavage, can certainly fill out
these sexy outfits and will bring big smiles to
Maurice and Mario as well!"

Once again, all of the ladies in the dress shop
burst out with humorous laughter and
suggestive screams. Now it was time to select
and purchase the clothing items from Madame
Moreau. Pamela Mae decided to buy a stunning
green and gold formal evening ball gown that
would match her Captain Mario LaGrande's
green cape and gold sword. In addition, she
picked out and bought a hot pink and black
bustier with matching garters and sheer thigh
length stockings. Pamela Mae completed her
feminine apparel shopping with a purchase of a
color coordinated and matching chemise,

petticoats, and other undergarments to compliment her dresses and hoop skirts.

Since Pamela Mae was "footing the bill," Gloria Faye chose to have just one formal dress and hoop skirt with suitable chemise, petticoat, and other undergarments. She selected a French navy blue evening gown to match Maurice's riding cape. Additionally, her friend and benefactor talked her into selecting a "ruby red bustier" with matching garters and high thigh length stockings.

Pamela Mae thanked Brigitte Moreau in her best French and English saying, "*Merci beaucoup Madame* (Thank you so much Madam) and I was wondering if you knew of a nice apartment for us to rent in this area of town? It would be for the four of us."

Madame Moreau quickly nodded her head and said, "It just so happens that on the second floor of this mansion, on the back half facing the stables, is a two-bedroom apartment. Each bedroom has an adjacent modern bathroom with a sink and bathtub and there is a parlor and kitchen area in the middle of the space. You may move in tomorrow if you like?" Her offer resulted in a huge smile, as Pamela Mae replied cheerfully "Yes, Yes, Yes, Ma'am, thank you so much," as she

hugged and kissed the soft cheeks of Madame
Moreau, Camille, and Gloria Faye.

"*Merveilleuse, très bien* (Wonderful, very
good). I will have Camille clean and prepare the
rooms. She can relocate your dresses,
undergarments, and lingerie to your second-
floor apartment," responded a very glad Madame
Moreau.

Pamela Mae and Gloria Faye expressed their
sincere appreciation to their host and future
landlady, and to Camille, and decided to walk to
a café, and have a late lunch. The small
restaurant was only about four blocks away from
their new home, down Letart Lane, and was
named "Barb's Coffee and Tea Shop." The
establishment is right across from a sunlit
square.

Our two attractive "Virginia Ladies" are
greeted by a very cute young waitress named
Lacie who greeted them and said, "Hello you-all,
have a seat over there and our special today is
'Green Pepper Stew' with cornbread, and it only
costs $1.99!"

The cook was a man in his fifties named Denny,
and he soon walked out of the kitchen to get a
closer look at his customers. He sees Pamela Mae

with her voluminous black hair, exquisite brown eyes, and long appealing eyelashes. He is speechless and thinks, *She is so 'easy on the eyes,' and has to be the most alluring and attractive young woman in all of Alexandria. Yes, Sir!*

Well, the owner, Barbara, who is very friendly and petite, returns soon thereafter and serves Pamela Mae and Gloria Faye tasty coffee before their meal. After the hot coffee and delicious stew, Pamela Mae asks Barb, in a subtle manner, a question, "We will be living in the *Mansion du Moreau* and desire to buy some beautiful flowers to decorate our rooms. What do you recommend?" Barb instantly replied, "I advise you to go down to Maple Street near the Army Hospital to the big flower shop called *'Las Hermosas Flores'* (The Beautiful Flowers). The business is owned and operated by a family who immigrated from Spain many years ago."

Pamela Mae's initial thought was, *This is fantastic. We can buy pretty flowers and I can practice mi Español (my Spanish), Ole!* Pamela Mae, who is very warm and affectionate, gives both Barbara and Lacie a farewell hug and waves good-bye to a smiling and winking Denny in the kitchen. Intuitively, she has a reverse déjà vu (already seen) moment, like both of these women and this man will be in her future.

Meanwhile, Gloria Faye is feeling elated, while enjoying her freedom and having many first-time experiences with her own human "Guardian Angel Pamela Mae." However, the good times would suddenly change for the worse as she first saw two drunken undesirable ruffians lurking about in a side alley. Pamela Mae smartly pulled out her pistol and was prepared to shoot, if necessary. Of course, the first mistake that the hooligans made was when the "Biggest Brute" of the twosome shouted out in a threateningly manner, "Hey, white girl, what are you doing with that black wench?"

Pamela Mae got upset with both of the scoundrels and thought back to the stories and times with her father, John. *I guess the darn fools don't know who they are messing with right now!* Suddenly, the smallest of the two lunged after Gloria Faye, who was quick enough to step to her left and then smacked the attacker with her right forearm which knocked him to the ground. The culprit then pulled out a switchblade. Pamela Mae reacted decisively and shot the man's right hand. He immediately moaned, screamed, and shouted obscenities, "That crazy b... shot me. Damn her!" He got up and ran down the opposite end of the alley.

The bigger man sprinted foolishly straight towards Pamela Mae, and she instinctually reverted back to her previous experiences and training. Pamela Mae did not hesitate as she kicked the vulgar stranger with her left foot square in the genitals. He was now in extreme testicular pain and was bent over. Then, Gloria Faye took over and pushed the rascal backwards into a watery horse trough, and then quoted Maurice saying in French, *"Voila* (there it is)!"

Coincidentally, a Lieutenant Leo Roush from the Provost Marshal's office who hailed from New Haven, Virginia (now West Virginia), observed the two incidents and arrested the defeated assailants. Pamela Mae gave her trusted companion a thankful and triumphant hug and looked up to the partly cloudy sky and said, "Thank You, Lord, for saving us once again. Gloria Faye, let's do something more pleasant and buy some pretty flowers for our new apartment!"

Within ten minutes, our "Virginia Young Women" walked along the streets of downtown Alexandria and then entered through the wooden doors of *"Las Hermosas Flores."* Pamela Mae and Gloria Faye are greeted and welcomed in Spanish and English by one of the co-owners, *"Buenas tardes, me Llamo Donita Flores* (Good

afternoon, I call myself Little Lady Flowers).
Welcome. My daughter, *Sofia*, will assist you."

Pamela Mae takes a careful, studious look at
Sofia, who is sixteen years of age and is very
attractive with long luxurious blonde hair and
thinks, *I have such a very heartfelt feeling in my
soul that I know this young lady, and she is like
family to me.* *Sofia* says casually and politely, in
Spanish and English, "*Hola, lindas señoritas*
(Hello, pretty young ladies), how may I help you?
I prefer to be called by my American name,
Shandy." Even the name sounded familiar to
Pamela Mae, as she looked intently at the
owner's daughter and said, "Well, Shandy, we
need flowers to be delivered tomorrow
afternoon about 1:00 p.m. to our new apartment
on the second floor at 17 Letart Lane right here
in Alexandria." Shandy led Pamela Mae and
Gloria Faye through the flower shop and onto the
deck and yard in back of the building. She
pointed to a beautiful array of flowers to the
right and exclaimed, "We just received a
shipment of the most heavenly tulips from
Holland, The Netherlands, this morning that you
will love, I'm sure!"

They were both overwhelmed with the
beauty, delicacy, and dazzling vibrant colors of
the tulips. After consulting with Gloria Faye and
scenting a few of the varieties, Pamela Mae, who

has Dutch ancestry, stated, "We will take a dozen each of the tulips in my favorite colors of pink, white, and red." Pamela Mae paid *Donita* the full amount and gave a three dollar tip to Sofia (Shandy) and bid farewell, saying in Spanish, "*Muchísimas gracias y vaya con Dios hoy* (Thanks a lot, and go with God today)!" It had been an adventurous, exciting, and successful day for Pamela Mae and Gloria Faye as they joyfully strolled on the uneven pavement towards the *Mansion du Moreau.*

Chapter 3
Four Day Pass "Alexandria"
July 28th – August 1st, 1861

It was circa 4:30 a.m. on that very early Sunday morning, July 28th, 1861, in the warm confines of Captain Mario LaGrande's tent. He awakes and looked at his own personal "Sleeping Beauty" in repose so contently. Mario briefly steps outside in the morning before sunrise, and looks to the east and sees Venus, the "Morning Star."

He also has a woman Venus, and she is asleep on the comforter. Mario is now inspired to sit down, light a candle, and with pen and paper write a poem about his "Lovely Virginia Lady" in English and Italian.

Mia Cara Pamela Bella
(My Dear Pretty Pamela)

You are my Bright Morning Star.
You are my Most Brilliant Venus, by far!

Your luxurious hair is so enticing.
Your luminous eyes are so mesmerizing!

I love your ruby red luscious lips, so inviting.
I love your talented tongue, so exciting!

Your beautiful breasts are so voluptuous.
Your captivating derrière is so vivacious!

Mia Cara Pamela Bella (My Dear Pretty Pamela),
I am always and forever, Your Mario Cavalier
Fella!

Mario decides to briefly lay down next to
Pamela Mae, his precious treasure, and read her
the poem while she is asleep. The ten-line poem
results in an endearing grin and sigh from his
"sweet natured" young lady.

Just before reveille, his "Darling Young
Woman," Pamela Mae, opens her gorgeous
brown eyes and said sweetly in Italian and
English, "*Buon Giorno, mio Mario Bello* (Good
morning, my handsome Mario), and all is right
with the world."

Mario smiles broadly and thinks in rhyme, *My
Pretty Pamela Mae is learning Italiano (Italian)
very well, I must say!* Captain Mario LaGrande is
overtly multi-lingual and is now fully dressed in
his "Union Uniform." He bends over and kisses
his "Dream Girl, "and said in Italian and French,
"*Ti amo, ci vediamo questa sera, ma Belle
Mademoiselle* (I love you, see you this evening,
my Pretty Young Woman)." Pamela Mae replied
in English and German, "Gloria Faye and I will be

traveling again today, and your Lady, will leave you a note, before we depart, *Mein schöner Ritter* (My handsome Knight)." Mario was a little puzzled about the note Pamela Mae mentioned and thought, *"My Lovely Southern Belle" must be planning a surprise, and I will surely enjoy the experience!*

Captain LaGrande was now back out of the tent and feeling thirsty, and he remembered his Greek course at the Military Academy, and a word for water was "*hydros.*" So, before he opened and drank from his canteen, he repeated out loud, "Hydros, *Hydros, Hydros* (Water, Water, Water)." Subsequently, Mario lifted his canteen and eyes towards the half-moon in the western sky, and quenched his thirst, and then said in Latin, *"Gloria in excelsis Deo* (Glory to God in the highest)!"

Yesterday, Captain Mario LaGrande heard unofficial communication that the Saint Albans' Mountaineer Regiment will be participating in the construction of defensive works and fortifications in the U.S. Capital Region of Alexandria, Arlington, and Washington D.C. The massive projects will continue next month in August, with the Vermont (Green Mountain) Brigade's participation.

The overall supervision of the operations will be directed by Major General George B. McClellan, who graduated as an Engineer, 2nd in his class at the United States Military Academy at West Point, New York, in 1846.

Well, Captain LaGrande, Captain Flambeau, and Captain Wei are ordered to attend an "Officer Meeting" after breakfast. During the meeting, all three Captains are overjoyed to know that A Company, B Company, and the Quartermaster Office will be granted a "Four Day Pass," which will commence at 6:00 p.m. that evening. Mario smiles and thinks in English and Italian, *I will get to spend the next four days straight with Mia dolcezza Pamela Bella (My very sweet Pretty Pamela). We will most certainly have the most adventurous and sensational time together each afternoon, evening, night, and after sunrise. Com'è bellissima fare l'amore a la mattina (How beautiful it is to make love in the morning)!*

Gloria Faye and Pamela Mae got dressed later, walked down to the Mess Hall, ate breakfast and drank coffee, and volunteered to help with the morning meal. Since it was Sunday morning, Pamela Mae convinced the "Union Food Service Sergeant" to allow two of his soldiers' time off. The soldiers both told her and Gloria Faye that they wanted to attend the 9:00 a.m. "Protestant Church Service" that was being conducted by Chaplain Kenneth L. Young who was from Ravenswood, Virginia (now West Virginia).

Later that morning, Captains LaGrande, Flambeau, and Wei were granted permission to do an all-day reconnaissance of the many man-made military obstacles that are currently being constructed and/or planned in defense of the "Double-A Virginia" towns of Arlington and Alexandria, in addition to the fortifications in Washington, D.C.

Meanwhile, Pamela Mae was back in Captain LaGrande's tent and left him a written note in English, French, and German which explained, "Mario Darling, you and Maurice are cordially invited by me and Gloria Faye for an exciting evening of tasty food, strong drinks, and delicious desserts. Our adventure will start exactly at 7:00 p.m. at 17 Letart Lane, Alexandria, Virginia. Please ride around to the rear of the *Mansion du Moreau* (Moreau Mansion) and the outside attendant, Henri, will meet you and take care of your Arabian stallions. You will need to climb up the backstairs and open the double doors and be ready for a very unique double surprise *mit liebe* (with love). Your Pamela Mae!

Soon thereafter, Pamela Mae stepped in the passenger seat, and with Gloria Faye driving, the two bold "Virginia Girls" departed the Saint Albans' Mountaineer Regiment campsite. Their one horse-drawn wagon was traveling straight to their new upstairs apartment in the "*Mansion du Moreau*" with the two very excited friends.

The very dependable and reliable Henri was near the "Carriage Entrance" waiting to greet them. He said to our "Prince William County" young ladies, "Madame Moreau and Camille have explained to me about your rental of the apartment on the 2nd floor upstairs. They will have your rooms ready in about thirty minutes. In the meantime, I can show you where your horse will be taken care of and there are two additional stalls for your gentlemen's horses."

Meanwhile, our three "Vermont Captains" have had a busy afternoon and finally returned to the Saint Albans' Mountaineer Regiment Camp area circa 6:00 p.m. Captain LaGrande relaxed and enjoyed the short respite and then found the note from Pamela Mae on his desk and then quickly told Captain Flambeau about the trip to the Moreau mansion. They both gathered a few clothing items and rapidly went to the orderly room, and gladly signed out and received a written "Four Day Pass."

By 6:30 p.m., Mario was mounted on his white and grey Arabian Stallion named *Marengo il Secondo* and Maurice was riding his dark brown Arabian Stallion named *Lannes*. Both friends were en route to their rendezvous location as designated by the instructions on Pamela Mae's suggestive note.

Back in the 2nd floor apartment in the expansive salon living room area was the glamorous Pamela Mae and the gorgeous Gloria Faye. They were so ready for their "Vermont Cavaliers" to come through the back doors. There was a variety of food on one side of the open room that included French hors d'oeuvres, cheeses, Italian sliced meats, Russian caviar, etc. On the opposite side of the room, near the kitchenette area, were a few different kinds of drinks to include: Champagne, *Vino* Bianco (White Wine), and Brandy from Spain.

Pamela Mae and Gloria Faye set up the rooms with the colorful tulip flowers to impress and please Mario and Maurice. The two ingenious women even rehearsed their novel and original greeting and options that will be presented verbally to their very handsome and virile "Vermont Officers."

In the middle of the room were a matching set of dark purple velvet "Victorian Chaise Lounge" furniture pieces. Pamela Mae was on her chaise lounge, wearing her very provocative hot pink and black bustier, with matching garters and sheer thigh length stockings. She was laying seductively on her left hip, with her right leg in an inverted V-position and was gazing imaginatively towards the doors.

Gloria Faye was on her left on the other chaise lounge wearing her very sensational ruby red bustier with matching garters and thigh length stockings. She was laying in an alluring manner, on her right hip with her left leg in an inverted V-position and was also closely observing the doors.

By 6:50 p.m., Captains LaGrande and Flambeau had arrived at the *Mansion du Moreau* and were immediately "flagged down" by Henri. He greeted them in French, "*Bonsoir, Messieurs* (Good evening, Sirs)" and took care of their Arabian stallions. Henri directed the "Union Officers" to ascend the back stairs to the 2nd floor balcony. Our two "Buddies from Burlington" were both in a hurry, of course, and bounded hastily up the twenty-one steps.

Mario was standing on the left and Maurice was directly to his right near the stone threshold. Consequently, our brazen "Vermont Cavaliers," opened the two big white doors together, walked into the large open room salon and were totally amazed by their super attractive "Virginia Young Ladies."

As they had rehearsed earlier that afternoon, Pamela Mae amusingly pronounced to Mario and Maurice, "Gentlemen, all of the scrumptious food is to your left" and then Gloria Faye stated, "Gentlemen, all of the delectable drinks are on your right!" At that moment, Pamela Mae and Gloria Faye both smiled naughtily and nodded to each other, and then told Mario and Maurice simultaneously, "And all of your delicious desserts are right here in the middle—with US!"

Well, Mario and Maurice were overjoyed and overwhelmed with their tasty options and with their irresistible "Beautiful, Brown-Eyed Girls." They both replied loudly in the exact same words, "We want to enjoy our delicious desserts, in the middle—immediately!"

Captain LaGrande swiftly advanced towards his tempting object of his affection who was in such a mystical mermaid position. He briefly thought poetically, *My marvelous "Sweetie-Pie" is such a fabulous teaser, squeezer, and pleaser!* Mario quickly takes off his boots, and holster belt and lays down on his right side on the chaise lounge, *faccia a faccia* (face to face) in a very Italian looking way with his Pamela Bella (Pretty Pamela).

Pamela Mae, who is oblivious to Gloria Faye and Maurice, was looking straight into the very charming blue eyes of her Mario Bello (Handsome Mario). She had her right arm around his back and tenderly said, "Darling, welcome to our new apartment! Give me your moist mouth, with your sweet lips, and hot tongue all through the evening, night, and morning!"

Mario complied with Pamela Mae's desire, directive, and proceeded to have his left arm upon her sleek back muscles. He kissed her boldly and often, and said romantically, "You are my enchanting and ravishing lover girl, and let's go to our bedroom right away!"

Maurice and Gloria Faye had already departed and entered their bedroom on the east side of the apartment. Mario got off the chaise lounge first, and Pamela Mae took him by the hand and walked to the west end and said venturesomely,

"Come with me you, my big hunk of a loving man!"

Mario's natural "Roman Ancestry" was definitely exhibited as he reached over and pinched each superbly contoured naked rear-end cheek of his "Lovely Virginia Lady." He soon responded in Italian to his Pamela Mae, "Sei tutto ciò che un uomo può desiderare e mia adorabile Signorina (You are everything a man could desire and my adorable Young Lady)! "When they arrived in the bedroom, Our "Vermont Cavalier," kissed the top of each of Pamela Mae's perfectly well-endowed breasts, and then he said gleefully, "Baby, you have the very best set of cleavage, enhanced by your hot-pink and black bustier. Ooh la, la!"

Pamela Mae had her initial new bedroom scene and *risqué* position all planned out. She directed her man, "My Love, close the outside door, get nude, and cover your eyes!" Meanwhile, Pamela Mae went to the near side of the bed, lifted her right leg up, placed her foot on the edge of the bed, and held on to the bedpost with her right hand. Her left foot remained on the floor as she presented herself in the most enticing fashion possible.

It only took a minute for Captain LaGrande to remove all his clothes and when he opened his eyes, Mario was visually stimulated by his immensely tempting Pamela Mae. Well, he moved closer to his "hearts' desire and wild fire." At this precise moment, he was completely energized and extended. Pamela Mae and her man stood up vertically and become one very interconnected and gyrating duo in the most enthralling position.

Pamela Mae caressed Mario's firm back, sighed, and then stated with a sultry voice, most passionately in Spanish *"Te amo mi caro con todo mi corazón* y mi alma (I love you my dear with all my heart and soul)."

After starting upright, Mario and Pamela Mae robustly traveled horizontally onto a softer surface. Our over-sexed couple continued loving each other in a variety of unique positions/ locations on every square foot of their king-sized bed. Mario told her in Italian and English, "Mia dolce cuore(My sweetheart), you look fantastic and feel tremendous. I adore you!"

After about an hour of frolicking fun, Pamela Mae and Mario joined Gloria Faye and Maurice in the big room. Both couples had the most satisfying expressions on their flushed faces as they enjoyed the scrumptious food and delectable drinks. The highly furnished salon, was decorated with numerous brilliant pink, white, and red tulips.

During their mutual time together, our two "Vermont Military Men" talked privately about their secretive plans for tomorrow. Also, Pamela Mae talked confidentially to Gloria Faye about going somewhere special on Monday to procure a few scented lotions, oils, and perfumes.

Alexandria
Monday Afternoon-Evening-Night,
July 29th, 1861

Captain Mario LaGrande felt much at home in the Mansion du Moreau that afternoon. He experienced the pleasure of being greeted by the owner, Madame Brigitte Moreau. They were both in the dining room, and in her native French, when she greeted him, *"Bonjour Capitaine, c'est un plaisir de vous rencontrer* (Good Day Captain, it is a pleasure to meet you)."He politely told her in French and English, *"Merci beaucoup, Madame* (Thank you very much, Madam), and what a privilege it is for you to open your elegant home to us!"

In addition, he was given a tasty appetizer plate by the chef Pierre, who was the husband of Camille, the maid. The expert baker and cook from Normandy, France, stated these words to Mario, "*Pour votre plaiser culinaire, jeune homme* (For your culinary delight, young man)." After tasting one of the *petit fours marzipan* cake, Mario told Pierre, "*C'est exquis, merci* (It is exquisite, thank you)." This caused him to nostalgically reminisce about the tender memories of his French speaking parents, Louie and Anna Rosa LaGrande. He missed them very much, as they were residing back home in Burlington, Vermont.

Captain Maurice Flambeau also felt very comfortable and nostalgic in the *Mansion du Moreau*. Especially when he was served a glass of French red wine (*Vin rouge Français*) from Camille as she politely said, "Une boisson savoureuse pour vous, *Monsieur* (A tasty drink for you, Sir)!" He fondly remembered his mother Suzanne Marie, who was back home in Vermont, who was also from Haiti. He, of course, missed her very much and the wise counsel of his Father Jacques Flambeau. Both of his devoted parents spoke French, like Maurice.

The young ladies from the Manassas , Virginia area, Pamela Mae and Gloria Faye, were still getting cleaned up and dressed. They will later venture out on a separate excursion that day into the business district of Alexandria.

Henri got ready the two Arabian stallions, as the fully uniformed Captain Mario LaGrande and Captain Maurice Flambeau departed the entry way of the *Mansion du Moreau.* Mario saw a very hopeful and lucky sign for today's diamond ring shopping. He recalled his Italian Mamma's words, "*Una bella pettirossa* (A pretty robin)," as he saw a foraging robin bobbing in the front yard of the mansion.

Meanwhile, Mario and Maurice rode their horses to the south side of Alexandria to buy an engagement ring for their brides to be, Pamela Mae and Gloria Faye, respectively. Madame Moreau recommended that they purchase the expensive diamond rings from a well-established business named "Kate and Amanda's Fine Jewelry."

Our "Vermont Officers" took their time as they rode for ten minutes and arrived at the jewelry store about 1:30 p.m. on that Monday afternoon: July 29th, 1861. Mario and Maurice heard that two sisters owned the establishment and were pleased to see the very well-dressed identical twin, curly blonde ladies, Kate and Amanda.

They were both smiling and waiting patiently on their clients.

Well, the customer service was excellent as Mario and Maurice purchased sterling silver engagement rings each which contained three "Blue Nile Diamonds" for Pamela Mae and Gloria Faye. The Roman Catholic Army Captains both wanted to honor the "Holy Trinity of the Father, Son, and Holy Ghost" in this most sentimental and spiritual method. In addition, Mario reminded himself that both he and Pamela Mae were the 3rd child of each of their parents' offspring. Maurice was also one of three children in his family. Kate and Amanda capped off the purchases with an appreciative and delightful farewell as they said in unison, "Thank you, Gentlemen, for your generosity and patronage, and God bless!"

It was now 2:30 p.m. and Pamela Mae and Gloria Faye were traveling in a carriage that Madame Moreau had allowed her new lady tenants to use for the afternoon. It was only a ten minute ride to the "Motions with Lotions, Perfumes, and Oils" store.

Our "Virginia Young Women," were welcomed by a lady from "South India" who was wearing a colorful blouse with a matching ornate *praavada* skirt. She had waist length straight black hair and dark brown eyes. Her name was *Sarika Doshi,* and she greeted Pamela Mae and Gloria Faye in Hindi and English saying, "*Namaste Mahilaon* (Hello Ladies) and how may I assist you this afternoon?" The "best friends" spent over an hour in the sweet aromatic store. They scented the fragrances, applied the lotions to their skin, and purchased a few products for themselves and "their husbands to be" which included the following luxury items: French perfume from the town of Grasse, Lavender lotion from Egypt, Coconut oil from the Philippines, and *Cologne* from Germany.

Later that afternoon, Pamela Mae and Gloria Faye decided to surprise their men and buy them gold cuff links to be worn with their white shirts for the "Military Ball." Coincidently, they also bought the men's accessories at "Kate and Amanda's Fine Jewelry." The initials MPL and MF were inscribed on Mario Patrizio LaGrande's and Maurice Flambeau's gold cuff links, respectively.

It was now after dinner that evening, circa 7:00 p.m., and Pamela Mae told Mario, "Darling, please disrobe and lay down on your belly with your head near the footboard of the bed!" Pamela Mae wanted to use her lotions and oils to give her "Vermont Captain" a relaxing full body massage.

She is standing on the floor, facing her man and leans slightly over the "Apple of her Eye."

Mario is in an inquisitive mental state, picks up a sensually stimulating scent of lavender, cologne, and an unrecognizable oil and thinks, *Something is telling me that Pamela Mae is going to give me an unforgettable massage with endless possibilities, and hopefully, some extra bonus activities, Mamma Mia (My Mom)!*

Pamela Mae just adores her very "Handsome Vermont Officer" and combines the lavender and coconut oil and starts to tenderly massage the hair and scalp of her man. She affectionately tells him, "Mario, my precious man, I love you and want to give you as much pleasure as womanly possible."

Pamela Mae has the most talented hands with nimble and sensitive fingers. She concentrates on the taut *trapezius* muscles of Mario's upper back, and then said in German and in English, "*Bitte tief durchatmen,* Please breathe deeply." Pamela Mae continues to massage the middle and lower back of her "Captain LaGrande" as she leans farther over her "American Hercules." Mario thinks in Italian, *Sono cosi infatuato della sua forma erotica e perfetta, Come Bella (I am so infatuated with her erotic and perfect shape, How beautiful)!* He sighs with a couple gasps of rapture and tells his "marvelous masseuse" in French, *"Merci beaucoup et tu es magnifique ma douce Mademoiselle* (Thank you very much and you are magnificent my sweet Young Lady)."

Pamela Mae now massages the perfectly shaped posterior muscles of her Mario Bello. She uses both hands to acutely rub the soothing oils onto his three very tight Gluteal muscles (*maximus, medius, and minimus*). Pamela Mae has now completed the brawny dorsal side of Mario, and thinks cleverly, *I could bounce a penny off of his rigid bottom.* Subsequently, Mario turned over and then looked up devotedly into the enamored chocolate colored eyes of his "Princess from Prince William County."

She tells him candidly and romantically, "Mario, I cherish you and love your anatomy and every inch of your powerful body." Pamela Mae takes a small amount of lotion and thoughtfully massages the noble face of Mario. She then bends over more to provide him a long vigorous French kiss as she coos with sensual pleasure. Pamela Mae is now massaging his bulging pectoral muscles, and then lovingly rubs the entire frontal length of her "Mario Bello (Handsome Mario)."

Pamela Mae now lays lengthwise on top of her "masculine hero," and places a very amatory moist kiss on the eager full lips of her lover. Mario responds in a very manly manner, as he "rises to the occasion" while holding Pamela Mae firmly. Presently, he massages her well-defined back fervidly, and repeatedly kisses her very amazing and luscious lips. The very well-connected twosome are pleasing and squeezing each other in the most memorable manner. Mario tells her in Italian, *"Mia Pamela Bella, amami follemente* (My Pretty Pamela, love me madly)."

"Our Lovely Virginia Lady and Our Handsome Vermont Cavalier" will be loving each other for the next couple of hours. The "heat of the night air" is matched equally by the external and internal heat of Pamela Mae and Mario. She gasps and sighs lustfully and tells him, "My Union Officer, I will do anything and everything to satisfy all of your desires." Finally, about 10:00 p.m., after a few good night kisses, and *Ti amo* (I love you), our devoted duo fall asleep in a very affectionate position. Pamela Mae calls it a "Mamma Hug." Mario is laying on his left side, facing the big middle room door and Pamela Mae is laying on her left side also with her hot, naked breasts on his back. In addition, she has her right arm wrapped around Mario, while clinging to the back of his right hand.

Alexandria
Tuesday Evening-Night, July 30th, 1861

It is now 6:00 p.m., Tuesday evening, in the elegant dining room of the *Mansion du Moreau*. Madame Brigitte, her cook Pierre, and his wife Camille are preparing and serving a very lavish and sumptuous *"dîner français* (French dinner)," to their special guests.

That evening, Captain LaGrande is wearing his dress "Hunter Green Army" uniform. He has the three stone diamond engagement ring in his breast pocket. The glamorous Pamela Mae Brewer is seated to his right, wearing her beautiful new green and gold formal gown, accented with an emerald green necklace, and adorned with gold ribbon in her luxurious hair. She chooses this color combination, in order to honor her Vermont (Green Mountain) Cavalier Officer, Mario Patrizio, who was born on Saint Patrick's Day in 1840.

Captain Maurice Flambeau is seated on the opposite side of the long mahogany table wearing his "French blue" colored dress Army

Uniform and he also has a matching diamond engagement ring in his jacket pocket. Gloria Faye is looking gorgeous in her new matching blue evening gown with a sapphire blue necklace with a red ribbon in her braided hair.

The very elaborate six course French meal will be served on porcelain plates and dishes from China, with "English Floral Whorls Silverware." The menu will have numerous delicacies, food choices, and culinary options to include:

L'Aperitif(Appetizers): Alsatian Cheese Tart, *Coquilles* (Scallops) Saint *Jacques*, and *Brie* with *Pesto*.

Entrée: Beef *Carpaccio*, Salmon *Mousse*, French Onion Soup.

Fish: Grilled Tuna with Vegetables and *Aioli* (Garlic and Olive Oil).

Salad: Spinach, Romaines, Carrots, Croutons, with *Vinaigrette*.

Cheese and Fruits: *Bleu de Bresse* (Blue Cheese), *Fromage* Blanc (White Cheese), Sliced Apples, and Red Grapes.

Desserts: Macarons, Crepes, and Sorbet.

After a few glasses and toasts with champagne, Captain Mario LaGrande rose up from his chair. He glanced to the head of the table and said to the Hostess and Owner in French, "*Madame Moreau, s'il vous plaît, pardonnez-moi* (Madam Moreau, please forgive me)."He then pulled out the diamond engagement ring from his pocket and bent down and placed his right knee on the floor to the side of Pamela Mae.

"Our Lovely Virginia Lady" became very emotional and her loving spirit moved her deeply and she thought prayerfully, *Thank You, dear Jesus. By Your grace, I will become a fiancée today and officially engaged to my beloved Mario!*

Captain LaGrande reached out and held his woman by her left hand and decides to "pop the question" in Italian and again in English as he asked, "*Mia Pamela Bella, mi faresti l'onore di essere mia moglie questo dicembre e per sempre?*, My Pretty Pamela, would you do me the honor of being my wife this December and forevermore?"

Pamela Mae instantly responded joyfully in Mario's three fluent languages in the affirmative, "Yes, Yes, Yes, Si, Si, Si, Oui, Oui, Oui!" Captain LaGrande then happily placed the radiant diamond engagement ring on her finger as the rest of the dinner party applauded and expressed congratulations to the happy couple.

Captain Maurice Flambeau was next as he asked Gloria Faye to marry him in French and English and she was overjoyed and accepted his proposal and replied faithfully, "Hallelujah. Thank You, Jesus. Yes, I will marry you, Maurice, and be your bride!"

The two military couples blissfully left the *Mansion du Moreau* soon afterward. Pamela Mae and Gloria Faye looked spectacular in their new formal evening gowns. Captain LaGrande and Captain Flambeau looked the picture-perfect role of "Vermont Cavaliers" as they both wore their shining gold 36 inch long French swords. They all rode comfortably to the "Vermont (Green Mountain) Brigade" military ball in a beautiful four seat "German Landau Carriage" owned by Wade's Transport Service.

The extravagant event would take place in the "Grand Ballroom" of the "Ellsworth Hotel" on Duke Street in downtown Alexandria, Virginia. Upon arrival at the hotel, Captain LaGrande exited first and waited patiently for Pamela Mae, who was giving him one her best "award winning" smiles. Mario extended his arms and held on to her very svelte 22" waist. He told her tenderly, "You are the most splendid feminine sight to behold, my Love. I adore you!"

Inside the highly decorated hall, Pamela Mae is practically "floating on air" as she danced upon the oak floor of the ball room with the "man of her dreams." She then suddenly had another *déjà vu* experience. She slowed the pace of her dance, hugged her handsome Mario Patrizio, and told him, "Darling, I previously had a dream of you and I dancing on this very floor a few years ago and now that wonderful dream has come true. I love you!"

Captain LaGrande smiled gleefully and felt that he was so truly blessed and most fortunate to be with his Pretty Pamela Mae in this festive environment. He gave her a big warm hug and whispered in her ear softly in a mix of English and Italian words, "You will always be mia Pamela Bella (My Pretty Pamela), and the future Mamma (Mommy) of our children. Ti amo (I love you)."

However, a few minutes later, he happened to survey the crowd and noticed two angry-looking sinister men who were lurking near the back of the expansive room. Mario made a mental note and then during a break, he confided to his fellow officer, Captain Maurice Flambeau, concerning the two suspicious strangers. Both Captains then proceeded to check their small revolvers that were hidden under their jackets.

Gloria Faye was so elated to be attending a military ball with Maurice.

She revealed her thoughts of rhapsody to her best friend and confidant, "Miss Pamela Mae, I am so grateful to you for giving me my freedom and to become engaged to Captain Flambeau. Also, thank you for buying me this very beautiful dress for our special military ball. Hallelujah!"

The two very joyful couples, Captain Mario LaGrande and Pamela Mae Brewer and Captain Maurice Flambeau and Gloria Faye Brewer, danced for two hours. They all imbibed a few alcoholic drinks and decided to bid farewell to their fellow officers and other guests and "call it a night."

Our Vermont Captains put on their swords once again and Mario had a "gut feeling" that there might be trouble outside. He told Pamela Mae about the two suspicious characters and the possible risky and threatening situation saying, "Sweetheart, I have a feeling that we may be attacked."

While Captain Flambeau was assisting Gloria Faye into the new Landau Carriage, there was an inebriated loud manly voice, heard from across the street who said, "Get the hell out of here "Bluebellies" and take that negro slave with you!"

Well this comment, of course, was very insulting to Captain Maurice Flambeau and he took out his pistol and ran across the street towards the belligerent man. At the same time, Gloria Faye laid down on the seat for safety and Pamela Mae went in front of the carriage to calm down the horses. Captain Mario LaGrande sprang into action and pulled out his sword.

Instantly, there was the sound of gunfire and the impact of a bullet upon metal. Captain Flambeau was hit by a round on his left side. Fortunately, the projectile struck the cross guard of his sword, just bruising his hip slightly. Even though it was mostly dark outside, Maurice was able to fire back and strike the adversarial attacker in his left thigh. The assailant screamed bloody murder and hobbled down a side alley.

Suddenly, a second shadowy attacker came around the back of the carriage and ran with a long blade in his right hand in an attempt to stab Captain LaGrande. Mario, who was very agile and an experienced swordsman, performed an evasive "swashbuckling maneuver." He then slapped the scoundrel with the flat end of his sword with full force which knocked over the culprit to the ground. The strong swipe of Captain LaGrande's sword severely bruised all three butt muscles in the rascal's rear end.

Pamela Mae merrily observed her "Vermont Cavalier" in action. She subsequently laughed whole-heartedly as the injured man yelled obscenities; while he rubbed his "black and blue buns." The thug screamed in pain, and stumbled down the street and was soon out of site.

Needless to say, Mario, Pamela Mae, Maurice, and Gloria Faye were so glad to arrive back at the *Mansion du Moreau*, just before midnight. Fifteen minutes later while they were upstairs in their rooms, Pamela Mae had a great idea and told Mario in English and Spanish, "Darling, stay here in the bedroom while I run our warm bath water, *por favor* (please)."

Mario would soon smell the very aromatic scents of rose hips, lavender, and orange blossoms wafting through the vents in the bathroom. He could hear the welcoming voice of his Pamela Mae saying, "Oh Baby, come in the bathtub with me, right away."

Our "naked as a jay bird" Mario LaGrande walks through the bathroom door and sees his stunning Pamela Mae in her original Valentine's Day, 1844 birthday outfit. She is wearing one of her most enchanting and mischievous smiles, along with thousands of sweet, scented bubbles. Mario could not resist and bent over and kissed her very wet luscious lips for a long while. He slowly reaches down into the bath water and massages her 38DD enticing mammary glands, one ideal breast at a time. Pamela Mae coos and expresses a delightful sigh and states, "I love you, today, tomorrow, and always! Now Sweetheart, please come into the bathtub with me."

Mario complies with her request and enters into the gigantic bathtub as he is able to lower himself down into a sitting position opposite his "Adorable Aphrodite." He then slides and maneuvers his legs against the outside of Pamela Mae's inviting thighs. Both of our lovers are now enflamed with carnal desire and are able to mate rhythmically underwater. He is amazed at his ability to be bonded aquatically with his "Lovely Virginia Lady." Mario expresses his pleasure salaciously in his three fluent tongues; French, Italian, and English "Ooh la la, mia Pamela Bella, (Oh wow wow, my Pretty Pamela), You are my magnificent mermaid."

Pamela Mae and Mario are amazing themselves as they smile, laugh, and ooze with erotic pleasure for the next thirty minutes. She comically tells him, "My Love, you definitely know how to bring enjoyment to your girl, on land and underwater. Ay, Ay, Ay, Ay (Oh, Oh, Oh, Oh)." Mario is currently overcome with such intense intimate feelings and responds poetically, "Pamela Bella (Pretty Pamela), you make all of my desires, dreams, fantasies, and wishes come true, and *Ti amo bene* (I love you so)."

Our amorous, sensational, and soaked couple become more active in the hot bubbly water as small waves are produced and sprinkle onto the mosaic floor. Pamela Mae remembers a cute phrase and alters it saying comically, "I guess it is the 'Size of the Ship' that is important." Mario recalls the same phrase and replies amusingly, "Yes, and we both know how to have fun with the 'Motion of the Ocean.' Oh Yeah!"

Well, the warm bath and wet lovemaking completely relaxed "Our Hot and Lovely Virginia Young Lady and Our Romantic and Handsome Vermont Cavalier." They soon exit the bathtub, dry off with very soft Egyptian towels, and find their way into their large comfortable bed. Within a few minutes, Mario kisses the very soft sensual lips of his Pamela Mae and says in Italian, *"Buona Notte e Buon Riposo, mia Pamela Bella* (Good Night and Good Rest, my Pretty Pamela). She kissed his appealing lips and replies in her very endearing voice, "Good night, My Gallant Knight." Pamela Mae turns and lays on her right side and Mario turns as well to his right. He presses his hairy chest firmly against her very desirable back and holds onto her left breast gently with his left hand. They lovingly refer to this sleeping position as the "Papa Hug."

Mansion du Moreau
Wednesday Afternoon, July 31st, 1861

The envelope was addressed to:
Captain Mario LaGrande
C/O Pamela Mae Brewer
Saint Albans' Mountaineer Regiment
Alexandria, Virginia

The letter was written by John Brewer who writes in German and English and it is included below. It was read out loud by Pamela Mae to her Mario in the early afternoon of July 31st, 1861.

July 29th, 1861
Anno Domini (Year of the Lord)
Prince William County

Meine Liebe (My Dear) Pamela Mae,

By the Grace of God, I was able to make it back to our "Sunshine Hills" plantation home to be with my loving wife, your mamma, Sarah Anne. Unfortunately, the perilous trip by horseback resulted in my wounded leg becoming infected and it is very painful to walk. I have requested to be placed on indefinite medical leave until my leg heals. I could surely use your managerial assistance immediately to help in the household and operate our businesses. In addition, our dear "Southern Nation" is at full mobilization and the War Department needs all of the horses, mules, livestock, foodstuffs, and other supplies to fight the "Union Invaders."

Furthermore, your military service is required in order to prepare for a special mission in the western part of our "Commonwealth of Virginia."

Dein liebender Vater (Your loving Father)

Captain Mario LaGrande listened carefully to the letter and gave his Pamela Mae a big hug and said, "Darling, I do not want you to leave, but I do understand that you have a sense of devotion to your family and have military responsibilities as well."

Pamela Mae places her lovely head on the comforting chest of her "Vermont Cavalier" and responded, "Yes, I must go and assist Papa and perform my Army duties, since I swore an oath to Virginia. However, I will miss and long for you every minute that we are apart, my Love."

She started thinking more about managing the family estate and resuming her role as Captain Pamela Mae Brewer again. *I surely need to be involved with seeing that "Sunshine Hills" is being operated efficiently. Also, I need to resume my training once again in order to serve as an Officer for our 1st Manassas (Virginia) Infantry Regiment as part of the Virginia (Old Dominion) Brigade.*

At dinner time, Pamela Mae broke the news to Madame Moreau about her departure tomorrow. She generously paid the owner for the next five months of rent so that Gloria Faye and Maurice could still use the 2nd floor residence of the *Mansion du Moreau.* Captain LaGrande decided to reside back in his Army tent while his "Wonderful Virginia Lady" was home and serving again with her regiment.

Henri procured a very fast male quarter horse named *Romano* (Roman) for Captain Brewer to use. Pamela Mae had to pack up a few of her things and would travel in baggy men's clothes in order to obscure her beauty and shapeliness. She would have a sufficient amount of cash, arms, ammunition, water, and find food at taverns to help ensure a successful return back to her "Sunshine Hills" residence.

Mario and Pamela Mae would spend the next few precious evening and night hours closely and intimately together. As they were lying in bed in a compassionate embrace, he looked intently into her very luminous dark almond brown eyes and said tenderly in Italian and English, "*Mia dolce Signorina, mia Pamela Bella* (My sweet Young Lady, my Pretty Pamela), You are the most superb of our dear Lord's creations, and I thank God that he has gifted me with you, *mia Tesora Preziosa* (my Precious Treasure)."

Pamela Mae replied, "Thank you, Darling, your affectionate, kind, and softhearted words mean the world to me." She then began to place her full lustrous ruby lips and talented tongue inside his awaiting mouth and kissed her Mario Bello enthusiastically, energetically, and exuberantly. Furthermore, she said, "Sweetheart, I love to wrap my arms around you, hold you oh so tight, and kiss you all over!"

Mario responded avidly and physically, *avec beaucoup de bisous français* (with many French kisses). He was holding onto Pamela Mae tightly and then rolled on top of his incredible and irresistible fiancée. He soon said salaciously in Italian and English, "*Ti voglio tanto bene, la mia leonessa selvaggia* (I want you so much, my wild lioness)."Pamela Mae reacted appropriately with a jungle-type feline scream and dug her nails along each half of Mario's super muscular back, and replied," I want you badly and will love you madly, my King of the Jungle."

The vigorous love-making continued for a couple of amorous and resilient hours. Pamela Mae and Mario were hugging strongly and kissing one another with fervor all over their king-sized bed. Mario was using his agility, flexibility, and versatility while he maintained his best mattress maneuvers to make his woman "ooh and aah." He thought provocatively, *It is every man's dream to have a gorgeous and well-endowed young lady to love, and I am truly fortunate to have my Pamela Mae to enjoy endlessly.*

Pamela Mae was having the utmost pleasure while loving her Mario in many different locations, positions, and with a variety of wonderful connections. She thought coquettishly, *It is every girl's romantic dream to have an ultra-muscular man who is so well-*

proportioned in the most important ways and uses his manliness to the utmost degree. His love-making ability propels me off the earth, by the planets, and through the "Milky Way of Exotic Ecstasy." Oh Me, Oh My!

It was now after 9:00 p.m. and Gloria Faye and Maurice were taking a break from their own *soirée d'amour* (evening of love) in order to get more water and food from the kitchenette in the big middle room. Gloria Faye giggled softly as she could hear the constant noise and the reactionary words emanating from the other room and could distinctly hear Pamela Mae saying, "Oh Baby, Oh Baby, Oh Baby, you are so fantastic!" Of course, Maurice laughed quietly as he could also hear the very familiar voice of his childhood friend Mario speak out and say the same exact words in Italian, *"O Bambina, O Bambina, O Bambina, tu sei piu fantastica."*

"Our Lovely Virginia Lady and Our Handsome Vermont Cavalier" were now completely exhausted as they concluded their extraordinary night of being joined as one loving body. They both heard the grandfather clock strike 10:00 p.m. on the first floor below. Mario had a very sweet endearing lullaby song to sing to his only love. He held her close and looked adoringly at her very beautiful face and in English and Italian sang;

"Lullaby, go to sleep mia Pamela Bella (My Pretty Pamela),

All the angels will keep you safe, it is true.

May the "Good Lord" hold you close mia Pamela Bella (my Pretty Pamela),

Close your eyes and sleep, your Mario Bello (Handsome Mario) loves you."

Pamela Mae squeezed her man tight, kissed him warmly, and responded excitedly, "I love my Mario Bello (Handsome Mario). I love him, I love him, oh I do love him so very much." Our "Southern Belle and Northern Gentleman" would sleep through the night peacefully together and once again dream adventurously, prophetically, and romantically of one another.

Chapter 4
Pamela Mae, Back to Home, "Sunshine Hills"
August 1st -23rd, 1861

It is approximately 4:30 a.m., on that very early Thursday morning, August 1st, 1861. Captain Mario LaGrande escorts his fiancée Pamela Mae Brewer to the "South Gate" of Alexandria, Virginia. Fortunately, there are only two Provost Marshal enlisted soldiers on duty. She dismounted from her horse *Romano* and took off the riding cap which revealed her long curly coal black hair.

Captain LaGrande was amazed to hear Pamela Mae talk casually to the guards. She gained their confidence and found out that they were brothers, Sergeant Johnny Buffington and his kid brother, Private Jimmy Buffington. They hailed from the town of *Guyandotte*, Cabell County, Virginia (now West Virginia).

Pamela Mae received a written pass from Sergeant Buffington and then subsequently hugged and kissed her fiancé, Mario, good-bye. She simply told him in Spanish, "*Vaya con Dios, mi Amor* (Go with God, my love) and he replied with an Italian blessing, "*Che Dio ti benedica, Amore Mia* (May God Bless You, My Love)." Pamela Mae put the hat back on her pretty head as she bravely traveled west to her ancestral home at "Sunshine Hills" in Prince William County, Virginia. Captain Mario LaGrande cried briefly and then headed back to his "Saint Albans' Mountaineer Regiment" bivouac area.

The early dawn light revealed that the road out of Alexandria was mostly vacant which allowed Pamela Mae to travel at a high velocity while making "very good time" on her fast quarter horse. During the ride, she thought faithfully and seriously, *I hope and pray, Lord Jesus, that You bless me and keep me safe from harm today. In addition, Dear God, help me explain to Papa how much I love Captain Mario LaGrande and that we are engaged to me married. Also, may I be of great assistance to my father on the plantation and have good fortune and luck with my military training and future missions. I pray in the name of the Father, Son, and Holy Ghost. Amen!*

Later in the morning during her trip, she began to see more people, wagons, and horses on the dusty road which included "Union Soldiers" who were probably on scouting assignments. By the "Grace of God," Pamela Mae was able to arrive at Fairfax Station, Virginia, just before noon. One of her favorite numbers is '3' as she is the 3rd child and is often blessed with that cardinal trinitarian number. Therefore, she was very elated and pleased to see that a nearby restaurant had a very obvious and prominent sign outside which read, "Welcome to The Three Sisters Tavern."

Pamela Mae was very curious by nature and wanted to meet all three sisters. In addition, she needed to inquire about Army soldiers in the area and any word about raiders and robbers. As Pamela Mae entered the well-kept tavern, she could scent the coffee and the many different fried meats. She took her hat off and was greeted by the youngest of the very attractive sisters, "Good afternoon, Ma'am. Welcome. My name is Rita!" Our "Lovely Virginia Lady" said politely, "Hello, my name is Pamela Mae. I am traveling towards Manassas. How is your coffee?" Rita replied sweetly with a dazzling smile saying, "Well, everybody likes it!" Pamela Mae giggled at her response and ordered her favorite drink and some nourishing food.

Well, our very thirsty and hungry traveler, Pamela Mae, was very ready for her coffee and a big bacon, cheese, and lettuce sandwich which was served by the middle sister Carol. She was able to tell Pamela Mae that, "We have a lot of our Virginia soldiers stop here and they are constantly looking for "Union scouts and spies."

Pamela Mae enjoyed the tasty coffee, delicious sandwich, and even ate a fried chicken leg before she settled the bill. She was also able to meet the owner's wife, Maryann, who was the oldest sister and she advised her, "Honey, you better 'keep your wits about ya.' There are a number of hooligans and thieves that travel down that main road to Manassas and prowl around the railroad tracks." Pamela Mae thanked her and had a clairvoyant feeling that she would encounter her fellow Confederate troops and a robber or two.

The first hour on the road towards Prince William County was without incident and then later, Pamela Mae encountered a small band of "Virginia Army" personnel who ordered her to halt. The leader was a young Lieutenant who identified himself as Eric Bolden, and he was from Culpepper, Virginia. He told her, "Ma'am, I can see that you are an excellent rider. Our scouting party is working for Colonel Stuart. Have you seen any Yankees or any suspicious looking men?" She decided to use her "girly charms" as she fluttered her long ebony hued eyelashes which accented her super attractive brown eyes. Consequently, with a heavy "Southern accent," she sweetly said, "No, I haven't Lieutenant, but I must say that you are a 'Handsome Officer,' and I will be sure to heed your words and will definitely notify the authorities of any Yankees or their deceptive spies."

Pamela Mae was able to once again get out of a difficult situation as she rode towards Clifton, Virginia, and thought, *Thank You Lord in heaven, you provided a secure way out of that precarious situation, and please bless Mario back in Alexandria, and Mamma and Papa at "Sunshine Hills." Amen!*

After a few more hours of vigorous riding on her very durable quarter horse *Romano*, Pamela Mae freely entered Prince William County, Virginia. She was able to go off the road to the west and located a good sized stream so that her steed could have a long drink. After the break, Pamela Mae continued by horseback towards her home outside of Manassas, Virginia. She was able to find a service road that ran parallel to the Orange and Alexandria Railroad.

Pamela Mae later heard a "flock of crows" making a fuss with their "annoying cawing" in the woods to her right, and she intuitively sensed trouble. She was approaching a crossroads up ahead and there were two men on horseback who were heading towards her from the east. They appeared to be drunk and moved erratically. Each man had a pistol and they yelled and fired their guns in Pamela Mae's direction.

She looked up briefly to the sky above and cried out, "Lord, have mercy," and since she is ambidextrous, Pamela Mae switched sides and shot her pistol three times with her left hand at the attackers. The lead rider was hit in the right shoulder and fell off his horse. The second bandit was wounded in the left arm and he slumped onto the neck of his equine. Pamela Mae did not look back at the wounded thieves and prayed and thought to herself, *I must keep riding in order to make it home by dinner time, Lord, help me!*

A few hours later, "Our Lovely Virginia Lady" galloped towards the tree lined entrance to her "Sunshine Hills" plantation home. Pamela Mae could now hear the friendly barking of her loyal German Shepherd dog, Butch, as she exclaimed, "Thanks be to God, I made it home. *Hallelujah!*"

She saw the very wonderful vision of her beloved mamma, Sarah Anne, waving at her daughter while standing on the front portico of the white painted two-story mansion. Her "dear mother" was smiling brightly and crying at the sight of her Pamela Mae who got off her horse and gave the reins of *Romano* to one of the stable workers who led the tired quarter horse to the corral.

Pamela Mae then heard the very familiar sound of her trusted white and grey Arabian mare, *Marenga la Primera,* neigh and whinny in the distance. She soon greeted her mother with a big hug and kisses and said, "Good Evening, Mamma, I am so very happy to see you. I missed you and Father so much!" Sarah Anne responded, "Praise the Lord you are safe and home again and your Papa is anxiously awaiting your return. He is at the dinner table drinking a large stein of *Deutsches Bier* (German Beer)."

Our two "Virginia Ladies" lovingly walked arm and arm through the large oak front doors and then saw their household servant, Lizzy, the mother of Gloria Faye, taking a tray of food into the dining room. Lizzy gently put the tray down on an end table and gave Pamela Mae a welcoming hug, and said, "Thank You, Jesus. It is so good to see you Miss Pamela Mae, and how is my girl, Gloria Faye, doing?" Pamela Mae continued to hug Lizzy and whispered in her ear, "She is doing well, is engaged to be married, and has a job working for the Union Army in Alexandria."

Lizzy looked at the left hand of Pamela Mae and saw the radiant diamond ring on her finger and said, "I guess you will have a lot to explain to your papa and mamma, and please follow me to the table, and I reckon you are very hungry!" Pamela Mae walked into the elegant dining room and saw her Papa at the head of the table. She affectionately greeted him in German and English, as she stated, "*Guten Abend Vater, ich bin hier, um dir zu helfen* (Good Evening, Father, I am here to help you), and I love you so! She hugged and kissed her father, John Brewer, on both cheeks and sat down beside him to his right.

He cried tears of joy and replied in German and English also, "*Gott sei Dank bist du zu Hause, meine wundervolle Tochter* (Thank God you are home, my wonderful daughter), and we need to talk after dinner." Pamela Mae knew she had to tell Papa the truth about her love and engagement to her fiancé, Captain Mario LaGrande. She thought about the words of Jesus in John 8:32, of the King James Holy Bible, "*And ye shall know the truth and the truth shall set you free.*"

Pamela Mae, her mamma, and her papa enjoyed a very scrumptious German style dinner cooked and served by Lizzy and Martha, the young teenage servant girl. The menu included the following delicious foods, desserts, and drinks:

Pork *Schnitzel*
Bratkartoffeln (Cottage Potatoes with Bacon)
Mohrengemuse (Carrot Side Dish)
Braised Green Beans, with chicken broth, butter, salt, and sugar
Pumpernickel Bread with creamy butter
Apfelstrudel (Apple Strudel)
Bavarian *Creame*
Dark Coffee from Columbia
Homemade White Wine

Pamela Mae told her parents about the 2nd floor apartment in Alexandria and the beautiful dress that she had purchased. A good time was had by all as they fondly reminisced about Pamela Mae's childhood. The good news, of course, was that their adventurous, courageous, and beautiful daughter was safely back home again in the bosom of her loving family.

After the very tasty evening meal, the "Master of the House," John Brewer limped with a cane in his right hand down the long hall into the library. He sat down in his dark green "Queen Anne Wingback" chair and waited for his only daughter to join him. Pamela Mae came into the room, sat down on the matching green sofa, and decided to tell her papa in detail about her "Vermont Cavalier" and the devoted love that she had for her Mario Bello (Handsome Mario).

"You know papa, Captain Mario LaGrande is the man who I dreamed of from childhood to this very day. He loves the color green, like you, and he and his fellow officers, Captains Flambeau and Wei bravely played a role in your escape from the temporary confinement. He loves me completely and has asked me to marry him. I told him, "Yes, and here is my engagement ring." At this point, Pamela Mae proudly displayed her triple diamond engagement ring to her father.

John Brewer knew that his daughter is a very accomplished, intelligent, and mature young woman. He pauses and ponders the situation thoughtfully, *I can see that she loves this "Yankee Officer" and is determined to marry him. However, I need her assistance. I must tell her a few important things.* Her papa replied sincerely, "Your Captain LaGrande must still ask permission from me before I give my final approval for the marriage. However, there is a 'War Between the States' happening right now. It hurts me to walk. You are indispensable to the plantation operation as I need your help to manage the property and servants, make business decisions, and deliver horses, etc. In addition, you must resume your training and be ready to comply with any orders from your Commanding Officer and Higher Headquarters!"

Pamela Mae felt really good about her "heart-to-heart" honest conversation with her father and responded in German and in English, "*Oh danke, lieber Vater* (Oh thank you dear Father), I am sure in the coming months, my Captain LaGrande will ask you for permission to marry me, when he visits our home here in 'Sunshine Hills.' In the next few weeks, I will surely assist in the operation and management of our plantation businesses and restart my military training and await any Army orders."

Pamela Mae said goodnight to her papa and mamma and then proceeded upstairs to her old bedroom on the 2nd floor. She washed up and changed into a nightshirt and fell fast asleep. Pamela Mae had two wonderful and astonishing dreams that night.

The first dream was very romantic and Pamela Mae was riding her Arabian mare, *Marenga la Primera*, at a moderate pace. It was early November, in the Commonwealth of Virginia and her beloved fiancé, Mario LaGrande, was in civilian clothes, which emphasized his impressive stature. He was riding alongside her, on his Arabian stallion, *Marengo il Secondo.* The very happy couple were enjoying themselves very much during the trip. They decided to stop for a rest and have their horses graze and get a drink by a small stream. Pamela Mae was in the "mood for love," and after tying up the horses to a rail fence, she got a blanket out and laid it over a section of grass. Mario was very aroused, and they had sweet intimate physical relations right there in the country. Pamela Mae said, "Darling, I have wanted to make love outside with you again ever since our first time at "Sunshine Hills" after the Battle of Bull Run/Manassas."

Pamela Mae woke up soon after the conclusion of her "marvelous dream" and got up and drank a glass of water and thought, *Oh my goodness, even in my dreams, Mario and I have the most wonderful ambrosial time loving one another in the outdoors under a tree."*

She went back to sleep, and in her second dream, Pamela Mae was again riding her trusted horse, *Marenga la Primera.* This time, she was traveling at a very high rate of speed and wearing her "Virginia Army Regimental Captain's Uniform." She noticed that her cousin, Captain Christopher Russell was riding his horse next to her and he is also in uniform. They appear to be on a training mission. Suddenly, there appeared a high-ranking flamboyant officer on horseback. He was wearing a grey uniform, draped in a big grey flowing "Cavalier-Style Cape," and he was chasing them. He had a trusted aide-de-camp with him, and they started to pursue our two Captains Brewer and Russell. Pamela Mae briefly looked over her shoulder and saw a Colonel and he had a full beard. Well, the amazing and perplexing dream ended, and Pamela Mae woke up and said to herself, "Who could this mysterious 'Cavalier Officer' be? I think he looks familiar. Lord, have mercy!"

Pamela Mae was up early that morning, got washed up, and dressed in a ranch work outfit. She quietly went down to the kitchen and saw Lizzy and Martha hard at work, brewing coffee and frying bacon and potatoes. Lizzy gave her a morning hug and then told her joyfully, "I am so glad you are home; I feel more secure when you are around, and here is your coffee and breakfast of bacon, eggs, potatoes, and fried bread with blackberry jelly."

After finishing her tasty first meal of the day, Pamela Mae took a piece of paper and a pencil. She thought logically to herself, *I should make an inventory of every animal, piece of equipment, amounts of grain, and number of field and stable hands who are available for work. Also, I should note any irregularities that I see and discuss the issues with Papa.*

Fortunately, Will helped with the inventory. Will was the common law husband of Lizzy and the father of Gloria Faye and was very fond of Pamela Mae and extremely loyal to her papa and mamma. He supervised the workers outside and knew a considerable amount about the details of the horse population and other businesses of the Brewer Family. Will was available for wise advice and sound information. He assisted her and identified the horses and other equestrian related animals which included:

3 Arabian Stallions and 2 Breeding Mares
7 Plow horses
3 Cuban *Criollo* Horses
8 Quarter Horses
6 Morgan Gelded Horses
5 Mules

In addition, Pamela Mae and Will counted:

3 Cows, 3 Calves, and 1 Bull
5 Hogs, 10 piglets
20 Chickens, 1 Rooster
24 Pieces of farm equipment
1 Ton of hay
1 Ton of straw

45 Bushels of Corn

Note: Sunshine Hills had twelve, strong colored and two white laborers who worked the land and fifty acres of bearded wheat and twenty-five acres of yellow corn that were in the fields.

Pamela Mae found out that the Confederate States of America's (CSA) War Department, had contracted with the Brewer Family and had already purchased twenty horses and mules, fifteen hogs, ten head of cattle, and two tons of hay since the start of the "Civil War."

In addition to her meticulous inventory of the plantation's many assets, Pamela Mae got reacquainted with her Arabian horse, *Marenga la Primera* and began to ride her daily.

She would spend the next three weeks from August 2nd through August 23rd, 1861, performing a variety of duties and functions, in place of the Master to include the sale of horses, cattle, and swine. She gained a lot of personal and professional enjoyment as her "Sunshine Hills" plantation and associated businesses were being managed to the utmost satisfaction of her father.

Of course, Pamela Mae thought often and faithfully of her Captain Mario LaGrande who was back in Alexandria with the "Union Army." *Dear Lord Jesus, please take care of my "Mario Bello," and may we be back in each other's arms, once there is a lull in the war. Amen.*

It was now Tuesday afternoon, the 20th of August 1861, and Pamela Mae was so elated and surprised to see her cousin, Captain Christopher Russell. He was on his old horse, Bluebonnet, and distinctively rode up towards the mansion. Pamela Mae smiled brightly at her dear cousin and fellow Captain. He is also an Army officer in the 1st Manassas (Virginia) Infantry Regiment.

Pamela Mae thought about him and about her military responsibilities. *Praise the Lord that Christopher is here and that we can train in earnest with our swords, pistols, rifles, ropes, and ride our horses as we try to simulate various battle actions, scenarios, and reconnaissance missions. Amen!*

Soon thereafter, Captain Pamela Mae Brewer and Captain Christopher Russell started to conduct military training maneuvers and rode their horses daily while they prepared themselves mentally and physically to return to combat and other relevant Army missions.

Pamela Mae will soon be very surprised when a "well known officer" comes to visit her and Christopher. Furthermore, the "Brewer Family" will welcome three additional residents to their "Sunshine Hills" plantation home near Manassas, in Prince William County, Virginia.

Chapter 5
Mario, Love Poem, U.S. Capital Region
August 21ˢᵗ, 1861

Saint Albans' Mountaineer Regiment
Vermont (Green Mountain) Brigade
Alexandria, Virginia
Wednesday, August 21ˢᵗ, 1861

Mia Cara Pamela Bella
(My Dear Pretty Pamela),

Good evening, Darling. I hope and pray to 'our Good Lord Jesus' that you are healthy and happy and have returned to the safety and security of your home in 'Sunshine Hills,' Prince William County, Virginia.

I have spent the last three weeks in command of "A Company" in Alexandria, Arlington, and Washington, D.C. Together, our soldiers, freedmen, horses, and mules have been constructing defensive works and fortifications. These challenging and complex tasks have been accomplished during extreme periods of heat throughout the United States Capital Region.

My good friend and fellow Vermont Officer, Captain Maurice Flambeau, has been expertly conducting similar military operations, in Command of his "B Company" troops. In addition, Captain Joseph Wei, our Quartermaster Officer, and mutual friend has been providing excellent logistical and quartermaster support to our entire regiment.

Alleluia (Praise the Lord), Gloria Faye is doing well and working in the food service (Mess Tent) area, as she helps prepare and cook three meals a day and brew coffee for our Army personnel and civilian workers. Maurice and Gloria Faye send their love and appreciation as they continue to enjoy their 2nd floor accommodations at the *Mansion du Moreau* (Moreau Mansion) in Alexandria.

Sweetheart, I miss you so much and long to kiss and hold you tight while we make passionate love once again. Baby, please be careful and write back when you are able and tell me about yourself and any adventures during the last few weeks. In addition, may God bless your father, mother, Lizzy, and others at your Virginia home.

I have written this enclosed poem in English and Italian to you, "My Lovely Virginia Lady." It is a small token of my devotion and dedication, *Mia Regina Bellissima* (My Beautiful Queen). Every word is filled with affection and tenderness from my amorous heart and joyful soul. *Ti amo per sempre* (I'll love you forever), my beautiful brown eyed girl!"

Con tanto affetto, (With much affection),

Tuo Mario Bello (Your Handsome Mario)

P.S. I Love You, and I paid a Sutler, named Ron McGavock, to hand deliver this letter to your home since he was traveling to Richmond, Virginia today.

My Lovely Virginia Lady,
My Pretty Pamela Poem
*(Mia Donna Virginiana Bellissima,
Mia Pamela Bella Poema)*

My Lovely Virginia Lady, My Pretty Pamela, You are my dream come true, and I am your Mario Fella.

(Mia Donna Virginiana Bellissima, Mia Pamela Bella, Sei il mio sogno che diventa realtà, e io sono il tuo Mario Amico).

You are adorable at seventeen, the royal vista of a beauty queen.

(Sei adorabile a diciassette anni, la vista reale di una reginetta di bellezza).

My Beautiful Brown Eyed Miss, with your ebony black luxurious hair.

(Mia Signorina Dagli Occhi Castani Belli, con i tuoi ebono lussuosi capelli).

Baby, you have the most enticing luscious lips, They are so irresistible, and with them, I must kiss.

(Bambina, Hai le labbra carnose più seducenti, Sono così irresistibili e con esse devo Baciarli).

Your brilliant smile brings infinite joy within my heart and soul.

(Il tuo sorriso brillante porta gioia infinita nel mio cuore e nella mia anima).

Your darling dimples are so cute, like a baby doll.

(Le tue care fossette sono più carine, come una bambolina).

Your voluptuous breasts are beautiful and
perfectly shaped.

*(Le tue mammele voluttuose sono belli e
perfettamente modellati).*

Pretty Pamela, your alluring walk with such a
captivating derriere, a superb figure, without
compare.

*(Pamela Bella, la tua passeggiata seducente con
un fondoschiena così accattivante, una figura
superba, senza paragoni).*

Your delicate hands, with light pink nails, are so
elegant.

*(Le tue mani delicate, con le unghie rosa acceso,
sono così eleganti).*

My Lovely Virginia Lady, My Pretty Pamela,
your faith in the Lord is steadfast.

*(Mia Donna Virginiana Bellissima , Mia Pamela
Bella, la tua fede nel Signore è salda).*

Your sweet personality, charming voice, and
friendly nature is so endearing to me.

(La tua dolce personalità, voce affascinante, e la

tua natura amichevole sono così affettuose per me).

Your generous spirit and charitable works are so inspiring.

(Il tuo spirito generoso e le tue opere di beneficenza sono così stimolanti).

You appear as Captain Pamela Mae Brewer on your Arabian steed, a magnificent sight to behold, indeed!

(Appari come la Capitana Pamela Mae Brewer sul tuo destriero Arabo, davvero uno spettacolo magnifico da vedere)!

My Darling Pamela Mae, our lives are so adventurous, and our enduring love is so tremendous.

(Mia Cara Pamela Mae, le nostre vite sono così avventurose e il nostro amore duraturo è così tremendo).

You are well known as Miss Robin Bea Goode throughout the land, defeating many scoundrels and villains.

*(Sei ben nota come Signorina la Pettirossa Sia
Buona, in tutto il paese, che sconfiggi molti
mascalzoni e cattivi).*

You are adept and exceptional with your sharp
saber, while fending off each challenger and
invader.

*(Sei abile ed eccezionale con la tua sciabola
affilata, mentre respingi ogni sfidante e
invasore).*

My Pretty Pamela, the love you share with your
handsome Mario is fabulous and fantastical.

*(Mia Pamela Bella, l'amore che condividi con il
tuo Mario Bello è favoloso e fantastico).*

Your sensational body united with mine is like
traveling in the Heavens, so divine.

*(Il tuo corpo sensazionale unito al mio, è come
viaggiare nei Cieli, così divino).*

Sweetheart, you are my precious treasure, your
fascinating amor results in my ultra pleasure,
forevermore.

(Dolce-cuore, tu sei la mia preziosa tesora, il tuo affascinante amore risulta nel mio ultra piacere, per sempre).

My Beauteous Princess, with such an exquisite touch, I love you so very much.

(Mia Bella Principessa, con un tocco così squisito, ti amo così tanto).

My glamorous southern belle, your northern gentleman has a very affectionate love for you, my passionate lover and good friend. Amen!

(Mia affascinante bellezza del sud, il tuo gentiluomo del nord ha un amore molto affettuoso per te, mia amante appassionata e amica buona. Cosi sia)!

It had been raining steadily in the "U.S. Capital Region" for two days straight on Tuesday, August 20th and Wednesday, August 21st. It was now the following morning, Thursday, August 22nd, 1861, and the Potomac River was flowing rapidly.

After having a substantial breakfast of: Southern Corn Pone Bread, fried potatoes, with onions and bacon, and coffee; Captain Mario

LaGrande led his A Company Saint Albans' Mountaineer Regiment out of their base camp. Captain LaGrande will manage today's work detail in the southern section of Alexandria. His personnel will be concerned with constructing defensive emplacements, earthworks, and parapets along the Washington and Alexandria Turnpike. This huge project is deemed necessary by the "Union Army" due to the many intelligence and reconnaissance reports of seeing "Confederate Cavalry" brigades within a twenty-mile half circle of Washington, D.C.

Mario often thinks, in English and Italian, of his beautiful and sweet fiancée, in a prayerful manner, *Dearest Lord Jesus and Blessed Mother Mary, please protect Mia Pamela Bella (My Pretty Pamela) and her family in Prince William County, Virginia. Prego nel nome del Padre, del Figlio e dello Spirito Santo, Cosi sia (I pray in the name of the Father, Son, and Holy Spirit. Amen).*

Captain LaGrande and his men will work closely with the soldiers of B Company, who are commanded by Captain Maurice Flambeau. His troops and civilian workers will be located to his left flank, just south of A Company.

Furthermore, Captain Joseph Wei will set up near the Potomac River, in order to provide construction supplies (cement blocks, hemp ropes, wires, wooden beams, etc.) and tools (sledge hammers, pick axes, pikes, etc.) to the respective work parties. His quartermaster location will be further south downriver in order to more easily access the cargo resupply boats.

Captains LaGrande and Flambeau are both feeling a sense of accomplishment as much progress has been made in the construction of the breastworks and artificial obstacles. Later in the afternoon, near the Potomac River, Mario told his life-long companion Maurice candidly in French and English, "*Mon bon ami et Capitaine* (My good friend and Captain), our day together has been successful. Let's give our soldiers and civilian workers a break and provide them some refreshments along the banks of the river. Captain Flambeau knew that there were a few bottles of "Hard Apple Cider" that were available and said in French and English, "*Oui, oui, Monsieur* (Yes, yes, Sir), I have access to some alcohol, so let's indulge our diligent working crews and give them something very tasty and spirited to drink!"

It was a very comfortable sunny day and many of the men were drinking the hard cider. Then later, a couple of the soldiers took off their hats, were joking around, and started a friendly wrestling match. Captains LaGrande and Flambeau were both enjoying the sweet drinks and watched amusingly as the two wrestlers got very close to the high and briskly flowing Potomac River. Mario had a comical thought and rhyme appear quickly in his mind, *The two wrestlers are playing around, vying for the advantage before they fall down.* Unluckily, the grapplers were in a mutual "bear hug," and then staggered and fell over sideways into the merciless moving current.

Unfortunately, neither of the soldiers could swim very well, as the current took their flailing bodies downriver towards Captain Joseph Wei and his quartermaster supply area. At this point, Captain LaGrande and Captain Flambeau saw the two soldiers in aquatic distress and took off their swords swiftly and dropped their loaded pistols to the ground and ran at full speed along the riverbank towards the drowning duo.

Fortunately, Captain Wei saw the entire incident and rapidly dragged out a hundred-foot rope. There happened to be an old sycamore tree that was down along the Potomac riverbank. Consequently, Captains LaGrande and Flambeau were able to take about fifty feet of the rope and swim out to the long branches of the downed tree. By the "Grace of God," our brave "Vermont

Cavaliers" were able to quickly grab and heroically rescue the very soaked troops from the unforgiving river. Amen!

It was now two days later, in the late morning of Saturday, August 24th, 1861. A Company and B Company of the Saint Albans' Mountaineer Regiment, commanded by Captain Mario LaGrande and Captain Maurice Flambeau, respectively, were now in the U.S. Capitol region on a different assignment.

Captain LaGrande briefly thought about yesterday's very sacred and touching mission, *It was an honor to assist in the initial construction of a cemetery on the grounds of "Arlington House." I also thank God that my future wife, Pamela Mae, and her good friend, Gloria Faye, were here last month to assist in the escape of my future father-in-law, Confederate Lieutenant Colonel John Brewer. Alleluia (Praise the Lord)!*

The mission today was to reinforce the banks of the Potomac River with huge rough stones. The Vermont Companies were operating near the U.S. Arsenal at the southern point of Washington, D.C. The industrious sergeants and privates utilized the very strong Morgan horses and mules to pull the heavy loads of big rocks on the reinforced supply wagons.

Suddenly, Captain Mario LaGrande heard a lot of noise and shouts of men who expressed many cheerful forms of "Hurrah, Hooray, and Huzzah," as he looked towards an officer who was receiving much attention from all the soldiers. A few minutes later, Captain LaGrande could see the very familiar face and form of Major General George B. McClellan. He was majestically riding his splendid tall purebred dark bay horse named Daniel Webster. The impressive steed was named in honor of that eloquent orator and famous senator from New Hampshire and Massachusetts.

Captain Flambeau was supervising his troops about thirty yards away near a copse of trees. Captain LaGrande turned towards his companion and fellow officer and yelled in French, "Capitaine *Flambeau, venez vite saluer le Général* (Captain Flambeau, come quickly and let's meet the General)!"

Shortly thereafter, Captains LaGrande and Flambeau ordered their respective Lieutenants to be in charge of A and B Company; as they hurried towards General McClellan. Captain Mario LaGrande, who usually takes the initiative and is extremely confident by nature, worked his way through the crowd of dedicated soldiers, curious civilians, and adoring women.

He finally got close to the "Union Commander, "and boldly greeted him, saying, "Good day, General McClellan. I am Captain Mario LaGrande from Vermont. Do you remember me being in Grafton last May and June in Taylor and Barbour counties and the Battle of Philippi, Virginia (now West Virginia)?"

Major General McClellan, who had an incredible memory, gave Mario a serious gaze as he easily recognized the junior officer and replied, "Yes, Captain LaGrande, I do remember that You had numerous reconnaissance, scouting skills, and briefing talents. Also, you were able to avoid precarious situations, to and from my Headquarters. Furthermore, I will have a need for experienced intelligence gathering 'Cavalier Officers,' like yourself for future missions. I will definitely keep you in mind for additional assignments!"

General McClellan and his entourage were pressed for time as they turned around and headed back towards the "War Department" located on 21st and Virginia Avenue. However, Captain Flambeau was able to have a minute with the obliging General and volunteered to accompany Captain LaGrande on any possible missions.

By this time, both of our good friends, Mario and Maurice, were feeling very good about their brief encounter, and the honor to converse with Major General McClellan. Consequently, Captains LaGrande and Flambeau resumed their defensive obstacles construction missions as they returned to be with their hard-working soldiers and civilian personnel of A and B Company of the Saint Albans' Mountaineer Regiment. Mario was inspired to think somewhat predictively, *In the future, there may be a promotion for me to Major, if I can perform my assigned duties in a superb manner!*

Captain LaGrande would later that evening enter his duties, anecdotes , and memorable time with the General and the overall spectacular reaction of the "Union Soldiers" to the Commanding Officer into his "Commonplace Book."

Chapter 6
Love Letter, Visitors, and Orders
August 24th, 1861

"Sunshine Hills"
Prince William County
Manassas, Virginia
August 24th, 1861, 5:00 a.m.

Mio Caro Mario (My Dear Mario),

Good morning, my darling sweetheart! Yesterday, I received your very affectionate and romantic letter that was hand delivered by that nice sutler gentleman named Mister McGavock.

Mario, my love, you are my very 'Handsome Vermont Cavalier' who I adore and love dearly. Thank you so much for the exceedingly amorous and sensual poem that you wrote about your devoted "Brown-Eyed Manassas Girl." You are the "true love of my very blessed life." You have exceptional writing skills, and I will forever cherish the "My Lovely Virginia Lady, My Pretty Pamela Poem" in both English and *Italiano*. I am convinced that you will be a brilliant author one day.

Baby, I think of you always and my heart is filled with love for you. My mind carries our fond memories of yesterdays and tender feelings for tomorrow. I will always and forevermore be *tua Pamela Bella* (your Pretty Pamela).

Honey, I have so much to tell you about what has occurred during the last twenty-four days as I write this long, detailed letter. A few of my stories about our special visitors will be summarized. I will also include some brief background information about my next reconnaissance and scouting assignment for the Virginia (Old Dominion) Brigade.

On that day that I left Alexandria, Virginia, I was surely blessed and protected by our Father, his Son Jesus, and the Holy Ghost. Amen. I was able to ride my very fast quarter horse *Romano* without incident to Fairfax Station, Virginia. I had the pleasure of enjoying lunch with coffee at a rest stop called "The Three Sisters Tavern." I was fortunate to meet and talk to the three very pretty, contented, and good-humored sisters named Maryann, Carol, and Rita. They also provided me with pertinent information that was useful for the duration of my journey.

After the delicious meal, I left Fairfax Station and was on the road towards Prince William

County, Virginia. I later encountered along the way a small group of Virginia troops led by a Lieutenant named Eric Bolden. I was able to use my pretty features, cleverness, ingenuity, and charming feminine ways to gather news about the possible dangers on the road to Manassas. In addition, I talked my way out of the awkward situation and departed from my fellow soldiers amicably.

Afterwards, I rode towards Clifton, Virginia and eventually made it across the county line. Consequently, I headed along a parallel thoroughfare in the direction of the Orange and Alexandria Railroad. I was once again protected by my "Guardian Angels" as I shot my way through an apparent robbery attack by a pair of suspected thieves. I was able to wound each of the scoundrels with bullets, which discouraged them from pursuing me. "Thank God" I made it through that dangerous ordeal and vanished from their sight unscathed.

I wanted to make it back to my plantation home before dinner, and the "Lord of all Mankind" blessed my arrival that evening. A few hours later, I was overjoyed to see the entrance to "Sunshine Hills" that has trees on each side of the picturesque, shaded lane.

Sweetheart, do your remember my "German Shepherd Dog Butch"? Well, my loyal companion was the first one to welcome me with his familiar 'arf, arf, arf, ruff, ruff, ruff, and woof, woof, woof,' greetings! Also, my trusted "Arabian mare," *Marenga la Primera,* sensed me immediately and welcomed me with 'neighs and whinnies,' with her distinctive equine voice.

First, I saw Mamma and we hugged, kissed, and cried warm tears of joy. Oh, Mario, please tell Gloria Faye that her "Mamma Lizzy and Papa Will" are doing well and asked about their only daughter. I reassured them that Gloria Faye was freed, doing well, and working for the "Union Army" in Alexandria, as a cook and food service assistant.

Papa was so relieved to see his daughter and we had a good long talk. I told him how much 'I love you,' and your proposal of marriage. I proudly showed him my radiant three-diamond engagement ring. Sweetheart, he wants you to ask him for permission to marry me and I said you would do that once there is a lull in this awful Civil War.

In addition, since Papa is hindered by his leg wound, he needed me to help manage our "Sunshine Hills" plantation, estate, and businesses. I have been busy and occupied with Will's assistance in the inventory of our animals, crops, equipment, and labor. We have sold corn, hay, and straw to the farmers and ranchers in the regional area. Furthermore, I have been involved with the breeding, delivery, and sale of our horses, cattle, and swine.

Personally, I have had the pleasure of my cousin, Captain Christopher Russell's, company as we train for our projected military service with our 1st Manassas (Virginia) Infantry Regiment. I must admit that I enjoy riding and maneuvering *Marenga la Primera* at very high speeds with my riding partner. Christopher has purchased a "Cuban *Criollo* Horse" from our breeding stock that he calls "Cisco," and talks to him in Spanish. His stallion is finely built and is very fast indeed!

In addition, we have been practicing shooting regularly with our .44 caliber revolvers and our long rifles and throwing knives at the designated targets in the woods near the corn fields. Also, I have been safely dueling and fencing with Captain Russell in order to maintain my sword fighting skills. He was born and raised in Texas, where he learned to speak Spanish and how to use a rope to *lasso*. I have had the most fun as I tie and throw my lassoed rope over manmade objects, horses, cattle, and upon my cousin Christopher, too!

My Dearest Love Mario, I want to tell you about a very unique dream that came true a couple of days ago. Christopher and I were on a trip together to another plantation near a small town named Warrenton, Virginia. We traveled west approximately twenty-one miles by horseback to the estate of Major (Retired) Daman Whitt, who was a Mexican War Veteran. He buys and sells quarter horses and we delivered a stallion and a breeding mare to him that afternoon.

On the return trip, about midway between Warrenton and Manassas, we stopped briefly for a rest for ourselves and our horses. We were underneath a grove of huge 'Northern Catalpa' trees. There was a slow flowing stream that *Marenga la Primera* and *Cisco* drank from in order to quench their thirsts. Christopher was feeling very confident with his new horse and riding abilities. Then he challenged me saying, "Pamela Mae, let's have a race back to 'Sunshine Hills' and I bet you twenty dollars that I will win!"

I thought about the proposed race, and I told him, "I accept your challenge and let's ride our best and not stop until we hear the sounds of Butch as he welcomes our return to the mansion.

"Of course, I knew that I had a distinct advantage over my opponent, since *Marenga la Primera* is an Arabian horse, and she 'loves to run.' I am sure that you know that this ancient breed, with origins in the "Middle East" goes back circa 4,500 years and is well known for its striking appearance. Most importantly, Arabian horses have superior speed and the utmost endurance during long races.

Well, it was about a ten-mile competitive race back to 'Sunshine Hills' and I was able to maintain a circa one-hundred-yard lead, within a mile of our home destination. Then, I raced around a big curve in the road and momentarily looked over my right shoulder and saw two men. They were wearing grey uniforms and were halfway between myself and Christopher. I could even hear my cousin yell out to me, "Pamela Mae, slow down. "However, due to my very competitive nature, I just had to finish the race and win! I then heard Butch barking as I approached our grand estate. I realized that my dream had come true. One of the riders was the striking "Cavalier Gentleman" who had an attractive full beard and was adorned in the most elegant flowing grey cape. He was one of the dashing "Confederate Heroes" from the July 21st, 1861, Battle of Manassas/Bull Run. His name is Colonel Joseph Ewell Brown (J.E.B.) Stuart. He was very polite, with impeccable manners, and is from Ararat, Virginia.

He and his aide-de-camp were on a double mission. Due to our reputation of having the highest quality horse stock, Colonel Stuart, who was from Patrick County, Virginia, had the individual incentive to examine, ride, and purchase an "Arabian stallion" for himself. Secondly, Colonel Stuart had written assignment orders in hand for me and Christopher from the Commander of the Virginia (Old Dominion) Brigade.

He told me personally, "Captain Brewer, you are well known throughout Virginia for your bravery and courage in battle. In addition, the Commander, Brigadier General Albert Morgan, is very knowledgeable of your exemplary intelligence gathering, reconnaissance, and scouting skills. Furthermore, I have seen you riding your horse in a very aggressive and yet controlled and rapid manner. Finally, on a personal note, you may visit my home in Patrick County, near Ararat, Virginia at any time and I will let my family know about this open invitation. Amen."

I did have a chance to talk privately to Colonel Stuart in our library and he admired my latest painting that is on the wall over the fireplace (see Grandma's Roses Painting). I thanked and told him, 'Sir, I was artistically influenced by that famous Italian-American impressionist painter, Lorenzo Giovanni Braggi. "Prophetically, I had this very bad spiritual feeling that Colonel Stuart would not survive the war and would die near Richmond, Virginia. I hugged him and whispered in his ear, 'Colonel Stuart, please be careful, I have a premonition that your life will come to an end near a Yellow Tavern.' May our Good Lord bless you and care for your family. Amen."

Note: J.E.B. Stuart would later become a Major General. He is considered by many historians to be one of the most charismatic, flamboyant, and gallant *beaux sabreurs* (handsome swordsmen) of the Confederacy.

Grandma's Roses Painting

Sweetheart, I have my orders in hand as I am assigned, along with my cousin, Captain Christopher Russell, to the Headquarters of the

Virginia (Old Dominion) Brigade for an indefinite period of time. The Brigade is currently located in Front Royal, Virginia. Colonel Stuart indicated that there is a necessity to confront the "Union Army" that is occupying many of the counties in the western portion of Virginia. There will be a need for me to write up an intelligence and reconnaissance report of my travels, with maps. The "Staff Report" must include intricate details of the various geographic locations of the 'Federal Troops and Movements' in a few counties of Western Virginia (now West Virginia). Mario, I am sorry that there is so much animosity, conflict, and misunderstanding between the peoples of the North and South.

Mamma and Papa are, of course, concerned about my going back into danger and harm's way. I showed my father the orders and apologized to him for my impending departure. He accepted and supported my military assignment and surprised me when he stated in German and English, "*Mach dir keine sorgen, meine freundliche Tochter* (Do not worry, my kind daughter). I am recovering better than I expected from my leg wound. Furthermore, we are also expecting visitors that will be of great help to your mother and me."

Oh Darling, the entire household received a very pleasant surprise yesterday. Butch alerted us all to the arrival of three significant visitors from Germany, with a wagon full of personal belongings and abounding supplies. Mamma, Papa, and I welcomed our cousins Franz Warner and his very robust wife Hannah and their ten-year-old boy, Leo, to our "Sunshine Hills" plantation. Their family and ancestors are from *Prussia* and have been farmers for many generations. Mr. Warner is very strong and has a considerable amount of agricultural training, animal husbandry knowledge, and is an expert horse breeder. Mrs. Warner is an accomplished seamstress and an excellent cook. Little Leo is very clever for his age and shares his witticisms freely with adults. They will sleep in my bedroom, while I am on my next military assignment.

Mio Mario Bello (My Handsome Mario), tomorrow I will soon be departing the comforts and pleasures of my "Sunshine Hills" plantation home. I will comply with the Army orders and travel west towards the 'Blue Ridge Mountains.' I composed this love poem as I most certainly have a perpetual fondness for You!

My Handsome Vermont Cavalier,
My Gallant Knight

My Handsome Vermont Cavalier,
My Gallant Knight,

You are so amazing and debonair, with
extraordinary courage and might;

I have dreamed, hoped, and prayed to the Lord,
to see you for many years.

Finally, at the Battle of Philippi is when you first
appeared!

Your very majestic frame sitting on your
Arabian steed,

Attracted your Virginia Dame with the utmost
aspiration, indeed!

I found out from Madam Carter that you were
Captain Mario LaGrande.

I knew from the beginning, you would become
my Northern gentleman!

At the Battle of Manassas, we were initially
against one another;

Later that night, we would be united as two
very amorous lovers!

Mario Bello (Handsome Mario), you have all the
best physical qualities.

I love the ways that you use your power,
strength, your perfect anatomy!

Baby, every time that you feel and kiss me,
enflames my inner fire.

Your hot, wet French kisses fulfills my most
passionate desires!

Darling Dear, even though we may be many
days and miles apart,

I will always and forevermore love you with all
my affectionate heart!

Toda Mi Amor (All My Love),
Your *Fiancée* Pamela Mae

It was very early on that Sunday morning,
August 25th, 1861, and Captain Pamela Mae
Brewer was getting dressed in her solid grey
Virginia uniform. She made sure that her "34-
inch Light Cavalry Saber" was sharpened and

securely placed into her matching silver scabbard. Also, Captain Brewer would be carrying two sidearms: a .44 caliber revolver and a .36 caliber LeMat revolver. She is blessed with ambidextrous skills and can wield a sword and fire a gun with either hand.

Will and one of the other stable hands were outside grooming and preparing to place the saddle and saddlebags on each horse. Captain Brewer would, of course, be astride on her remarkable Arabian mare, *Marenga la Primera,* and Captain Christopher Russell would be riding his new Cuban Criollo horse, *Cisco.*

Pamela Mae could see the pale sunrise light of that summer morning coming through the big windows in the front of the mansion. She was now on the 1st floor and was walking down the hall, past the green *baize* covered side table from France. Her dear cousin, Christopher, who is also an "early bird," was already seated in the dining room. He had just finished drinking a cup of dark South American coffee while he made the initial notes for his "Staff Report." Lizzy was in the kitchen and assisting with the food preparation and would fetch Captain Russell another cup of coffee before eating.

Hannah Warner was up early and patiently brought in a hot cup of coffee with cream for Captain Pamela Mae Brewer. Hannah, who has a very inquisitive nature, was astounded and impressed to see Captain Brewer in her complete Confederate Army uniform with sword and pistol. She felicitously and formally greeted her attractive cousin, Pamela Mae, who had a full curtain of luxurious black hair. Hannah stated in German, *"Guten morgen, Captain, und haben sie hunger (*Good Morning, Captain, and are you hungry)?" Captain Brewer did not hesitate and replied in her father's tongue, *"Ja bitte, ich bin ausgehungert* (Yes, please, I am famished)."

Frau (Madam) Warner prepared a very delicious Prussian and Bavarian style farewell meal for Captains Brewer and Russell, and the rest of the household. The very delectable culinary items included:

German *Spaetzle* Dumplings, with bacon
Weisswurst (Bavarian veal sausage)
Spiegelei (fried eggs)
Rührei (scrambled eggs, with *Tilset* cheese and parsley)
Hot out of the oven, Baked Pumpernickel Bread
A Big Pot of Dark Roast Coffee

After saying grace and a few scrumptious bites, Pamela Mae thought prayerfully, *Oh my goodness, Hannah's food is so delicious, I know Papa, Mamma, and the rest of our extended family will thoroughly enjoy themselves this morning. Hallelujah (Praise the Lord)!*

Captain Brewer had just finished her breakfast when her father and mother came downstairs to say their blessings and good-byes. Mamma Sarah Anne kissed her teary cheeks and hugged her tenderly and said,

"My Pretty Pamela Mae, God bless and protect you. Farewell and be careful my Sweet Girl. Amen!" Our "Lovely Virginia Lady and Army Captain" replied with an emotional voice, "Oh Mamma, thank you. I love you so much, and by the 'Grace of God,' I shall return."

Her papa, John Brewer, who is feeling sad and worried, struggled to get his words out and said in German and English, "*Möge unser Herr Jesus Sie im Namen des Vaters, des Sohnes und des Heiligen Geistes segnen. Amen!* (May our Lord Jesus bless you in the name of the Father, Son, and Holy Ghost. Amen)! Please give my regards to the Brigade Commander and be alert my dearest daughter and Virginia Army Captain. I want to be there at your wedding to escort You down the aisle." This brought "tears of joy" to Pamela Mae's beaming gorgeous brown eyes as she told her Father happily, "Yes, Papa, I will be alert and careful and pray to 'our Good Lord,' that we will all be together joyfully for my nuptials with Captain LaGrande." Captain Pamela Mae Brewer left her "Sunshine Hills" mansion and turned around and waved to her loving parents who were on the front portico. Lizzy and Will came out of the side doors to also wave good-bye to both Captain Brewer and Captain Russell. Even her cousin, "Little Leo," opened the 2nd floor window of her brothers' old bedroom. With his father, Franz, and mother, Hannah, next to him, Leo shouted a blessing in German, "*Tschüss Pamela Mae, Gott sei mit dir* (Bye Pamela Mae, God be with you)!"

With Captain Russell on his horse, Cisco, to her right, Captain Pamela Mae Brewer rode her Arabian mare, *Marenga la Primera,* through the tree lined lane out of "Sunshine Hills." She began her official duties, in accordance with her military orders. However, Pamela Mae mused and thought fondly and prayerfully of her personal "Hercules and *Romeo," Mario, my Precious Treasure, with your beautiful azure eyes, you are everything to me. You are the answer to all my desires, dreams, hopes, and wishes. I long and want to kiss you endlessly and be with you again in your strong loving embrace. You are my Vermont Cavalier, Italian Stallion, French Musketeer, and Roman Soldier All in One. In honor of our Father, Son, Holy Ghost, and Saint Patrick, May our Good Lord Jesus hold you in the palms of His hands. Amen!*

Chapter 7
Western Virginia to Pocahontas County
August 25th, 1861

Captain Pamela Mae Brewer and her cousin and fellow officer, Captain Christopher Russell, departed their "Sunshine Hills Virginia Home" at 5:30 a.m. and were riding west on that rainy August 25th, 1861, morning. Their mutual objective was to arrive in Front Royal, Virginia by dinner time that evening. Captain Brewer was making extensive mental notes of the prominent terrain features along the very muddy route. The substantial amount of rain coming down had made travel arduous and exceedingly slow. The "Southern Army Officers" wanted to be at the Headquarters of the Virginia (Old Dominion) Brigade by 6:00 p.m. as stipulated by their orders.

At approximately 11:00 a.m., the rain ceased and the sun came out for a while. Pamela Mae looked upwards towards the partly cloudy skies and said out loud, "Thank You, Lord God, for the break in the weather!" Captain Brewer then thought of something individually for herself, *If I can excel in my assignment as a reconnaissance and scouting officer, perhaps Brigadier General*

Morgan would give me the honor of a promotion to Major.

After taking a lunch break and a couple more hours of travel by horseback, Captains Brewer and Russell came upon a muddy mountain landslide of dirt, rocks, and trees. There was a solitary sorrel female quarter horse with saddle that was alone on the east side of the road. The abandoned horse was apparently searching for her master. Captain Pamela Mae Brewer quickly dismounted from *Marenga la Primera* and gave Captain Russell the reins to her mare.

Captain Brewer got the attention of the unoccupied horse by whistling and saying, "Come here, Girl. You will be alright, Sweetie." The horse responded in a positive manner and approached "Our Lovely Virginia Lady." She took hold of her reins and petted the "Sorrel," and then the horse led Pamela Mae to the edge of a steep slope. Captain Brewer carefully looked over the edge and could see a partial view of a man in uniform that was clinging to a tree stump. He appeared to be either dazed, sleeping, or unconscious.

Captain Pamela Mae Brewer took a brief moment and thought spiritually back about her previous rescues as Robin Bea Goode, *Thank You*

Lord, once again, You placed me in a situation to help someone out of trouble, Amen! Well, her "Gracious God" utilized the innate instincts of the "Sorrel horse" as the equine creature shouted out a very loud and vibrant whinny and squeal, which awakened the man. Pamela Mae then called out to him in an endearing and reassuring voice, "Hello, Sir. Do not worry. We are here to help you. It will be alright!" All she heard were faint groans emitting from the soldier's weary and injured body.

Shortly thereafter, Captains Brewer and Russell devised a plan to use their ropes and for Pamela Mae to rappel down the precipitous hill and bring the soldier back to the road. Captain Christopher Russell had a bottle of fine whiskey that was contained in his haversack and gave the "spirits" to Captain Brewer. Pamela Mae had not practiced rappelling; but she had read about the technique and saw it illustrated in a book. Christopher gave his cousin a quick verbal rappel tutorial and Pamela Mae understood the instructions.

Captain Russell expeditiously fixed the lasso at the end of his fifty foot rope and tossed the circular end of the rope in the direction of the man near the tree truck. The lasso landed right in front of the soldier and then Captain Russell secured the other end to the horn of his saddle. He then held on tight to the rope line, about three feet from his horse, *Cisco*. Captain Brewer started to rappel down the slope while carrying the whiskey bottle in her haversack. She also had bandages, a balm to treat the abrasions/cuts to the man's flesh, and another piece of rope if needed.

Captain Pamela Mae Brewer continued to rappel nicely and descended carefully down the hill and she could hear the soldier groan and say, "Help me, Someone!" Pamela Mae thought briefly and faithfully about her heroics as a younger girl, *Oh Lord, one more rescue* of this *pitiful man, and may You revive him please, I pray. Amen!* Mercifully, her prayers were answered as the man cautiously stood up and said, "Hallelujah, the Lord has sent me an 'Angel' to save me." Captain Brewer turned around and secured the lasso to the tree and said, "Do not worry, Sir, Miss Robin is here!" Pamela Mae was surprised to hear herself say that and then properly introduced herself and found out the man's name was Captain Jeffrey Boyd.

Captain Brewer used the healing balm for the cut around Captain Boyd's left upper arm, bandaged his wound, and gave him a "wee bit" of whiskey. Consequently, she attached the lasso around his waist, and then held on to the tail end of the rope to ascend the hill with the injured officer. Subsequently, with a shout and a whistle from Pamela Mae, Captain Russell and his horse *Cisco* backed up along the road. The pulling actions with the horse and lassoed rope by Captain Russell enabled both Captain Boyd and Captain Brewer to slowly climb safely to the top of the steep slope to the rocky road above.

Captain Russell was able to untie the weary officer from the rope with the assistance of Captain Brewer. Captain Jeffrey Boyd was originally from Franklin, Virginia (now West Virginia). He was also en route to Front Royal and assigned as a "Reconnaissance and Scouting Officer" to the Virginia (Old Dominion) Brigade. As Pamela Mae was sharing her canteen of water with Captain Boyd, she sweetly thought about her *Mario Bello* (Handsome Mario), *It is truly amazing that her "Vermont Cavalier" Captain Mario LaGrande and his two very close friends, Captain Maurice Flambeau and Captain Joseph Wei, are like "The Three Musketeers." I wonder if myself, Captain Russell, and Captain Boyd will also be like those three brave "French Cavaliers and Swashbucklers."*

The rest of the journey would be slower due to the injury to Captain Boyd. Fortunately, there would be no further incidents or worries as "The Three Virginia Captains" arrived before supper that evening. Upon arrival to the camp, the tired officers reported promptly to Brigadier General Albert Morgan, who was the Commander of the Virginia (Old Dominion) Brigade. The brigade commander was taken aback by the dazzling great form of Captain Pamela Mae Brewer. He thought to himself, *Everybody I talked to commented that she has the most luxurious long black curly hair, the most luminous chocolate brown eyes, with the most inviting kissable lips, and they all were correct indeed!*

Brigadier General (BG) Morgan knew he must act professionally as he warmly welcomed all three of his new "Reconnaissance and Scouting Officers." Thereupon, he directed his aide-de-camp to have the "Mess Sergeant" bring the evening meals with strong coffee to the "Officer Briefing Tent."

After the tasty roast beef, potatoes, and carrots supper, Captain Brewer thought about her papa back in Prince William County and took the initiative and said, "Sir, my father, Lieutenant Colonel John Brewer of the 1st Manassas (Virginia) Infantry Regiment, sends his best regards to you. I also want to thank you for considering myself and Captain Russell for this important mission. We will do our utmost best to comply with your directives and orders while honoring and serving the Commonwealth of Virginia and the Confederacy!"

BG Morgan nodded his head in appreciation and was impressed with the communication skills of Captain Brewer. The Brigade Commander gave the following briefing. "Newly assigned officers to the Virginia (Old Dominion) Brigade, our distinguished and honorable President, Mr. Jefferson Davis of the Confederate States of America (CSA), is very concerned about the western counties of Virginia (now West Virginia). The 'War Department' in Richmond has received reports of a number of hostile 'Yankee Soldiers' in the following counties of Virginia: Pendleton, Pocahontas, Webster, and Nicholas."

Brigadier General Morgan hesitated for a moment and asked for comments and/or questions. Captain Jeffrey Boyd was quick to comment, as he bravely stated, "Sir, I lived and worked in Franklin, the County Seat of Pendleton, and I am also very familiar with the roads and stores/taverns and with many prominent citizens who reside in these four counties."

The Brigade Commander, was very pleased to hear this intriguing news from Jeffrey Boyd and responded, "Very good, Captain Boyd, and now I want to introduce all three of my 'Virginia Officers' to a trio of Sergeants who will be your assistants during your western mission." At this point, Captain Pamela Mae Brewer was surprised to see three very attractive Sergeants in their 20s, and she had a familial feeling about the men. They introduced themselves as Sergeants Pete, Earl, and Ralph Boone. The brothers and soldiers hailed from the Summersville area in Nicholas County, Virginia (now West Virginia).

Brigadier General Morgan continued his briefing and stated, "The Boone Brothers are also very familiar with: Pendleton, Pocahontas, Webster, and Nicholas Counties and will be invaluable to the operations. My staff will provide you with topographical maps and Captains Brewer, Boyd, and Russell, along with your three Sergeants, will act as the 'Vanguard' during the deployment of the Virginia (Old Dominion) Brigade."

In addition, BG Morgan explained, "Captain Brewer will be the 'Officer in Charge,' and all officers are tasked to make daily intelligence, reconnaissance, and scouting reports of the location, movements, and number of 'Federal Soldiers.' Furthermore, you will provide me information concerning any friendly 'Virginia Units,' you encounter. You will perform these very important duties, while ensuring that the "Main Body' is kept informed and secure as we move towards our objective of reaching the Tygart Valley River by September 9th, 1861."

The briefing concluded as all the officers and enlisted personnel stood up and saluted Brigadier General Morgan. Captain Brewer found a suitable location to bed down for the night, as her trusted Arabian mare, *Marenga la Primera,* was in a makeshift stall close by.

During her sweet slumber, Pamela Mae had the most amazing dream that she recorded in her journal. "I was a young teenage girl in a very big house that was full of my relatives. The home overlooked the Ohio River. I remember that the adults referred to the area as 'West Columbia,' and my grandma's name was Virginia and her daughter, Lois Ann, was there. I had an enchanting little sister in my dream, and she was like an Angel. Then I saw the three sisters from the restaurant in Fairfax Station: Carol, Maryann, and Rita and surprisingly the girls were joking and talking in a very friendly manner with the Boone Brothers: Pete, Earl, and Ralph.

Subsequently, to my delight, there was a very handsome man in an officer's uniform and he was smiling at me and the whole family and said in Italian, '*Come bella avere una famiglia numerosa* (How wonderful to have a large family).' I unashamedly gave the attractive gentleman one of my patented big smiles and winked at him. Then I realized at the very end of the dream that the man was Captain Mario Patrizio LaGrande, my *fiancé*, my love, and my Vermont Cavalier."

It was now Monday morning, August 26th, 1861, in Front Royal, Virginia. Just after the "crack of dawn," Captain Pamela Mae Brewer led her six member "Virginia (Old Dominion) Brigade Vanguard" in a southwest direction towards Harrisonburg. She remembered from her "History Studies" that the city was named after Thomas Harrison and is located in Rockingham County, Virginia. Harrisonburg would be the initial objective of this "Advance Party" and the Captains wanted to be on schedule. Captain Brewer directed Sergeant Pete Boone to be the "Point Man" since he was so familiar with the approximate sixty-four mile journey. He candidly told her, "Ma'am, I recommend that we try to make it to the south end of Luray, Virginia by dark, which is *circa* twenty-five miles away."

Captain Brewer heeded Sergeant Boone's advice and notified Captain Jeffrey Boyd, who was riding alongside Sergeant Earl Boone in the middle of the formation. Shortly thereafter, Earl rode back and updated Captain Christopher Russell and Sergeant Ralph Boone, who were bringing up and securing the rear end of their small group movement.

After a few hours of steady riding, Captain Brewer decided to take a break by a sizable creek that was flowing along the west side of the dusty tan colored road. Her horse, *Marenga la Primera*, and the other horses were very thirsty, as were all of the officers and enlisted soldiers. Pamela Mae sat down and then gazed at the beauty and majesty of God's creation in the lush Shenandoah River Valley.

She could easily see and then marveled at the very majestic scenery of the "Blue Ridge Mountains" to the east and the impressive "Massanutten Mountain Ridge" to the west. She thought prayerfully of her "Captain LaGrande" back in the "United States Capital Region."

My Mario, who loves Mamma Natura (Mother Nature), would certainly appreciate the abundant beauty of this part of Virginia. He would probably identify the variety of coniferous and deciduous trees and bushes that grace the mountains to include Fraser Fir, Red Spruce, Yellow Birch, Southern Red Oak, White Oak, Mountain-Ash, Hobblebush, and Mountain Laurel. Lord in heaven, please bless him today and keep him safe. Amen!

During the rest stop, Captain Russell talked to Pamela Mae and said, "Captain Brewer, Sergeant Ralph Boone made contact with the "Main Body" of our Virginia (Old Dominion) Brigade and they are intact and have departed the base camp and are about one hour and a half behind our Vanguard." Along their journey, our bold three captains and brave three sergeants were able to pass through a quaint community with overarching Beech, Maple, and Oak trees called New Market, Virginia. They were warmly greeted by the friendly towns-folk who waved to their "Virginia Heroes," and gave them gifts of bread and sweet rolls.

Captain Brewer and company were most appreciative of the New Market citizens, as she thought, *God bless them, Lord, for their generosity, and I believe these trees will look even more spectacular in the fall with brown, orange, and red leaves. Amen!*

It took Captain Pamela Mae Brewer and her entire "Advance Party Vanguard" two full days to make it safely to Harrisonburg, Virginia. Thankfully, there were no remarkable incidents and there was zero contact with "Federal Forces." On that morning of Wednesday, August 28th, 1861, Captain Brewer was leading her six member military unit down the narrow rough road west out of Rockingham County towards Franklin, Virginia (now West Virginia).

She could hear and see a number of ugly black crows that were perched in a couple of trees in this very wooded section. Captain Brewer knew from her previous experiences that the sighting of many crows that are "making a fuss" could be an ominous sign of impending danger. They continued to "caw and croak," and she tactically decided to reverse the order of the formation.

Captain Brewer and Sergeant Pete Boone would now maneuver to the rear of the "Vanguard" and Captain Russell and Sergeant Ralph Boone would take the front, while Captain Boyd and Sergeant Earl Boone would be in the middle. Within one hour of their journey towards Franklin, Captain Pamela Mae Brewer's premonition was soon about to materialize. Suddenly, a scouting party of five "Yankee Troops" on horseback attacked the rear element.

She heard pistols and rifles being fired with bullets flying perilously close to herself and her accompanying Sergeant Pete Boone!

They decided to go off the thoroughfare, dismount, and shield their bodies and horses behind a number of protecting "Red Maple Trees" in the woods. Foolishly, the "Union Soldiers" forcefully made a direct assault that completely exposed themselves to a counterattack. Captain Brewer pulled out both of her loaded pistols as she was ambidextrously able to hit the first two of the "Scoundrels" in their respective shoulders. The penetrating bullets knocked both of the "Federal Soldiers" off their horses into the ditches along the road. Subsequently, Sergeant Pete Boone, who is a superb marksman, used his revolver which had a japanning shine, to wound the other three attackers.

Wisely, all five of the defeated transgressing "Yankees" surrendered to Captain Brewer and Sergeant Pete Boone. Soon thereafter by an intervention of "Divine Providence," there arrived on the scene a "Confederate Group" of around thirty soldiers that were traveling east. The "Officer-in-Charge" was a Major, who wore a grey pelisse coat, and he agreed to handle the prisoners. His men were able to load the wounded soldiers in a couple of weathered clapboard lined supply wagons and take them to a prison in Harrisonburg, Virginia. He would notify the "Main Body" of the Virginia (Old Dominion) Brigade about the fight with the "Federals." Pamela Mae was very relieved and looked up into the sunny "August Sky" and joyfully exclaimed, *"Hallelujah, Hallelujah, Hallelujah!"*

Soon thereafter, Captains Brewer, Boyd, and Russell, along with the "Boone Brothers" regrouped. Captain Pamela Mae Brewer described the successful skirmish to all, concerning the intruding "Union Troops," and there was a short discussion of their current situation. As a consequence, Captain Jeffrey Boyd took the initiative and firmly told the "Vanguard Group" in a direct manner, "Since, I am very familiar with the route to the town of Franklin and Pendleton County, I will gladly lead us along with Sergeant Earl Boone."

Captain Brewer agreed with Captain Boyd, as she felt it prudent for her and Sergeant Pete Boone to be in the middle while Captain Christopher Russell and Sergeant Ralph Boone took to bringing up the rear. Captain Brewer realized that she must include this fight with the

"Union Raiding Party" from her perspective in the staff report by the end of the day!

Within a few more hours of westward travel towards the evening sun, Captain Boyd smiled and saw a familiar sight. On the right side of the narrow road was a painted wooden sign. It stated, "Welcome to Franklin, Virginia." Captain Boyd and Sergeant Earl Boone stopped and waited for Captains Brewer and Russell to join them, along with Sergeants Pete and Ralph Boone.

Fortuitously, there appeared to be a couple of travelers who were about one hundred yards in front that were heading in a western direction. The officers and soldiers caught up with the two people on foot. After the greetings and polite conversation, the Captains asked a few relevant questions and were able to gain some routine and then some very pertinent information from the husband and wife couple. Their names were Norman and Victoria Proctor and they resided in Franklin in a fine home on a hill with a white picket fence in the front yard. They even proudly pointed towards their residence to the inquiring Virginia military group.

Mister Proctor spoke as his wife remained silent, "I am not one to brag, but I served as a scout out west in Kansas as a 'Cavalry Sergeant' under the command of Lieutenant J.E.B. Stuart. I was wounded in my right arm and no longer able to fire a rifle accurately, so I am sitting out during this 'crazy war.' My wife and I are very loyal to Virginia. I must advise you that I observed from our hilltop home a 'Federal Regiment' of over three hundred soldiers with a Lieutenant Colonel in charge. The rough looking 'Yankees,' passed through our peaceful little town a few days ago. Word is that those 'Union Soldiers' will be joining forces, with their fellow 'Bluecoats' in Webster County, Virginia (now West Virginia). Also, y'all may stay the night with us and Victoria will be glad to cook you a homemade chicken dinner."

At this point, Captain Boyd advised Captains Brewer and Russell that it would be smart for their military group to travel tomorrow towards "Germany Valley" to gain more valuable intelligence and reconnaissance information. However, after much ethereal prayer thought and "divine assistance," Captain Brewer came up with a daring alternative plan. "Since I speak German, I will travel with Captain Russell and Sergeant Pete Boone and ride towards where the 'German People' live in order to gather insight on any further Union Soldiers' activities. Captain Boyd, you and the other Boone Sergeants will remain here in Franklin and make contact with our 'Main Body' and bivouac and set up camp south of town."

It was now the late morning of Friday, August 30th, 1861, and Captain Pamela Mae was amazed and delighted to see this lush green mountain valley in that western section of Virginia (now West Virginia). She could tell that the land was bountiful as the corn was growing high and there were a numerous amount of cattle grazing. Sergeant Pete Boone, who had been there before, pointed to a far-off elevated mountain ridge that was over 4,500 feet in height.

Early in the afternoon, Captain Brewer and her small scouting party were able to stop a father and daughter pair who were riding in a buggy. Pamela Mae had a very good intuitive feeling about meeting the man and young woman, who were dressed in traditional "Pennsylvania Dutch" style clothing. She politely greeted them in German saying, *"Guten Tag Herr und Fraulein, wei geht es dir heute?* (Good afternoon, Lord and Young Lady, how are you today)?"

Well, speaking in German to the man and pleasant young woman enabled Captains Brewer and Russell to gain their trust and acquire personal and then more important relative information about the "Federal Troops" who traveled through the area earlier in the week.

The father's name was Aaron Ritter and his daughter's name was Sarah and interestingly enough, today was her 14th birthday! Captain Brewer felt a special connection to the girl, who also had pretty brown eyes and an enchanting smile like Pamela Mae.

Mister Ritter then spoke in his German and accented English affectionately, and said, "*Meine liebe Kapitän* (My dear Captain), on Monday, there were about 100 Union Soldiers with three cannons on wheels who were from Ohio. They bought three horses and six head of cattle from me. *Danke Gott* (Thank God), their Major commander paid full price in United States currency for the animals. I did overhear the men, who spoke English and German, that they were on the move and their destination was Webster County and Nicholas County, Virginia (now West Virginia). Now, excuse me, we must get back to our farm, *und möge der Herr Sie segnen!* (and may the Lord bless you)!"

At this point, Captain Brewer figured it was prudent to turn around and ride back to Franklin and hopefully meet up with Brigadier General Morgan and the "Main Body" of the Virginia (Old

Dominion) Brigade. Within a couple of hours of riding south, just outside of Franklin, Captains Brewer and Russell and Sergeant Pete Boone were greeted by Captain Boyd and Sergeants Earl and Ralph Boone, and told to, "Follow us to the bivouac site."

Within thirty minutes, all six members of the "Advance Vanguard Group" entered the camp of the Virginia (Old Dominion) Brigade. They were soon escorted to the "Officers' Briefing Tent," and Captain Pamela Mae Brewer greeted and briefed the Brigade Commander, Brigadier General Albert Morgan. "Good evening, Sir, your advance party has pertinent and relevant intelligence, reconnaissance, and scouting information to provide you whenever you are ready."

The commanding officer responded, "Yes, Captain Brewer, I understand that your 'Vanguard Party' has been very active and fought off 'Union Attackers' and have been talking to the civilian population. Yes, I and my staff are ready for your 'Situational Briefing' right now."

Captain Pamela Mae Brewer took a deep breath and then said, with confidence and eloquence, "Yes, Sir, that is correct. By the 'Grace of God,' Sergeant Pete Boone and myself were able to defeat and then capture a five member 'Union Raiding Party.' We were on the road west of Harrisonburg and another Confederate Unit took the hapless scoundrels to a prison."

Captain Brewer continued the briefing and stated, "In addition, we met a couple named Proctor from Franklin. Mister Proctor was good enough to tell us about an estimated three-hundred-man regimental-sized unit of 'Federal Soldiers' with a Lieutenant Colonel in charge. He figured they were heading southwest towards Webster County."

She hesitated momentarily and concluded her military intelligence, reconnaissance, and scouting "Situational Brief" saying, "Finally, in the 'Germany Valley,' we encountered a Mister Aaron Ritter and his lovely daughter Sarah. I utilized my German fluency to find out that an approximate one hundred man 'Yankee Unit' from Ohio purchased horses and cattle from the Ritter family farm and paid valid money for the beasts. Mister Ritter mentioned that they had three artillery pieces/cannons and the 'Union Soldiers' were commanded by a Major and were likely marching towards Webster County and Nicholas County."

At this point, Brigadier General Morgan stood up and said, "Excellent staff work, Captain Brewer. Tomorrow, I am ordering you to lead your 'Advance Party/Vanguard Group' and to arise early and ride towards Pocahontas and Webster Counties. The 'Main Body' will proceed later while you maintain contact with us and attempt to locate other loyal 'Confederate Virginia' soldiers and units. You will need to gain military intelligence and reconnaissance data from them; and, of course, you may observe and see additional 'Enemy Troops.' Try to avoid a fight but defend yourselves as required."

It was now the early morning of Saturday, August 31st, 1861, and Captain Pamela Mae Brewer was awake "before the roosters" and had such an unusual spiritual feeling. She thought, *August 31st seems to be a very special day for me in the future. Dear Lord, please bless me today and I wonder what significance this particular end of the month of August day can be?*

The three Captains, Brewer, Russell, and Boyd, started out of camp along with the three Boone Sergeants, Pete, Earl, and Ralph as they left the outskirts of Franklin and travelled through Pendleton County that day. The Brigade Commander's goal was to make it all the way to

Marlinton, Virginia (now West Virginia) by
September 3rd, 1861.

Once again, the 'Main Body' of the Virginia (Old
Dominion) Brigade would be a couple of hours to
the rear of their "Advance Vanguard Party."
Captain Jeffrey Boyd and Sergeant Earl Boone
would again be the lead pair. Captain
Christopher Russell would be in the rear
element, with Sergeant Ralph Boone. Sergeant
Pete Boone accompanied Captain Pamela Mae
Brewer, who was in the center of the six-member
group. Pamela Mae was in a comical and
humorous mood, while she thought, *It is funny
that even though I am the youngest child in our
family, I do feel like the "Middle Sister" when I am
placed in the central section between these
officers and brothers!*

Well, the next few days of the approximate 63
mile trip would be "over hill and dale," through
the valleys and woods of this beautiful
picturesque western Virginia landscape. Pamela
Mae observed "God's Creation of Mother Nature"
as she prayerfully and tenderly thought of her
family back home in Prince William County, and
Mario, Gloria Faye, and Maurice in Alexandria.
*Our Precious Heavenly Father, I thank You and
praise You for this abundant world that You gifted
us. Please bless and keep safe Mamma, Papa,*

Lizzy, Will, and others in "Sunshine Hills." Also, a special blessing for Mio Mario Bello (My Handsome Mario) and my best friend Gloria Faye and her man, Maurice. I further pray that we will all be together in happier circumstances one day in the future. I ask this all in the holy name of Jesus. Amen.

Fortunately, this four-day movement of the "Vanguard" leading the "Main Body" of the Virginia (Old Dominion) Brigade was without incident or tragedy for the officers and enlisted men as well. There was a limited amount of civilian folks on the roads to talk with, and a few acknowledged that they have seen "Confederate and Union" forces in the area and there were no reports of skirmishes.

Just as planned, the lead Virginia element commanded by Captain Pamela Mae Brewer with her men, arrived near Marlinton, the seat of government for Pocahontas County, on Tuesday, September 3rd, 1861. Captains Brewer, Boyd, and Russell with the Boone brothers were delighted to meet up with a separate Virginia company from Webster Springs, Virginia (now West Virginia). The unit selected the name, "Webster Mountaineers" and was commanded by Captain Timothy Culp.

Captain Brewer once again felt blessed by "The Lord," especially since Brigadier General Morgan directed her to gain intelligence and reconnaissance information from military personnel. This chance meeting would be the best opportunity so far for her "Advance Guard Group." All the officers and Sergeants talked with their counterparts and gained timely and valuable details about the size and movement of "Confederate and Union" forces in the three county area.

Captain Pamela Mae Brewer was able to gather and consolidate the tactical and strategic facts, statistics, and predictions as follows:

First, the "Webster Mountaineers" have been on a reconnaissance and scouting mission themselves for the last two weeks. Their light cavalry unit of seventy troops had spotted over 500 "Union Infantry Soldiers" from three different units. They counted a total of six light artillery pieces. Captain Culp said, "During the last couple of days, my company was able to capture four 'Federal deserters/stragglers,' who talked freely about where they were from in Ohio and they were fed up with this 'senseless war' and were walking home. I gave them a 'parole document,' took their rifles, and gave them some food. They skedaddled in a northwest direction."

Secondly, his "Webster Mountaineers" had recently been assigned to the Headquarters of the "Army of the Kanawha" commanded by Brigadier General (BG) John Buchanan Floyd. BG Floyd was a former governor of the Commonwealth of Virginia and owned property in Abingdon, Virginia. He was projected to have an estimated 2,000 soldiers under his command and available for combat against the "Yankee Invaders." Captain Culp revealed to Captain Brewer and others that he and his company will depart on September 4th, and travel thru Pocahontas, Webster, and Nicholas Counties and rendezvous with the General and his staff by September 9th, 1861.

Finally, intelligence reports indicate that there may be approximately 5,000 "Federal Troops" converging in the Tygart River Valley in Nicholas County, Virginia (now West Virginia). Reliable military sources indicate that those soldiers are from Ohio, Illinois, and New York. The "Union Troops" will be under the command of a "U.S. Military Academy" graduate named Brigadier General (BG) William S. Rosecrans.

Captain Pamela Mae Brewer took many circumstantial and copious notes of the important military information that was explained to her by Captain Culp and relayed to her by her fellow "Vanguard Officers," Captain Russell and Captain Boyd. Furthermore, the "Boone Brothers" provided her many examples of terrain features that will be experienced and viewed on the mountain roads to Nicholas County.

Immediately thereafter, Captain Brewer wisely prepared a "situational brief" to be presented to Brigadier General Albert Morgan when the "Main Body" arrived that evening near Marlinton, Virginia! She thought to herself prayerfully, *Lord, have mercy on us all, it appears that a sizable battle will take place within a week or so. Amen!*

Chapter 8
Captain Brewer to Webster County
September 4th, 1861

Captain Pamela Mae Brewer provided Brigadier General Albert Morgan, Commander of the Virginia (Old Dominion) Brigade, with a complete situational brief yesterday evening. She included military specific details, in her presentation concerning friendly "Virginia Soldiers" and hostile "Union Troops" in the western counties of Pocahontas, Webster, and Nicholas, Virginia (now West Virginia).

It was, once again, an early departure on that cooler Wednesday morning of September 4th, 1861, for Captain Pamela Mae Brewer and her "Vanguard Advance Group." Sergeant Pete Boone volunteered to be the "Point Man "as he astutely, confidently, and yet guardedly led the way through the "breathtaking," bucolic landscape. He told his trusted Captain, "Ma'am, I would recommend that we try to make it for lunch to a tavern called, 'Sherman's Shack' near the 'Williams River,' by 1:00 p.m. this afternoon. Mister Sherman Hamilton and his lovely wife Laura are very well acquainted with the creeks, rivers, and streams of this very mountainous area. In addition, Sherman will entertain us with his lively banjo music. Also, he is a military veteran and could provide us with valuable information about the 'Federal Forces,' and our fellow 'Virginia Regiments,' traveling in the vicinity."

Captain Brewer notified Captain Christopher Russell and Captain Jeffrey Boyd about the day's goal. The weather in that early afternoon was now ideal and perfect for their reconnaissance and scouting duties. Pamela Mae marveled at the beauty and glory of the "Good Lord's" handicraft, as was illustrated by the variety of the wild flowers on the hillsides, to include mystical black-eyed susans, sparkling goldenrods, rust colored iron-weeds, hot pink sweet peas, and bright yellow sunflowers.

The six-member advance group arrived at "Sherman's Shack" just after 1:30 p.m. and they heard banjo music and singing from the back of the old structure. Sergeant Pete Boone and his brothers, Earl and Ralph, knew about the faithful and humorous man who was loyal to the "Southern Cause." Sherman continued to play his banjo, which he amusingly called his "banger," and sang in a bluegrass music gospel style:

Oh, the marvelous Marlinton mountains are so dear to me,

Their greatness is inspirational, as I sing about them to thee!

Folks around here say, "It's like heaven in the west half of Virginia,

With all of the beautiful rivers, trees, and wildlife near ya!"

The hills are in my heart and soul, as I often humbly pray,

"Oh Lord up above, bless our wild, wonderful homeland night and day!"

Captain Brewer was feeling very good about arriving at this unique rest stop in a timely manner and spiritually thought about Sherman and Laura in reference to their changing situation. *Dear Lord, I wonder how much this gentleman knows about the Armies in the area; and perhaps his wife can also assist us in our tactical and strategic missions!*

All three Captains and the "Boone Brothers" were hungry, thirsty, and were invited to go into the tavern to have lunch. The hostess and server approached our "Virginia Advance Party" group and greeted the visitors and formally and politely stated, "Good afternoon and welcome y'all to 'Sherman's Shack.' Most folks around here call me 'Aunt Laura.' Our special today is fried cabbage with bacon bits and onions and fried green tomatoes with cornmeal. In addition, we are known for our sweet tea!"

Pamela Mae was immediately impressed by the friendliness and warmth of "Aunt Laura," who seems familiar to her. She decides to have both of today's specialties. Well, the food and drink were very enjoyable and savory. Aunt Laura told Captain Brewer privately, "Ma'am, we have had a steady amount of 'Union Ohio and Confederate Virginia,' troops come through here the last few days and they are marching and riding towards the Gauley River, near Summersville in Nicholas County. Furthermore, my woman's intuition tells me that there will be a ' Big Fight' soon enough!"

After the satisfying and substantial lunch, Captains Brewer, Russell, and Boyd were able to talk to Sherman about the movements of soldiers with their equipment and horses. Mister Hamilton, who had a good memory and had military experience in the United States Army years ago, explained, "I can verify that three regiments of 'Union Soldiers' from Ohio passed through this area en route to Webster and Nicholas County that include the 23rd Ohio

Infantry Regiment commanded by Major Rutherford Hayes, 30th Ohio Infantry Regiment commanded by Colonel Hugh Ewing, and the 47th Ohio Infantry Regiment commanded by Colonel Frederick Poschner

Captain Pamela Mae Brewer was very pleased with the intelligence gathering information received from Sherman and Laura Hamilton. That evening, she was able to provide an updated "situational brief" to Brigadier General Morgan, the Commander of the Virginia (Old Dominion) Brigade.

That night alone in her small tent, Pamela Mae went to sleep and had another one of her distinctive unique dreams that would be prophetic as she later described the experience in her journal. "Our 'Advance Guard' group of six were traveling by horseback upon a series of 'long, bending, and winding roads' in Webster County, Virginia. Our 'tight-knit' crew happened to stop at a dry goods store that had the very appropriate name of 'You Want it, We Sell it.' Myself and the other officers and soldiers were all in uniform and in need of additional and essential items for our mission to include bullets, haversacks, and ropes, etc."

"The dream continued, as we happened to see a distinguished looking couple in the establishment. The handsome gentleman had a good demeanor and looked at me with a slight grin and said in a Scottish-Irish accent, "Good afternoon, my beautiful Army Captain!" His attractive petite wife was very friendly and we had a more lady-like conversation. The couple's names were Samuel and Martha Raye Davis and they lived about ten miles south of the dry goods store near the Elk River by Webster Springs, Virginia (now West Virginia). I woke up a few minutes later and pondered what the dream could mean and wanted to meet the charming couple."

It was now Saturday, September 7th, 1861, and Captain Brewer and her fellow Captains Russell and Boyd were together on the road in Webster County, Virginia. Sergeants Pete, Earl, and Ralph Boone were once again accompanying the officers as they were providing essential escort, guard, and guide duties with the very well-known mountain roads. Captain Jeffrey Boyd was in the front with Sergeant Earl Boone by his side.

Suddenly, out of the blue skies on a green hill ahead, Sergeant Boone saw a solitary image of a figure about ninety yards away from the six-soldier group. He could see that it was a young lad, and he was carrying and playing a drum. The numerous "rat-a-tat-tat" sounds were easily recognizable to the experienced enlisted man. As he approached the boy, Earl Boone was shocked to see his youngest brother, Johnny Boone, smiling and playing the drum with enthusiasm.

Within a few minutes, Sergeant Boone dismounted his horse, and shouted out in an upset "Southern Manner" to the younger fella asking, "What in tarnation are you doing all alone here in Webster County?" Well, the youngest of seven boys replied fearlessly, "Last week, I told Ma and Pa that I was exiting Summersville and going to join up with my big brothers. I was leaving home with my drum set and a knife to join up with the famous Virginia (Old Dominion) Brigade." Johnny Boone hesitated a few moments and continued, "And by the way, where are my other brothers, Pete and Ralph?"

Earl was dumbfounded by the appearance of Johnny and thought, *What the hell! The boy is so mature for his age, and he is brave, clever, and has endless energy and could connive a squirrel out of his last acorn. We will send him back to the "Main Body" of our Brigade and they can have him perform various duties. Lord, have mercy on us all!*

That night, the four Boone Brothers, Earl, Pete, Ralph, and little Johnny were all together around a camp fire in the friendly confines of the Virginia (Old Dominion) Brigade. Captain Pamela Mae Brewer felt a deep kinship to the Boones and decided to join the family group. Johnny was very outspoken and talkative and wanted to know about any skirmishes with "The Federals" and yelled out loud, "The 'Virginia Soldiers' need to kick the butts of those 'Damn Yankees' all the way north of the Mason-Dixon line."

Captain Brewer was amused with the humor and laughter of Johnny and his older brothers but knew seriously in her heart that the Northerners would be in her beloved home state of Virginia for many years. However, as Pamela Mae later settled down for the night, she thought fondly and lovingly of her northern "Vermont Cavalier Captain" and said the following prayer, "Dear Heavenly Father, I thank You for this day and every day on Your 'Good Earth,' and please bless and keep *Mio Mario Bello* (My Handsome Mario) in Your loving care and protection. Amen!"

It was now the afternoon of September 8th, 1861, and just like in her dream, Captain Pamela Mae Brewer and her "Advance Vanguard Group" saw a store on the road to Webster Springs. Pamela Mae thought to herself, *Oh my goodness, this looks like the same dry goods store in my dream a couple of days ago!* Sure enough, as the "Virginia Crew" got closer, Captain Brewer said out loud, "You Want it, We Sell it," as she read the sign of the weathered looking business establishment.

Initially, Captain Brewer and Sergeant Pete Boone went into the store to shop for a few essentials. Pamela Mae walked to the big counter in the back of the store and saw the couple from her dream. The distinguished looking husband and wife team were in their best "Sunday-go-to-meeting clothes." The very pretty, petite, and friendly lady spoke up and said to Pamela Mae, "Good afternoon, my name is Martha Raye Davis, and my husband Samuel and I just left church. Oh, my gracious Miss, I can see that you are a Lovely Virginia Lady and Army Captain."

While the two women were enjoying their "girl talk," Captain Brewer could hear Mister Davis, who is a traveling businessman, say to the owner in a consequential manner, "We got 'Union Troops' coming and going in the area, and I want to buy a couple more guns and ammunition in order to fight against the damn invaders of my cherished mountain home!"

In addition, Captain Brewer could hear Samuel Davis say confidentially to the proprietor, "I feel confident about defeating 'The Federals' ever since I found out last week that at least six Virginia Regiments were en route to Nicholas County."

Well, Captain Brewer really got along with Martha Raye and found out the nice lady was originally from Georgia and fell in love with "Sam, her Virginia Mountain Man." Mrs. Davis invited Pamela Mae to visit her 'Hellenbrook Mansion,' that evening. Martha Raye would be sure to provide Captain Brewer a scrumptious "homemade dinner," and Mister Davis would provide her and the Virginia (Old Dominion) Brigade with some additional relevant reconnaissance and scouting information.

The entire Virginia (Old Dominion) Brigade was together that afternoon and once again Captain Pamela Mae Brewer gave a succinct "situational brief" to the Commander, Brigadier General Albert Morgan. Captain Brewer included in her briefing that, "Sir, we believe that there are at least six Virginia Regiments that are en route to Nicholas County, and I feel that a significant battle between our 'Confederate Forces,' and the 'Belligerent Yankees' is imminent. Furthermore, I request that I be permitted to travel to the

Davis Home near Webster Springs in order to gain more military intelligence information from Mister Samuel Davis."

Brigadier General (BG) Morgan was pleased with the reconnaissance and intelligence situational briefing from Captain Pamela Mae Brewer and assigned Sergeant Pete Boone to accompany her to the mansion called "Hellenbrook."

The Davis Family Hellenbrook Mansion in Webster County

In addition, BG Morgan had more specific intelligence information to present to his "Advance Vanguard Group" leader saying formally, "Captain Brewer, I have had communication from a dear colleague of mine from Mason County, Virginia (now West Virginia). His name is Colonel John McCausland and he is Commander of the 36th Virginia Infantry Regiment, 2nd Kanawha Infantry."

The commander of the Virginia (Old Dominion) Brigade, BG Morgan paused momentarily and said, "Tomorrow, the 36th Virginia Infantry Regiment will join up with the loyal 'Confederate Forces' commanded by Brigadier General Floyd. Colonel McCausland is well aware of your bravery, ingenuity, and military skills, to include: horse riding, marksmanship, and your sword fighting abilities. He is in need of an experienced cavalier, reconnaissance, and scouting officer. Therefore, Captain Pamela Mae Brewer, you are hereby ordered to ride into Nicholas County along with your assigned Sergeant. You must meet up with the 36th Virginia Infantry Regiment by the morning of September 10th, 1861, near the Gauley River in Nicholas County outside of Summersville, Virginia (now West Virginia). As I said before, you have my permission to visit with the Davis family this evening, to gather vital information and make any and all decisions independently en route. Also, you are authorized to enlist and commission 'Virginia Citizen-Soldiers,' as required." Note: The Virginia (Old Dominion) Brigade will be held in reserve for the upcoming battle.

Captain Brewer acknowledged and understood her new assignment and told Sergeant Pete Boone about the mission as they prepared to travel towards Webster Springs. It was now approximately 6:00 p.m. that September 8th, 1861, evening when Captain Pamela Mae Brewer and Sergeant Pete Boone approached the very elegant looking "Hellenbrook Mansion" home of Samuel and Martha Raye Davis. Pamela Mae thought faithfully, nostalgically, and romantically about the *Mansion du Moreau* in Alexandria, Virginia, that made many indelible memories for her. *Oh Lord, it would be such a blessing to be back in the Victorian home of Brigitte Moreau with mio Mario Bello (my Handsome Mario). However, he and I would surely love this grand home that was probably built in the 1850s. I love the covered front porch and the eight rectangular windows in front. God bless us. Amen!*

They were soon on a brick drive way, as the horses made several clip-clop sounds with their hooves. Captain Brewer and Sergeant Boone were initially greeted by a very friendly chocolate Labrador Retriever dog named Max as they dismounted their horses near a stable by the house. Samuel Davis came out of the mansion with a shotgun and realized that the expected visitors were friendly and invited them into the kitchen. Martha Raye Davis was busy cooking and preparing the scrumptious meal. The savory smell of "Georgia Style" fried chicken was prevalent and wafted pleasantly into the beautifully furnished dining room.

Captain Pamela Mae Brewer and Sergeant Pete Boone sat on one side of the long table. A young servant girl and Martha Raye placed all of the appealing food and drink items on the table, while Martha Raye sat down next to her husband, Samuel Davis, as he said Grace. "Dear Heavenly Father, we thank You and praise You for this time of fellowship and nourishment together. Thank You, Lord, for the abundant food that you provide for us that my wife and our cook prepared exquisitely. Gracious God, please bless our beloved and endangered Commonwealth of Virginia soldiers, women, and children. We pray this all in the Precious Name of Your Son Jesus, by the power of the Holy Spirit. Amen!"

The scrumptious dinner menu meal and tasty drinks included:

Georgia Style Fried Chicken
Blackberry Wine
Mashed Potatoes with Mushroom Gravy
Colombian Coffee
Golden Brown Hush Puppies.
Scotch Whiskey
Corn on the Cob, with salt and butter
Fried okra
Collard Greens with bacon bits
Buttermilk Cathead Biscuits
Peach Cobbler with raisins for dessert

Sergeant Pete Boone and Captain Brewer had the most delightful and enjoyable time, as Pamela Mae expressed her heartfelt appreciation to her host and hostess saying, "Thank you so much, Martha Raye and Samuel, for your charitable hospitality and the very delicious foods and flavorsome drinks. God bless you both and Virginia, our wonderful Commonwealth. Amen!" Samuel and Martha Raye Davis then gave Captain Brewer and Sergeant Boone a quick tour of the downstairs.

While walking through the living room, the host and hostess pointed to a very valuable painting upon the mantle above the fireplace.

Captain Pamela Mae Brewer gasped and then wept, as she gazed in wonder upon an original and magnificent portrait of her military hero, General Robert E. Lee, see photo.

General Robert E. Lee Portrait

After regaining her composure, Mister Davis invited Captain Brewer and Sergeant Boone into the Library to discuss the possible battle scenarios between "Union Soldiers and Confederate Troops" in a couple of days in the future. Samuel Davis had topographical maps of both the Webster and Nicholas County areas. He detailed what he knew about the landscape and roads from his extensive travels in the bi-county region.

Mister Davis spoke candidly and frankly, "Captain Brewer, I estimate that 'The Yankees,' will have more than twice as many Ohio, New York, and Illinois soldiers on the ground as compared to our 'Virginia Troops.' I believe more than 4,000 'Bluecoats' will be against our men! I am not one to boast, but I am a U.S. Army veteran of the 'Indian Wars' out west and have spent thousands of hours in the saddle. Furthermore, I am an expert sharpshooter and can hit targets hundreds of yards in a distance. Since, you need to be in Nicholas County by the Gauley River/Carnifex Ferry area by September 10th, 1861, I will gladly volunteer to help scout, traverse the terrain, and combat the 'Union Aggressors' if necessary."

Captain Brewer was very interested and made notes on what Samuel Davis had to say about the "Union Forces" while feeling confident in his terrain knowledge of the two counties mentioned. Also, his combat experience, horse-riding, marksmanship, resolve, scouting abilities, and skills would be invaluable to the mission. She told him sincerely, "Mister Davis, my good Sergeant and I would appreciate your assistance and military services, and I will make you a Brevet Lieutenant in the Cavalry!"

Martha Raye was tasked to sew on "silver bars" on an old Army jacket and Captain Pamela Mae Brewer gave Samuel Davis the "Officer Oath." Lieutenant Davis would lead the movement to Nicholas County, early the next morning. All three of the "Virginia Troops," subsequently shared in a congratulatory toast with "Scotch Whiskey" and salutes to each other and to the "Confederate States of America."

It was quite an eventful day for Sergeant Boone and Captain Brewer, and she was shown to her bedroom on the first floor, off the main entrance to the "Hellenbrook Mansion." That night, Pamela Mae had the most fanciful, fascinating, and wondrous dream. "I was attending a military ball in a grand hall in Virginia with a giant chandelier in the center and I was wearing an elegant Italian royal blue gown."

The amazing and fascinating dream continued. Pamela Mae recalled, "There in attendance were Mamma and Papa and many officers representing the "Confederate States of America." J.E.B. Stuart was now a 'General Officer' and he was talking with General Thomas Jonathan (Stonewall) Jackson. Both of the officers were laughing and were the epitome of 'Southern Gentility.' Soon thereafter, the Commanding General of the Army, Robert E. Lee arrived. He was wearing the exact same stunning blue uniform with the gold sash and long ornate sword that he wore in the portrait at the 'Hellenbrook Mansion.' He removed his sword and gave the weapon to his aide-de-camp and politely asked me to dance. He was an excellent dance partner and General Lee spun and whirled me around and around the dance floor for many minutes. I thought to myself prophetically, *Generals Lee, Jackson, and Stuart will be remembered as the "Greatest Generals" in all of Virginia and the South!"*

The fantastic dream became even more marvelous when I saw a very attractive dark haired, blue-eyed officer in a "Verdant Green" uniform. Amazingly and thankfully, the gentleman was my 'Handsome Vermont Cavalier,' Mario Patrizio LaGrande. He was wearing gold Major leaves on his epaulettes. He smiled and said sweetly in Italian, *"Buona Sera mia Pamela Bella, Ti amo bene* (Good evening, my Pretty Pamela, I love you well)!"

Chapter 9
To Nicholas County and Carnifex Ferry
September 9th, 1861

Pamela Mae woke up from her very enjoyable and fanciful dream and had such a glorious feeling in her heart and soul that everything would be alright. Before dawn, Captain Brewer got ready quickly and met up outside in the back with Lieutenant Samuel Davis and Sergeant Pete Boone.

It was now "Oh Dark Thirty," as they say in the Army, on that very early morning of Monday, September 9th, 1861. Captain Pamela Mae Brewer was fully dressed in her grey "Virginia Officer" uniform. She had two handguns, a .44 caliber revolver and a .36 caliber revolver along with her 41" long, light "Cavalry Saber." She was majestically mounted upon her Arabian mare, *Marenga la Primera.*

Lieutenant Samuel Davis also had a .44 caliber revolver and a custom-made sharpshooter rifle in his possession. He was mounted on a swift roan colored male quarter horse named "Piper" and he will lead the bold three-member group in the morning darkness.

Sergeant Pete Boone had his trusty "British Made" .45 caliber double action revolver and the standard musket. He had a very fast male bay horse named "Bubby." Pete was also very accustomed with the roads and the way towards the Gauley River since he lived and traveled extensively in Nicholas County. Captain Pamela Mae Brewer was bringing up the rear in the first part of the day's 38 mile trip. She had confidence in Lieutenant Davis and in Sergeant Boone since they had travelled these mountain and valley roads numerous times before. Captain Brewer thought extensively about her mission and knew they had to ride the entire day and meet up with Colonel McCausland and the 36th Virginia Infantry Regiment, "2nd Kanawha Infantry," by the morning of September 10th, 1861. She earnestly prayed and thought, *Dear Lord in Heaven above, your "Virginia Lady" humbly asks for You to clear a path for us; even-though, we may encounter adversity and travel through the "valley of the shadow of death" today and tomorrow. In addition, Gracious God, please bless and keep safe Mamma and Papa, Lizzy, and Will back home in 'Sunshine Hills,' and, of course, watch over and protect my "Vermont Cavalier," Mario Bello (Handsome Mario), Gloria Faye, and Maurice in Alexandria, Virginia. Amen!*

Well, the first few hours of their long journey were going well with no incidents. However, the circumstances changed abruptly, once Captain Pamela Mae Brewer, Lieutenant Samuel Davis, and Sergeant Pete Boone crossed the line and entered into Nicholas County, Virginia (now West Virginia). Our two courageous officers and intrepid sergeant were riding their horses at a moderate pace through an area which had boulders and thickets along the shoulders of the granulated road.

Suddenly, Captain Brewer and her adventurous crew came under attack from a faraway hill. The sounds of bullets could be heard pinging and ricocheting off the hard ground and big rocks around the "Virginia Soldiers." Fortunately, the attackers were off their intended marks, as the errant rounds flew past them. Pamela Mae's worried prayers and thoughts included, *Oh Lord, have mercy on your servants, Please be our shield, and lead me to my next course of action, Amen!*

With due haste, rapidity, and swiftness, Captain Brewer shouted out the following instructions, "Men, take immediate cover behind the huge boulders and safeguard our horses." Sergeant Boone was the first to heed the orders, hiding behind the oversized rocks, and volunteered to hold on to the reins of *Marenga la Primera*, Piper, and Bubby.

Captain Pamela Mae Brewer expeditiously pulled out her "10x50" field binoculars and was able to detect and see two scoundrels on the summit of the hill that was approximately two hundred yards to the south. She relayed that vital information to Lieutenant Davis, and he also took a look through the sophisticated looking devise and nonchalantly said, "No problem, I can knockout the varmints with a few shots!"

Consequently, Samuel got out his custom-made sharpshooter rifle with five bullets. Soon thereafter, Captain Brewer loaded both of her handguns with six shots each and then informally told Lieutenant Davis, "Sam, I will carefully move about thirty feet to the right and will shoot sporadically at the attackers in order to get their attention, and then give out a loud scream. This should distract the ambushers enough for you to eliminate and silence the threat."

"Thanks be to God," the imaginative plan worked perfectly as Captain Brewer relocated to her next position, fired at the shooters, and screamed.

Within a few seconds, the rascals moved to unsecured spots on the hilltop and Lieutenant Davis was able to clearly wound both of the culprits. He could hear the injured personnel shout in pain, "Son of a ..." and fall into some brush. At this point, all of the gun fire ceased and Captain Brewer signaled for Sergeant Pete Boone to move the horses about one hundred additional feet to the west. This enabled all three of the "Virginia Scouting Party" to exit the area without injury, Praise the Lord!

Sergeant Pete Boone was thinking that, *Perhaps it would be more prudent for our three person Army crew to take a less traveled alternate route towards Summersville and the Gauley River.* He contemplated their perilous location and after some rough analysis, said frankly to Captain Pamela Mae Brewer, "Ma'am, I advise that you allow me to lead us on a different way, back to my home area. Do not fret, I believe we will still be able to join up with the 36th Virginia Infantry Regiment by supper time!"

Captain Brewer, who was totally unfamiliar with the terrain and its paths and roads replied discreetly, "Sergeant Boone, please describe the secondary roads to Lieutenant Davis. If he agrees with you, then we will proceed with your recommendation and carry on with this daunting excursion of ours."

Lieutenant Davis remembered that different passage through Nicholas County and concurred with Sergeant Boone, who was now the "point man and pathfinder" on the narrow roads towards Summersville and the Gauley River. Well, the next two hours were difficult traveling for Captain Brewer, Lieutenant Davis, and Sergeant Boone. However, they all breathed a collective "sigh of relief," when the group entered a wide open area and had a view of a regimental size unit.

Captain Pamela Mae Brewer boldly took the initiative and introduced herself to the "Officer in Charge." Providentially and thankfully, the military organization was the 22nd Virginia Infantry Regiment, 1st Kanawha Infantry, and it was commanded by Colonel Christopher Tompkins. Pamela Mae briefly thought fondly of her cousin Christopher, and said a little prayer for Captain Russell, *"Heavenly Father, please bless Christopher and the entire Virginia (Old Dominion) Brigade, who are probably at least a day behind us, Amen!*

Captain Brewer summarized her assigned mission to Colonel Tompkins, the regimental commander and he replied, "My 22nd Virginia Infantry Regiment is in the same Brigade and will be lined up right next to Colonel McCausland and his 36th Virginia Infantry Regiment. Captain Brewer, you and your men should ride with me in the center of our formation, and we will give you a personal escort. Furthermore, I will brief you along the way on the current situation, in respect to our friendly 'Confederate Forces,' and what I know about the 'Union Troops,' who most likely will be our opposing enemy tomorrow!"

"Our Lovely Virginia Lady" and "Phenomenal Army Captain" was feeling more secure about the current "state of affairs" and listened intently to Colonel Tompkins details for several miles. "I estimate that our 'Virginia Forces' will number between 1,700-2,000 soldiers and we will be grouped at what is now called 'Camp Gauley.' Our 'Confederate Troops' will be lined up in a very strong defensive position on the Patterson Farm which is approximately one mile from the 'Carnifex Ferry' operation on the Gauley River. Furthermore, we have intelligence reports that General Rosecrans and his 'Federal Forces' had left Summersville earlier and are heading towards our planned position.

Historical Note: Carnifex Ferry was a flat boat operation across the local rivers that was named after the Carnifex family.

Captain Pamela Mae Brewer was now getting a more enhanced visual in her mind about the disposition of the "Virginia Units" and asked Colonel Tompkins, "Sir, what is the estimate of the number and size of the 'Union Forces' that we will be fighting?" The "Commanding Officer" of the 22nd Virginia Infantry Regiment paused and responded in a calculated manner, "Yes, Captain Brewer, our plight will be risky and the odds will certainly be against us. Our reliable and savvy scouting sources have reported that Brigadier General Rosecrans had moved his 5,000-7,000 three Brigade 'Yankee Army,' southward from Clarksburg, Virginia (now West Virginia). The Federals' objective is to control and occupy the Western Section of Virginia, and to secure the major rivers to include the Ohio, Kanawha, and Monongahela. Of course, we will be there to try to repulse his advances inside our beloved "Commonwealth of Virginia."

Pamela Mae was disappointed to find out that the "Virginia Troops" would be vastly outnumbered against the "Union Army" as she prayed silently in her faithful mind. *Oh Lord Jesus in Heaven, I pray that our loyal "Southern*

Soldiers" will fight well, and I humbly ask that none of our men will be killed in the next couple of days. In the name of the Father, Son, and Holy Ghost, Amen!

Within a couple more hours of steady travel by horseback, Captain Brewer could see a grey wooden two-story house in the distance. She also had a partial view of hundreds of soldiers wearing a variety of butternut-colored outfits, gray and dark brown mismatched uniforms. It was supper time in "Camp Gauley" and the vast majority of the Virginia fighting men were either eating or drinking, cleaning weapons, and/or talking casually with one another. She also thought briefly and personally about the Commanding Officer, Brigadier General John Floyd. *I recall that John Floyd had a successful "Law Practice" and lived in a stately mansion in the wonderful town of Abingdon, Virginia, and he later became Governor of our "Great Commonwealth."*

Then an imposing and robust looking gentleman exited his personal tent and saw the most beautiful officer in uniform. Due to his written note from Brigadier General Morgan, Colonel John McCausland was expecting the arrival of Captain Pamela Mae Brewer. As she took off her riding hat, shook her luxurious hair, and removed her cape, the Commanding Officer of the 36th Virginia Infantry Regiment saw the "Lovely Virginia Lady and Officer" up close. He looked her over carefully and thought to himself, *She is so very pretty and stunning in appearance, with cute doe-brown eyes, perfect in form, and the most intriguing woman to watch walking towards me!*

She saluted crisply and formally stated, "Good Evening Colonel McCausland, Captain Pamela Mae Brewer, Lieutenant Samuel Davis, and Sergeant Pete Boone reporting for duty, Sir!" The Commander of the 36th Virginia Infantry Regiment, 2nd Kanawha, invited all three of the specialized crew into the "Officer Briefing Tent" and had them sit down. The "tough talking," Colonel McCausland began his brief and stated, "I welcome you to my command. Our regiment has marched and traveled over one hundred miles from the Kanawha River Valley to this very good tactical position. Brigadier General Floyd and I, anticipate an attack by those 'Damn Yankees' tomorrow! Are there any questions?"

Captain Brewer smartly spoke up, "Sir, Sergeant Boone and I have excellent riding skills and we can both shoot on the run. In addition, Lieutenant Davis is an exceptional marksman and would expertly assist the Command with his long-distance shooting abilities!" Colonel McCausland explained other situational details to the threesome for about fifteen more minutes, and concluded his remarks with, "Get a good night's sleep, and be ready 'bright and early' for any special assignments that will be required to defeat the Union Invaders."

Pamela Mae had a late supper and a serious talk with her two subordinates, Lieutenant Davis and Sergeant Boone. Samuel Davis was a "man of faith" and offered up a group prayer and Captain Brewer accepted his soulful supplication. "Benevolent and magnificent Lord in heaven above, we praise and thank You for our precious time here on earth. Please be with and protect Captain Brewer, Sergeant Boone, and myself as we defend our homeland tomorrow. In addition, gracious God, I humbly request a special blessing with a hedge of protection surrounding my beautiful wife Martha Raye at home in Hellenbrook! We pray this all in the name of the Father, Son, and Holy Ghost. Amen!"

Captain Pamela Mae Brewer was spiritually moved by the prayer and replied, "Amen Brother" as she departed her loyal crew and found accommodations for the night. She reflected upon all that transpired that day and the previous sixteen days since she and Captain

Russell departed their "Sunshine Hills" home on that rainy morning of August 25th, 1861. She began to think historically about all of the battles, skirmishes, and wars that her family members had participated in while living in the colony and state of Virginia. Pamela Mae recalled that Mamma told her about maternal grandfathers, uncles, and cousins who had fought in the "French and Indian and Revolutionary Wars" to include the "Battle of Point Pleasant" in Mason County, Virginia (now West Virginia). Finally, Pamela Mae remembered reading many poems about famous and legendary heroes in her school days.

She went to bed shortly thereafter and late that night, "Our Lovely Virginia Lady" had the most astonishing dream. "I was living as a young teenager in Massachusetts, and it was the spring of 1775, the month of April. My bedroom was on the second floor of an old house in a small village. The walls and windows were both thin in construction and the cool air was coming through. I could hear the pounding of horseshoes on the hard cobblestone streets. Papa was away from home on 'Militia Duty' and I screamed for Mamma to come to me!"

Pamela Mae hesitated a few moments and continued recounting her bewildering dream.

"Mamma opened the window and yelled at the rider, inquiring about all the commotion. The man replied excitingly, 'The British are Coming, the British are Coming.' We found out the next morning that the exuberant courier and horseman was 'Paul Revere' and he was on his famous 'Midnight Ride.' I was not sure about the meaning of the dream, but I had a feeling that I would be in for a very special ride the next day. Lord, help me. Amen!"

It was the morning of September 10th, 1861, in "Camp Gauley" near Carnifex Ferry, Virginia (now West Virginia). Captain Pamela Mae Brewer, Lieutenant Samuel Davis, and Sergeant Pete Boone would start off on the battle line, with the 36th Virginia Infantry Regiment, 2nd Kanawha Infantry. The Commander, Colonel John McCausland was "fired up" and ready to "defeat the Yankees!"

Brigadier General William Rosecrans did not commit his entire force of "Union Soldiers" that day but decided to use a limited number of men to attack Brigadier General John Floyd's entrenched "Virginia Troops" near the Patterson House. The "Battle of Carnifex Ferry" commenced with the offensive by the "Federal Troops" and it was repulsed numerous times by the very proficient "Confederate Soldiers" who fought bravely and were very accurate in their withering shots towards the "Charging Yankees." Along the well-entrenched lines of the 36th Virginia Infantry Regiment, 2nd Kanawha Infantry, Captain Pamela Mae Brewer was patiently waiting for specific orders from the Commander. The battlefield was very noisy with the continuous constant cracks and sounds of bullets. In addition, there were hundreds of orders being given by the officers, the cries and screams of wounded soldiers and the thunderous shrieking of numerous artillery shells that were fired by both of the combative sides.

It was now 11:30 a.m. when Captain Brewer calmly approached Colonel McCausland and asked, "Sir, my men and I are ready for any unique special assignment/orders. What do you want us to do to help relieve our current situation?" Well, the Commander hesitated a little while and then pointed to the Virginia left flank and yelled over the harsh cacophony din of prolonged sounds, "I want Lieutenant Davis to initiate fire upon the enemy artillery battery redoubt that is over yonder on that distance hill, to disable their operations. Captain Brewer, I want you and Sergeant Boone to make an end around ride to disrupt the right flank of that "Yankee Regiment."

Captain Pamela Mae Brewer replied, "Yes Sir," and got her three man crew together and explained the individual assignments and initially gave directives and orders to her subordinate officer. Lieutenant Davis was given a pair of binoculars, so that he could have a more acute and exact view of the artillery emplacements and redoubts on that "yonder hill." He could see that the Union Batteries had the older and bigger M1857 Napoleon 12-pounder weapons and the newer and smaller 10–pounder Parrot Rifles. He would spend the next hour loading bullets and firing his "Sharpshooter Rifle." He successfully harassed, disrupted, and made ineffective the work of that Union Right Flank's' heavy weapon's operations.

Captain Brewer walked Sergeant Boone back to the temporary holding pen for the horses, while explaining the mission. "By the 'Grace of God,' you will be riding your horse "Bubby" to my left and I will be on your right upon my mare, *Marenga la Primera.*" She continued and pointed to the left and yelled, "We are going to travel swiftly behind the right flank of those 'Federal Regiments.' Here, take one of my pistols. As you fire your guns, while being 'My Wingman,' through the 'Yankee Units,' I have a plan in mind to impede and interfere with the enemies' military actions."

Our daring and valiant "Virginia Duo" would proceed and perform a wide half circle route behind the lines of the "Bluecoats" while Captain Brewer was thinking of an audacious plan in her analytical mind. *I can remember reading about the "Mexican-American War" and stories about saving and capturing the regimental flags.*

This special mission would ensue, with the very electrifying sight of Captain Pamela Mae Brewer as she was gallantly riding her white and gray Arabian horse. Her long, black, voluminous hair was bouncing in the wind over her long flowing cape while she had her curved 41" cavalry sword in her right hand pointed upward. She thought faithfully and momentarily about her very hazardous mission, *Oh Lord of all mankind, may Sergeant Boone and I make it through this gauntlet of guns and sabers unscathed. Amen!*

Within ten minutes of riding a circuitous route around the "Union Right Flank" of mostly Ohio soldiers, with Sergeant Boone on her left firing his guns with either hand, Captain Brewer was galloping behind the enemy lines. The "Yankee Soldiers" were perplexed and startled to see a woman "Confederate Officer" on horseback. Some of the soldiers just gazed and looked at her and her sidekick with their mouths open. Other

"Union Soldiers" yelled at her and fired their pistols and muskets in the air and in her direction.

Captain Pamela Mae Brewer became very animated in her determined expression and was feeling very patriotic, as she called out, "Onward for a Free and Independent Virginia and Victory." The words she spoke even surprised herself and their "Federal Opponents." She could hear the "roar of battle," and could sense the bullets going by her left and right side and overhead. She could now see a "Union Army Colonel" with his sword obviously raised up to try to settle his men. Captain Brewer slashed her extended 41"cavalry sword to a few of her opponents; as she intelligently eyed the colorful Ohio white and red regimental flag with a buckeye themed insignia being held by a young "Color Guard Soldier."

Even though Captain Brewer knew and tried to obey the commandment, "Do not steal," she figured the capture of the flag would cause confusion with the "Bluecoats." The color bearer was "all shook up" and nervously dropped and then lost control of the ornate flag.

Athletically and fluidly, Captain Brewer was able to reach down and scoop up the "Buckeye State" regimental flag and then continued her ride through that disrupted "Northern

Regiment." Colonel McCausland was completely amazed to see Captain Brewer perform such a compelling, "Hey Diddle Diddle, right up the middle" action through the center of the "Yankee Unit." He couldn't help himself when he yelled out, "Ride like the wind all the way here, Pamela Mae. God bless her!"

Fortunately and miraculously, Sergeant Boone, who had provided cover with his two pistols, and Captain Brewer, were not injured or wounded, as they both made it back safely to the "friendly confines" of the cheering lines of the welcoming 36th Virginia Infantry Regiment, 2nd Kanawha Infantry. This courageous and risky foray into hostile territory would eventually be called and referred to as, "The Midday Ride of Captain Pamela Mae Brewer."

Note; The "Virginia Legend and Lore of Miss Robin Bea Goode" continued for generations through the storytelling of many of her family members about her daring Cavalier ride at Carnifex Ferry. *Hallelujah!*

Colonel John McCausland was very impressed by all three of the outstanding members of the Virginia (Old Dominion) Brigade. Their bravery, courage, and successful actions helped deter the "Federal Forces." He would later promote the trio, individually. Captain Pamela Mae Brewer will now be advanced to Major Brewer and Lieutenant Samuel Davis will become Captain Davis, and Sergeant Pete Boone will now be known as Lieutenant Boone.

Consequently, the battle went very well for the "Virginia Soldiers" as the "Union Troops" were confounded and outmaneuver by "The Southerners" and ceased the futile attack. Tactically, the "Confederate Forces" fought superbly and came out on top with approximately 30 casualties and zero deaths. Note: Pamela Mae's prayer was answered by her "Lord and Savior" when all of her fellow troops survived the battle. In contrast, the "Northern Troops" were worse off as they suffered 130 injured/wounded with circa 30 killed.

Historically, the "Battle of Carnifex Ferry" was considered a strategic triumph and victory for Brigadier General William Rosecrans and his Union Army as they maintained the ground. The subsequent decision of Brigadier General (BG) John Floyd, who was wounded during the battle, and the "Confederate Army" to withdraw from their Nicholas County position was controversial.

BG Floyd blamed Brigadier General Henry Wise for the strategic defeat because he failed to send his troops to the "Carnifex Ferry" battlefield site. In addition, the withdrawal of the Confederate Forces from Nicholas County and the adjacent counties would ultimately result in the "Yankees" maintaining an increasing amount of command, control, and occupation of the 52 counties of western Virginia.

Historical Note: Consequently, these western Virginia counties would become even more "Pro-Union" in the following two years. Many prominent business, government, and political leaders would later organize and vote to create a new entity, the State of West Virginia. Statehood would officially happen on June 20th, 1863, and the West Virginia Motto would be the Latin Phrase *Montani semper liberi* (Mountaineers Are Always Free).

Presidential Note: Rutherford B. Hayes and William McKinley, both from Ohio, fought for the Union during the "Battle of Carnifex Ferry." They would later become the 19th and 25th President of the United States of America, respectively.

Chapter 10
Mario, Letter, Construction, Friends, Mission
September 16th, 1861

Captain Mario LaGrande wrote in his very private journal some of the recollections of his amorous and fanciful dream. "I was in the 'Mansion du Moreau,' in Alexandria, Virginia in the bedroom with Mia Pamela Bella (My Pretty Pamela). I could view her beautiful sight of luxurious dark hair, with gorgeous chocolate brown eyes that sparkled like precious jewels, enticing sensual lips, and a scintillating smile; while I was climbing marvelous mountain tops; as I traveled through a luscious valley of erogenous hot springs of fabulous love. I remembered all the love-making details of the fabulous dream of mine, and woke up and stated in Italian, "*Mamma Mia, sicuramente amo e mi manca Mia Donna Virginiana Bellissima* (My Mom, I surely love and miss My Lovely Virginia Lady)!"

It had been over a month and a half since Mario had been with his beautiful "Southern Belle and Army Officer." He had the entire day off for himself and tenderly held Pamela Mae's last letter in his hand. Mario wanted to respond affectionately to her activities, plans, and words in a "love letter." Also, he was concerned about her health and safety after receiving an informal report about the recent "Battle of Carnifex Ferry" and the amazing story of a heroic "Confederate Woman Captain" riding around and through the "Union Lines."

In addition, Captain LaGrande would recap what he has been accomplishing and doing for the last six weeks. Finally, Mario wished to conclude the long letter with a love-filled poem in his three main languages: English, Italian, and French.

Monday, 16th of September 1861
Alexandria, Virginia

My Dear Pretty Pamela Mae,
Mia Cara Pamela Bella,
Ma Cheri Pamela Belle,

Oh Darling, how I long and miss everything about you: emotionally, personally, physically, socially, and spiritually. It has been such a long time since we saw one another and frequently made mad passionate love. My love for you grows stronger each moment and it is your health and safety that I pray for to "Our Good Lord" each day.

Sweetheart, It sounds like you have had some wonderful visitors at your "Sunshine Hills" home last month. It must be nice to have cousins from Germany who "*die Deutsch sprechen* (who speak German) to converse with. I know about J.E.B. Stuart and his fame as a "Cavalry Officer" during the "Battle of Manassas/Bull Run." I do believe Colonel Stuart will be a great General in the future.

Baby, I know how much you love your father and mother and honor them and your close relationship with Lizzie and Will, Gloria Faye's parents. By the way, Gloria Faye and Maurice are talking about marriage and having a baby. Both of them want me to express their fondness, love, and God's blessings upon you.

Captain Brewer, it sounds like the military training that you and your cousin Captain Christopher Russell were conducting has served you well in skirmishes and battles. I have heard reports that you made a daring "Cavalier Ride" in Nicholas County, Virginia last week and captured an "Ohio Regimental Flag during the "Battle of Carnifex Ferry."

My "A Company" soldiers of the Saint Alban's Mountaineer Regiment have continued our "Garrison Engineer Projects." At least six days a week, we perform a variety of construction assignments in the United States Capital Region. As their Captain and Commander, I proudly lead and supervise them, along with free blacks and poor white civilians. We are being directed at the regimental level by Lieutenant Colonel (LTC) Jonathan Wilson, who became an "Engineer Officer" after graduating from the United States Military Academy at West Point, New York. LTC Wilson is the Executive Officer and Training Officer of the Saint Albans' Mountaineer Regiment and was also my instructor at the Saint Albans' Military Academy when I was a cadet.

There is a real sense of anxiety by Major General McClellan and the War Department that there will be attacks upon our "Union Soldiers" here in this region. The last two months, our regiment along with several other "Northern Units" has built numerous defensive works in Washington D.C., Alexandria and Arlington, Virginia. The many construction projects that are needed to counter the possible "Confederate Advances" include the following:

a. Erections of numerous barricades along the Potomac River
b. Reinforcements of the gates and river walls

c. Constructing artillery redoubts and permanent emplacements
d. Digging trenches to thwart possible cavalry and infantry attacks
e. Building brick and stone walls to shield infantry soldiers
f. Extending protective fences around critical buildings and other vital infrastructure

I have been spending a lot of my days working and socializing with my dear friends and fellow Vermont Officers Captain Maurice Flambeau and Captain Joseph Wei, who is now assigned as the Commander of C Company. We have been spending many evenings in order to maintain our military abilities while conducting "Cavalier and Officer" training to include: horse riding, knife throwing, marksmanship, and sword fighting. Captain Wei continues to instruct Maurice and myself in "hand to hand combat" through the utilization of the ancient martial art discipline of *"Kung Fu"* actions and movements.

We have had military balls that I have helped organize and served as the 'Officer in Charge" of security for the event. Maurice and his pretty fiancée, Gloria Faye, and Joseph and his sweet fiancée, Marie Louise Yang, have really enjoyed themselves during these festive occasions. At

times, I have had to help get my friends and
fellow officers back to their quarters when they
have had too much wine and brandy. It has been
all "Good Fun." Maurice and Gloria Faye want to
thank you again for their 2nd floor apartment at
the "*Mansion du Moreau*" in Alexandria.

My Precious Pamela Mae, I have been making
lots of notes in my journal over the last 45 days
about my warm feelings and amatory thoughts
about you and I. Therefore, I have decided to
express my love for you in the enclosed poem, by
again using my three main languages of English,
Italian, and French.

My Beautiful Young Lady
Mia Signorina Bellissima
Ma Belle Mademoiselle

Pamela Mae, I express my love for you in three
linguistic ways,

With my trio of fluent languages of English,
Italiano, and Français.

On February 14th, you were born so lovable
and kind,

A cute girl, you are my everyday Valentine,
Valentina, Valentin.

My "Lovely Virginia Lady" with your attractive
hair so voluminous,

Covers your sleek back in a manner so
luxurious, lussuosa, luxueuse.

Your luminous brown eyes move me deep
inside my amorous heart,

Like the appealing colors of rich chocolate,
cioccolato, and chocolat.

With perfectly shaped lips that are irresistible,
kissable, and luscious,

Contours your savory mouth pure delicious,
deliziosa, and délicieuse.

My Darling young woman with a pretty face,
most captivating,

I long to see your vista so enchanting,
incantevole, enchanteresse.

My adorable Angel on earth, you have a
physique most Heavenly,

A great form that arouses me so excitedly,
eccitata, and excitée.

Honey, you have all the supernatural beauty of a
radiant red rose,

All the charm, with a countenance that glows, si
illumina, la lueur.

I hope that we will someday walk on a beach
romantically,

With fingers interlocked devotedly,
devotamente, dévouement.

I have a wish that we will once again be dancing
and drinking wine,

You in a beautiful dress and looking extra
divine, divina, divine.

I dream of seeing you in a lace wedding gown,
walking down the aisle,

A bouquet of fresh flowers, and your radiant
smile, sorriso, sourire.

Dearest Love, I desire to be in a warm embrace
with you nightly,

To be alone with you and hug you so tightly,
stretta, fermement.

My precious wife to be, I vow to be dedicated
and loyal to You,

To spend the rest of my life sharing a love, oh so
true, vero, vraie.

We will be a good Papa and Mamma and have a
wonderful family,

The strong bond we share will last through
eternity, eternità, éternité.

Con Tanto Affetto (With Much Love),
Tuo Mario Bello (Your Handsome Mario)

P.S. Pamela Mae, when you get time, please write
back and tell me about your military and
personal adventures.

P.S.S. I love you so much, *ti amo tanto bene, je
t'aime beaucoup.*

It was now the morning of Tuesday, September
17th, 1861, and Captain Mario Patrizio LaGrande
was up early, shaved, washed, and dressed in his
"Vermont Green" officer's uniform. That day, he
was surprised to meet a young sergeant during
the morning's "Muster Formation" and his name
was Leopoldo Simoni. The new Sergeant was

also from his home state of Vermont. In addition, Sergeant Simoni was an excellent marksman, horse rider, and scout. Captain LaGrande was able to have Sergeant Simoni assigned to "A Company" so he would be one of his subordinate men.

Furthermore, Captain LaGrande found out that Sergeant Simoni's mother was from the Italian speaking section of Austria and his father's family were stonecutters from the Alps in northern Italy. The Simoni's were very prominent in the carving and making of tombstones and grave markers throughout Vermont and could speak Italian. His family could also speak German, too, like his *Pamela Bella* (Pretty Pamela).

Captain LaGrande took an immediate interest in his fellow *paisano* (countryman) who also spoke Italian and loved to sing "Opera" songs. In fact, Leopoldo Simoni, who had a strong tenor voice, was later heard that day singing a few verses from the well-known Italian composer, Gioachino Rossini and a very famous and popular song, *Largo Al Factotum*.

Note: The verses below are from the opera, <u>The Barber of Seville.</u>

Mario heard the very pleasant Italian sounds coming from the mouth of Leopoldo who was in the "Mess Tent" helping out, and they nostalgically reminded him about his mother. A humorous and sarcastic excerpt from the song and the translation is written below:

Largo Al Factotum (Make Way for the General Servant)

Uno alla volta (One at a time)
*Per carita!, per carita! per carita! (*For charity!, for charity!, for charity!)

Uno alla volta, uno alla volta (One at a time, One at a time)

Uno alla volta, per carita! (One at a time, for charity!)

*Figaro! Son qua (Figaro! I'm here)
Ehi, Figaro! Son qua (Hey, Figaro! I'm here)

Figaro qua, Figaro la, Figaro qua, Figaro la (Figaro here, Figaro there, Figaro here, Figaro there)

Figaro su, Figaro giu, Figaro su, Figaro giu (Figaro up, Figaro down, Figaro up, Figaro down)

Note: *Figaro is the name of the heroic comical servant and main character of <u>The Barber of Seville Opera.</u>

Mario LaGrande was very fluent in Italian and he smiled broadly and laughed at the very funny rendition by Leopoldo, who imitated with his hands and facial expressions the charming Italian Barber Figaro so perfectly. Captain LaGrande couldn't help himself, as he ventured into the "Mess Tent" and in the classical "Italian Style," shouted approvingly, *"Bravo, Bravo, Bravo Maestro* (Well Done, Well Done, Well Done Master)."

On Saturday afternoon, September 28th, 1861, Captain LaGrande was continuing to command his "A Company" soldiers of the Saint Albans' Mountaineer Regiment. His unit was working that day near the War Department on a few defensive barricades.

Consequently, Captain Mario LaGrande was approached by a very friendly and loquacious officer, who had the afternoon off. He was a military scholar, and he introduced himself as Major Michael Sampson. He was from east central Illinois. Soon thereafter, Major Sampson proceeded to compare Major General (MG)

George McClellan with other famous American Generals.

Of course, Mario was intrigued by the gregarious Major Sampson and paid attention to every iota of his historical comparisons, summary, and predictions. He told Mario in part, "Captain LaGrande, I firmly believe that our Commander, MG McClellan will lead our brave "Union Troops" into a number of huge battles. General McClellan will be great like General George Washington was in his victory over the Hessians at Trenton in 1776. He will be celebrated like Brevet Major General Andrew Jackson was in his victory over the British at New Orleans in 1815. And, also, MG McClellan will become very well-known as Major General Zachary Taylor, due to his victory over the Mexicans at Buena Vista in 1847." Captain LaGrande continued to listened attentively to the talkative Major Sampson and thought pleasantly, *This Officer is just like me, an aficionado of famous American Generals and Army Battles and like Major Sampson said, I hope and pray that MG McClellan will also be an accomplished and successful General in this United States Civil War.*

It was now near the end of the "Lord's Day" on Sunday, September 29th, 1861. Captain Mario

LaGrande, Captain Maurice Flambeau, and Captain Joseph Wei were summoned to report to the Executive and Training Officer, Lieutenant Colonel (LTC) Jonathan Wilson, in the briefing tent.

Each of our "Vermont Officers" did not know what to expect but were hoping for orders to get them away from their daily construction duties performed in garrison. Captain LaGrande was thinking to himself, *I am getting bored with these last two months of constructing defensive works in the Alexandria, Arlington, and Washington D.C. areas. I pray that LTC Wilson will provide us information about a new assignment. Amen!*

Captain Mario LaGrande will soon find out that his thought and prayer would be answered as he arrived first to the officers' briefing tent of the Saint Albans' Mountaineer Regiment. Within the next five minutes, his two best friends and fellow officers, Captain Maurice Flambeau and Captain Joseph Wei, walked nonchalantly into the large white tent and sat down next to Captain LaGrande.

Mario reverted to his Italian and said, "*Ciao amici miei, come state?* (Hello, my friends, how are you)?"Maurice decided to answer in French,

"*Je vais bien merci*! (I am fine thank you)!"Joseph, of course, responded in Mandarin Chinese, "我对简报很好奇！ *Wǒ duì jiǎnbào hěn hàoqí!* (I am fine, and curious about the briefing)!"

Captain LaGrande noticed that Lieutenant Colonel (LTC) Jonathan Wilson was about to enter the tent and leaned over and told his fellow Captains, "I am curious, too, and I am sure we will find out soon about any future assignments and missions." They all took deep breaths and waited momentarily.

Then, one of the Sergeants called out, "Attention Officers!" Immediately, Captains LaGrande, Flambeau, and Wei sprung to their feet. Their "Executive and Training Officer" instructed them to be seated. LTC Wilson began the short brief saying, "Gentlemen, we have received much praise from our higher headquarters and from the Commander of the Vermont (Green Mountain) Brigade for our excellent construction of the defensive works in the Washington D.C., Arlington, and here in the Alexandria, Virginia region. We are ahead of schedule on our construction mission, and now Major General George McClellan wants selected personnel from our regiment to be assigned to his command. This is necessary in order for the

Commanding General to gain valuable information concerning "Confederate Troops" and their military movements and operations in the adjoining counties north and west of Arlington, Virginia.

Lieutenant Colonel Jonathan Wilson paused and continued the briefing. "Our regiment has been tasked to select seven officers/sergeants to be assigned to train for a special upcoming mission and operation for a minimum of 30 days. Our regimental commander has tasked myself to be the 'Officer in Charge,' and to lead and train my subordinate crew of Captains LaGrande, Flambeau, and Wei." LTC Wilson waited for a minute and stopped to read a short missive delivered by a courier.

Captain Mario LaGrande immediately thought this special mission may be similar to his first assignment in May and June of 1861. *I can remember traveling for a few weeks all the way from my home in Burlington, Vermont to Taylor and Barbour Counties in western Virginia (now West Virginia) and back to my beloved "Green Mountain State." I also recall meeting Major General George McClellan for the first time in Grafton and afterwards performing intelligence gathering, reconnaissance, and scouting duties in the area down to Philippi, Virginia. Finally, I will*

*never forget my first combat action during the
"Battle of Philippi" when I fondly saw the
gorgeous, luscious, and voluptuous "Young Lady"
of my dreams, the beautiful Captain Pamela Mae
Brewer, by the covered bridge.*

LTC Wilson continued his briefing about the
necessity to determine the size and current
operations of the "Rebel Forces" north and west
of Arlington, Virginia through the utilization of
experienced intelligence gathering, scouting,
and reconnaissance Cavalier officers and
enlisted personnel. Captain LaGrande was right
in his assumption that his future mission will be
comparable to his assignment in Western
Virginia. LTC Wilson concluded his briefing by
saying, "Gentlemen, each Captain will select a
Sergeant to be your assistant in this mission by
the evening of October 1st, 1861. Make sure that
they are brave, dependable, excellent horsemen,
and can expertly fire a pistol and a rifle as well."

The next day, Captain Mario LaGrande asked
Sergeant Leopoldo Simoni to be his right hand
man on the reconnaissance and scouting mission
that will begin next month. Sergeant Simoni
quickly agreed to work for Mario and replied in
the affirmative in Italian saying, "Sì, Capitano
LaGrande, assolutamente (Yes, Captain
LaGrande, absolutely)." Captain LaGrande was

very pleased with his positive response and thought, *"Sargento (Sergeant) Simoni will be valuable to our assignment especially with his linguistic abilities in the making of coded messages that will greatly complement his military skills.*

That same afternoon, Captain Maurice Flambeau would convince a volunteer from Quebec by the name of Sergeant Jacques DuBois (Wood) to be his enlisted partner in the mission. Sergeant DuBois' ability to speak French and his many martial skills will be a welcome addition to the seven-man crew. However, Captain Joseph Wei was not able to find an enlisted man who spoke "Mandarin Chinese." Furthermore, he was able to convince a bold "hard charging" Sergeant by the name of Dan Bailey to accompany Captain Wei on their intelligence gathering, scouting, and reconnaissance mission. He happened to be a relative of the famous "Mad Anne Bailey" who was a very brave courier, scout, and Indian fighter in Virginia during the Revolutionary War and after.

Mario went to sleep that night as he contemplated his future "Army Adventure" and wondered if everything worked out if he could be promoted to Major and wear the gold leaves.

He liked the Italian sound of being addressed as "Maggiore LaGrande (Major LaGrande)."

Finally, Mario LaGrande thought faithfully and romantically about his "Lovely Virginia Lady" and prayed in French, *"Seigneur dans le ciel ci-dessus, s'il vous plaît bénissez et protégez ma Pamela Belle* (Lord in heaven above, please bless and protect my Pretty Pamela), *au nom du Père, du Fils, et du Saint-Esprit, Amen* ! (in the name of the Father, of the Son, and of the Holy Spirit. Amen)!"

Chapter 11
Captain LaGrande and Ball's Bluff
October 4th, 1861

It had been three days since Lieutenant Colonel (LTC) Jonathan Wilson had begun his role as the "Officer in Charge" of his seven-man unit that included himself, Captain Mario LaGrande and Sergeant Leopoldo Simoni, Captain Maurice Flambeau and Sergeant Jacques DuBois, and Captain Joseph Wei and Sergeant Dan Bailey. LTC Wilson led his officers and sergeants to depart their home camp of the Saint Alban's Mountaineer Regiment in Alexandria and to travel north of Arlington towards Leesburg and the southern section of Loudoun County, Virginia.

LTC Wilson had directed each of his officers to proceed with their "Sergeant Partner" and conduct daily intelligence gathering, scouting, and reconnaissance duties and then report back, by coded message, to a remote and safe location. LTC Wilson would then review each officer's report, consolidate the information, and transmit the summary findings by Army Courier" back to the Headquarters of the Vermont (Green Mountain) Brigade in Alexandria. Subsequently, the Brigade Commander would review the summary report, comment, and relay the information to the Headquarters of the Commander, Major General George McClellan.

Major General George McClellan Official Photo

Captain Mario LaGrande reflected on the morning of Friday, October 4th, 1861, and thought affectionately and prayerfully of his Italian mother, Anna Rosa, and that she honored San Francesco di Assisi (Saint Francis of Assisi), on his name day. *It is both ironic and sad that on a day that* Mamma Mia *(My Mom) honors Saint Francis as a "Man of Peace" that I am preparing for war each day. Please forgive me Lord Jesus because you are the "Prince of Peace." Amen!*

On today's sun-filled venture into Loudoun County, Captain Mario LaGrande admired the pastoral and silvan beauty of the maple and sycamore trees in the woods. He was once again impressed with the "Lord's Creation and Re-creation" of the picturesque "Autumn Season." Mario thought again in Italian, English, and Greek about the "Patron Saint of Italy," *San Francesco would certainly delight and enjoy the colorful view of God's earthy handicraft. Kyrie eleison, Christe eleison, Kyrie eleison (Lord have mercy, Christ have mercy, Lord have mercy). Amen!*

Mario was, of course, mounted upon his majestic looking "Arabian stallion," *Marengo il Secondo,* while Leopoldo was sitting upon his smaller multi-colored horse, Raffaello (Raphael), who was named after the brilliant Italian Renaissance painter of the same name.

Captain LaGrande and Sergeant Simoni were near a copse of huge Liriodendron tulipifera (tulip poplar) trees and the two soldiers were partially camouflaged, since they were wearing their "Hunter Green Vermont" uniforms. Well, the beautiful and peaceful scene would abruptly change. Sprinting down the dusty road in their direction on two very sweaty quarter horses, came two "Confederate Soldiers." They were obviously galloping at an alarming rate in such a hurried manner.

Captain LaGrande candidly told Sergeant Simoni in Italian and English, "Sargento (Sergeant), I believe these two "Rebel Riders" are disoriented and heading in the wrong direction. Let them pass southward down the thoroughfare and we will follow them in order to ascertain their intentions, va bene (all right)?"

Sergeant Simoni just nodded his head and about a minute later, our two-member "Union Reconnaissance and Scout" team vacated their position behind the trees and started to pursue the "Southern Troops" from the rear. Captain LaGrande was very puzzled about why the two "Virginia Riders" were heading south towards Arlington County in such a frantic state. He instantly deduced that they were under the influence of alcohol and did not know "where the Hades" they were going!

Within five minutes of the hot pursuit of the "Running Rebels," Captain Mario LaGrande spotted the friendly sight of his best friend and fellow Vermont officer, Captain Maurice Flambeau. He could see Maurice, who is a larger figure, and was to the left at an intersection of a road that was approximately fifty yards in the distance. Captain Flambeau was upon his brown "Arabian Stallion," Lannes. He was standing alongside his enlisted partner, Sergeant Jacques DuBois, who was on a light brown Morgan horse called Bon Ami (Good Friend).

Alertly, Captain Flambeau and Sergeant DuBois maneuvered into a defensive position in the middle of the road. This action would block the path of the two fleeing "Virginia Duo." The suspected officer took out his sword and was prepared to charge straight towards Captain Flambeau, who also alertly pulled out his saber with his right hand.

Captain Mario LaGrande was riding as fast as his gray/white horse, *Marengo il Secondo*, could take him and was near the rear of both of the "Confederate Soldiers." He could vividly see Lannes perform a quick sideways hop to his right. Instantly, Captain Flambeau switched his sword to his left hand and slashed the enemy across his torso. This nifty move resulted in the "Virginia Officer" being knocked off of his steed.

Consequently, Captain LaGrande dismounted his horse, and subdued the fallen officer by taking a strong piece of rope and tying his wrists behind his back. Mario found out that the defeated rebel was named Lieutenant Richard Skaggs and he was from the "Bluegrass State of Kentucky."

Meanwhile, Sergeant Simoni shot the accompanying enemy soldier in his right shoulder, which caused the wounded man to slump over his horse. Then, Sergeant DuBois swiftly dismounted and pulled the injured man off of his steed, who happened to be called Sergeant Jonas Lowe and he was from Montgomery County, Virginia.

Captain Mario LaGrande was very skilled at communicating with people and was able to gain valuable intelligence information from the two captured "Rebel Men." Lieutenant Skaggs, who appeared to have had a few alcoholic drinks casually mentioned that he liked to be called Mickey, and he was from the 8th Virginia Infantry Regiment commanded by Colonel Eppa Hunton. He proudly bragged about an approximate two brigade "Confederate Force" close to 2,000 soldiers that was slowly forming between Leesburg, Virginia and the "Potomac River" near a prominent terrain feature called "Ball's Bluff."

Captain LaGrande, Captain Flambeau, and Sergeant Simoni decided to utilize their multiple coding and language skills to write a message that will be delivered to fellow officer and experienced linguist Captain Joseph Wei. Captain Wei was located circa five miles away, north of Arlington, Virginia.

Note: All three Captains have been using, practicing writing, and deciphering coded messages since their college days years ago before "The War."

The short coded general military message was completed in Mandarin Chinese, Italian, French, Greek, English, Latin, and then a repeat of the languages as follows: Duìzhǎng Due Ancien domain αιχμάλωτοι … Also, circa duo mille στρατιῶτες near flumen Jiéwěi.

The translation of the short message above was Captain, 2 Old Dominion captives... Also, approximate two thousand soldiers near river (Potomac) end. The message was meant to be somewhat confusing so that if an enemy intercepts the words, it would be difficult to understand.

Captain Flambeau would, upon arrival, explain the message and tell Captain Wei verbally in more specific details. This will include additional information about the significant number of enemy soldiers being located east of Leesburg,

Virginia and about the very prominent terrain feature called Ball's Bluff. Shortly thereafter, Captain Wei and Sergeant Bailey will take their prisoners and translate the coded message to the rear so that LTC Wilson could properly incarcerate Lieutenant Skaggs and Sergeant Lowe and reroute the updated intelligence report to their Higher Headquarters.

Captain Maurice Flambeau and Sergeant Jacques DuBois proceeded to transport the two "Dixie Prisoners" to Captain Joseph Wei and Sergeant Dan Bailey, who were a short horse ride from their current position. Meanwhile, Captain LaGrande and Sergeant Simoni decided to take a break in place. Mario thought prayerfully and reflectively, *Oh Dear Lord above, I have this intuitive feeling that there will be a battle near Leesburg and that all seven of us: LTC Wilson, Myself, Sergeant Simoni, Captain Flambeau, Sergeant DuBois, Captain Wei, and Sergeant Bailey will be directly involved in the fighting, God help us. Amen!*

Saturday, October 12th, 1861

Captain Mario LaGrande was proudly thinking of his "Italian Heritage" when in confidence he told his enlisted partner in Italian, English, and

Latin, "Sargento Simoni, oggi celebriamo Cristoforo Colombo (Sergeant Simoni, today we celebrate Christopher Columbus) and his discovery of America in 1492, Anno Domini (In the Year of Our Lord)." This October 12th, in the year 1861, would be similar to the previous two weeks as the special intelligence gathering, reconnaissance, and scouting mission would continue in Loudoun County, Virginia.

The latest situational update from Major General McClellan's "Headquarters Staff" indicated that Brigadier General (BG) Charles Pomeroy Stone would lead the "Union Forces." The Federals would have over 1,500 troops at their disposal to shield the U.S. Capitol from a possible attack.

Once again, the brave and courageous Captain Mario LaGrande and his trusted Sergeant Leopoldo Simoni would be the lead twosome of their seven-man special military intelligence, reconnaissance, and scouting unit. The "daring and dynamic duo" would conduct a secret mission behind enemy lines. It was now the early afternoon of Saturday, October 12th, 1861, and each soldier would carry an extra-large civilian jacket and pants in their saddle bags.

Fortunately, Captain LaGrande and Sergeant Simoni are now dressed in eccentric looking civilian gentlemen swallowtail jackets and matching trousers and just happened to come across a couple of black male field slaves. The farm servants they met were on a piece of fallow ground east of Leesburg, Virginia, on the edge of a big plantation near an old outlying building. The "undercover soldiers" found out that their Master and foreman were preoccupied at the mansion and the workers had a few hours to themselves.

Captain Mario LaGrande lied to them and said that his name was Mister Charles Finely and he was from Frederick, Maryland. Sergeant Simoni, was pretending to be Mister Finely's assistant, a.k.a. *Giuseppe* (Joseph). Mario then asked the two hard working farm laborers whether they knew "the whereabouts" of any "Confederate Troops" in the vicinity. The older man said, "Yes, Sir, there are hundreds of 'Them Rebels' on the west side of the Potomac River. There are many slaves, men and women amongst them, doing cooking, supply, and teamster work, and we are very familiar with the area."

Mario, a.k.a. Mister Finely, took a few mental notes of what the older man summarized about the enemy. He used his acute communication abilities and persuasive skills to talk the two workers into spying for "The Union" in exchange for some cash money. The suspicious negro men paused and looked all around to see if there was anyone else in the area. The two future civilian spies were named Caleb and Ezekiel. They received a ten-dollar bill each as an incentive to work for Mr. Finely and Giuseppe. Captain LaGrande thought it was quite appropriate to have a spy named Caleb, *"I remember in the "Book of Numbers" when Moses sent Caleb and others to spy for the Hebrews in the Negev and the surrounding area.*

Caleb was the leader and he walked quickly down a narrow wooded side path that took them to within 100 yards of the big encampment of the "Confederate Regiments." Ezekiel, Captain LaGrande, and Sergeant Simoni, did not see any enemy pickets, and followed close behind Caleb. Rapidly and wisely, Captain LaGrande took out his binoculars and was only able to view two regimental flags and two artillery weapons; as the numerous amount of trees obscured his view of the rest of the "Southern Forces" and their heavy weapons.

"Mister Finely" then allowed Caleb and Ezekiel to look through the binoculars and instructed the two men how to determine a regimental flag and an artillery weapon. Mario then told them, "Caleb and Ezekiel, I want you to walk around the camps of the 'Rebel Troops' and perhaps bring them food and water while you count the number of regimental flags and the number of artillery pieces. My assistant Giuseppe and I will wait here for an hour and a half. If we encounter anyone, we will leave and meet you behind the outbuilding on the plantation where we first met you. Do you understand? Also, if you are successful, I will give you each an additional five dollar silver coin, alright?"

Both Caleb and Ezekiel's eyes got real big and they displayed happy grins, and just nodded their heads in the affirmative. Within ten minutes, the intrepid twosome walked into the "enemy camps." They were shrewd enough to talk one of the cooks into giving them a few loaves of bread and a wooden bucket filled with water, and a long handled metal ladle. Then, in a very casual manner, Caleb and Ezekiel began to ingratiate themselves to the "Confederate Troops" by offering them each a chunk of bread and a cup of cool water and started to count the flags and artillery pieces.

Captain LaGrande, a.k.a. Mister Finley, and Sergeant Simoni, a.k.a. Giuseppe, heard some unwelcome noise coming from their front. Also, they had now waited ninety minutes in the woods and then decided to return to the edge of the plantation land. They would find the wooden structure and hide behind the building as planned.

The two adventuresome civilian spies, Caleb and Ezekiel, spent circa two hours walking around the "Rebel Camp" and found out that most of the troops were from either Mississippi or Virginia. In addition, as directed, Caleb and Ezekiel counted five very ornate regimental flags and a total of six artillery pieces in their reconnoiter. They were able to return the empty bucket and silver ladle back to the generous cook, and then slyly slipped away and returned to the woods.

Caleb prayerfully thought to himself, *Lord have mercy on us, may we get out of here safely and back to our plantation land and find those two generous "white men."* Well, our two brave "colored men" were initially disappointed when they could not see "Mister Finely and Giuseppe" in the woods. However, Caleb and Ezekiel carried on anyway as planned and eventually approached the outbuilding on their plantation.

Heretofore, Captain LaGrande and Sergeant Simoni heard the two negros coming and they came around the side of the building. The risk taking "Union Men" were now out of their civilian clothes and looking dignified in their military uniforms. They gladly received the reconnaissance report from Caleb and Ezekiel. Caleb proudly told them, "Sirs, we did just what you told us and we counted a total of five very fancy (regimental) flags and six very big guns (artillery weapons)."

Mario was elated at the news and quoted the words of Jesus in the "Parable of the Talents" in Matthew 25, and told them, "Well done, my good and faithful servant(s)." Captain LaGrande then gave Caleb and Ezekiel each a five-dollar silver coin and shook their rough hands.

He expressed sincere gratitude in his three languages, English, Italian, and French, to the temporary Union spies, "Thank You Men, *Grazie Uomini, et Merci les Hommes.*"

Well, the two field workers were so happy and then they waved good-bye to the departing "Yankee Soldiers." Caleb spoke on behalf of the working men, "Thanks y'all, we have never been treated so kindly, God bless you two." Wisely, the two plantation servants decided it would be prudent to stash the money somewhere as they soon dug a hole inside the old building, buried it in the ground and subsequently put a bunch of firewood over the spot.

Captain LaGrande was going to write another coded message to be delivered to Captain Flambeau concerning what he and Sergeant Simoni found out about the enemy location, strength of the Mississippi and Virginia soldiers, and their "heavy weapons."

Monday, October 21st, 1861
Battle of Ball's Bluff

It was now 2:00 a.m. on the very early morning of October 21st, 1861, and Sergeant Leopoldo Simoni was on guard duty. He received and read an urgent message from the Headquarters of the Vermont (Green Mountain) Brigade. It read in part, "Union Military operations have begun a probing action and a reconnaissance in force across the Potomac River near a prominent terrain feature called 'Ball's Bluff.' Reinforcements are needed urgently as soon as possible."

Immediately, Sergeant Simoni left his post and ran to the tent of his Officer, and woke him up and said, "Capitano LaGrande, we are directed to get dressed and saddle up immediately. Our seven-man crew is ordered to ride right away towards the Potomac River east of Leesburg, Virginia. Our Higher Headquarters predict that the 'Confederate Troops' are ready to go on the offensive. We have orders to meet up, as soon as possible with the "Union Soldiers," commanded by Brigadier General (BG) Charles Stone and his subordinate Colonel Charles Devins."

Captain Mario LaGrande was expecting the news and was prepared to get quickly washed and ready in his dress blue uniform, with green cape. He would be sure to take both of his .44 caliber revolvers, and his very sharp 41 inch Cavalry Sword. He had an innate feeling that each of his fellow officers and sergeants would need a 100 foot long rope in case there might be a "river crossing or rescue."

Even-though there was much "hustle and bustle" going on in their Saint Albans' Mountaineer Regiment bivouac camp; Mario took a few moments to amorously think and lovingly pray about his Pamela Mae. *She does have the most enchanting, soft, splendid, and enticing brown eyes and I long to kiss her adorable, delicious lips once again. Good Lord in Heaven, Please keep Mia Pamela Bella (My Pretty Pamela) safe and warm and protected from harm, and may I be able to be with her next month at her Prince William County, Virginia home, Amen!*

It was now 3:00 a.m., on that cool October 21st, 1861, autumn morning, and all seven members of our indomitable "Vermont Group" were gathered at the Headquarters of the Vermont (Green Mountain) Brigade. LTC Jonathan Wilson found a "Loyal Union," Loudoun County civilian resident, named Gerald Dabney to be their guide/pathfinder. They headed off cautiously into the obscure darkness towards Arlington and then traveled in a northwest direction towards Leesburg, Virginia.

Each member of their Saint Albans' unit would have a long rope in their possession, attached to their respective saddles. Captain Mario LaGrande and Sergeant Leopoldo Simoni would ride just behind LTC Wilson and would be followed next by Captain Maurice Flambeau and Sergeant Jacques DuBois. Captain Joseph Wei, who hastily procured the ropes would bring up the rear element along with Sergeant Dan Bailey.

Captain Mario LaGrande is a little concerned about traveling at night. Wisely, LTC Wilson instructs Mister Dabney to ride at a moderate pace, while carrying a torch for the first fifteen miles. At the approximate three-quarter point of the journey towards Leesburg; the officer-in-charge decided to take a half hour break to reorient themselves with the topographical map.

At approximately 5:00 a.m., LTC Jonathan Wilson wanted to take a well-deserved break, look at the map, and brief his officers and sergeants. "My fellow 'Vermont Soldiers,' Mister Dabney, our guide has determined that our group is approaching the town of Farmwell (Now Ashburn), Virginia. Also, we may have to eventually cross the Potomac River; having been assigned to support our "Federal Forces" of the 15th Massachusetts Infantry, commanded by Colonel Charles Devens." LTC Wilson paused for a few minutes, as he saw a Union courier, who provided him a succinct updated situational status of the conflict.

Captain Mario LaGrande was listening intently to the brief, and then during the pause, confided casually and privately to his two best friends, Captain Maurice Flambeau and Captain Joseph Wei. "Maurice and Joe, I have this very spiritual feeling that things will not go well for our 'Northern Brothers,' today, so please be cognizant of the danger ahead of us. I will pray for you, as you pray for me, that Our Lord Jesus will carry us through with our duties, and that Saint Michael the Archangel will protect us, Amen Brothers." Captains Flambeau and Wei nodded in the affirmative as they exchanged handshakes and encouraging pats on their respective backs.

Well, the "Vermont Intelligence, Scouting, and Reconnaissance Crew" would arrive soon after the commencement of a major combat action from both sides. LTC Wilson, Captains LaGrande, Flambeau, and Wei, along with Sergeants Simoni, DuBois, and Bailey could easily determine that the "Confederate Forces" of mainly Mississippi and Virginia soldiers had many advantages.

"The Rebels" were better organized and prepared and maintained the disposition of troop placement and held the high ground to effectively utilize their artillery. In addition, their Commander, Colonel Nathan G. Evans, was a West Point Graduate, Class of 1848 and he was an experienced "Indian Fighter" and served brilliantly during the Battle of Manassas/Bull Run earlier in July 1861.

Au contraire, the "Union Men" were in an untenable position, with their backs against the West Bank of the Potomac River. The "Yankee Soldiers" were inexperienced and they were commanded by two inept high level officers, Brigadier Charles Stone and Colonel Edward Baker.

As they arrived on the scene during the daylight, Captain Mario LaGrande and the others could hear explicitly the screams of wounded

men, shouts from stressed out officers, and the
frightful sounds of musket fire and artillery
shells. It was obvious that the situation was
already going horribly wrong for their fellow
"Federal Troops." After 8:00 a.m., LTC Wilson
directed his seven-man Vermont detachment to
position themselves on the left flank down river
from the 42nd New York Infantry Regiment. The
unit was commanded by Colonel Milton
Cogswell.

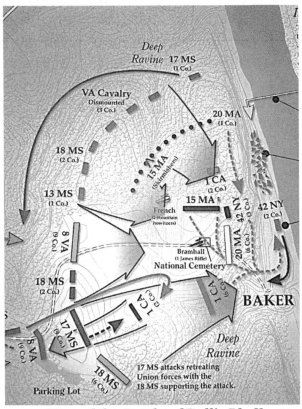

Map of the Battle of Ball's Bluff

Right away, Sergeant DuBois and Sergeant Bailey took the initiative and cared for the vulnerable horses. The "Good Sergeants" grabbed the reins and brought the steeds to safety on the banks of the Potomac River, that were fortunately lower than the elevated field of combat above themselves and their animated equines.

Sergeant Leopoldo Simoni luckily located a good sized egg-shaped boulder that was circa three feet high. He crouched down and loaded his rifle and began firing at the advancing "Mississippi Soldiers." He felt badly, thought and prayed in Italian, "*Mi dispiace Signore per aver ucciso i nostri compagni americani, ti prego perdonami, Cosi sia* (I am sorry Lord for killing our fellow Americans. Please forgive me. Amen). Sergeant Simoni was an expert marksmen and hit at least four of "The Rebels" in the first hour of fighting.

Captain Mario LaGrande had both of his .44 caliber revolvers loaded and he was able to wound three of the enemy men as he alternated the firing of his hand-held weapons ambidextrously. Shortly thereafter, he gazed at a location that was about one hundred yards to his right and could see that the line and ranks of the 42nd New York Infantry Regiment were breaking down. Captain LaGrande had an instinctive feeling that the "New Yorkers" would have to retreat and that they could be possibly driven into the inexorable Potomac River by the advancing "Virginia and Mississippi" troops. He swiftly moved to his right and told Captain Flambeau to take his previous position.

Captain Mario LaGrande subsequently asked LTC Jonathan Wilson, "Sir, may Captain Wei and I be granted permission to come to the aid of the distressed men of the 42nd New York? I feel like they will be forced to flee their positions and they will end up in the river!" LTC Wilson nodded his head affirmatively and replied, "Yes, Captain LaGrande, I trust your judgement completely. Go forth and Godspeed."

"Captain Joseph Wei, come with me and we will get our horses and proceed up along the west side of the Potomac River to assist our struggling comrades," yelled Captain LaGrande over the noisy din of countless rounds of ammunition and exploding shells. It was an impressive sight as the two Vermont Captains, LaGrande and Wei, mounted their gray/white and black Arabian stallions, respectively. The beautiful horses were in the temporary care of Sergeant Dan Bailey who took his own horse and rode to the left of Captain Maurice Flambeau.

Ten minutes later, Captain LaGrande and Captain Wei could see their fellow "Union Soldiers" flee the combat lines and go into the river. Mario LaGrande knew that the long ropes would come in handy. Right away, he took the 100-foot length of the coarse cord in hand and went into the flowing water himself upon his trusted steed, *Marengo il Secondo*. Joseph Wei followed his good friend and leader and took his horse Han Xin (who was named after a famous Chinese General from the 3rd Century before Christ) into the water also. Both horses were very brave and loved to swim.

For the next hour or so, Captains LaGrande and Wei threw their long ropes into the Potomac River and provided a lifesaving line for over forty dire "Union Soldiers" who clung to the ropes and were pulled to the eastern shore of the river. Fortunately, there was a "Federal Doctor" on the dry land that viewed the heroic deeds of the "Vermont Officers." He noticed the flamboyant officer who was wearing the dark green cape in his rescue efforts. The handsome doctor had been treating the soldiers who had almost drowned and many had suffered wounds. He was a French Canadian from Montreal and he volunteered to join the "Union Cause" and his name was Major Arthur L'Amende (Fine) and he spoke French and English, too.

Unfortunately, on the last trip "to and fro" across the cold waters of the Potomac River, Captain LaGrande was shot in the back of his lower left leg and Captain Wei was shot in the back of his lower right leg. By the saving "Grace of God," Doctor L'Amende directed Mario and Joseph in English to lay on their stomachs as he stopped the bleeding and wrapped white cloth bandages around the wounds. The "Good Doctor" later found out that the officers understood French as he praised them saying, *"Vous avez été très audacieux dans l'action, Mes Braves Capitaines. Magnifiques* (You were very bold in action ,My Brave Captains. Magnificent)!"

Meanwhile, on the west side of the Potomac River, Sergeant Dan Bailey took the initiative and rode his horse in a rowdy and wild manner into the thick of the fighting. He valiantly fought "The Rebels" and was able to rescue a fallen member of the 42nd New York Infantry. He then firmly placed the soldier on his horse. Sergeant Bailey made a quick decision and, with the soldier, rode south along the banks of the Potomac River to the safety of an advancing Union Infantry Company. Captain Maurice Flambeau was able to observe Sergeant Bailey in his conspicuous action and thought, *This soldier looks like a crazy and mad man but he sure was uncommonly brave on the battlefield.* That courageous battlefield action resulted in that brazen man receiving the nickname of "Mad Dan Bailey." Captain Flambeau soon after performed his own heroic deeds as he fired his .44 caliber revolver numerous times at the advancing "Confederate Troops" and later was able to pick up and resolutely save a regimental flag from the 20th Massachusetts Infantry color guard.

Colonel Nathan Evans was exceptional and outstanding in his command and direction of his "Confederate Soldiers" in the resounding victory over the opposing "Union Troops." His effective and superb orders and management expertise earned him a promotion to Brigadier General effective the day of the battle on October 21st, 1861. His mostly Virginia and Mississippi troops fought bravely and outmaneuvered the defeated pathetic "Federal Soldiers" which resulted in their retreat into the frigid waters of the Potomac River. Evans' men experienced far less casualties than the "Hapless Bluecoats."

The "Battle of Ball's Bluff" was a disastrous defeat for the Union Army with the following amount of estimated Union casualties: 223 killed, 226 wounded, and 529 missing with close to 100 men who were reported as drowned in the Potomac River. Colonel Edward Baker, who was a United States Senator from Oregon at the time, was killed in the battle. Furthermore, the humiliating loss to "The Rebels" upset Major General George McClellan and other high ranking government officials in Washington, D.C. The embarrassing defeat to the Confederate States of America (CSA) was initially blamed on the deceased Colonel Baker. However, later on, the U.S. Congress got involved and the blame and scapegoat for the defeat was directed at Brigadier General Charles Stone who was overall in command of the field forces. He was later arrested, confined, and was threatened with an "Army Court Martial." However, he was eventually released from prison without a trial.

The "Good News" was that all seven members of the Saint Albans' Mountaineer Regiment's group of intelligence gathering, reconnaissance, and scouting personnel survived the "Battle of Ball's Bluff." Captain Mario LaGrande and Captain Joseph Wei recovered from their wounds and were promoted to Major for their bravery in rescuing their fellow soldiers from the river and devotion to duty. In addition, Captain Maurice Flambeau was promoted to Major for his heroics in combat and the saving of a "Union Regimental Flag." Furthermore, Sergeant Simoni was promoted to Lieutenant for his excellent marksmanship and bravery in action. Finally, Sergeant "Mad Dan" Bailey was promoted to

Lieutenant for his frenetic boldness and lifesaving actions during the hostilities.

Major Mario LaGrande was extremely happy with his promotion. He smiled and thought happily in Italian and in English, "*Che meraviglia, Sono un Maggiore dell'esercito. (How wonderful, I am a Major in the Army) and I really like the way it sounds— Maggiore LaGrande!*

However, he was saddened to have witnessed the wounding and death of so many of his fellow "Union Soldiers." He was now very encouraged to find out that he would be on a sabbatical leave for the next two months or more. In addition, Major LaGrande was hopeful that he will soon be with the "Woman of all his desires, dreams, fantasies, prayers, and wishes"— his very "Lovely Virginia Lady and Officer" Pamela Mae Brewer.

Chapter 12
Pamela Mae's Letter and Mario's Travels
October 28th, 1861

Newly promoted Major Pamela Mae Brewer, while at home again in "Sunshine Hills" in Prince William County, was feeling very good about her recent advancement in rank. Obviously, her Papa, John Brewer, and her Mamma, Sarah Anne, were so very proud of their daughter's accomplishments as an officer and as a young "Virginia Lady."

Pamela Mae was sitting in her chair at the dining table drinking a cup of her favorite dark rich "Colombian Coffee" with cream. She remembered that her father, who was so intelligent, told her in German and English a few years ago, "*Mein kostbares Mädchen und mein Schatz* (My precious Girl and my Treasure), coffee was first introduced into Colombia in the early 17th century by 'Roman Catholic Jesuit Priests' who had arrived with the Spanish settlers."

That Monday morning of October 28th, 1861, was crisp and cool in Prince William County, Virginia. Gloria Faye's mother, Lizzy, was kindly brewing coffee and she was making a ham, cheese, potato, and vegetable omelet with sweet corn bread and butter for the entire "Brewer Family."

Pamela Mae had been spending the last five weeks back at her picturesque "Plantation Home" near Manassas, Virginia. She had been assisting in a myriad of duties and responsibilities to include household planning, business dealings, animal husbandry, sales, and delivery of livestock, and more.

Fortunately, Mister Ronald McGavock, the sutler, was staying overnight on the property and he had brought her father a newspaper, called "The Baltimore Beacon." Her tender heart warmed when she read an article written about the recent "Battle of Ball's Bluff" that was considered a significant victory for the Confederate States of America (CSA). In addition, the newsworthy item mentioned that there was a heroic "Union Army Captain" wearing a green cape and riding a gray/white "Arabian stallion." The valiant officer had been seen rescuing "Yankee Soldiers" with a long rope from the cold waters of the Potomac River east of Leesburg, Virginia.

Pamela Mae thought prayerfully and lovingly, *Oh Gracious Lord Jesus in heaven above, that brave "Federal Captain" sounds like my Mario*

Patrizio LaGrande. Please may he be safe so I can see his very handsome face, hug his super muscular body while kissing his very alluring lips. In addition, I ask that Mario will be able to come see me on a future "glorious day. Amen."

Major Pamela Mae Brewer's 1st Manassas (Virginia) Infantry Regiment strength had been depleted significantly over the last three months and the unit had been subsequently disbanded. The enlisted soldiers are now assigned to a regiment in the "Stonewall Brigade" which became famous by their Commander, Brigadier General Thomas Jonathan Jackson. Major Brewer requested to be on personal leave to the first of the New Year, January 1st, 1862. Yesterday, she had received written approval to be on leave from her higher headquarters, the Virginia (Old Dominion) Brigade, and was hopeful to be with her Mario Bello (Handsome Mario) once again.

Mister McGavock would be departing "Sunshine Hills" that afternoon for the Washington D.C. area. Therefore, Pamela Mae needed to hurry and write a short letter and poem to her "Vermont Cavalier Officer" so that McGavock would be able to deliver it personally. She wished to invite Mario LaGrande to travel right away to her home and ask her Father John

Brewer for "her hand in marriage." Pamela Mae would utilize three of her languages: Spanish, English, and German to give the letter more of a "European Flavor."

Mi Caro Mario Hermoso,
October 28th, 1861
(My Dear Handsome Mario),
Manassas, Virginia

Guten Morgen (Good Morning) my charming fiancé and husband to be. I pray that you are well and safe back in Alexandria. I love you so much and I long to be in your strong and warm embrace in the near future. Please give my love to Gloria Faye and let her know her father and mother, Will and Lizzy, are well and send their love and tender regards.

Darling, I have so much to tell you. First, I performed my intelligence gathering, scouting, and reconnaissance mission duties in August and September of this year and was in the "Battle of Carnifax Ferry" in Western Virginia. By the "Grace of God," I survived the battle and was promoted to Major for bravery and for the capturing an "Ohio Regimental Flag."

Second I have been assisting Papa and Mamma with the numerous business and plantation duties. I especially enjoy being involved with the breeding of the livestock. In addition, it is very rewarding to train the horses and the subsequent sale and delivery of the farm animals.

Third, I have continued to take time out of my very busy day to maintain my Cavalier and Army Officer skills. Thank God, my Arabian mare, *Marenga la Primera* is healthy. I ride her often at very high speeds while performing many attacking and evasive maneuvers. Furthermore, Will has been making cloth and straw dummies so I can use my saber to execute a variety of fencing and sword fighting techniques. Also, I have been practicing with my pistol and rifle so as to maintain my marksmanship proficiency. Finally, I am enjoying my knife throwing training with Papa and I have a lot of fun making and throwing my lassoed rope.

Sweetheart below is a short affectionate love poem for you.

Mario, My Dream Came True

In Philippi that morning, by the covered bridge,
my dream came true,

At Manassas by the Bull Run Creek, I saw and
rescued you.

On the master bed at home we kissed, and my
desire was for you.

When we first made mad passionate love, all my
fantasies came true.

We woke up in each other's loving arms, and I
felt brand new,

As we walked hand in hand on our plantation
lands, I said, "I love you too."

During amorous times in Alexandria, you
proposed. My prayers came true.

In Elk Garden, Virginia, when we get married
near the mountains of blue,

I will be your wife forever, and all of our
dreams will begin again anew.

Con amor (With Love)
Pamela Mae

P.S. I love and miss you so much and please come to see me as soon as possible so that you can ask Papa for my hand in marriage and we can be united in love once more.

November 1st, 1861

Major Mario Patrizio LaGrande held the brief, sweet, informational, and love letter with a poem titled "Mario, My Dream Came True" in his right hand. A few moments later, he looked up to the heavens and said in Italian, "*Gloria a Dio nei luoghi altissimi (*Glory to God in the Highest)." Mario read the wonderful words in Pamela Mae's letter and poem and was feeling so elated that he could be together again soon with his "Lovely Virginia Lady."

He was at his "Vermont Camp Site" in Alexandria, Virginia and was able to go on an extended medical sabbatical leave due to his wounded leg. He thought to himself, with a plan in mind and a prayer, I *will have to wear a "Southern Gentleman" gray style suit complete with hat and cane. I will need to bring my pistol and revolver and carry enough .36 caliber and .44 caliber ammunition for a full day of riding upon my Arabian stallion, Marengo il Secondo. Finally, "Good Lord in heaven," it would be a blessing to have a travel partner who was familiar with the main and secondary roads from Alexandria to the "Sunshine Hills" Brewer Mansion in Virginia.*

It was now 6:00 a.m. on that Friday, November 1st, 1861. Major LaGrande was in a nostalgic mood and fondly remembered years ago in Burlington, when he and his father and mother all went to mass together and honored the "Saints of the Roman Catholic Church." He said a short prayer while walking to the "Mess Tent" for breakfast, "Dearest Jesus, Saint Mary, Saint Anthony, Saint Francis, and Saint Patrick, please ensure that I ride safely to see Pamela Mae and may I have a reliable guide and travel partner. I ask this all in the name of the Father, Son, and Holy Ghost. Amen!"

Suddenly, Mario saw a familiar looking negro man in a plain navy blue jacket with matching trousers. He approached Major LaGrande smiled broadly, and stated confidently , "Good Morning Sir, and congratulations on your promotion, for your heroics at 'Balls Bluff.' Remember me? I am Samuel d'Union and I was the man who assisted Captains Wei, Flambeau, yourself, and the enlisted soldier with our travels between Centerville, Prince William County, and back to Alexandria, Virginia, in July of this year. Furthermore, I had my surname legally changed to d'Union in appreciation for my freedom and work with the Union Nation."

This time, Mario smiled broadly and stated, "Alleluia (Praise the Lord). Samuel, I do remember you vividly, and you are an answer to prayer. Let's have breakfast and talk intelligently about how we could work together again. I am planning a return trip back to see my fiancée, Pamela Mae Brewer, at the 'Sunshine Hills' plantation and I will need your assistance during my travels."

Mario LaGrande told Samuel that he would be paid fifty dollars up front for being his guide and scout and would receive fifty more dollars upon a successful trip. The two men further discussed the need to wear gray civilian clothes and have forged identification and travel documents while carrying dried meat and two canteens of water each. They decided to travel mostly on the secondary paths and roads. In addition, Samuel d'Union would play the role of a servant once again while Major LaGrande would once more portray the civilian character of Mister Charles Finely. Samuel would be riding Joshua, his solid ebony-colored quarter horse which will help when traveling under limited visibility and nighttime conditions. Mario would personally carry the handguns and have the long rifle inserted into his elaborate saddle baggage. He felt and thought that their plan was sound, *But, if captured, I could be imprisoned, sent to trial, and hung for being a spy. Lord, have mercy on us. Amen!*

It was now close to 11:00 a.m. and Major Mario LaGrande, a.k.a. Charles Finely, and Samuel were close to departing Alexandria. Samuel candidly told Major LaGrande, "Sir, I am afraid if we are stopped and questioned by any Confederate soldier or government official, that your northern accent will give you away and make you suspicious. I recommend that I tell them that you have laryngitis and can only barely whisper and can write out answers."

Mario realized how clever and realistic Samuel was and he would take his trusted aide's advice, if necessary. Major Mario LaGrande and Samuel got everything together for the difficult trip. Soon thereafter, Major LaGrande briefly told his best friend and fellow Union officer, Major Maurice Flambeau, about his plan. He also asked Maurice to escort himself and Samuel to the Provost Marshal's location at the south end of Alexandria, which was only a few miles away from the "Vermont Camp."

Well, Major Maurice Flambeau talked to the two sergeants manning the "South Gate" and signed out the "two civilians" on the Provost Marshal's paperwork log. Soon afterwards, the two lifelong friends shook hands and gave one another farewell hugs much to the surprise of Samuel and the Union Sergeants on duty. Mario told his confidante Maurice in Italian, "*Mille Grazie mio amico buonnissimo* (Thousand thanks my very good friend)."

As Major Mario LaGrande and Samuel exited the gate and headed west, they could hear the clear French voice of Maurice giving a heartfelt benediction, "Que notre Seigneur Jésus vous bénisse et vous protège jusqu'à votre retour, Amen (May our Lord Jesus bless you and protect you until your return. Amen)!"

Mario and Samuel decided to make rest and water stops near the following two communities en route to "Sunshine Hills" to include Burke's Station and then Clifton which are both located in Fairfax County, Virginia. Samuel reminded Major LaGrande that, "Sir, of course it will probably be dark by the time we cross into Prince William County. By the "Grace of God," I am very comfortable traveling at night through these backwoods areas."

Mario, a.k.a. Charles Finely, nodded his head affirmatively and they were off on their current adventure.

Samuel rode ahead on his very fast steed, Joshua and Major LaGrande followed about 100 yards to his rear on his majestic appearing Arabian stallion, *Marengo il Secondo*. There was no obvious sign of any "Confederate Troops" on the main route for the first hour. However, during the second hour of travel on the road leading west, Samuel spotted a company-sized element of butternut and grey uniformed Virginia soldiers. He could see that the men were marching towards "Burke's Station." He wisely signaled to Mario to veer off to the left on a secondary route.

This was a slower and yet safer way to travel as they encountered only a few pedestrians, black and white, along with peddlers driving their one horse wagons. Even though Major Mario LaGrande was very anxious to see his beloved Pamela Mae, he realized that this narrow road would be more prudent for both of them. He thought prayerfully, *Dear Lord in heaven and my Guardian Angel, I know that you are caring for and guarding me along the way. Please guide Samuel and may you deliver us from evil. Amen!*

It was now approximately 2:00 p.m. and our daring duo were able to take a rest on the southern edge of "Burke's Station." Major LaGrande and Samuel found a clear stream to water their horses near a field of Autumn grasses to graze upon. Mario took out some of the dried meat and one of his canteens and was able to eat a little food and drink some water for about fifteen minutes.

Mario asked his guide, "Samuel, what is the estimated travel time to our next stop in Clifton?" Mister d'Union hesitated for a few moments while calculating the distance and travel time and replied, "Major LaGrande, Sir, I would guess that if we remain on the secondary roads that it will be another two more hours of riding and we will be near Clifton, Virginia by 4:00 p.m. Also, just in case we encounter any trouble on the next leg of this journey, let's agree to meet on the west side of Clifton, all right?"

"Our Vermont Cavalier" concurred with the suggestion and they departed within a few moments and the first forty-five minutes of the ensuing trip were peaceful until they heard gunfire. Samuel was in the lead and he instantly reacted to the sound of lead cast bullets flying over his head. He heard angry shouts of, "Hey Boy, surrender and stop right there," and instinctively decided to head in a southwest direction and within 400 yards found a safe path through a mostly coniferous wooded area of loblolly and Pinus echinata (shortleaf pine trees).

Major LaGrande, a.k.a. Mister Charles Finely, found himself alone and knew from his geographic experience and military training that most of the rounds were coming from a northeastern direction. He thought to himself spiritually, *Oh Lord, be my navigator, refuge, and save me for my Pamela Mae. Amen!* Mario and his Arabian stallion, *Marengo il Secondo*, swiftly accomplished a 180 degree dressage equestrian maneuver which resulted in "Our Vermont Cavalier" heading in a southeast direction. He took out his loaded .36 caliber revolver and fired a few random shots and was riding his trusted steed at a breakneck pace of over 30 miles per hour.

Mario felt so unusual to be running away from danger, but he remembered the words of William Shakespeare in his play of Henry IV, Part 1, "The better part of valor is discretion." Within ten minutes, Major LaGrande was temporarily "out of harm's way" and found a safe place to stop and took out his topographical map and compass. As he gazed at the map and found the agreed upon rendezvous point west of Clifton, Mario figured it may be an additional seventy-five minutes of travel by horseback to meet back up with Samuel.

He was standing face to face with his devoted gray and white male Arabian horse and spoke to him in Italian and English like a human being saying, "Va bene Mio buon amico (Alright my good friend), we find ourselves on another adventure, il Signore Gesu' e Michele il arcangelo (The Lord Jesus and Michael the Archangel) have protected us each. So we trust that we will be safe during the rest of the day. Amen!"

Major Mario LaGrande made the sign of the cross upon himself and upon the head of *Marengo il Secondo* and briefly thought about Napoleon Bonaparte and his father Louie LaGrande and said in French, "Au nom du Père, et du Fils, et du Saint-Esprit. Amen (In the name of the Father, and the Son, and the Holy Ghost. Amen)." Mario, with his "military thinking cap on," determined the most logical and practical path to his next objective. He said out loud, "Lord, have mercy" and began to gallop towards the main road.

By the "Grace of God," the next forty-five minutes of travel west were free from any incident and then he saw a carriage full of finely dressed Virginia civilian personnel traveling west also. He heard an angelic voice tell him, "Mario, get to know the people and offer to give the younger children rides along the way."

This was such a new religious experience for him and he was able to ride alongside the civilian group in their lavish vehicle. The occupants of the carriage appeared to have a mother and father in the front seats with two boys of about eight and ten years old with a young woman in her twenties in the back. Major Mario LaGrande, a.k.a. Charles Finely, had this intuitive spiritual feeling that the passengers in the carriage were familiar with French.

Mario rode along the right side of the conveyance as he got the attention of the people and greeted them in French, "*Bonne après-midi à tous* (Good Afternoon to everyone)! By "Divine Providence," Major LaGrande heard a very understandable and welcome response from the oldest boy as he replied, "*Bonsoir Monsieur, et je reçois des cours de français, de Mademoissele Fountaine avec mon frère* (Good evening, Sir, and I am receiving lessons in French from Miss Fountain along with my brother.)"

A very normal, polite conversation in French ensued for about thirty minutes as Monsieur Finely portrayed the role of a visitor from France who was en route to Richmond to conduct business with the government of the Confederate States of America. Mario even took turns and gave each of the boys a ride on top of his horse while "Rebel Soldiers" passed by without much suspicion.

Major LaGrande thought of his very unique situation, *It felt like the "Southern Troops" are assuming that I am with this family and maybe an uncle of the boys. Thank the Lord that I am not being asked questions by the soldiers so that I can maintain my French conversation as I talk to the children. Amen."*

By the "Grace of God," our "Vermont Cavalier," who was incognito, enjoyed this part of the journey and had to finally say, "Au revoir et que Dieu soit avec vous (Good bye and God be with you)!" He then galloped and ran his mighty horse, *Marengo il Secondo*, at a very fast pace. It was about 30 minutes later as Mario slowed down and thankfully there was no trouble ahead as the daylight was vanishing steadily as he approached Clifton, Virginia.

"Sir, Mister Finely, I am on the side of the old empty shack off the road." Mario heard the voice of Samuel, his trusted aide. Major LaGrande turned partially around and located the freeman and they enjoyed a brief cheerful reunion.

Darkness was nigh and Major Mario LaGrande asked his assistant, "Samuel, how much longer till we make it to Sunshine Hills?" Samuel hesitated and said, "Sir, if we stay off the main routes, maybe we are three hours away from Manassas. However, I have heard talk that there are a number of "Confederate Troops" on the roads looking for us!"

Mario thought for a minute, and then said to Samuel, "As anxious and excited that I am to see my beautiful and sweet Pamela Mae later this evening, perhaps it would be more judicious for us to stay the night and start off before dawn tomorrow."

Samuel expressed his thoughts with Mario, and he answered, "Major LaGrande, I agree that it would be wise to stay overnight en route to Prince William County. In fact, one of my colored friends named Elkanah lives about thirty minutes down the road and we could possibly stay with his family for a few hours until we leave early tomorrow."

It was just over thirty-five minutes later as Mario and Samuel saw the shape of a modest two-story house and fortunately, Elkanah was out front. Samuel greeted his older friend with a welcoming whistle and they met each other and exchanged handshakes and hugs.

Samuel happily relayed the good news to Mario saying, "Praise the Lord Jesus, Elkanah says his master has 'gone off to war' and his wife and children are staying the night elsewhere with some relatives. We can stay in the 'Big House,' tonight and Elkanah's woman can cook us a late supper."

Mario was feeling so good about their accommodations for the night that he replied in a typical Italian manner, with emphasis, "Bravo, Samuele, Lavoro Eccellente (Well done, Samuel, excellent work)!

Chapter 13
Pamela Mae and Mario Reunited
November 2nd, 1861

The chickens and the roosters were making their pre-dawn cackling and crowing sounds as Pamela Mae Brewer rolled over onto her left side. It was after 7:00 a.m. on that Saturday morning, November 2nd, 1861, and "Our Lovely Virginia Lady" just finished her most amazing dream. She saw a very tall and handsome man in a gray outfit riding a majestic looking horse down the tree-lined drive towards her "Sunshine Hills" mansion home.

In her very fascinating dream, Pamela Mae was sitting on the swing on the front portico and she is anticipating, hoping, praying, and wishing to see her Mario Bello (Handsome Mario) ride up the lane. Suddenly, she can hear the neighing sounds of her horse, *Marenga la Primera,* and then the barking sounds of her German Shepherd dog, Butch, alerting her and the family that there are visitors on the premises.

Pamela Mae woke and arose quickly and fondly recalled her wonderful dream. The house was silent upstairs and she determined the need to wash up speedily and get dressed into a bone-white house dress with a matching belt. She could smell the fantastic aroma of fresh brewed coffee and the culinary combined scent of bacon, eggs, and potatoes in the frying pan.

Her mother and father were still in bed as she descended to the first floor and can view Lizzy busy in the kitchen. Pamela Mae greets Gloria Faye's mother, her Mammy, house cook, and maid, with her customary hug and kiss on her right cheek and said, "Guten Morgen (Good Morning) Lizzy and I will just have a cup of coffee first and take the strong brew to the front porch. I just had a very realistic dream and I have this very strong feeling deep in my heart that "my Mario" will be arriving soon, Good Lord willing." Lizzy responds, "Sakes alive, Honey Child, I know about your dreams and feelings so I will keep your breakfast warm whenever you are ready."

Pamela Mae takes her hot morning drink outside, sits on the swing, and takes three sips of the delectable coffee and closes her "resplendent brown eyes." She hopes and prays in a soft voice, "Heavenly Father, I praise you. Hallelujah and I only ask and wish for one thing to happen on this early morning? Please, may the 'love of my life and future husband, Mario Patrizio LaGrande' appear upon his Arabian stallion, *Marengo il Secondo*, in the next hour or so. Amen!"

After about ten minutes, Pamela Mae was now very surprised to hear her Arabian mare, *Marenga la Primera,* make a number of very eager and excited neighing sounds. This is followed by the "woof, woof, woof" barking noises of Butch as he is greeting the visitors riding up the lane. Pamela Mae then sees a negro man in the lead and he is talking to one of the field hands who is pointing towards the front of the mansion. At this point, she realized that a very elegant Italian-French looking gentleman in a gray suit is riding his impressive mount and in his typical European way starts to sing his favorite Italian song in a very audible manner for his young woman to hear.

**"*Pamela Bella, Pamela Bella, Ti Amo*
(Pretty Pamela, Pretty Pamela, I Love You)..."**

Well, when Pamela Mae heard those very amatory words from the voice of her fiancé, she immediately got up from the swing, screamed delightfully, and had tears of joy in her luminous brown eyes. Quickly, Pamela Mae ran like the wind to see her "Handsome Vermont Cavalier." Mario LaGrande dismounted promptly, gave Samuel $50, his thanks, and the reins to his horse. He walks rapidly towards his adorable, irresistible young woman with her coal black luxurious hair bouncing and saw her radiant smile and very enticing luscious ruby lips. Mario extended his muscular arms wide open and grabbed and hugged Pamela Mae tightly and spun her three times around.

He instantly thought , *Dearest Lord Jesus above, You have answered all my prayers, as I am with "my love so true." Alleluia and thank You!*

Pamela Mae told him excitedly, "Darling, I had a dream that you would be riding down the primary lane of my 'Sunshine Hills' estate this morning, and praise the Lord, here you are. Our dreams came true when I saw you. Hallelujah!" Mario responded to his "young lady and beautiful dreamer" in a very fond manner, saying in Italian and in English, "Pamela Bella, tu sei mia Tesora Preziosa (Pretty Pamela, you are my Precious Treasure) and my ultimate hope and nascent dream came true, too." Well, our very amorous and "Lovely Virginia Lady" and our equally amorous and "Handsome Vermont Cavalier" continued their very warm embraces and moist kisses for a long time in the early morning sunshine, oblivious to anyone who was watching their outwards displays of affection.

By this time, John and Sarah Anne Brewer, the Master and Madam of the home, are also outside as they hear all of the commotion and noise. For the first time in their lives, they witness their daughter hugging and kissing the distinguished looking man in gray, continuously and without embarrassment or interruption. Her papa turns to his wife of twenty plus years, hugs her, and says, "Sarah Anne, let's give them some time together, and it is obvious that Pamela Mae loves Mister LaGrande very much and I believe we are going to have a "son-in-law" and a wedding to attend, Gott sei Dank (Thanks be to God)!"

Circa fifteen minutes later, our very devoted and loving couple walk mano e mano (hand and hand) towards the "Main House." Mario had a creatively positive indulgent thought, *I should honor Pamela Mae's parents and greet them initially in German.* As they walked up the front porch stairs together, Mario LaGrande extended his right hand towards Pamela Mae's father and stated, "*Guten morgen, Herr und Frau Brewer, es ist mir eine Freude, Sie kennenzulernen* (Good morning, Mister and Mrs. Brewer, it is my joy to meet you)!"

After giving his future father-in-law, John Brewer a firm handshake, Major Mario LaGrande takes the extended right hand of his future mother-in-law Sarah Anne and in the typical "French Style," kisses the top of her hand. Pamela Mae is so very impressed by the very honorable and respectful manner of her husband to be and smiles beamingly and says, "Hallelujah, my prayers are surely answered this morning. We are all here together at last!"

Lizzy, of course, was listening to all of the talk outside and loving every moment. Soon thereafter, she decided to call out in a loud voice, "Is anyone hungry for some delicious breakfast vittles?" Pamela Mae answered on behalf of herself, Mario, Mamma, and Papa saying, "Yes Lizzy. Yes, we will all be coming inside right away for the tasty meal!"

Pamela Mae took Mario by the hand and escorted him down the long hall into the grand dining room. Her father sat down at the head of the table and her mother was seated to his right. Pamela Mae sat down on the chair closest to her father on his left side while Mario was seated to her left. John Brewer said, "Grace" and they all enjoyed the friendly conversations and the savory breakfast foods of cheesy eggs and parsley, fried potatoes and onions, bacon, freshly baked hot apple turnovers, and steamy hot coffee.

Sarah Anne noticed how happy her daughter looked as she was glowing with such a joyful countenance on her gorgeous, illuminated face.

Pamela Mae and Mario held hands at the table which resulted in her mother thinking and praying, *I can really see the devoted and loyal love that Pamela Mae has for her "Northern Gentleman." Dear Lord, he is so very attractive and handsome and I can truly see how my daughter would fall in love with Mario. I pray that their children and our grandchildren will resemble our good-looking couple. Amen!*

Major Mario LaGrande was being very charming as he utilized his multi-lingual skills during the meal.

He raised his coffee cup and said in Italian, "*A La Salute al Padrone e alla Padrona di questa casa e alla loro bellissima figlia*! (Salute to the Master and Mistress of this home and to their very beautiful daughter)!" He then expressed his appreciation and politely told Lizzy in French, "*Merci beaucoup, Madame, le repas était délicieux* (Thank you very much, Madam, the meal was delicious)."

He then remembered his Father Louie's words in Latin, "*Carpe diem* (Seize the day)" as he decided it was as good a time as any to ask permission from Pamela Mae's father. Mario LaGrande took her left hand and interlocked his fingers with hers securely. He looked at John and

Sarah Anne Brewer and made the following request, "*Herr und Frau Brewer* (Lord and Lady Brewer), I have been dreaming of a beautiful brown eyed girl since I was a child back in Vermont. I first realized in June of this year by the covered bridge at Philippi, Virginia, that the woman officer riding the gray and white Arabian horse like mine was the lovely lady of all my dreams and thoughts for those many years. I love Pamela Mae with all my heart, soul, mind, and strength and promise to be her dedicated and steadfast husband until my last breath here on earth. She is so very precious to me and I will cherish and honor her always. Therefore, I humbly ask your permission for her 'hand in marriage'? and pray that Jesus our 'Good Lord in heaven and Savior' will richly bless our lives together and that we will have many children. Amen!"

At this point, Pamela Mae and her mother began to cry as her father carefully stood up and walked behind his daughter and her "Union Officer." John Brewer placed his right hand on the back of his daughter and his left hand on the back of his son-in-law to be and stated in English and German, "Major Mario LaGrande and Major Pamela Mae Brewer, I give you permission to marry wholeheartedly and may our dear Lord above richly bless your marital lives together. *Ich bete dies alles im Namen des Vaters, des Sohnes und des Heiligen Geistes. Amen* (I pray this all in the name of the Father, Son, and Holy Ghost. Amen)!"

Pamela Mae saw her dear mother nod her head affirmatively and was so very thrilled to have her father and mother's approval and blessing of her impending marriage and wedding. She again responded out loud, "Hallelujah. Thank you." She decided to tell her parents about her dream and plans. "Mamma and Papa, I had the most amazing dream this last August while I was bivouacked and sleeping overnight in Front Royal, Virginia. In my dream, Mario and I were in front of a stately white mansion located in Elk Garden, Virginia. It was the first day of the frigid season, the 'Winter Solstice.' In German style, the stately home was highly decorated for the Christmas Season to include *ein Tannenbaum* (a Christmas Tree) and I was dressed in a white lace wedding gown and Mario was wearing his dress blue Army uniform."

She paused for a few seconds and closed her lustrous brown eyes and then continued, "After the wedding ceremony, my beautiful great grandmother Elizabeth was there next to me under the portico. Great grandma Elizabeth put her left arm around my waist and told me the most phenomenal things, "Pamela Mae, look towards Cedar Creek. There are your maternal great great grandparents, Thomas and Sarah (Van Hook) Hendricks, with their white 'Great Pyrenees' dog. They are waving to their great great granddaughter and want you to visit them and have your wedding ceremony right here."

Sarah Anne was emotionally and spiritually affected by her daughter's dream of her deceased grandmother and great grandparents. She calmly got up and walked around the table and gave Pamela Mae a very warm embrace and kissed her teary cheeks. Sarah Anne responded, "Darling, that is so wonderful that you saw my grandmother Elizabeth and my great grandparents, Thomas and Sarah, in Elk Garden. It is definitely a sign from our 'Good Lord' above that they totally approve of you and Mario getting married. I will help plan your wedding in December at our ancestral home in Elk Garden, Russell County, Virginia. Lord, have mercy and bless us all."

Even though it was still the morning, Mister Brewer told his faithful servant, "Will, bring out our best German Cognac and French Brandy. In addition, get six small liqueur glasses in order to honor this very special day for Mario and Pamela Mae." Lizzy poured out all the drinks, as John

Brewer gave the celebratory toast in German and English, "*Ich möchte einen Toast auf Pamela Mae und Mario ausbringen* (I would like to raise a toast to Pamela Mae and Mario) for a long and prosperous life together and many children. Prost (Cheers)." Everyone who had a drink gave their own cheers and salute to one another as they smiled and cheerfully clanked their glasses together.

Pamela Mae was bursting with jubilation as she told her fiancé, "Sweetheart, I adore and love you so much. My travel bags are currently packed and ready to go. I will tell Mamma and Papa that we will be departing later this morning to Woodbridge, Virginia. I am sure that we can stay the night at the "Old Mason Mansion" near the Occoquan River. Mister Mason told me and directed his servants that I could stay overnight whenever necessary. I have delivered horses there a few times and I am very knowledgeable of the route." Mario gave her a big smile, a tight hug, and a soft kiss and replied, "I would go anywhere confidently with you my love because you mean the world to me."

"Our Lovely Virginia Lady" knew that she would have to dress in one of her soft tan buckskins "riding outfits" figuring that she and her "Handsome Vermont Cavalier" would have to ride very fast and outmaneuver anyone who could be a threat during their journey to the southeast section of Prince William County, Virginia.

Samuel helped Mario LaGrande get his Arabian stallion, *Marengo il Secondo*, ready for the trip while Will prepared Pamela Mae's Arabian mare, *Marenga la Primera*. It was once again a tearful farewell for all of the family present as Mamma Sarah Anne called out, "Pamela Mae, please write to us and God bless you on your excursion." Papa John Brewer followed up and gave a benediction in German, "*Möge unser Herr mit Ihnen sein und Sie beschützen.* Amen (May Our Lord be with you and keep you safe. Amen)."

While mounted up on their distinguished looking horses, Mario gave his fetching "wife to be" a caring smooch and told her poetically, "A kiss for luck, and I am on my way with my adorable and lovable Pamela Mae." She smiled brightly and winked at her "Handsome Officer" and led the way down the drive of her "Sunshine Hills" home.

Pamela Mae expertly knew the seventeen miles of paths and secondary roads to the Woodbridge, Virginia area and figured that herself and Mario could hopefully arrive there harmlessly by nightfall. She mentally recalled her "Virginia History" and folklore about the area and the prominent family. *Yes, I remember that the Mason Family bought and received a substantial amount of land there and Thomas Mason had a toll bridge built, hence the name Woodbridge, in the late 18th century. Also, one of the prominent family members was George Mason and he was one of the "Founding Fathers" and very influential in the development and initiation of the "United States Bill of Rights." Also, Mason County, Virginia (now West Virginia) was named in his honor.*

Thankfully, the first half hour of the trip was uneventful. However, the circumstances changed abruptly when Pamela Mae observed a sinister pair of motley looking men who appeared to be lurking and waiting for someone to rob. The scoundrels did not notice Mario and Pamela Mae riding eastwards towards them. However, there was an innocent elderly couple from Fairmont, Virginia (now West Virginia) who were riding a one horse wagon traveling west. Pamela Mae slowed down and candidly told her daring Vermont Cavalier, "Darling, it seems that 'Our Lord in heaven' has placed me in a position to be 'Miss Robin Bea Goode' once more." Immediately, our two Majors in civilian clothes heard gunshots to their front.

Mario had a few personal and spiritual thoughts as he viewed his "courageous and valiant" military officer and daring damsel spring into action. *Pamela Mae is so incredible as she takes out one her very sharp "throwing knives" and yells at the two bandits. I will be her back-up if things get out of hand. Lord, have mercy. Christ, have mercy. Lord, have mercy."*

Well, our very brave and intrepid "Miss Robin Bea Goode" threw the first knife with her left hand and it stuck deep into the upper right back shoulder of the culprit on her left. This caused the wounded man to painfully scream, "What the hell was that," as he dropped his pistol and slumped over the neck of his chestnut-colored quarter horse.

The second robber reacted by turning around on his painted pony. He then pointed his revolver at Pamela Mae. By this time, our heroic "Virginia Lady" who is equally ambidextrous, took her second knife into her right hand and accurately threw the shining blade into the upper right bicep muscle of the unsuspecting man.

Mario came upon the wounded men, who were amazed and shocked to find out that a young woman defeated them handily. He helped

Pamela Mae further subdue the attackers while confiscating their weapons.

"Thank God" neither the blameless man or the upright woman was hurt and by the "Grace of the Lord," they were a doctor and nurse team. Fortuitously, the medical duo were devout Christians who were very forgiving. They subsequently removed the knives from the injured culprits, stopped the bleeding, and bandaged the wounds. The nurse further admonished the thieves and gave them both some biblical advise when she stated, "Go forth and sin no more."

The doctor, who did have a handgun and had a very relieved expression on his face, asked, "What are the names of our rescuing hero's and how can we repay you?" Pamela Mae humbly smiled and gave the healthcare man and woman both hugs and replied in an amusing and candid manner, "Folks in Prince William County just call me 'Miss Robin.' I call my fiancé and trusted assistant, Mario Bello (Handsome Mario). We are on our way to stay the night in Woodbridge, Virginia and you don't have to repay us. Please just give a monetary donation to your church this Sunday in order to honor Jesus, 'Our Prince of Peace.' Amen!"

Our very bold and heroic young woman told her intimate traveling partner in Spanish and in English, "*Mi Querdisimo Amor* (My Dearest Love), I would say that 'By the Grace of God,' we just concluded another Pamela Mae and Mario adventure, without injury, so that's a very good thing." Our rugged "Northern Gentleman" smiled and replied in Italian and English, "*Mia Cara Dolce-cuore*, (My Dear Sweetheart), Yes My Love, and I cherish every adventurous, exciting, and intriguing moment that we share. I hope and pray arduously that we arrive unscathed at Woodbridge, Virginia later this evening. Amen!"

Fortunately, there was a slow flowing crystal clear creek with cool water that Mario and Pamela Mae could freshen up with as their horses got plenty to drink themselves. Major LaGrande hugged and kissed his overtly appealing young lady, and thought, *Oh what a lucky man I am!*

Since Pamela Mae was very knowledgeable about the terrain and the roads ahead, she decided to take the initiative and comically told her horse, *Marenga la Primera,* Mario, and *Marengo il Secondo* in Spanish stating, "*Vamos amigos valientes y caballos rápidos* (Let's go brave friends and rapid horses)." Our "Italian-French-American Officer and Gentleman" had the pleasure of seeing his *Pamela Bella* (Pretty Pamela) take-off in an instant on her swift Arabian mare. He definitely admired her horse-riding technique and tried to follow her at a safe distance on his Arabian stallion.

After a very steady ride of seventy-five minutes, Pamela Mae recognized the very elegant "Mason Mansion" in the distance. This picturesque three-story structure was built in the "Eighteenth Century" close to the Occoquan River according to highest standards of the "American Colonial Period" near Woodbridge, Virginia.

Pamela Mae and Mario dismounted from their weary horses as they were greeted by a couple of stable workers. The men readily remembered the unforgettable "Lovely Virginia Young Lady" with the resplendent coffee colored brown eyes, long curly black hair, and likable personality. The older of the two grooms stated, "Good evening, Ma'am, and welcome back. We will take good care of your horses and Miss Sally, the cook, will have a yummy supper for you in the dining room."

Mario followed his precocious and socially brave Pamela Bella (Pretty Pamela) into the huge double front doors and heard her say,

"Excuse us, Miss Sally, it's Pamela Mae Brewer and my fiancé, Mario, and we are hungry!" Mario took a discerning look down the long decorated hall as he saw a colored woman wearing an apron approaching them. He was once again pleasantly surprised to see Pamela Mae greet Miss Sally with a big hug as the cook took her by the hand into the opulent dining room. Mario noticed that there was an elaborate bronze, glass, and gem chandelier hanging down from the ceiling in the center of the grand room.

Miss Sally told her two guests, "The Master and his family are away for a few days so you two sit together here on this side of the table and I will bring in one of my original specialties. Soon thereafter, she carried out two good-sized "Beef and Cabbage Stew" bowls with fried bread." This was one of Pamela Mae's favorite dishes that her Mamma Sarah Anne made. She recalled some of the main ingredients to include beef (chuck steak), shredded cabbage, beef broth, potatoes, carrots, celery, onions, salt, and black pepper.

Pamela Mae and Mario enjoyed the "delicious and nutritious" supper so much and it was further enhanced by two glasses of "Sweet Cherry Wine." Miss Sally told her after supper, "Miss Pamela Mae, you and your man may use the guest bedroom upstairs and I will have my daughter, Abigail, who is a house servant, fill up the big tub in the bathroom with hot water from the stove in the kitchen. She will provide you with scented flowers and spices to place in the water, shampoo, and two full length towels.

Mario decided to go outside to the stables to see how their Arabian horses were faring. Apparently, *Marengo il Secondo* and *Marenga la Primera* had plenty of green hay, fresh water, and yellow straw for bedding. He was about to return to the mansion when he heard his stallion and Pamela Mae's mare performing their equine mating ritual. He amusingly thought to himself, *Well, they say that our horses tend to take on the activities and characteristics of their owners, so as we say in French, Voila (There you are)!*

By the time "Our Handsome Vermont Cavalier" arrived at the 2nd floor guest room, he could scent the enchanting floral aromas of gardenia, jasmine, and lavender that Abigail inserted into the hot steamy water. Mario walked into the tiled bathroom and he was overwhelmed by the beauteous sight of his superbly formed "Lovely Virginia Lady" in the heated *Aqueous* (Water), with thousands of pink and white rose scented bubbles covering her shining cleavage.

Pamela Mae was extremely hot and consumed with desire for her fiancé and lover as she cleverly and seductively told him, "Baby, please disrobe 'Quick Time' and come join me in this bathtub of liquid delight." Mario took off his clothes smartly while he gazed at the most gorgeous, luscious, scrumptious, vivacious, and voluptuous of all young women in the universe— his captivating and entrancing Pamela Mae.

Mario soon slipped into the water with his charming Signorina and Mademoiselle (young lady) as his "Italian and French" ancestry and heritage were accentuated. He gasped and stated, "Oh, com'è fantastico stare con te(Oh, how fantastic it feels to be with you). Ooh La La, Mia Pamela Bella (Oh there there, My Pretty Pamela)."She had her impeccably shaped legs with her skinny tantalizing ankles on each side of the bathtub as her "Italian Stallion" fit perfectly in front of her.

Needless to say, our very erotic and sensual couple were very excited and enflamed with passion as they connected perfectly with one another under the humid water. At this point, Pamela Mae was very stimulated as her luminous big brown eyes became even larger and her dainty ebony eyelashes fluttered joyfully while her curved dark eyebrows raised up noticeably towards her attractive coal black hair. Mario LaGrande's Italian feelings and language were stimulated as he looked lovingly at his young vibrant and vivacious woman. Subsequently, he told her affectionately, "*Pamela Bella, tu sei la mia piu bellezza, carezza, e dolcezza ragazza dagli occhi castani belli e ti voglio tanto bene* (Pretty Pamela, you are the most beautiful, dearest, and sweetest girl with the prettiest brown eyes, and I want you so much)."

Pamela Mae responded instantly and expressed her sensual and sultry enjoyment with several aroused coos and sighs. A few seconds later, she shouted out in a variety of English, Spanish, and German choice words to include, "Oh Baby, Oh Baby, Oh Baby, *Ay, ay, ay, ay bebé'*(Oh, oh, oh, oh baby) *und Ja, Ja, Ja baby* (and Yes, Yes, Yes baby). You are all of my dreams, fantasies, and wishes come true, and I adore and love you!"

They continued to be "as one body" while moving in the water and washing one another: feet, legs, arms, breast and chest areas. Mario and Pamela Mae delicately washed each other's hair with an imported soapberry shampoo from India. This exotic lotion resulted in Pamela Mae's voluminous black hair becoming even more luxurious and soft.

After about thirty minutes of the most amatory, salacious, unique, and wonderful aquatic experience imaginable, Mario allowed Pamela Mae to exit the soothing sweet bathtub waters first. When she stood up and grabbed a thick Egyptian made beige towel, Mario was overcome sensually as he looked and lusted at his Pamela Bella (Pretty Pamela). She appeared like Aphrodite coming out of a cool spring fountain on a Greek island in the Aegean Sea. He was mesmerized and couldn't take his ocean blue eyes off of his fabulous fiancée. She initially dried off her waist length hair and then continued using the towel on her frontal and dorsal sides.

Fifteen minutes later, it was time for our six foot thee inch "Vermont Cavalier" to get out of the bathtub as Pamela Mae grabbed a second towel to dry off her muscular fiancé and dream man, *Mario Bello* (Handsome Mario). Since "Our Lovely Virginia Lady" measures in at five foot eleven inches, "a tall glass of water" herself, it was relatively easy for her to reach up and dry off the dark brown locks of her "Brawny Beau." While only wearing her, "Valentine's Day Birthday" outfit, she continued to desiccate the wetness off of Mario. She removed the water that was upon his tight pectoral muscles that were covered with dark curly hair as well. Pamela Mae even added some levity to her movement of the towels, when she told Mario, "Darling, raise your hands towards the ceiling while I dry off your 'Army pits.'"

At that moment and remark, Mario laughed heartily as he grabbed his irresistible young woman and proceeded to give her a lengthy "French-Style kiss" and big "Italian-Style hug." Pamela Mae was definitely relishing those very intimate and pleasurable physical activities as she held on to the towel and managed to dry off his broad back while eagerly kissing her "Northern Gentleman."

Well, all of this mutual carnal activity accelerated the adrenaline glands greatly and the sexual hormones rigorously of both of our leading characters. Pamela Mae and Mario made the short walk towards the king-sized bed. Major LaGrande was feeling his intense desire for Pamela Mae in a very personal and military manner as he got her on the bed and decided to immediately "Storm the Breastworks." He expressed his feelings in a unique "French Fashion" when he spoke romantically to his fiancée, *"Je t'adore, Je t'aime, et Je ne peux pas vivre sans toi, Ma Mademoiselle Pamela Belle* (I adore you, I love you, and I can't live without you my Young Lady, Pretty Pamela)."

Pamela Mae placed both of her sleek arms around the upper back of her *Mario Bello* (Handsome Mario) as she kissed and hugged her lover energetically and tightly. She responded to his amorous words and fervent love making and remembered a phrase from reading a "Spanish Romance Novel" and she replied, *"Te amo con toda mi corazon y alma, y cada dia te querio mas* (I love you with all my heart and soul, and each day I love you more)."

Mario rolled smoothly over onto his right side while shifting his darling Pamela Mae onto her left side. There were two honey-scented candles on each of the lamp tables as he kept his eyes upon the endearing face of his only love. Mario LaGrande had the most pleasurable smiling expression on his good-looking face as he expressed his sentiments poetically to her saying, *"Mia Pamela Bella's* (My Pretty Pamela's) eyes are so exceedingly alluring to observe and view. They are absolutely two spectacular objects of the outmost beauty. Darling, your adorable eyes are exceptionally cute as a baby deer. They are totally delightful and illuminate my life completely."

Pamela Mae hugged and kissed her ever-loving man even more vigorously as she responded in Italian and English, "*Mio Mario Bello, Mio Tesoro Squisito* (My Handsome Mario, My Exquisite Treasure), my brown eyes see you as my ultimate gift and I love every moment that we share together in each other's arms and I love you with every ounce of my yearning body."

Well, of course, "Our Lovely Virginia Lady and Handsome Vermont Cavalier" kept up their enthusiastic love-making, physically and verbally, in a variety of different positions on the bed and various locations in the bedroom. They both believed that they were "making up for lost time" while they were performing their military duties.

After about forty-five minutes more of kissing, hugging, and loving each other gladly and without inhibition, our two "love birds" were secure in their temporary nest and said their respective good nights. Pamela Mae used her father's German language and creatively told her husband to be, "*Gute Nacht, mein tapferer Ritter* (Good night, my gallant Knight)."

Mario responded to her affectionate words appropriately as he said in his mother's Italian language, "*Pamela Bella, Pamela Bella, Ti Amo e Buona Notte e Buon Riposo la Mia valorosa donna Cavaliere* (Pretty Pamela, Pretty Pamela, I Love You and Good Night and Good Repose My valorous Cavalier Lady)." She smiled endearingly and understood every word of her Italian speaking man.

As they entered together the nocturnal world of rest and slumberland, Pamela Mae had a very divine faithful thought of appreciation, *Thank You, Lord in heaven for getting me safely through this day, and for blessing me with Mario. He is my companion, partner, and love of a lifetime. Amen!*

At precisely the same time, Mario had his own very faithful thought of appreciation, "*Lord of all creation and mankind, it is no coincidence, but "Divine Providence" that I am securely here tonight. Thank You for saving and blessing me with Miss Pamela Mae Brewer who is full of life and will be on one beautiful Winter's Day, my lovable and marvelous wife. Amen!*

Chapter 14
Travel to and Days in Alexandria
November 3rd - 12th, 1861

It was close to 7:00 a.m. on that Sunday morning of November 3rd, 1861, in the very comfortable and cozy guest bed of the Mason Mansion in Woodbridge, Virginia. Mario had his Pamela Mae in a warm "Papa Hug" as they were both laying on their right sides. He had his hairy chest on her welcoming back and his left arm wrapped around her tender breasts.

This peaceful "spoon-like repose" between "Our Lovely Virginia Lady and Our Handsome Vermont Cavalier" was suddenly interrupted with seven "Rap, rap, rap, rap, rap, rap, rap" made on the wooden door and Abigail entered the room with a small lighted whale oil lamp. "Excuse me, I am sorry Miss Pamela Mae, Miss Robin Ma'am, you and your man have to get your clothes on and leave quickly. There is a search party outside, and the men say that they are looking for Yankee Spies."

Pamela Mae and Mario disengaged swiftly and rose up and got dressed in a couple of minutes. She then looked intently at the house servant and asked in a low whispering voice, "Abigail, how in the world do we get out of our predicament without being caught?" Miss Sally's brave and clever daughter replied with confidence, "Miss, Don't you fret none. I got a key that unlocks a secret door in the closet that leads to a private stairs in the back of the house. Let's hurry!"

At that point, Pamela Mae and Mario could hear the angry loud shouts of men on the first floor as they began to climb up the long twenty step staircase and the uniformed leader and officer yelled out for everyone to hear, "Where the hell did you hide them?"

By the "Grace and Mercy of the Lord," Abigail went into the closet between the hanging dresses and coats and unlocked the interior door. Pamela Mae and Mario followed her closely as he shut the regular closet door behind him while they were able to get on the other side securely. Immediately, Abigail locked the second door with the metal key. Right away, she led them all down a long wooden staircase with cobwebs hanging down. They briefly stopped and regrouped on a brick landing that was right in front of a five foot high tunnel that was about three hundred feet in length.

Pamela Mae was amazed at the audacity and ingenuity of Abigail and stated and inquired in an excited and inquisitive way, "A thousand thanks Abigail, but what about our horses?" Abigail replied assuredly, "No worries Ma'am, my brother Ephraim, who is a horse trainer, was told to move the Arabians to the exit of the tunnel which is close by the bridge and river. Lord, have mercy on us!"

Mario was the last one to enter the tunnel as he had to crouch down for more than a foot, lift his left hand towards the ceiling, while covering his mouth with a handkerchief. While they walked on the very wet rocks and stones, he had an inclination and a notion that Pamela Mae, himself, Abigail, and her brother Ephraim were in for a truly extraordinary adventure. He thought faithfully and sentimentally about his exceptional Pamela Mae and the two negro servants who were helping them escape. *Lord of Heaven above, please show benevolence to my bold and skilled Pamela Mae and I. Thank you for the courage displayed by these two young servants who are enabling us to escape to safety. I know in the Bible you often use the least of your people to perform great acts of valor. Amen!*

Meanwhile, Pamela Mae was navigating her way behind Abigail who had the lamp. She had to also lift her left arm up and cover her mouth and prayed and thought personally, *Oh Lord, this time*

I am the one who is being saved and I am led to recall some of the words of David in Psalm 23: Even though I walk through the "Valley of the Shadow of Death," I will fear no evil.

Soon thereafter, Pamela Mae and Mario heard the very encouraging words of Abigail who happily stated, "Thank You, Jesus. I can see the light at the end of the tunnel and Ephraim is waiting patiently with your gray and white horses. Hallelujah!"

Mario and Pamela Mae were ecstatic to be outside of the tunnel as they swiftly cleaned themselves off and then stood on the damp grounds that were adjacent to the Occoquan River and the old wooden bridge. Pamela Mae gave Abigail a very grateful hug and told her, "My dear 'Saving Angel,' thank you so much for rescuing me and Mario. I now give you the legendary nickname and title of 'Miss Robin Bea Goode, the Second.' Ephraim, thank you, too, for bringing out our horses. You are a Godsend, also. Finally, here is $20 each for your brave deeds and hurry and hide from the search party."

Our heroine, Pamela Mae, and our hero, Mario, briskly became Major Brewer and Major LaGrande as they mounted their horses and soon located the entrance to the bridge. In the distance behind them, our Army Officers in civilian clothes could hear gunfire and the many shouts of the angry "Confederate Soldiers" who were frustrated and unsuccessful in the attempted capture of the suspected "Yankee Spies." Once again Pamela Mae took the initiative and was in the lead position. She unshakably shouted out, "Mario, my love, follow me. I will lead us for the next eleven miles to Mount Vernon, Virginia, where we can rest and get something to eat."

They soon crossed the Occoquan River Bridge as Majors Brewer and LaGrande rode towards the Potomac River. Within twenty minutes, "Our Lovely Virginia Lady and Our Handsome Vermont Cavalier" were able to find a three-foot-deep ford in the water which allowed for an easy traverse of the Potomac. By the "Grace of God," the balance of the journey was without incident as they identified only a few carriages and pedestrians who appeared to be family members and who were obviously traveling to attend worship services in their best-looking outfits.

Pamela Mae slowed up halfway on the road to Mount Vernon and relayed a story to Mario about her one and only trip to the historic "Presidential Mansion" that was once owned by George and Martha Washington. "Darling, when

I was fourteen years old in 1858, Mamma, Papa, and I had the pleasure of visiting the very 'Historic Washington Family' three story mansion called 'Mount Vernon.' It was during the exceedingly floral and picturesque month of April when the Eastern Redbuds, flowering Dogwoods, and some wild Crabapple trees were in full bloom. We were invited to a dinner party in the evening and stayed overnight. I really enjoyed myself and found the stately mansion to be extremely fascinating."

Mario was listening intently to his Pamela Mae who had the most charming mannerisms and endearing story-telling voice as she recalled her "Mount Vernon" visit from three years ago. He thought to himself, *I will give "My Lovely Virginia Lady" my complete attention and am so excited to visit the elegant home of America's most celebrated and famous Army General, Founding Father, and President. I am so interested in finding out more about General Washington and about his property and how he lived at his family estate and mansion.*

After about ten minutes of slow riding with an interesting story, Pamela Mae said out loud in a strong voice in German and in English, "*Mein nördlicher Gentleman und meine großartigen Pferde* (My northern gentleman and my grand horses), let's make haste and travel expeditiously to Mount Vernon!" Mario replied to the directive of his Virginia Officer in a compliant, pleasant, and loving manner, "Major Brewer, I will follow you 'over hills, dales, and rivers' and from mansion to mansion and hopefully there will be breakfast and coffee available when we arrive, Good Lord willing."

Pamela Mae was the first to spot the imposing and majestic looking "Mount Vernon" villa and the surrounding well-kept estate of five hundred acres, adjacent to the Potomac River.

Photo of Mount Vernon, Virginia
Mansion and Grounds

Much to the delight of Mario, his "Lovely Virginia Lady met a groundskeeper and was able to get with a cook and they were "fixed up" for breakfast.

One of the "Mount Vernon" cooks named Mama Bertha was very generous and provided fresh hot coffee with cream and a "good old traditional Southern Style" breakfast. The savory foods were right from the oven/stove and included biscuits with pork gravy, corn grits, and hash brown casserole with dried parsley and thyme.

After the very delectable and filling breakfast, a very kind Lady by the name of Imogene Cordan, from the "Ladies Historical Society" gave Pamela Mae and Mario a one hour tour of Mount Vernon. It was an extremely fascinating and informative presentation. Our very inquisitive couple, walked hand and hand. They had lots of questions about the historical structure and about the personal and military details of George Washington. In addition, Pamela Mae was intrigued to find out relevant ancestral and cultural facts about Martha Dandridge Custis Washington.

Even though Pamela Mae was having an enlightening and diverting time, she took a moment to stop and whisper into Mario's ear in English and Spanish, "Sweetheart, I am very much loving our special time at Mount Vernon. However, let's talk to one of the foremen and find out the best route to Alexandria and this time you can lead the way, *Mi Amor* (My Love)."

Only about ten minutes of time elapsed and this time Mario said in his funny, poetic, and sweet English and French way, "Darling, how about *un petit baiser français* (a little French kiss), and I will be on our next adventurous way with my dream-girl Pamela Mae." The very affectionate couple went ahead and kissed for luck, right in front of Mount Vernon. Being incognito, Major Mario LaGrande proceeded to mount his noble horse, *Marengo il Secondo,* while our clandestine Major Pamela Mae Brewer followed along upon her fetching horse, *Marenga la Primera.*

Fortunately, the approximate eight mile trip was made in about two hours. Even though halfway to their destination, they were stopped by a four member group of "Union Provost Marshal" soldiers. Pamela Mae remembered two of the men as Captain Workman and Sergeant Snyder who easily recognized her from their encounter in July 1861. Of course, Pamela Mae utilized her beauty and amiable personality to once again endear herself to the security personnel. Mario helped to negotiate a pass from Captain Workman so that he and his fiancée could routinely enter the "South Gate" of Alexandria, Virginia.

It was thirty minutes past the noon hour on that sunny November 3rd , 1861 day as Pamela Mae and Mario rode up and once again saw the very refined *Mansion du Moreau* (Moreau Mansion). The "Holy Spirit" was moving once again as they viewed Henri driving the fancy carriage that was carrying Madame Brigitte Moreau up the driveway. She was dressed in a spectacular looking orange and red day dress that, of course, reminded Pamela Mae of her favorite song bird, the robin.

Major LaGrande greeted the "Lady of the House" in her native French language in a congenial and proper manner, *"Bonjour Madame et quel plaisir de vous revoir* (Good day, Madam, and what a pleasure it is to see you again)." Pamela Mae approached Madame Moreau and gave her a heartfelt embrace and kissed her tenderly on both cheeks "European Style." She had memorized a few of the French phrases taught to her by Mario LaGrande as she told her hostess, *"Vous êtes si belle Madame et c'est super d'être de retour* (You look so beautiful, Madam, and it is great to be back)."

Madame Moreau was so pleased to have her two Army Majors, Pamela Mae and Mario, back in her 2nd floor apartment in Alexandria. Brigitte Moreau thought back in French and English when she was seventeen in *"le gai Paris, (gay Paree),"* *I too was a very gorgeous and ideally shaped brown eyed young lady and most of the men would gaze and want to be with me. While many a "Femme envieuse (Envious Woman) would want to possess my beauty and style. Back then, I was also so very happy that I would have my future husband Julian as my fiancé.*

She could intuitively sense and obviously see that Major Brewer and Major LaGrande had a rough day of riding their horses and was certain that they had encountered a dangerous situation or two along the way. Therefore, the "Madame of the Mansion" instructed Camille, her maid from Haiti, to clean up their upstairs bedroom and provide her tenants with two porcelain pitchers full of hot water and almond scented soap and coconut oil. In addition, Camille put clean sheets and linens on their bed.

Also, she took up some night clothes, scarves, and a few dresses for the enchanting Pamela Bella (Pretty Pamela). Brigitte Moreau remembered, *Pamela Mae has a well-defined 38x22x38 figure and is the same size that I was at her age.*

While Pamela Mae and Mario were waiting for their rooms to be tidied up, Brigitte Moreau instructed the staff to prepare a light *hors d'oeuvres* type lunch for the lovely couple. The very much appreciated foods and drink included Cheese puffs, chicken *canape'* upon *baguettes*, and melted *Brie* with *Pesto*. Camille also brought out one of Madame Moreau's favorite *vins Blancs* (white wines) called *Sœur cadette* (Younger sister). When Mario told his sweet fiancée Pamela Mae about the name and meaning of the wine, she replied happily, "I love that since I am the "younger sister" of my Brewer family.

Major Mario LaGrande, Major Pamela Mae Brewer, and Madame Moreau enjoyed the light meal and conversational time together. She informed them that their good friends and fellow Vermont officers Major Maurice Flambeau with his fiancée, Gloria Faye, and Major Joseph Wei with his fiancée, Marie Louise Yang, were presently vacationing in *Havre de Grace*, Maryland.

Well, the delicious foods and savory wine was an ideal meal for Pamela Mae and Mario. He kindly expressed his gratefulness to their superb hostess in French saying, "*Merci beaucoup Madame et excusez nous s'il vous plait* (Thank you, Madam, and excuse us, if you please)."

Pamela Mae and Mario walked out the front door and around the back to the stables and checked on their Arabian horses and they were doing fine. Then, they proceeded to climb the steps and at the top of the landing, Mario picked up Pamela Mae and held his exquisite young lady in a "Fireman's Carry" and crossed the threshold into the apartment. He told her, "Darling, I just wanted to practice for our wedding night." She giggled and replied amusingly, "Honey, I so much look forward to that marvelous night when we can maintain that wonderful custom and tradition."

"Our Lovely Virginia Lady" hurried to the bathroom and then to the sink while she began to disrobe. She placed all of her clothes into a wickerwork receptacle and began to wash up, utilizing the heated pitcher of water and the scented soap at the "Italian Marble" basin. The door into the bathroom was open as Mario was slowly removing his clothes. He was, of course, looking at his own "Angelic Athena" getting prepared for a session of an "Early Afternoon Excite." Pamela Mae came out of the bathroom wearing a sweet flowering fragrance and apologized saying, "Sweetheart, I am sorry that you had to wait for me." Mario responded back to her lovingly, "Darling, I would wait for hours and days for the ultimate pleasure of being with you because I adore and love you."

It was now "Our Handsome Vermont Cavalier's" turn to freshen up in order to be more aromatically pleasing for his luxuriously attractive and magnificently shaped "Virginia Young Lady." Meanwhile, Pamela Mae was very curious to see what Madame Moreau chose for her to wear. She walked over to a new "Rosewood Oriental Armoire" and soon discovered a see through sky-blue "Cashmere Scarf." Pamela Mae thought to herself, *My very romantic Mario Bello (Handsome Mario) will be even more invigorated and stimulated when he sees me wearing this sheer lavish lightweight one piece lingerie.*

After about ten minutes of Mario splashing around with the water and the soap in the basin, Pamela Mae positioned herself near the bedpost that was at the foot of the bed closest to the bathroom. She wore the bluish lightweight scarf open in the front which emphasized and exhibited her superbly formed pair of very firm breasts. "Her Lover Man," who was wearing only his "Saint Patrick's Day Birthday Suit," was very fresh, crisp and clean. He was indeed invigorated and stimulated. .

Mario was visibly excited and moved by the intoxicating sight of his arousing and desirable "Virginia Lady." Within a few seconds of seeing her wearing only a very big "ear to ear smile and a little ole scarf," he told her in his typical French and Italian mode, "*Ooh la la, mia Pamela Bella, Ti voglio tanto bene* (Oh there there, My Pretty Pamela, I want you so much)."

Our hyper exhilarated muscle-bound "Northern Gentleman" walked closer to his Pamela Bella (Pretty Pamela) as she opened her arms wide. Pamela Mae gave Mario a very big "bare and bearhug" as they embraced and kissed one another in the upright position. The Cashmere scarf from India fell off of the inviting dorsal side of Pamela Mae and dropped lightly to the floor without a sound.

At this inspiring point, "Our Lovely Virginia Lady" became especially enflamed and acted like a "Lady Leopard." She kissed "Our Handsome Vermont Cavalier" with numerous and vigorous "French Kisses." Pamela Mae grabbed her Mario Bello (Handsome Mario) and dug and moved her nails across his rock-hard back and told him in a sensual and sultry voice, "Babe, you bring out the 'Wild-Cat' in me and let's make love in a fantabulous feline way."

Mario responded eagerly and instantly to Pamela Mae as he laid her erotically upon the awaiting bed and kissed her energetically and romantically upon her delectable and delicious ruby red lips. Subsequently, our animated gentleman then placed both hands upon her very appealing temples while he tenderly caressed her coal black hair. Mario thought to himself in Italian and English, *Mia Cara Pamela Bella (My Dear Pretty Pamela) is the most captivating and charismatic young lady in the world. I love her deeply and every sweet moist kiss from her succulent lips and tantalizing tongue brings me the utmost pleasure.*

This time Major LaGrande expressed his love for her in French and English saying, *"Ma Magnifique Mademoiselle* (My Magnificent Young Lady), you are the most delicious and desirous of all delicacies and I am overwhelmed with your beauty and buxomness, *Ooh la la!"* Pamela Mae responded verbally to the kissing and sexual movement of her superb lover as she said, "Oh Darling, every kiss from your ravishing lips and massaging tongue sends me into the upper atmosphere of my feminine fantasies."

Major Brewer now took the initiative and performed a nifty roll-over maneuver that resulted in her being on top of her very own "Italian Stallion." Fortunately, Mario ended up near the bedside table where there laid an open jar of coconut oil from Sri Lanka. He could detect the alluring scent and then alertly reached to his right and got an ample amount of the oriental liquid on both of his hands.

Pamela Mae was moving her exquisite mobile hips forwards and backwards and became even more enthusiastic when Mario began to warm up the soothing oil by rubbing his hands together. He soon began to massage both of her perfectly proportioned bountiful breasts in a clockwise and then counterclockwise series of motions. All the while, Mario is fully engaged and extending his pulsating physique in a series of upward movements that causes his woman to experience the utmost level of all-encompassing rapture. While seemingly defying gravity, Pamela Mae and Mario travel jointly, physically and metaphorically, in flight through the universe of sensory amour. She told her man with a sexy voice, "Oh Baby, you have the most delicate and skillful hands. I super enjoy the way you effleurage and massage my mammary glands. I love it and I love you so."

"Our Amorous and Lovely Virginia Lady" continued her verbal response with aahs, coos, and sighs and then said in Spanish and English, "*Mi corazón y tesoro, Tengo el máximo amor y pasión por ti* (My Heart and treasure, I have the ultimate love and passion for you). Sweetie, let's spend the next couple hours inseparable while kissing, hugging, massaging one another, and Baby, we know the rest!"

"Our Amorous and Handsome Vermont Cavalier" replied affirmatively and happily in French and English, "*Oui, Oui, Oui Ma Merveilleuse Mademoiselle* (Yes, Yes, Yes, My Marvelous Young Lady). I cherish and only want to be with you, as I provide as much emotional and physical pleasure as possible."

Mario and Pamela Mae will spend the next few days, afternoons, and nights loving one another in a variety of novel positions and locations, inside and outside of the *Mansion du Moreau*. In addition, Pamela Mae spent many hours planning her wedding with Mario and sent her Mother Sarah Anne a detailed letter of her ideas for a "Winter Wedding."

It was now the fifth day of their current stay in their comfortable upstairs dwellings at the *Mansion du Moreau* in Alexandria, Virginia. They decided to rent an enclosed carriage with driver and take a ride to Arlington, Virginia. Pamela Mae had many thoughts in her mind prior to leaving, *I would love to go back to "Arlington*

*House," the former home of General Robert E. Lee
and his wife Mary Anna Randolph Custis Lee. I
hope and pray "Dear Lord" that none of the "Union
Soldiers" recognize me from when I rescued my
Papa John Brewer who was a "Lieutenant Colonel
and Confederate Prisoner" back in July of this year.
However, if someone does recognize me, I better
take cash, liquor, and a revolver just in case there
is an incident. Lord, have mercy and protect us.
Amen!*

Mario could tell by looking at his contemplative
and prayerful *Pamela Bella* (Pretty Pamela) that
she was thinking about the trip to Arlington and
then he heard a carriage pull up. The elegant
conveyance was near the stables when he looked
out the back windows. He saw a very lavish
burgundy colored enclosed two seat Brougham
carriage pull up with two horses and a well-
dressed gentleman as the driver.

Pamela Mae went onto the covered balcony of
the back porch and saw that the carriage was
modest in size. She turned to her handsome
Officer and told him, "Darling, I shouldn't wear a
big hoop skirt and dress today. It would be better
to wear one of the long pretty crimson red ankle
length day dresses with an ivory colored
petticoat underneath."

Mario gave her an understanding smile and replied with a pertinent compliment in Italian and English, "Dolce-Cuore (Sweetheart), I am sure that the outfit you choose will greatly benefit from your "easy on the eyes" splendorous appearance!"

The driver and owner of the ornate Brougham carriage was a man named Francois Thompson whose mother was French. Fifteen minutes later, Mister Thompson looked up at the top of the long outside stairs and first saw a very handsome young man (Mario LaGrande) exit the door. A few minutes afterwards, Mister Thompson looked up and was totally amazed as he saw the loveliest young lady on two feet— Miss Pamela Mae Brewer.

Mario knew that Francois spoke French so he greeted the driver politely saying, "Bonjour Monsieur, et s'il vous plaît, emmenez-nous au domaine Lee à Arlington (Good day, Sir, and please take us to the Lee estate in Arlington)." Our Vermont Officer noticed that there were curtains on the small windows as he took the initiative and closed them.

As the carriage ride was traveling on the main route to their destination, Pamela Mae was holding hands with her fiancé and began to be aroused by the cozy intimate confines of the enclosed vehicle. Her Hispanic words came to mind as she told Mario romantically, "*Bésame, bésame con mucho pasión mi cariñoso Amor* (Kiss me, kiss me with much passion my affectionate love)."

Well, Mario complied with her amorous directive and then in just one instant, a hot tender kiss was all it took. Our super stimulated lovers became fully engaged on the cushy carriage seat. Mister Thompson chuckled and smiled as he heard the love-making actions and sounds from the rear and could feel the carriage swaying from right to left from left to right and back again. He couldn't hold back as he exclaimed "*Ooh la la*" and amusingly and understandably thought, *It would be better if I take my time and slow down since it appears that my two guests are practicing for their wedding night. Voila!*

Pamela Mae and Mario were having the very best time as the engaged couple enjoyed their first experience of agile and mobile love-making. Mario, who has the gift of comical and amatory rhyme, took a short break and said to her in Italian and English, "*La Mia Amore piu' Cara* (My Dearest Love), a beautiful Virginia Woman and her Vermont Gentleman will join together every chance they can!"

Their love-filled ride continued for about twenty minutes until Mister Thompson, his horses, and clients approached the south end of the "Arlington House" property. All of the traveling group clearly heard the words from a soldier stating, "Halt, and get out of the carriage now!" Pamela Mae alertly moved the curtains and peeked through the small side window of the ornate carriage. Immediately, she recognized the face of the young soldier during that encounter on the rainy evening of her father's rescue on July 26th, 1861.

Pamela Mae could tell from Mario's body language that he was a little anxious and wanted to boldly talk to the Union security soldiers to mitigate any trouble. She quickly sized up the precarious situation and put her left hand on top of the right thigh of her future husband and calmly told him, "Sweetheart, I will get out and talk to the youthful soldier who I recognize from the situation when Gloria Faye and I assisted Papa. As you remember, back in July of this year, I used my charm and wit during Papa's escape from confinement on the grounds in back of that mansion. Please talk to the officer in charge and give me ten minutes and turn the carriage around and head back towards Alexandria."

Mario could tell by looking at his lovely lady that she was in her Major Pamela Mae Brewer and Miss Robin Bea Goode characters and simply nodded his head in the affirmative. Her intrinsic abilities and analytical skills were correct as the soldier took one look and recognized her very luxurious black hair and gorgeous indelible face with the most impressive sparkling pair of brown eyes. The Union soldier thought for a brief moment and said," Excuse me, Ma'am, but aren't you the lady who was pregnant on that wet night in July when that 'Rebel Colonel' escaped?"

Pamela Mae, who possesses an excellent memory for details and names responded, "Let's you and I take a walk towards Alexandria." Of course, the young soldier could not resist the beauty or the charm of the young woman and willingly went along with her as they walked arm and arm down the road towards the old shack. While they were alone, Pamela Mae candidly said, "Yes, you are correct young man and I remember that you are Frank Garnett from Baltimore, Maryland, who likes liquor and congratulations on your promotion to Sergeant, I bet your parents are so very proud of you!"

Well, her evasive plan of action worked to perfection as Pamela Mae walked for ten minutes with Sergeant Garnett towards the old shack. She had utilized the dilapidated structure as a temporary refuge in July 1861 during the escape of her father. Pamela Mae was able to persuade the Union Sergeant to keep their previous meeting a secret while she pulled out a twenty dollar bank note and a small bottle of "Scotch whiskey" and gave both of the valuable items to the cooperating Federal soldier. She gave Garnett an appreciative hug as the burgundy Brougham carriage pulled up and Mario got out.

Soon thereafter, Mario and Pamela Mae got back into the carriage as Francois drove them back towards the friendly and safe confines of the *Mansion du Moreau*. She recounted her ten minutes that were spent with Sergeant Garnett and Mario said with a happy look on his face, "My Lovely Virginia Lady, Army Major, and Miss Robin Bea Goode, you are totally incredible in how you can solve a potential serious situation with your irresistible charm, unforgettable beauty, and clever methods. You are my *Bellefleur* (Beautiful Flower) and amazing partner. *Brava Donna* (Well done, Lady). "

November 12th, 1861, Alexandria, Virginia

It was now the evening of Tuesday, November 12th, 1861, on the 2nd floor of the *Mansion du*

Moreau in Alexandria, Virginia. Mario LaGrande and Pamela Mae Brewer, Maurice Flambeau and Gloria Faye Brewer, and Joseph Wei and Marie Louise Yang were all enjoying themselves immensely during a "Going Away Party" for our Vermont Cavalier and our Virginia Lady.

The six-member celebratory group had a number of culinary delicacies to eat and savory beverages for drink to include Russian caviar, French cheeses, Chinese sweet and sour pork, Italian breads, German beers, sweet French and English port wines, and more. There was much laughter and smiles amongst the congenial friends.

After about an hour of the happy and joyful festivities, Pamela Mae Brewer decided to make a formal announcement about their upcoming wedding date, location, and other specifics. "My fellow Army Majors and Young Ladies, Mario and I have decided with the grace of our "Good Lord Jesus" and His guidance to inform you about our marriage plans. During the late afternoon of the "Winter Solstice," December 21st of this year, Mario and I plan to get married at the 'Hendricks Mansion' in Elk Garden, Virginia. Gloria Faye and Marie Louise, it would be my individual privilege for you to be two of my maids of honor." At this point, all three of our pretty young women shared moments of excitement, happiness, and jubilation as the close knitted friends cried, hugged one another, and smiled cheerfully.

Fifteen minutes went by and this time, Mario felt the need to talk to everyone present. He got their attention and spoke to his intimate group in his three languages of English, French, and Italian. "Ladies and Gentlemen, of course I will need to have two more individuals to attend our wedding in Elk Garden. Therefore, I am inviting Maurice and Joseph to be my two best men. *Chiedo che ognuno di noi indossi le nostre uniformi blu abbinate anche* (I request that each of us wear our matching dress blue uniforms, also). *Prenons un verre pour honorer cette occasion spéciale avec du vin doux Français* (Let's have a drink to honor this special occasion with sweet French wine)."

At this point, each of the three engaged couples raised their glasses upwards and looked at one another merrily as Mario said, "*Questo vino, molto fino, a la salute alla nostra buona amicizia* (This wine, very fine, to the health of our good friendship)." After a few more drinks, Major Mario LaGrande become somewhat nostalgic and wanted to reminisce and share a short story about himself, Maurice, and Joseph during their trip from Vermont through part of New York and into Canada.

"Maurice and Joseph, do you recall in June of 1857, concerning our adventure with the horse thieves? I was riding my horse, Leonardo. Maurice, you were on Lamont and Joseph was mounted on Wǒ de mǎ (my horse). We were a few hours north of Burlington when we heard gunshots and, 'Stop, you damn horse thieves.' The bad robbers stole three horses from a farmer and we were all able to subdue the scoundrels by the 'Grace of God' while utilizing our own horses, guns, swords, and quick actions to get the horses back. Then, the farmer husband and his wife were so grateful that they fed us and we slept overnight." Joseph and Maurice nodded their heads and shook hands and exchanged many pats on one another's backs and shoulders as they re-celebrated that successful recovery of the equines.

Pamela Mae listened intently to Mario's story in Vermont, with his buddies over four years ago when he was seventeen years old and thought, *It is so wonderful to hear my Vermont Cavalier recall and share his memories before he enrolled in the military academy. I am so proud of him.*

Now it was time for Maurice, who was inebriated, to tell one of his fondest and longest memories of that trip to Montreal, Canada to the whole group. This adult level story will be heard for the first time by Gloria Faye, Pamela Mae, and Marie Louise. Maurice amusingly thinks of the three young women in Montreal, *In French they say,* "L'amour est un oiseau rebelle (*Love is a rebellious bird) so I want to tell this story to all in an entertaining manner!*

"A day after we caught and subdued the two horse thieves, Mario, Joseph, and myself, upon our brave and strong horses, crossed the *Rivière Richelieu et à Montréal* (Richelieu River and into Mont Royal). We were, of course, very much in need of food, alcoholic drinks, and some feminine companionship." Mario and Joseph both laughed hard and gave one another a knowing look and wink as Pamela Mae, Gloria Faye, and Marie Louise looked perplexed and did not know what to expect as they giggled and smiled.

Maurice paused for many moments and then continued the story. "Well, I must first apologize for our indulgent consumption and naughty behavior. However, I must admit at the time that it all started at the tavern when we encountered the first of the near identical triplet sisters,

Danelle. She was petite with blue eyes, dressed in a red, white, and blue outfit and had a mole near her mouth. Well, the "public house" was busy and the service was slow with our order of *vin dous rouge (*sweet red wine). After a while, the situation became most confusing when we mistook *Danelle* for her sister *Geeselle*, who was identical to her sister. We found out that *Geeselle's* particular mole was on a different side of her mouth, and she finally brought the wine."

Major Flambeau laughed heartedly and so did Mario and Joseph, and Pamela Mae, Gloria Faye, and Marie Louise laughed along with the apparent ensuing "comedy of errors" tale. The barroom/tavern scene went on as Maurice recalled, "Things really improved on the 'food front' when we were served the specialty French leg of lamb meal with potatoes and then met the third sister named *Mishelle* who was also identical, but her mole was on another location around her enticing mouth. We totally enjoyed the meal and then imbibed on shots of Cognac and it must have affected our good judgment." Pamela Mae thought to herself jovially, *That sounded a bit like a disclaimer!*

After another drink, Maurice continued and went back in time with his very detailed account. "We should have known better after more drinks when we were offered a unique dessert, a la Français (French style) that would cost a gold coin each, three in total. We took turns, as Joseph, me, and Mario went outside for a petite dessert Français with one of the triplets, not really knowing whether we were with *Danelle, Geeselle, or Mishelle.* Of course, we should have figured out that the clever and conniving young French women were deliberately playing us as fools in order to make some extra cash."

The attentive and listening ladies on the 2nd floor of the *Mansion du Moreau* figured out the next scene as Maurice laughed again and recalled, "Our shy Joseph was now the most drunk and volunteered to go first outside. He performed his "manly function" for the first time with Danelle, he thinks, who was one of the seductive triplets and he definitely looked like a satisfied 'first time' customer when he returned. I was next and this was not my first time, and I was on the lawn with another one of the 'French Girls' who I think was the temptress *Mishelle.* Finally, Mario outdid us all when he was with the captivating *Geeselle.* I have to admit he was the most athletic of the 'Three Vermont Cavaliers and Musketeers' as he stayed connected with his adult playmate when rolling down the riverbank into the water. *Ooh la, la, et voila* (Oh there, there and there it is)!"

Pamela Mae listened intently to Maurice's "Tales of the Three French Triplets" and tried to think logically, *Oh my goodness, this is the "first time" that I heard about my Mario and his escapades with the Montreal waitresses and yet I have not told him my "first time" with Bobby Ray Jones during the overnight "Virginia Regimental" training bivouac in 1860, so I guess we are even!*

It was now Major Joseph Wei's turn and he continued the next exciting story when the three "Burlington Boys" went towards the bank in Montreal the next day. Joseph recalls the incident like this, "We first completed some transactions at a few businesses in Montreal on that fateful June 1857 morning. Mario, Maurice, and I were on our way to the *Première banque provinciale du Québec* (First Provincial Bank of Quebec) and we were not expecting any trouble.

Then, we heard clearly in French from a terrified bank teller shouting out, '*Vol de banque, arrêtez ces voleurs* (Bank robbery, stop these thieves).' We could see the bank robbers with the stolen money riding their horses in our direction."

Joseph continued his exciting story, "Well, 'to make a long story shorter,' our 'fearless leader,' Mario LaGrande, devised a quick plan to interrupt the fleeing thieves. Mister LaGrande is upon his horse Leonardo and takes his sword and slashes the first escaping rascal robber on the back. Right afterwards, Mario was able to shoot the second robber and Maurice strongly wrestled him to the ground. Meanwhile, by the "Grace of God," I used my best and favorite 'Kung Fu' moves in defeating and subduing the third robber to include in Mandarin with the following actions: *Lóng* (the Dragon), *Shé* (the Snake), and *Bàozi* (the Leopard). Eventually, all of the notorious criminals were captured and delivered into the hands of the authorities."

Pamela Mae, Gloria Faye, and Marie Louise once again marveled at their heroic men: Mario, Maurice, and Joseph with amazement. Our Lovely Virginia Lady thought to herself in a faithful manner, *Lord in heaven above, over time You have shown mercy to our men and to each one of your young ladies who are here together. Please guide and protect all six of us and may I be able to have my wedding ceremony in peace with my "Handsome Vermont Cavalier" next month at the "Hendricks Mansion" in Elk Garden, Virginia. I pray this all in the name of the Father, and of the Son, and the Holy Ghost. Amen!*

Chapter 15
Ararat and Bristol, Virginia and Tennessee
November 13th – 24th, 1861

Pamela Mae Brewer woke up on that chilly morning of Wednesday, November 13th, 1861, and slowly disengaged from her affectionate and warm "Mamma Hug" with her Vermont Cavalier, Mario LaGrande. She had to get out of bed and write a short letter to Mrs. Elizabeth Letcher Pannill Stuart and ask about staying with her overnight with Mario, her fiancé. Elizabeth Stuart was the mother of Brigadier General J.E.B. Stuart (CSA) who had last summer given Captain Brewer an open invitation to visit his family at the Laurel Hill Farm near Ararat in Patrick County, Virginia.

About ten minutes later, Mario woke up and looked around and saw his Pamela Bella (Pretty Pamela) at the small oak desk and she was writing the letter. They planned on departing their ideal accommodations at the *Mansion du Moreau* and subsequently from Alexandria no later than 8:00 a.m. that morning. She gazed at her "Dream Man" come true. "Mario, Darling, I love you dearly," Pamela Mae said affectionately, "and I always will."

Later on, Pamela Mae was riding her Arabian mare, *Marenga la Primera,* and Mario was astride upon his Arabian stallion, *Marengo il Secondo,* as they arrived at the South Gate of Alexandria at circa 7:50 a.m. They were pleasantly surprised to once again meet up with SGT Johnny Buffington and his brother, the newly promoted Sergeant Jimmy Buffington, who were from out west hailing from Cabell County, Virginia (now West Virginia). The two "Provost Marshall" soldiers were very upset. Yesterday, November 12th, 1861, the two brothers and sergeants had received disturbing news about their hometown of Guyandotte, Virginia (now West Virginia). On November 10th, 1861, Guyandotte was the site of a Confederate Cavalry victory over Federal Soldiers and recruits. Additionally, Union troops travelled primarily by boat and came to the town the next day on November 11th, 1861, for revenge and burned many of the homes, businesses, and churches. They just hoped and prayed that their sisters, Mary Jo and Lisa Buffington, were alright. Furthermore, the worried brothers were concerned about the welfare of their nice neighbor lady, Mrs. Mary Carroll and her family. Her two-story elegant home and property was where the Buffington brothers and sisters played with the Carroll family as children. Pamela Mae was emotionally moved by their family and personal stories and told the two western Virginia men, "I am so sorry about the bad news of your scenic hometown of Guyandotte. I remember reading that it is on a very panoramic location at the awesome confluence of the Guyandotte and Ohio Rivers. God bless you soldiers and your sisters, too!"

Well, Majors Brewer and LaGrande were now on their way as they successfully passed through the security area. The good looking couple were attired in very comfortable traveling civilian clothes as they headed in a southwest direction on a circa 240 mile trip towards Ararat in Patrick County, Virginia. The calculating officers figured that they would attempt to travel approximately thirty to forty miles per day upon their Arabian horses who were known for their stamina, maneuverability, and velocity.

On the second day of their journey, Mario and Pamela Mae crossed the mighty *Rappahannock* River into the very historic and picturesque town of Fredericksburg, Virginia. Pamela Mae marveled at the appealing beauty, the many examples of 18th century architecture, and the antebellum splendor of the well maintained city. She told her fiancé and traveling partner, "Darling, I recall from my 'Virginia History class' studies that Fredericksburg was named for

Frederick, Prince of Wales, son of King George III and Queen Charlotte, and Spotsylvania County played prominent roles in the development of 'British Colonial America.' Furthermore, the 'Washington Family' influenced the area and even Mary Bell Washington, the mother of our great President George Washington, resided in Fredericksburg. Finally, on a personal note, Papa was very fond of conducting business at the plantations along the Rappahannock River. He especially liked the times that he would converse in German with his fellow immigrants from *Deutschland* (Germany) and enjoyed their cultured and tasteful cuisine."

Mario was once again impressed by the information that his Pamela Mae knew about that historic area and her very charming and pleasant method of explaining the facts to him. They were both hungry and thirsty and it was during supper time when they spotted an eye-catching sign in a store front window that read, "*Das beste Essen aus Sachsen.*" He inquired about the meaning of the sign and our trilingual leading lady replied, "Mario, the translation of those German words are 'The best food from Saxony.' Honey, would you like to go inside to eat?"

Our Vermont man thought, *My very intelligent young woman will surely lead me through another*

"Pamela Mae and Mario Adventure" into the German world of fine dining. He decided to reinforce *her* Germanic heritage as he replied in her father's native tongue, *"Ja, Ja, Ja meine liebe Dame* (Yes, Yes, Yes, my dear Lady)." They both soon dismounted and found the owner of the livery stable to care for their horses.

Our undaunted twosome, led by Pamela Mae, walked into the delicatessen and restaurant combination establishment as our leading lady saw a blonde buxom waitress who was wearing a long pair of braided pigtails. She gave the pretty server a traditional greeting, *"Guten Abend, wei geht's dir heute* (Good Evening, how are you today)?" Well, the very polite Germanic salutation resulted in a very welcoming atmosphere as Pamela Mae and Mario sat down for an especially piquant meal and very savory drinks. The scrumptious variety of foods and beverages from Saxony included:

Bratwurst (Grilled pork sausage)
Schnitzel (Breaded veal cutlet)
Bretzel (Pretzel)
Braised Cabbage
Bratkartoffeln (Fried potatoes).
Eierschecke (Layer cake)
Radeberger beer
Riesling wines

Near the conclusion of the fine supper, Pamela Mae paid the bill with a generous tip and then asked the friendly waitress, by the name of Gretchen Huffman, in German, "*Junge Dame, wo würden sie uns empfehlen, heute Nacht zu übernachten* (Young Lady, where would you recommend for us to stay tonight)?" *Fraulein* Huffman was remarkably happy with the indulgent extra money, smiled delightfully, and replied in German and English, "*Mein Lieber Vater* (My Dear Father) owns a modest bungalow on the scenic area of Marye's Heights. The good news is that the house is available for one night, it comes with maid, livery service, and a delicious breakfast tomorrow morning." Gretchen paused for a few seconds and then interjected suggestively, "I am sure you two lovebirds would look forward to the benefit of having a very lavish 'queen-sized' bed which will be ideal for relaxing and other nighttime activities."

Well, Pamela Mae and Mario looked at each other while their eyes lit up and exchanged understanding winks as Pamela Mae responded, "*Wunderbar, wir nehmen es* (Wonderful, we'll take it)!" Shortly thereafter, they exited the premises and retrieved their horses.

Mario and Pamela Mae enjoyed the post sunset ride which was partially illuminated by the candles in the residences along the way. They received very detailed directions in how to get to the house on Marye's Heights while they could see a few lights glimmering on the Rappahannock River.

A stable boy had been alerted that a handsome looking gentleman and very lovely young lady, on horseback were on their way. They were greeted upon arrival as the youth took care of *Marengo il Secondo* and *Marenga la Primera*. After feeling the positive effects of the delectable Saxon food and the inducing effects of the flavorous drinks, our ultra inspired duo wasted no time and rapidly took off their traveling clothes and placed them in a hamper in a side room. Miss Huffman was indeed correct as Pamela Mae took the initiative and clasped Mario by the left hand and nudged him on the "queen-sized" bed. She retrieved from her outstanding memory of the "Old Testament" the story about the sumptuous royal woman leader from the ancient world. Pamela Mae then smiled seductively and spoke out with an evocative voice, "Mario, my Darling, tonight you will be my eminent King Solomon of Israel and I will be your luxuriant Queen of Sheba!" Well, Major LaGrande's big blue eyes got even larger while he placed both of his very strapping arms around the lustrous back of his ravishing *Pamela Bella* (Pretty Pamela).

"Our Lovely Virginia Lady and Our Handsome Vermont Cavalier" will spend the next couple of hours fully engaged and immersed in a variety of amatory activities on the very accommodating mattress. The hugs were so exotically warm and the kisses were romantically hot. Mario's Italian linguistic skills were motivated as he exclaimed poetically, *"Mia Cara, poiche' il fiume scorre sempre attraverso la valle, la mia passione per te sara' eterna* (My Dear, as the river always flows through the valley, my passion for you will be eternal)!"

She was experiencing the utmost contentment with every cuddling caress, erogenous embrace, and savory smooch as Pamela Mae imagined in her wondrous mind, *Mio Mario Bello (My Handsome Mario) expresses himself emotionally and physically with every affectionate word in his many languages and with every tender touch from his talented hands and adorable lips.* This time, Pamela Mae's Spanish skills were induced as she responded poetically, *"Mi Caro, como el mundo siempre da vueltas, mi pasion por ti sera' infinita* (My Dear, as the world is always spinning around, my passion for you is infinite)!"

It was now close to 10:00 p.m. as both of our very active lovers were winding down and getting very sleepy. Mario LaGrande gave his Italian nocturnal salute as he routinely stated in his mother's native tongue to his Darling, "*Buona Notte e Buon Riposo Mia Pamela Bella, Ti amo* (Good night and good rest my Pretty Pamela, I love you)." Pamela Mae Brewer replied in kind in her father's native tongue to her Darling, "*Gute Nacht und guten Schlaf mein hübsche Mario, ich liebe dich* (Good night and good sleep my handsome Mario, I love you)."

That night would bring lightening, rain, and loud thunderstorm noises upon the temporary dwelling of Pamela Mae and Mario. The last hour of tranquil repose would be interrupted violently in the mind of "Our Vermont Cavalier." He could vividly see and hear in his nightmarish dream the prophetic images and sights of thousands of bloodied "Blue Coated Soldiers" sobbing for their mothers. The hapless dead and wounded men were subject to relentless artillery and musket fire from the top of the hills. He remembered the consistent crying out for aid and water on the slopes of Marye's Heights.

Historical note: During the December 11th – 15th, 1862 Civil War battle, the "Confederate Forces" of General Robert E. Lee were victorious over the defeated "Union Forces" under the command of General Ambrose Burnside in the Battle of Fredericksburg. There were thousands of casualties that were inflicted against both sides, especially upon the area called Marye's Heights.

November 20th, 1861

It had been a very satisfying and wonderful seven days of being together. Pamela Mae Brewer and Mario Patrizio LaGrande had traveled the very panoramic countryside through several Virginia counties in a southwest direction. Late in the morning after many miles of traveling, they noticed an old wooden black on gray sign and crossed the line into Patrick County, Virginia. Mario was pleased in how coincidental it was since his middle name was Patrizio in Italian which means Patrick in English. He thought to himself, *I feel that Pamela Mae and I will be very fortunate and lucky during our time in this county and our eventual trip to the Stuart homestead near Ararat.*

Well, it was close to noon on Wednesday, November 20th, 1861. Our adventurous and valiant couple were unsure about the most direct route to the "Stuart House at Laurel Hill Farm" near Ararat, Virginia. By the "Grace of God," Pamela Mae, with her superb eyesight, spotted a

small, aged building with a front porch in the distance. Mario, with his acute audio abilities, heard the sounds of music emanating from that weathered structure.

As Pamela Mae and Mario advanced closer, they could see a few men in their thirties attired in long sleeved shirts, rugged overalls, and floppy hats. It was a three member band and the trio were playing their instruments and singing away. The group concluded the song and Pamela Mae and others clapped their hands approvingly.

Mario took out a silver coin and said in Italian and English, "*Bravo Uomini, Eccellenti* (Well done Men, Excellent), could you play one of my favorite songs, 'Camptown Races'?" The musical group knew the melody and the words; however, they first introduced themselves to their new visitors. The leader of the band was a tall man named David Perry and he sang and played the fiddle. The good-looking, well-built guitar player and lead singer was named Andy Fife, and the slim harmonica player was called Barney Taylor.

Soon thereafter, Mario gave the group the coin as an incentive and he and Pamela Mae were so happy to hear that very popular "Camptown Races" song by Stephen Foster with two verses listed below:

De Camptown ladies, sing dis song, Doo-dah!
doo-dah!
De Camp-town race-track five miles long. Oh!
doo-dah day!

It was such a fun time for our daring and
dynamic duo as they were also able to get a
sandwich and a cup of coffee inside the tavern.
Mister Perry was the owner of the "little ole"
eating, drinking, and musical establishment. He
was originally from south of the Virginia/North
Carolina state border from a very small
community that would later be known as Mount
Airy. He was a childhood friend of J.E.B. Stuart
and very familiar with the route to the quaint
"Laurel Hill Farm" and gave Mario and Pamela
Mae specific directions in order to expedite their
trip.

At approximately 4:30 p.m. that late afternoon,
Pamela Mae and Mario arrived at the attractive
two story home and were warmly welcomed by
the owner and widow of Archibald Stuart, Mrs.
Elizabeth Stuart. The conversation was mostly
about the Stuart's ancestors and how influential
and numerous were the amount of Scotch, Irish,
German, and English immigrants who settled in
southwest Virginia during the Colonial period.

Pamela Mae reminisced about the day that Colonel Stuart visited her at her "Sunshine Hills" home.

She and Mario, with their kind hostess, enjoyed a wonderful meal of roast beef with mushroom gravy, buttered carrots, cooked cabbage with bacon bits and onions, and fried bread. In addition, the guests were served homemade blackberry wine. Mrs. Stuart talked fondly of her son, J.E.B. Stuart, and that the "Laurel Hill Farm" was his birthplace and how he was blessed by the Lord Jesus in maintaining his devout Christian faith through the turmoil of the "War Between the States."

She could tell immediately that Mario and Pamela Mae were deeply in love. After the culinary delights of the meal, the influence of the flavorsome wine, and with a big smile on her pretty face, Madam Stuart told her visitors, "My house servants have the guest room ready and you will be able to sleep on a mattress of spun cotton and the pillows are filled with goose down. In addition, you are welcome to utilize the furry bear rug with its softness for your nightly fancies!"

Mario listened intently to what the lovely lady just said and remembered the witty French expression of his father Louie who would say in situations like this, "*On n'a pas des offres comme ça tous les jours* (One does not get offers like that every day)!"

Pamela Mae responded in a very courteous manner to Elizabeth Stuart with an appreciative smile and a playful wink, "Thank you so much, Ma'am, for your very generous hospitality that is so much appreciated. Yes, I am sure the comfortable mattress, luxury pillows, and bear rug will be most suitable for our delights this night!"

Mario walked *mano nella mano* (hand in hand) with his irresistible fiancée Pamela Mae up the stairs and to the guest room which had three cinnamon scented candles from India spaced in the form of a triangle. They noticed the very large black bear rug that was at the foot of the bed. Mario went into the bathroom to disrobe. Pamela Mae then proceeded to the dressing table where she found a bottle of "French perfume" with the label, "*Une touche de pétales de rose*' (A touch of rose petals)."

Approximately five minutes elapsed and Mario looked for his captivating young woman on the bed. Pamela Mae was not on the soft cotton mattress and sheets. "Our Lovely Virginia Lady" had moved to the floor and was seductively laying on her back as her long luxurious and voluminous coal black hair matched perfectly with the ebony cozy furry bear covering. Mario thought lovingly of the "Girl of his Dreams" come true, *Along with my Pamela Bella's beauteous hair, her long black eyelashes, and delicate eyebrows are exactly the color of the bear's fur. How marvelous!*

Well, once again there was an electro-magnetic super attraction-like phenomenon taking place, this time in the "Stuart guest room." Pamela Mae and Mario began the night's amatory activities in an ancient manner going back to the early days when humans laid upon animal fur. She was feeling like her amorous ancestors and thought, *Mario Bello is covering my fervent body as I can feel each ounce of his desire for me while every cell and neuron of my stimulated skin is full of rapture from my* Hercules-like lover. Ay, Ay, Ay, Ay!

Mario was exceedingly inspired and invigorated by his exceptionally animated and vibrant Pamela Mae. They soon switched their acrobatic reproductive positions while she caressed and massaged the rock-hard deltoid muscles of her man.

He could not resist kissing the abundantly sweet nectarine lips and darling dimples of his enchanting lover. He thought of the Old Testament royal women and poetically of his real-life Esther beauty in Italian, English and French, *Mia Pamela Bella (My Pretty Pamela) is so supremely blessed with the classical facial vista of a "Majestic Queen." She has the most perfect pair of bountiful breasts complemented by an exquisite tiny waist as her posterior muscles are ideally shaped. Combien Magnifique (How Magnificent)!*

After about thirty minutes of very erotic and salacious love-making on the wild animal skin, our mutually adoring twosome got up and proceeded upon the welcoming bed. The ardent kissing, affectionate hugging, and more continued for the next hour or so. Then Mario expressed his love for Pamela Mae and admitted to being sleepy as he said in Italian, *"Buona Notte e Buon Riposo Mia Cara Signorina Bellezza* (Good night and good repose my Dear Beautiful Young Lady)!"

Pamela Mae conveyed very similar sentiments as she responded in Spanish, *"Buenas Noches y Buen Descanso, Mi Señor Hermoso* (Good night and good rest my Handsome Lord)." Once again, our lovable couple got on their left sides in the

"Mamma Hug" position as Pamela Mae hugged Mario's broad back and reached around her right arm while tenderly placing her right hand on his pectoral muscles. Pamela Mae then sweetly said one of her favorite statements, "And all is right with the world."

The following morning, Mario and Pamela Mae enjoyed a light breakfast of eggs, bacon, cornbread, and coffee made by the very friendly house cook. In addition, Mrs. Stuart made certain that there were enough sandwiches and apples prepared for the next two days of travel towards Bristol, Virginia/Tennessee. Pamela Mae showed her appreciation to Elizabeth Stuart with a very long embrace, a couple of kisses, and then told her, "Ma'am, thank you so much for all of your charity and hospitality."

After their respectful farewell's, Majors Brewer and LaGrande mounted their individual horses and gave an impressive joint *Pesade* to Mrs. Stuart and her household. This classical dressage movement involved both *Marengo il Secondo* and *Marenga la Primera* raising their front legs off the ground as Mario and Pamela Mae saluted the beneficent Elizabeth Stuart.

November 22nd, 1861

Pamela Mae and Mario had been "making good time" during their last day and a half of steady travel in a mostly westward direction. It was the afternoon of Friday, November 22nd, 1861, when our enterprising military pair were on the "Road to Damascus" and found out from a passerby that they could water their horses in "Laurel Creek."

Of course, Mario and Pamela Mae recounted the Apostle Paul and his fateful "Damascus Revelation" as it was recorded in the "Book of Acts." They were both lounging on the soft grass by the creek and were eating one of the delicious red apples given to them by Elizabeth Stuart. After the brief and casual break, they remounted their horses and rode further down a hard path and then stopped at a fork in the road and looked at their map. They decided to travel south and then instantly they could hear gunfire coming from their rear.

Major Pamela Mae Brewer's soul was immediately stirred by the "Holy Ghost" and she could hear an angelic-like female voice say, "Ride backwards in the saddle like you did with your cousin Christopher years ago." Pamela Mae briskly performed an acrobatic-like maneuver above and upon her saddle which placed her in the leather seat facing the rear and the fastly approaching shooters. After pulling out both of her loaded revolvers, she gave Major LaGrande the reins to her horse, *Marenga la Primera*. "Our Lovely Virginia Lady," who is very ambidextrous, resolutely told her very perplexed and surprised Vermont Cavalier, "Darling, don't worry, just hold on the reins of my horse and ride along at a fast pace and I will, by the "Mercy of Our Lord,' fend off the bushwhackers."

Well, everything went as planned by our creative and ingenious Major Pamela Mae Brewer as she started firing at the attackers to her rear. The apparent robbers and scoundrels were not wearing any sort of recognizable uniforms while the four men were firing forwards towards the two moving targets. In addition, the assaulters were riding in a tight formation with a pair in front and two in the back. Major Brewer was able to confidently and expertly shoot the first two thieves in their upper right arms that caused them to drop their weapons, curse up a storm, and scream out in agony. She thought to herself faithfully, *Oh Lord, why do people feel the need to attack each other and please forgive me for firing in self-defense. Amen!*

Meanwhile, Major Mario LaGrande was holding the reins steadily that were attached to Pamela Mae's horse as his steed, *Marengo il Secondo,* was galloping along stride for stride at a synchronized pace with *Marenga la Primera.* Mario was also in faithful thought of their uncertain circumstances as he glanced to his left and saw his astonishing woman in action. He thought for a few seconds in Italian and English which resulted in this abbreviated prayer, *O Caro Signore nei cieli (Oh Dear Lord in the heavens), Please be our vision as you guide and protect my Darling Pamela Mae and I while You save us once again. Amen.*

Circa five minutes later, the second set of cowardly marauders suffered a similar fate as Pamela Mae wounded them each on their upper left arms. Her actions resulted in those two hapless assailants shouting fruitless obscenities as they gave up the pursuit.

After only ten minutes of Pamela Mae riding backwards and firing her handguns to the rear, the dangerous situation was averted. At that time, Mario led them and their horses to a safe and secure place behind a thicket of bushes and shrubs. Pamela Mae and Mario decided to dismount from their athletic and brave horses.

He then stated in Italian and English, "*Pamela Bella* (Pretty Pamela), you were so sensational in the way that you rode your horse in a rodeo-like manner backwards while firing both your revolvers expertly with superb ambidexterity. You are amazing in so many ways!"

Pamela Mae humbly accepted the compliments from her "Riding Partner" and replied in a positive manner in Italian, English, and German, "*Mario Bello* (Handsome Mario), you were also amazing as you rode at a constant pace and kept our horses in unison, *Du warst so wunderbar* (You were so wonderful)!" Our very adoring lovers exchanged hugs and kisses and Mario remembered the geography of the states and said to his Pamela Mae, "Sweetheart, let's continue traveling south until we cross the border into Tennessee and then head west to find out the most sensible route to the train depot in Bristol, alright?" Pamela Mae was elated and responded with an affirmative smile, "Of course, my love, Mario, I would travel all over America and abroad as long as we are together!"

Fortunately, within forty minutes, they met a local Tennessee farmer and he estimated that it was another 30 miles of travel towards the setting sun before they could arrive at the very busy "Bristol Depot" railroad complex in Virginia near Goodson. He further stated, "Folks, if you like good barbecue and music, you will love the Bristol area!"

November 24th, 1861

It was just after 11:00 a.m. on that Sunday morning of November 24th, 1861, as the sounds of a *pianoforte* and gospel singing were emanating from a small church down the street from the Bristol train station. Pamela Mae was verily inspired when she recognized and heard one of her favorite hymns, *Amazing Grace*. Those inspirational and soul-saving words by John Newton included "Amazing Grace, how sweet the sound to save a wretch like me" pulled upon the "Holy Spirit of Our Leading Young Lady."

This would be the "first time" for Mario Patrizio LaGrande to be inside a "Methodist Episcopal Church." Growing up as a Roman Catholic, he was mostly familiar with ancient chants and hymns that were recited and sang in Latin and Greek. After a time of praise, prayer, and supplication, the Preacher, Graham William, gave a sermon that was from Jesus' Sermon on the Mount from the Gospel of Saint Matthew, Chapter 5, verses 3-5: "Blessed are the poor in Spirit, for theirs is the kingdom of heaven. Blessed are they that mourn, for they shall be comforted. Blessed are the meek, for they shall inherit the earth."

It was a grand blessing for both Pamela Mae and Mario to attend that uplifting worship service. The closing hymn's lyrics were written by Charles Wesley and it was the first time for Mario to hear those precious religious words, "O for a Thousand Tongues to Sing, My Great Redeemer's Praise..."

It was now after 12:00 noon and Mario and Pamela Mae were adjacent to the bustling Bristol Train Depot and it was a very active sight of hundreds of Virginia and Tennessee soldiers, along with numerous civilian personnel, black and white, with lots of baggage and supplies stacked up in various locations. They were both feeling hunger pains and lo and behold, there was an enterprising young couple selling pulled pork barbecue sandwiches, fried cabbage, and corn pone for $1 a plate. The sweet savory scents of the classical "Southern Food" were simply irresistible to our "Virginia Lady and Vermont Gentleman." They sat down with their food in their laps on the floor of a wooden platform.

Our traveling couple enjoyed the flavorsome lunch meal and then saw a man with a banjo and his son walk towards the seated Mario and

Pamela Mae. The man took off his weathered old straw hat and placed the open-faced hat on the dirt in front of him. He then tossed three coins inside the headwear in order to encourage his listeners to throw in "tip money."

Pamela Mae liked a variety of music and dance and was especially fond of buskers (street musicians and singers). Since it was the "Lord's Day," the banjo player, whose name was Darrell Pritt, started out playing his instrument and singing in a strong baritone voice the old time Gospel song *Rock of Ages*. His son Daniel, who looked to be about eleven years old, bowed his head and sang along with a dulcet tenor voice. Pamela Mae, with her endearing Virginia soprano voice, joined in during the opening words of "Rock of Ages, cleft for me, let me hide myself in Thee..."

Mario was once again joyfully impressed as he heard the sweet voice of his Pamela Mae and the many ways that she connects with others. She clapped her hands after the completion of the grace-filled hymn and exclaimed, "Amen Brothers," as Mario got up and took out a couple coins and dropped them in Darrell's hat.

Aura Lea was a beautiful ballad song that had just been released in 1861 and sung in the North and South. It was the second song performed by the "Father and Son" duo that afternoon. Pamela Mae and Mario were not familiar with the softhearted "Love Song" as they stood up and hugged, kissed, and slow danced with each other fondly. While in a very comforting and long embrace, Mario gazed into the lucent brown eyes of his only love and sang, "Sunshine came along with thee and swallows in the air..." As this very romantic melody came to an end, Pamela Mae pulled out a silver coin and placed it in the open pale yellow hat, and then requested that Darrell and Daniel perform *Dixie*, a celebratory song, so that her and Mario could dance enthusiastically.

Darrell Pritt played his five string banjo in a zealous manner as his son Daniel sang with charismatic emotion. This was one of "Our Virginia Lady's" favorite songs as she and Mario held hands with their arms fully extended and twirled and whirled fancifully in circles. Pamela Mae was so excited that she sang out loud with her delightful voice, "In Dixie Land where I was born in early on one frosty mornin,' Look away, look away, look away, Dixie Land." It was over three minutes of pure merriment as Mario remembered, *It is so fitting for Pamela Mae to sing this song especially since she was born in the South on a frosty February 14th Saint Valentine's Day morning.* Mario was singing along too and

recalled his classmate at the "Saint Albans'
Military Academy," Preston Garrett, who years
ago first sang this song to him and his best friend
Maurice.

After the very joyous song ended, the two very
happy dance partners went towards Mister Pritt
and his son and Mario LaGrande said to his
beautiful young woman, "Pamela Mae, I believe
it is time for us to depart and travel towards the
town of Abingdon, Virginia." Darrell heard her
name for the first time and responded, "Sir, you
and I are fully blessed to have a beautiful woman
to cherish and they both have the exact same
first name— Pamela. In fact, my wife's name is
Pamela Kaye, and I adore and love her so."

Having just experienced that very enjoyable
and incredible melodic and singing experience,
our dreamy and predictive Pamela Mae thought
about the future music in the 20th century. She
prophetically stated with confidence to all who
could hear her voice, "I feel profoundly that
Bristol will be the birthplace of country music!"

Chapter 16
Washington County and Abingdon, Virginia
November 24th – 25th, 1861

"Our Lovely Virginia Lady and Our Handsome Vermont Cavalier" were on the road again and riding their well-groomed Arabian horses in a mostly northeast direction in Washington County, Virginia. Pamela Mae Brewer and Mario Patrizio LaGrande were traveling on the main thoroughfare between Bristol and Abingdon, Virginia. Mario, who loved trees, took mental note of the vast variety of the "Gentle Giants" that he could thoughtfully identify. *Even though most of the leaves have fallen, I can still see numerous portentous looking white and red oaks, massive tulip poplars, and russet red and sugar maples, and Pamela Mae's favorite, the magnificent Magnolia (Magnolia virginiana).*

It was now the late afternoon of Sunday, November 24th, 1861, and Pamela Mae and Mario were able to water their horses in "Spring Creek" en route to their destination. They were on the western outskirts of Abingdon when Pamela Mae noticed a sign with an arrow pointing north towards Russell Road which read "Sinking Spring Cemetery." She felt the action of the "Holy Spirit" upon her heart and soul and told Mario, "Darling, let's turn left, as I feel that

'The Lord' wants us to pay our respects to a fallen soldier."

Pamela Mae and Mario entered the six-foot-tall iron gates of the cemetery that belonged to the Presbyterian Church. They went in respectfully and dismounted their horses and tied them to a hitching post nearby. She looked to her right along a narrow path and saw a funeral service being conducted for a recently deceased "Virginia Soldier" by a minister named Brian Scott. Mario and Pamela Mae could distinctly hear the preacher quote the words that Jesus told Martha about her brother Lazarus as recorded in the Gospel of John 11:23, "Thy brother shall rise again."

At the conclusion of the "Christian Burial Service," Pamela Mae found out that the only living family member present was the sister of the lamented soldier and she appeared to be approximately twenty years old. Our sympathetic leading lady walked over and hugged the grieving sibling and told her, "Ma'am, may our Dear Lord bless and console you during this sad time."

Before leaving the cemetery, Pamela Mae was again being influenced spiritually and thought about the Ohio River Valley and the States of

Kentucky, Ohio, and Virginia and the name Morgan. She held onto Mario tightly and told him prophetically, "Sweetheart, I have this innate feeling that a famous "Cavalry General" will lie here one day in the future." Mario comforted her and quoted his father Louie once more, "My Dear, don't worry, everything will be alright."

Historical Note: After his funeral and procession, the famous "Southern Cavalier" Brigadier General John Hunt Morgan's deceased body was temporarily laid in a tomb at the Sinking Spring Cemetery in Abingdon. Virginia. He rested there from September 6th through September 13th, 1864.

At this point in their journey, Mario LaGrande and Pamela Mae Brewer took the advice of Reverend Scott and headed towards "The Tavern" on East Main Street in Abingdon and wished to have supper there. When they walked in the establishment, they were promptly greeted by the owners' daughter. Her name was Casey Sainte Genevieve and she was a very attractive blonde, blue-eyed woman who was tall like Pamela Mae. Casey proudly told them that their business was first established in 1779 during the Revolutionary War.

The two attractive, shapely women became very friendly right away as Pamela Mae asked, "Miss Casey, would you possibly have a pretty dress that I could wear this evening and a place to wash up and prepare for dinner?" Miss Sainte Genevieve smiled brightly and responded right away and said, "Yes, Miss Pamela Mae, I have a lovely blue evening gown that would fit you perfectly and you may use my ultra-modern bathroom to get cleaned and dressed for your handsome man.

Pamela Mae told Mario about her plans to get a borrowed dress to wear and a place to wash up and get ready. He understood and decided to go outside in the back of the tavern to enjoy a couple of glasses of "blackberry wine" while awaiting for his "Lovely Virginia Lady."

Casey took Pamela Mae over to her family's home that was down a side street and offered their guest room for the night. In addition, the hospitable hostess explained to her beautiful visitor some of the local history of Abingdon which is the governmental seat of Washington County, Virginia. "Well, immediately before the Europeans settled here, the Cherokee Nation inhabited the area. The land was first surveyed between 1748-1750 by Thomas Walker, who called it the 'Wolf Hill Tract.' Colonel William

Byrd III ordered the 'Great Road' to be built which connected current day Abingdon and Kingsport, Tennessee. Also, many well-known Americans have been to this community to include Daniel Boone and Andrew Jackson. Furthermore, three of Virginia's Governors have resided here to include Wyndham Robertson, David Campbell, and John B. Floyd."

Our historical and military minded Major Pamela Mae Brewer added personally saying, "Thank you, Miss Sainte Genevieve for explaining those fascinating historical facts to me and Brigadier General Floyd was the Commander of our "Virginia Soldiers" when we fought at the Battle of Carnifex Ferry in Nicholas County, Virginia (now West Virginia)."

Miss Sainte Genevieve continued to tell her new friend, "I wanted to tell you about the caves and tunnels that we have in Abingdon that are sometimes used by the 'Underground Railroad' to hide and temporarily shelter runaway slaves. These are perilous times for Abingdon since this terrible war began."

Casey hesitated awhile, remembered something, and then went over to a storage cabinet and pulled out a very unique item and gave it to Pamela Mae. "Oh, by the way, I will gift you a bottle of 'Olive Oil infused with lemon' from Greece that you and your fiancé could enjoy and utilize sensually to your hearts' desire later tonight on the bed in our guest room."

Pamela Mae knowingly smiled at her personal remarks and yet she was so interested in all that Casey Sainte Genevieve had to tell her about the local history and well-known famous men. Pamela Mae thanked her for demonstrating such extraordinary congeniality and generosity to herself and Mario as well. She smiled and winked and told Casey, "You are so very kind to Mario and I and we do love to massage one another so the scented olive oil is so much appreciated. *Danke* (Thank you). "

In the meantime, Mario was outside "The Tavern" enjoying the sweet blackberry wine where he happened to encounter two gentlemen travelers. The dark haired, brown-eyed men were dressed very well in three-piece suits. He was so amazed when he heard the older man say in Italian, "Paisano, *ricorda l'anno scorso quando combattemmo sotto Garibaldi nella battaglia del Volturno* (Compatriot, remember last year when we fought under Garibaldi at the Battle of the *Volturno*)?"

Well, *Maggiore* (Major) Mario Patrizio LaGrande was doubly surprised and thrilled to hear Italian being spoken in Abingdon, Virginia and the military related language. He thought felicitously to himself, *Che buona fortuna (What good luck)*. Mario is exceptionally bold by nature as he interrupted the two men saying, *"Vi prego di scusarmi Signori, potreste parlarmi di quella battaglia in Italia* (Please excuse me Lords, could you tell me about that battle in Italy)?" The older man then introduced himself as Gaetano Soldato and said that his younger friend and fellow officer's name was Antonio Fratelli.

The two former *Capitani dell'esercito* (Army Captains) who were under the influence of more than a few alcoholic drinks agreed to summarize their combat role to Major LaGrande with the English translation included below, "It was during October of 1860 and we were amongst a battalion of 'Southern Italian (Sicilian and Calabrian) Volunteer soldiers' under the command of General Giuseppe Garibaldi. We were each company commanders as our battalion's troops were in mortal combat, near the Volturno River, in south central Italy against Bourbon men from Naples. There were approximately close to fifty thousand warriors total and there were over five thousand casualties from the conflict and Garibaldi was victorious."

Signore (Mister) Soldato discontinued his "Battle of the Volturno" story when he first saw the most loveliest of the "Fair Sex." It was the moment that Pamela Mae Brewer came onto the patio and was seen by all the people in the back of The Tavern." Antonio Fratelli gazed at the entrancing youthful female and thought in Italian, *Com'è squisitamente bellezza questa Signorina della Virginia dall'aspetto splendente davanti a noi questa sera (How exquisitely beautiful is this resplendent looking Virginia Young Lady before us this evening.)*

Her long thick black hair was adorned with a gold and diamond jeweled tiara. Pamela Mae's immensely enchanting brown eyes were gleaming under the glowing moonlight. Those fuchsia hued lubricious lips were very glossy and accented her radiant smile that provided additional light to the outside atmosphere. Pamela Mae was feeling chilled and told her handsome Cavalier gentleman, "Mario Darling, let's go inside and get warm by the fireplace."

Mario escorted his *Pamela Bella* (Pretty Pamela) into the back door of "The Tavern" and she had the most awe-inspiring and dream-like vision of General George Washington standing before the huge fireplace. He was in his full Colonial uniform. The famous General gazed at the irresistible Pamela Mae and paid particular attention to her voluptuous cleavage that was enhanced by the low-cut blue sapphire gown. He grinned and winked at her and thought, *She is the most adorable woman in all of the British Colonies!*

Shortly thereafter, the image of the "Father of Our Country" disappeared as Pamela Mae cautiously whispered in the left ear of her fiancé, "Sweetheart, I just had an apparition of seeing General George Washington by the fireplace, and he pleasantly admired my breasts." Mario chuckled and smiled at her experience and responded, "*Mia Pamela Bella* (My Pretty Pamela), I totally believe you since you have such extraordinary sensory gifts. Additionally, I am sure our famous 'General and National Hero' was very impressed by your glamorous and fascinating appearance and irresistible top-level form."

Pamela Mae and Mario were seated by the candle lit window on the west side of the first floor. Casey was back at "The Tavern" as she greeted them once again in French and English and said, "Bonsoir *Mademoiselle et Monsieur*

(Good Evening Young Lady and Sir), and what would you like to drink and eat?" This time, Mario took the initiative and said, "*Bonsoir à vous ma chère hôtesse* (Good evening to you my dear hostess). We would love to have a bottle of your finest '*Vino Bianco Dolce Italiano*' ('sweet Italian white wine') to drink and what are your favorites that You would recommend for us from your menu?"

Miss Sainte Genevieve smiled wittingly, winked, and told them , "I personally love our 'Chesapeake Bay Oyster Stew,' one of my all-time favorite seafood specialties while being an ideal choice for 'young lovers' like you two!" Pamela Mae smiled broadly on the outside and the inside as she encouraged Mario to have two full bowls of the oyster stew with crackers, saying, "Darling, you should definitely have additional oysters for our partners' dance and romance later on." She knew the aphrodisiac effects that the oysters will have on the "Male Libido" and that later in the evening her "Vermont Cavalier" would be physically stimulated even more during their nighttime exercises. *Ooh*, la, la.

The next "fruit of the sea" course would be "Black Mussels" from the North Atlantic, which has the Latin name of "*Mytilus trossulus*" and was sprinkled with lemon juice to add to the flavor of that culinary delicacy. There was also a mixed vegetable medley of sliced carrots, green beans, and peas with melted butter. Mario commented in his positive Italian manner about the food saying, " *Lo stufato di ostriche e le cozze nere sono davvero deliziosi e splendidi* (The oyster stew and black mussels are very delicious and splendid)!"

After the vegetables were consumed, Pamela Mae inquired to Casey about the "Maryland Crab cakes" that were being eaten by a number of her fellow diners at the tables nearby. Miss Sainte Genevieve responded delightfully, "As you can see from their very happy faces and expressions, everybody likes them!"

At the conclusion of the very scrumptious supper and the payment of the bill with a plenteous tip, Pamela Mae offered the toast with a small glass of German Cherry Schnapps," a heartfelt salute to our gracious and lovely hostess and blessings to 'The Tavern' and 'Abingdon, Virginia' and may they all remain charming and welcoming to all visitors. *Prost* (Cheers)."

At approximately 7:30 p.m. on the late evening of November 24th, 1861, Mario and Pamela Mae were all comfy/cozy in the guest bedroom provided by the gracious Casey Sainte Genevieve. Pamela Mae had the bottle of Grecian olive oil with infused lemon in her hand. She slowly poured an adequate amount of the soothing lubricant and then warmed it with her hands.

Her "Vermont Cavalier" was laid out on his back and was completely naked. He was primed and more than ready to feel the sensitive and strong touch of the talented hands of his "Virginia Lady" upon his bulging pectoral muscles. She massaged Mario's ideally shaped chest muscles in a clockwise and then a counterclockwise manner and then reversed her hands periodically. Pamela Mae told her beau, "Darling, I do love to massage your superior body form and give you as much pleasure as possible."

Mario exhaled and sighed with gladness and responded in French and English, "*Ma très chère jolie fille* (My dearest lovely girl), you definitely know how to please your man." Furthermore, he complemented her in Italian saying, "*Mia Signorina fantastica, tu sei bellissima, bravissima, buonissima e ti amo tanto bene* (My fantastic Young Lady, you are very beautiful, very brave, very good, and I love you so much!"

Pamela Mae continued to massage the entire front side of Mario's physical structure and she delicately rubbed every toe on his size twelve feet and each finger of his manly hand. Pamela Mae was totally in love with her "Northern Gentleman" and had these precious thoughts, *I am the most blessed and most fortunate young woman on earth to have a man to love while expressing my affection through the ancient art of massage. I do adore him and truly admire his abdominal muscles that are so tight. I love to feel his well-proportioned quadricep muscles in my hands. In addition, his super fit calve muscles makes me think of the statues of the gladiators and soldiers from Ancient Rome. What a man! Furthermore, I do like to thoroughly stroke his hands and feet and overall, I love his strength.*

After Pamela Mae completely massaged Mario with the imported olive oil, he responded, "Thank you so much my love, and now it is time for us to switch positions and I will give you a deluxe massage. *Va bene* (Okay)!" Of course Pamela Mae agreed and was now laying on her stomach with her long lavish coal black hair extended down to her waist.

He decided to get the appropriate amount of the Hellenistic and sweet-scented olive oil and warm the fluid by vigorously rubbing his hands together. Mario determined to begin with the back of her appealing feet, alluring ankles, and darling calves. Our expert massage therapist started on each side of Pamela Mae's lower right leg, and then left leg as she cooed and suspired with contentment. She took a deep breath, exhaled, and said, "Sweetheart, every touch of your especially masterful fingers and adroit palms sends multiple impulses of arousing enjoyment throughout my entire body. Ooh Baby, Baby!"

Mario loved her complimentary language and then continued to move his hands and proceed up towards her finely defined hamstring muscles in which he ardently rubbed the olive oil, with lemon upon until they were completely relaxed. Pamela Mae then took her right hand and moved her immense lengthy voluminous hair off of her fetching back and over her right shoulder. Her very loving "Northern Gentleman" with a broad knowing smile on his handsome face, moved upward to massage all three of her perfectly contoured gluteal muscles. Subsequently, Mario rubbed the Grecian olive oil all over her exquisite back. He affectionately and tenderly told her in Italian, English, and French, "Mia *Regina Bellezza, ti amo da sempre* (My Beautiful Queen, I have always loved you), and you are the 'Good Lord's' most magnificent creation. *Oui, Oui, Oui, ma Cheri Mademoiselle* (Yes, Yes, Yes, my Dear Young Lady)!"

The two massages lasted well over ninety minutes and the very relaxed and well lubricated couple continued their very intimate night time activities. During the last ten minutes of their very zestful *l'amour* la *nuit* (love at night), Pamela Mae had a few poignant carnal thoughts, *The sensuous vibrations of My Vermont Cavalier were pulsating and stimulating his Virginia Lady so thoroughly inside that each throbbing artery and vein were heated to a fever pitch of 103 degrees. Oh Me, Oh My!*

Our especially enamored couple continued their dynamic intimacy until after 10:00 p.m. that night.

Mario and Pamela Mae were now face to face in a very warm embrace. She recited the devout nightly prayer for herself and her "True Love" and concluded the supplication with, "In the name of Jesus, and in the name of the Father, and the Son, and the Holy Ghost. Amen!" Mario softly kissed Pamela Mae three times upon her satiny lips and sang in Italian to his "Lovely Virginia Lady" like this:

"Mia Pamela Bella, Mia Pamela Bella, Ti Adoro tanto bene.

(My Pretty Pamela, My Pretty Pamela, I adore you so much).

Tu sei Mia Signorina dagli occhi castani bellissima.

(You are my beautiful brown eyed Young Lady).

Tu sei Mia Principessa con il piu   sonrisso splendido.

(You are my Princess with the most splendid smile)

Mia Pamela Bella, Mia Pamela Bella, Ti Amo tanto bene.

(My Pretty Pamela, My Pretty Pamela, I love you so much)

"Our Lovely Virginia Lady" was so happy and bid goodnight in her father's German language by saying, "*Guten Nacht Mien Herr* (Good Night My Lord). Within a few seconds, "Our Handsome Vermont Cavalier" replied in his father's French language, "*Bon nuit ma Dame* (Good Night my Lady)." Shortly thereafter, Pamela Mae rolled onto her right side and Mario did likewise while he embraced her with his left arm while clinging to her supremely endowed breasts. Within a minute, our leading man and lady were asleep in a very cuddly "Papa Hug."

November 25th, 1861
Abingdon, Virginia

Mario and Pamela Mae had just finished a light breakfast and decided to walk around the neighborhood to admire the elegant 19th century architecture of the nearby aesthetically pleasing residences off of Main Street. It was very cold on that Monday morning, November 25th, 1861.

By chance, they encountered a distinguished looking lady who was wearing a light green and white day dress with a matching full length woolen fur cloak with hood. Our beautiful and gregarious young "Southern Belle" politely greeted the well-dressed lady saying, "Good Morning, Ma'am, my name is Pamela Mae Brewer and this is my fiancé, Mario Patrizio LaGrande, and excuse us, but are you acquainted with the homes and the prominent families in this section of Abingdon, Virginia?"

The very neighborly gentlewoman responded in a friendly manner, "Well, Good morning, my Dear, my name is Mrs. Doris Floyd-Preston. Yes, I am acquainted with the homes and also related to the General John B. Floyd and General Francis Preston families here in our fair city."

Pamela Mae was very impressed by the manners and the very beautiful outfit of the outgoing woman and said, "Mrs. Floyd-Preston, it is surely a blessing to meet you and I really love your luxurious dress and cloak ensemble that you are wearing today!" The elegant elderly lady smiled and replied, "You are very kind Miss Brewer. I own a fabric and dress shop here in Abingdon. Shelby Tyler, my best seamstress, made this entire outfit in two weeks with Virginia Cotton, Irish Wool, and Chinese Satin." Pamela Mae made a mental note and thought, *Good Lord willing, Miss Shelby could make a white wedding gown and matching long hooded cloak for me!*

Mrs. Doris Floyd-Preston volunteered to give Mario and Pamela Mae a tour of the Floyd and Preston estates and homes up the hill going west along Main Street in Abingdon. In addition, she would provide them with personal, military, and governmental information about General Floyd and General Preston, respectively. She pointed to the left towards the prominent home and stated, "You can see that he owns that elegant mansion in the heart of Abingdon and the finely maintained landscape that surrounds the home.

His entire family is very proud of John Buchanan Floyd who is continuing to proudly serve his beloved Commonwealth of Virginia as a General in the Confederate States of America (CSA)."

Pamela Mae decided to tell Mrs. Floyd-Preston, "Yes, it was an honor for me to serve under the Command of Brigadier General Floyd as a Captain when we defeated the "Union Troops" at the "Battle of Carnifex Ferry" in September of this year. I was, in fact, rewarded for my bravery with a promotion to Major." Doris was very much surprised to hear that Pamela Mae Brewer was also an Army Major.

However, she continued to talk about John B. Floyd saying emotionally, "He was a prominent attorney in Washington County, a member of the Virginia House of Delegates, the 31st Governor of Virginia, and the 24th United States Secretary of War. As a family, we are very blessed and honored to have him and I pray for him daily as he leads our brave soldiers into battle."

At this point, Pamela Mae gave Mrs. Floyd-Preston a big hug as Mario adoringly watched his compassionate fiancée and thought, *Mia Dolce Pamela Bella (My Sweet Pretty Pamela) is such an empathetic young woman and expresses her love*

*so wonderfully. She is such a joy to be around and
her presence is very supportive.*

Pamela Mae and Mario continued to walk
alongside of their very interesting guide as they
approached the former grand property and
residences of the Preston family. Mario was
amazed at the immensity of the multi-level
mansion and thought, *This reminds me of Mount
Vernon and surely a great general and a very
wealthy family resided here.*

He was correct, as Mrs. Floyd-Preston led the
way towards the magnificent brick and stone
edifice and confidently stated, "This opulent
stately mansion was originally the home of the
famous War of 1812 Hero, General Robert
Preston. In 1832, it became the family abode of
General Francis Preston who was an Army
Officer, a Virginia legislative member, and in the
U.S. House of Representatives. He had a very
lovely wife named Sarah Buchanan Preston." She
paused and giggled a little and then said, "Yes,
they were very fond of one another as Sarah gave
birth to nine children."

Mrs. Floyd-Preston paused for a few seconds
and then continued her talk saying, "However, in
1858, the Preston family mansion and estate was
purchased for $21,000 dollars and it is now 'The

Martha Washington College' for young women. I often visit there to see how the young ladies are doing and have tea in the original living room while admiring the long classic staircase up to the 2nd Floor. Due to the war, the facility has been used to quarter and treat our dear 'Southern Soldiers' who are sick and/or wounded in battle."

Note: The Martha Washington College went through multiple changes, purposes, and renovations over more than 150 years and is now operating as an upscale Hotel in the heart of Abingdon and it is called "The Martha Washington Inn and Spa."

Pamela Mae was very interested in everything that Mrs. Floyd-Preston told her and then felt the need to talk about her maternal great great grandparents at this point saying, "Ma'am, that information about the Preston family and home is so fascinating. Coincidentally, my great great grandfather Thomas Hendricks was in the Indian War and "American Revolutionary War Patriot." He married Sarah Van Hook and their union resulted in nine children also," Doris replied with an amazed expression on her face, "Oh my gosh, I have known the "Hendricks Family from Elk Garden" for many years and now I do see that you have many of their women's beautiful features in your countenance."

At this point, Mrs. Floyd-Preston invited Mario and Pamela Mae to visit her home and business with the very appropriate name of "Fancy Fabric and Dazzling Dress Shop" that was located near the "Woman's College" on Cummings Street. Upon entering the shop on the south side of the two-story house, our lovely young lady instantly noticed the many types of fancy domestic and imported fabrics to include cotton, cashmere, linen, satin, silk, and wool, etc. In addition, there were a variety of dazzling rich vibrant dresses and gowns that were arrayed on hangers and fitted on numerous mannequins. Right away, she noticed her favorite colors in the room decorated with eye-catching outfits to include blue, fuchsia, green, lavender, magenta, pink, turquoise, and numerous shades of white.

Shelby Tyler had the tape measure as the attractive Virginia young lady disrobed and was wearing only a beige cotton chemise thigh length one piece. Miss Tyler wrapped the marked cotton band around the bosom of the shapely Miss Brewer and she whispered, "Forty inches." Pamela Mae verbally reacted with, "Forty inches, are you sure?" Shelby responded with, "Yes, Miss Pamela Mae, that's what the tape indicates."

Well, the measurements, design, and fitting process continued with Mrs. Floyd-Preston in attendance. Pamela Mae understood that her family was related to Queen Victoria and she wished to have a wedding gown that was similar to the famous British *Regina* (Queen). Furthermore, the wedding will be conducted on the first day of Winter, December 21st, 1861. "Our Lovely Virginia Lady" told both women, "It will probably be very cold on Mario's and my wedding day. I would love for you to make a full-length matching woolen white cloak with hood for me to wear when I go outside at night."

Mrs. Floyd-Preston concurred with Pamela Mae's request and provided an estimate of the total cost. Miss Tyler agreed and said, "The wedding gown and full length cloak could be delivered to the Hendricks Mansion on Elk Garden Road in Russell County, Virginia within two weeks."

Pamela Mae Brewer was overjoyed as she hugged and kissed her fiancé, Mario Patrizio LaGrande, and he just had to say, "You will be the most gorgeous and radiant bride in all of America and I will be the most blessed and joyful bridegroom in history, *Ti amo tanto bene mia*

Pamela Bella (I love you so much my Pretty Pamela)." She was so very exuberant and proceeded to show her appreciation and hugged and kissed Mrs. Floyd-Preston and Shelby. Mario and Pamela Mae soon departed the premises and walked back to the livery stable to retrieve their Arabian horses. Before they mounted their horses, Mario affectionately told the love of his Life in "Italian Romance" language, "Mia Pamela Bella, *vieni cui vicinissimo e dammi un grande baccio Francese* (My Pretty Pamela, come here closer and give me a grand French kiss)." Pamela Mae was instantly compliant as they smooched while their Arabian horses neighed with delight! While riding west along Main Street in Abingdon, our devoted couple contemplated their trip towards Lebanon, the county seat, and eventually to Elk Garden, Virginia.

Chapter 17
Lebanon and Elk Garden, Virginia
November 26th, 1861

Pamela Mae Brewer, "Our Lovely Virginia Lady" was riding her graceful Arabian mare, *Marenga la Primera*, as she descended a very "pretty as a picture" hill en route to Lebanon, Virginia. It was midmorning on that Tuesday, November 26th, 1861, a chilly and yet sunny day. She had superb eyesight and happily noticed a sign off the right side of the road. Shortly thereafter, Miss Brewer joyfully read out loud, "Welcome to Russell County, Virginia." Mario Patrizio LaGrande, her "Handsome Vermont Cavalier," was on her left side while he was riding his dignified Arabian stallion, *Marengo il Secondo*. Mario could obviously hear and see that Pamela Mae was elated, excited, and he commented, "Oh Sweetheart, I am so glad that you and I will be visiting the ancestral homeland of your maternal grandparents. *Alleluia!*"

A decision was made to commemorate that very special event as the traveling couple took a break near the sign. As Pamela Mae and Mario got closer, they could both see that the boundary line between Washington County and Russell County was clearly delineated. Mario had an idea that he knew would appeal to Pamela Mae as he told her endearingly, "Darling, let's dismount and tie the reins of our horses to that white birch tree. Come with me and we will stand face to face and hand in hand with one foot in Washington County and our other foot in Russell County."

At that bi-county location, Mario and Pamela Mae warmly embraced and shared a very long celebratory kiss. She told him tenderly, "Sweetheart, I love the way that you observe the special moments in our lives together. We will be united as one on our wedding day when we become Mister and Mrs. Mario Patrizio LaGrande.

May our 'Good Lord' in heaven bless us and the "Hendricks Family" and friends these next few weeks during our time in Lebanon and Elk Garden, Virginia. *Hallelujah.* Amen!"

The huge clock at the Russell County Courthouse in Lebanon, Virginia chimed three times as the long red minute hand was straight in the middle of the 12 and the short black hour hand was in the center of the 3. Pamela Mae wanted to conduct about an hour's amount of research into the land granted to her great great grandfather, Thomas Aaron Hendricks, back in the late 1700s. She told her wonderful beau, loyal friend, and steadfast fiancé sincerely,

"Mario Darling, I hope and pray that we will find out specific information about my great great grandparents, Thomas and Sarah (Van Hook) Hendricks, from the official deeds and court filings. By the 'Grace of God,' may we meet a 'Kind Soul' who would be generous and give us the time in our pursuit for family documentation. Amen!"

There was indeed an appropriate answer to prayer when Mario and Pamela Mae entered a large office that was filled with binders and files. She noticed that the copies of the documents were categorized by years on the outside of the containers and there was a lady there who appeared to be one of the clerical staff.

Pamela Mae walked towards a petite and pretty woman by the name of Helen Bowen who took one careful look at "Our Lovely Virginia Lady" and told her, "Excuse me, young lady, for my inquisitive expression but are you related to the Van Hook family; in particular, the matriarch Sarah Hendricks and/or one of their daughters: Phoebe, Sarah, Elizabeth, Margaret, or Eunice? You really have the classic gorgeous appearance of that family's Dutch ancestry!"

Of course, Pamela Mae was profoundly delighted to meet Miss Bowen who was a retired

English and History teacher, and she responded blissfully, "Thank you and praise the Lord Ma'am, you are truly an answer to my prayer. Yes, Elizabeth Hendricks was my great grandmother and Sarah (Van Hook) Hendricks was my great great grandmother. We are traveling to Elk Garden and wanted to gain some relevant facts about my Patriot, Thomas Aaron Hendricks, and his deed/property that was granted to him for his military service."

Helen Bowen replied gleefully, "Miss Pamela Mae, it must have been 'Divine Providence' that brought us together today. Through my extensive historical and genealogical research, I have discovered that we are distant cousins due our mutual relationship to the heroic 'American Patriot' David Musick."

Miss Bowen hesitated and continued saying, "In addition, I know that in 1769, Thomas Hendricks received a 'Crown Right Patent Land Claim' of 400 acres from King George III for his militia service to the British Crown during the French and Indian Wars." Pamela Mae was pleasantly surprised to hear about her great great grandfather being honored and rewarded in this manner and responded, "Ma'am, I am very astonished and so very proud to know that about my heroic ancestor."

After a momentary pause, Miss Bowen carried on and provided the engaging Hendricks' descendant even-more ancestral news. "Moreover, our very famous historical figure and former Virginia Governor Patrick Henry awarded a 'Land Grant' of 400 acres to Thomas Hendricks on the 26th of June 1786. Mister Hendricks provided essential service to the Commonwealth of Virginia and was compensated with that large amount of property. That land was officially located in Washington County, Virginia on the north and south side of Cedar Creek, a tributary of the Clinch River."

All the while, Mario and Pamela Mae were listening intently to every aspect of Helen Bowen's detailed account of the Hendricks' Elk Garden property holdings that were originally in Washington County but are now located in Russell County, Virginia! Miss Bowen provided the following additional intersecting elements, "In fact, my mother, Elaine Bowen, worked at the Old Russell County Courthouse located near Dickensonville, Virginia in the early 1800s. She fondly remembered Thomas and Sarah Hendricks when they conducted official legal business with the county clerk. Also, she took me along on a visit to the 'Hendricks Mansion' and estate when I was a child."

Pamela Mae was so very blessed and pleasantly surprised to find a knowledgeable woman like Helen Bowen whose family knew her Hendricks' family to learn from and asked her, "I was thinking, Ma'am, does this Russell County Courthouse here in Lebanon, Virginia have a copy of the Hendricks' property deed and survey that I may observe and read?"

Helen Bowen nodded her head affirmatively and walked down to where the deeds and survey sections of the official records were stored. Pamela Mae was able to locate that specific information. She was amazed to read how Thomas Aaron Hendricks and his assistants, to include Sarah's brother Samuel Van Hook, performed and recorded the survey.

The very heavily wooded and thicketed land that is now located on both sides of Elk Garden Creek, Russell County, Virginia was surveyed by the use of transits, theodolites, and rods. Pamela Mae read the particulars of the very intricate survey and was interested to find out that the survey included a reference to a white oak and a dogwood sampling. She contemplated the survey and thought, *This is so incredible that my great great grandfather, Thomas Hendricks, and others would utilize numerous 16 and ½ foot rods to measure and record their findings. I just love it that the surveyors traveled by foot to and fro between arbor plants to include beech, pine, oak, and maple trees.*

Mario was also fascinated by the survey methods and data. However, he was getting "mighty hungry" and asked Miss Bowen directly, "Excuse me, Ma'am, where would you recommend for Pamela Mae and I to eat this evening?" Well, Helen Bowen responded without hesitation, "My favorite restaurant and tavern is called, 'Patricia's Country Diner' and is located on the same road as the courthouse east of here towards Elk Garden. Furthermore, they are well known and proclaim that they have the 'Best Food' in the Clinch River Valley."

It was nearly 5:00 p.m. when Mario LaGrande and Pamela Mae Brewer arrived on their impressive looking Arabian steeds, *Marengo il Secondo* and *Marenga la Primera*, respectively, at the front of "Patricia's Country Diner." This well-known eating establishment showcased and had a famous book written by Mary Randolph with the popular title of "The Virginia Housewife." Pamela Mae picked up the book and showed it to Mario as they both looked at a few of the mouthwatering "Southern Recipe's." She later purchased the absorbing book for $3.50.

Our Lovely Virginia Lady and Our Handsome Vermont Cavalier Love Story Book 3

A dark haired beauty of a waitress named Heather Jo, greeted her new customers with a welcoming smile and said, "Good evening, Folks, and I can see that you have been reading and purchased Mary Randolph's book. We serve our own version of each one of her Dixie Dishes." Well, Pamela Mae and Mario were more than delighted and decided to celebrate their very successful day in Lebanon by indulging in a few of Miss Randolph's culinary choices.

They started with the appetizing "Okra Soup" which was additionally flavored with tomatoes, lima beans, potatoes, carrots, diced onions, and beef chunks. Mario, who appreciated and loved a variety of cuisines, met the cook and told him in English and Italian, "Sir, the okra soup *era molto delizioso* (was very delicious)."

After consulting with her fiancé, Pamela Mae decided to request two orders of the "fried catfish" for her and Mario. Heather Jo, who has a good sense of humor, informed them in a comical way of describing the food by saying, "The ingredients that were used on the 'Meow Meow Fish' included peanut oil, cornmeal, salt, paprika, pepper, and fried with 'yummy for the tummy' bacon grease."

Mario enjoyed the "Pesce *Gatto* (catfish), so very much and Pamela Mae was equally satisfied as she told her waitress politely in German and English, "*Dieser Fisch ist überaus wunderbar* (This fish is exceedingly wonderful). My compliments to the chef."

Pamela Mae and Mario decided to top off their flavorsome supper with another one of Mary Randolph's specialties, "Appoquinimink cakes, with Colombian coffee." Pamela Mae asked the baker, named Bette Locker, about the short beaten biscuit and she replied, "Ma'am the ingredients include flour, eggs, butter, salt, and new milk as I make it into a paste and form a dough. I beat it with a pestle for about 30 minutes and then roll the paste thin. I cut it into round cakes and then bake them on a gridiron. I am careful not to burn them." Pamela Mae replied considerately, "Thank you, Bette, for the explanation. They are delicious with coffee."

After the conclusion of the very filling and tasty meal at "Patricia's Country Diner," Mario and Pamela Mae travelled back west on Main Street in Lebanon, Virginia. Helen Bowen had told them previously about the Elizabeth Garrett Home saying, "I knew your lovely great grandmother Elizabeth and have been inside her well-built three-bay, two-story brick house with attic and it has a high basement." Elizabeth Garrett was Pamela Mae's maternal great grandmother and she had appeared to her in a dream earlier in November 1861. She thought about the home intently, *I pray to You, oh Lord, and wonder if the current occupants would allow Mario and I to stay overnight?*

It was only a ten minute trip to the imposing residence as Mario LaGrande and Pamela Mae Brewer rode their horses to the back of the "Garrett House" on West Main Street in Lebanon, Virginia. "Our Lovely Virginia Lady" looked upon the home of her ancestor while she was feeling a little apprehensive, especially emotional, and eminently spiritual. After dismounting their horses, Mario took Pamela Mae by the hand and told her tenderly, "Darling, don't be preoccupied or worried, I am sure that the people here will be amicable and invite us in to their charming abode."

Of course the prayer was answered as the oldest girl named Margaret (Maggie) Garrett came to the back door and yelled back into the kitchen saying, "Hey Ma, we have a couple of visitors and they have the prettiest pair of horses. Can I pet them?" Well, her mother, Eunice, replied, "Surely Honey-Child and invite the couple in for something to eat and drink. I will tell Pa about our guests."

James Garrett and Pamela Mae Brewer both had something important in common: they both shared Elizabeth Garrett as their great grandmother. The Garrett Family wholeheartedly welcomed Pamela Mae and Mario into their happy home that was constructed in 1832. The entire family and guests gathered around their father James in the living room by the warm fireplace. He was obviously the gracious husband and Papa as his noble wife Eunice and mother of four children brought out food and drinks. Maggie helped with the vittles and beverages as her younger sister Angelina (Little Angel) and brothers Michael and Timothy looked on and smiled cheerily. Maggie sweetly asked Mario first, "Sir, would you like to have some of Mamma's corn fritters, blueberry jam, and hard cider?" Mario loved children and replied in Italian and English, *"Si,' Si, mia Cara Piccina (Yes, Yes, my Dear Little One)*, my mamma taught me to never turn down generosity and kindness!"

Pamela Mae was also provided with flavorous food and tasteful drinks and commented graciously to her host and hostess, "I am so thankful for your tender hospitality and I propose a toast to our great grandmother Elizabeth, to you James, Eunice, and your precious children who seem to be so familiar to me with a salute to the entire Hendricks-Garrett family. Amen!"

James Garrett was overwhelmed with Pamela Mae's gorgeous face and excellent personality. He began to compare "Our Lovely Virginia Lady" and then talked fondly about their beloved great grandmother saying, "Pamela Mae, you do have a few of her exquisite pretty features as you favor the women on our side of the family. Frankly, Elizabeth Garrett, at times, appears in this grand house to me in my dreams and encourages me to keep up my Christian faith. Great Grandma Elizabeth lived here for many years and I have such wonderful memories of her 'Christian Spirit' and singing the old-time church hymns while playing the harpsichord beautifully. I am blessed with her musical abilities and skills. Please join us as we honor our Lord Jesus and Grandmother Elizabeth while I play my 'Appalachian Dulcimer' and we sing together, *Come Thou Fount of Every Blessing.*"

Pamela Mae started to cry "tears of joy" while she remembered singing this sacred song written by Robert Robinson in her church back near Manassas, Virginia. She closed her resplendent brown eyes and heard the family faithfully sing in unison, "Come, Thou fount of every blessing, tune my heart to sing Thy Grace; streams of mercy, never ceasing." Pamela Mae had the most profound grace-filled thoughts, *Oh Dear Lord, even though our Commonwealth of Virginia is in the midst of this uncivil turmoil, Thy presence and love is still amongst our Garrett and Hendricks families. Hallelujah for your tender mercies, and please hold Mario and myself in Thy Holy hand, and guard us in all Your ways. Amen!*

Mario saw his sensational young woman with her eyes closed as he held his Pamela Mae's hand and could feel her love and prayers coming through her cherished touch. Well, it was now after 8:00 p.m. and Papa James told his four lovable children, "Youngins, it is very close to bedtime, but we do have time for one more song. What will it be?" Angelina, who was very fond of animals, was the first to speak up when she requested boldly, "Papa, please play that new folk song, *Old MacDonald had a Farm.*" Angelina and Maggie proudly led their younger brothers with the words and the traditional animals voices while Mario and Pamela Mae joined the chorus excitedly with the customary farm yard noises. James Garrett played his dulcimer with energy and smiled merrily. Here are some of the very funny verses that were sung:

Old MacDonald had a farm.
Ee i ee i oh.
And on his farm he had some cows.
And on his farm he had some pigs.
Ee i ee i oh.
With a moo-moo here.
With an oink-oink here.
And a moo-moo there.
And an oink-oink there.
Here a moo, there a moo.
Here an oink, there an oink.
Everywhere a moo-moo.
Everywhere an oink-oink.
Old MacDonald had a farm.
Ee i ee i oh.

Old MacDonald had a farm.
Ee i ee i oh.
And on his farm he had some chicks.
Ee i ee i oh.
With a cluck-cluck here.
And a cluck-cluck there.
Here a cluck, there a cluck.
Everywhere a cluck-cluck.
Old MacDonald had a farm.
Ee i ee i oh.

It was now 11:00 p.m. on that cold Tuesday, November 26th, 1861, night. Mario and Pamela

Mae were invited by James and Eunice to stay overnight at the "Elizabeth Garrett House" and our two love-birds were fast asleep in a spare bedroom on the 2nd floor.

Pamela Mae will have three different dreams with the first two similar in nature which she recounted to Mario early the next day before sunrise. "During my first dream, I can recall that it was the middle of April 1861. It was a week after the defeat and surrender of the Federal Troops at Fort Sumter, South Carolina. It was a rainy spring day and her young relatives, Michael and Timothy Garrett, were playing hide and seek in the 3rd floor attic of this very house."

She paused momentarily and then said, "The boys heard the pounding of horse hooves on the hard surface in the alley and the Southern accented shouts of Virginia officers commanding, 'Find every young man you can, and bring them to me immediately.' The very scared boys looked out the back windows to see numerous soldiers. Michael and Timothy then swiftly went in reverse and walked to the front side of the attic and opened the windows. They immediately saw a few teenage boys loitering on West Main Street below and yelled out, "Fellas, get out of here and run away quickly or the

Rebels will make you Privates of the Confederacy!"

Mario held onto to his Pamela Mae tightly, kissed her darling dimpled face in an understanding manner, and then she recounted the next night time story:

"It was now in May of 1861 before the Battle of Philippi, Virginia (now West Virginia). Once again, my youthful cousins, Michael and Timothy, were upstairs in Great Grandma Elizabeth's attic and it was beginning to get hot on the 3rd floor. This time the boys could hear the noise of soldiers marching and horses clopping their horseshoes on the 4" by 8"paving bricks on Main Street. Michael and Timothy took a quick look through the front windows and saw the blue coated soldiers and heard the Northern accented officers screaming, 'Get every last one of the single men in this two bit town and bring them to the County Jail for enlistment.' The boys now went to the rear of the attic and opened the windows and called out vociferously, 'The dang Yankees are in Lebanon, head for the hills.'"

At this point, Pamela Mae's serious countenance and voice changed to a more agreeable state as she remembered vividly her last and best dream when her great grandmother, Elizabeth Garrett, appeared and talked to her. "Grandma Elizabeth and I were walking arm and arm and we were on the opposite side of Elk Garden Creek. She said to me tenderly, 'My dear Pamela Mae, I can recall the days before the Mansion was built on the hill across the way. My mamma, Sarah (Van Hook) Hendricks, your great great grandmother, and I were in the kitchen of our modest two story house and she taught me how to bake with plenty of butter and to cook with lots of bacon grease. We made the most delicious pastries and dinner meals in Washington and Russell County. They included the following:

Baked Goods/Pastries that included
Fried Apples with butter, sugar, and nutmeg
Gingerbread with wheat flour, molasses, cinnamon, and allspice
Tea cake cookies with eggs, buttermilk, sugar, and baking soda

Dinner Meals that included
Pan-fried chicken with collard greens, mashed potatoes, and cornbread
Stewed duck with minced ham, chopped onions, sage, and parsley
Family mince pie with beef chunks, beef suet, salt, currants, and cloves

Pamela Mae told her great grandmother Elizabeth, "Grandma, I cherish, love, and thank you for telling me about the times that you spent with Great Great Grandmother Sarah. I hope and pray that I will see her on my wedding day." Pamela Mae then closed her eyes and hugged her Mario Bello (Handsome Mario) until they both dozed off once more.

November 27th, 1861
The Hendricks Mansion,
Elk Garden, Virginia

Mario Patrizio LaGrande and Pamela Mae Brewer had a simple breakfast of hot coffee with cream and a big slice of "Hendricks-Garrett pecan pie" that was ever so savory and then rode their horses east and north towards Elk Garden, Virginia. Pamela Mae had her recent dream with Great Grandma Elizabeth to ponder and thought faithfully and wonderfully, *I certainly cherish the heavenly dream with Grandma. I do have a mental picture of what the Hendricks property and houses might look like and I am very curious and excited to see Elk Garden Creek, the Waterfalls, the Brick Grist Mill, and the General Store. In addition, I pray that the current master of the house, Aaron Lilburn Hendricks, who is my cousin, and his second wife Martha Meliss (Fuller)*

Hendricks will open their home and agree to host our wedding next month. Amen !

Pamela Mae was of course mounted upon her magnificent gray and white Arabian mare, *Marenga la Primera*, while Mario was riding his majestic gray and white Arabian stallion, *Marengo il Secondo*. They were close to the right turn off of the Tazewell Turnpike. Consequently, they both looked to their left at the same time and encountered a very handsome looking gentleman who was sitting astride an impressive looking dark brown Morgan stallion. He had a sidearm on his right hip and a long sword strapped on his left side.

The man's name was John F. Maxwell and he was a writer from New York and he wanted to research and write a book about Thomas Aaron Hendricks and his wife Sarah's two brothers: Samuel and Lawrence Van Hook. His particular interest was to gain insight and knowledge about their participation in the French and Indian War and the Revolutionary War.

Pamela Mae led the way down the "curvy, long, twisting, and winding road." John Maxwell and Mario LaGrande were behind her and had an interesting discussion about military life and their mutual interest in "Ethan Allen and The

Green Mountain Boys," Mister Maxwell candidly revealed as he told Major LaGrande, "Young Man, I had the very personal thrill of visiting Fort Ticonderoga, New York before the 'Civil War' and I am still amazed that a small force of New York and Vermont militia soldiers could capture such a gigantic mighty fort from the British Army on May 10th, 1775."

Mario replied, "Yes, my fellow officers and friends of mine, Maurice Flambeau and Joseph Wei, and I visited there before 'The War Between the States.' We conducted a 'training scenario' in which we tried to recreate the events of that great American victory."

After about fifteen minutes of horse riding, all three of the small party came to a rise on the road as Pamela Mae was the first to see the panoramic vista. She exclaimed with a very excited voice, "Mario, my Dear, and Mister Maxwell, come see the spectacular view of the Appalachian Range and the Clinch Mountains and the lush river valley with the amber farming land fields of wheat, hay, and many cattle grazing in the grass." Mario was indeed impressed at the very picturesque and riveting sight of this section of the "Appalachian Mountains." He was inspired by the scene and responded in Italian, *"Si, mia Dolce Signorina, come belle le Montaigne sono questa mattina* (Yes, my Sweet Young Lady, how beautiful the mountains are this morning)"

Within another ten minutes of slow riding upon the dirt road that was lined with a variety of bushes, shrubs and trees, Pamela Mae was once again the first one to spot the sign which read "Elk Garden General Store." She dismounted quickly from the Arabian mare and tied her to the hitching post. She was very fortunate to meet up with the owner of the General Store and Grist Mill and Master of the Plantation, Aaron Lilburn Hendricks, her cousin.

Photo of Elk Garden, Virginia Grist Mill, built between 1823-1840

Mister Hendricks was expecting his cousin to arrive sometime near the end of November from the letter her mother, Sarah Anne Brewer, wrote to him last week.

However, Master Hendricks was not prepared to meet the most attractive young woman in all of his 39 years of life on earth. He was initially speechless, but he gazed at her and thought pensively, *Miss Pamela Mae Brewer is such a beauteous and "Lovely Virginia Lady." Her long thick coal black hair crowns the most bright and soft complexion. Pamela Mae's candescent coffee colored brown eyes are accented by her extended curly pitch black eyelashes. She surely has the desirable and enticing crimson lips of a temptress. My buxom cousin is a delight to behold and I truly envy her fiancé Mario who is lucky to have such a divinely wonderful young woman for his own.*

Mario and Pamela Mae were given a personal tour of the General Store which is on the roadside of Elk Garden Creek and the brick Grist Mill with the powerful waterfalls which is on the opposite side of the flowing water. Aaron Liburn Hendricks mentioned during the interesting walk that, "My father, Aaron Hendricks, built this 'Elk Garden Grist Mill' which grinds corn, wheat, and buckwheat, and feed for livestock similar to our Dutch ancestors built their mills in Holland

and continued their craft in New Netherlands, New York, New Jersey, and right here in Virginia."

Pamela Mae could feel the spiritual and working presence of her ancestors and said, "Sir, thank you so much for explaining and showing Mario and myself the particulars of the Store and Mill and its history. I would now love to go and see the "Hendricks Family Mansion" that my grandparents, uncles, and workers built in the early 1800s."

Mister Hendricks replied, "You are welcome, Pamela Mae. Please take your time and retrieve your horses and I will send a servant to the 'Big House' to alert my wife Martha that you will be gracing our home with your initial visit. I will see you both again later today, I pray."

Well, Mario was the first to get his horse, *Marengo il Secondo,* and went up ahead about seventy yards and gazed to his left and was stunned at what he saw. He felt the happiness of a surprised child and automatically turned around and called out, "Darling, hurry up, you have to see this!" Within thirty seconds, Pamela Mae rode swiftly upon her horse, *Marenga la Primera,* and caught up with her "Vermont Man." She took one long look at the elegant and magnificent looking edifice with the six vertical carved "Greek Style Columns."

The Hendricks Family Mansion, Elk Garden,
Russell County, Virginia

Pamela Mae gasped, sighed, and began to joyfully cry tears of nostalgia and told Mario, "Sweetheart, I feel like I have in many ways come home to a place that I dreamed and longed for in the innermost part of my consciousness and heart. *Hallelujah*, and I thank God that you are here with me right now to savor and share these precious and treasured moments. Amen!"

One of the house servants named Miriam answered the front door and said politely, "Good morning, Sir and Ma'am. Mrs. Martha Hendricks will be with you shortly. Please have a seat in the parlor!" Within five minutes, the twenty-five year old Madam of the Mansion, Martha, walked in and warmly greeted her guests, the future bride and groom to be. She stated, "Welcome to you both, and would you like to have tea with pies and tarts or take a tour of your great great grandparents' home first? "

Pamela Mae was so excited to be in the house where her ancestors, Thomas Aaron Hendricks and his wife Sarah (Van Hook) Hendricks, resided. Martha Hendricks showed them the grand ballroom and "Our Lovely Virginia Lady" pictured herself as the radiant bride in her lace white gown dancing with her "Handsome Vermont Cavalier." She had the most romantic thoughts of her Mario, *He will look so sensational in his Army dress blue uniform as we spin, sway, and twirl around the dance floor amongst our honored guests.*

Mario and Pamela Mae were both affected by the stylishness of the bisectional mahogany staircase that ascended up to the 2nd floor. Pamela Mae held onto Mario's hand during their time in the upper level corridor and whispered tenderly to him, "I can feel the spiritual presence of my great great grandparents as I sense that they are walking the halls with us now. Praise the Lord." Mario stopped and hugged his Pamela Bella (Pretty Pamela) and spoke softly in a mixture of English and Italian idioms, "Sweetheart, your great great grandparents are such a primary part of your emotional, mental, physical, and soulful being and they love you profoundly and are so jubilant that you are in your ancestral home *e ti amo tanto bene anche* (and I love you so much too!")

Pamela Mae became even more spiritually moved when Mario and her were in the master bedroom. Martha Hendricks could tell that her beautiful guest was having a special moment and kindly told her, "Please sit down on the bed which belonged to your great great grandparents, Thomas and Sarah. In addition, my husband Aaron wants you to spend your wedding night in this very room. Well, needless to say, Pamela Mae was overwhelmed by sitting on the bed while holding Mario's hand and thought, I *thank You, Lord and Savior, You have blessed Mario and myself abundantly and I praise You and please guide and be with us these next few weeks. Amen!*

Mario and Pamela Mae would spend the next several days residing in the Hendricks' guest house behind the Grist Mill which had the distinction of being the only brick mill in Southwestern Virginia. Pamela Mae loved to walk hand in hand with Mario as they walked the hills, fields, and dales. They enjoyed viewing and taking moments to hug and kiss while they travelled by foot across the earth of the 800 plus acres of lush and valuable property awarded and deeded to her great great grandfather, Thomas Aaron Hendricks.

They spent many days traveling and meeting the Hendricks, Van Hook, Garrett, and Booth family members throughout the Virginia Counties of Washington, Russell, and Tazewell. Mario and Pamela Mae were so impressed with the astounding topography of the Clinch and Blue Ridge Mountains as they rode their Arabian steeds through the rocky terrain. They were fortunate to have teas, lunches, and dinners with many of the prominent families and to tour their elegant mansions. Pamela Mae and Mario wrote and sent out numerous invitations to family and friends during this time.

In addition, Pamela Mae spent many days in planning her upcoming wedding and reception with Mario through personal visits and writing letters to Casey Sainte Genevieve at "The Tavern" and Mrs. Doris Floyd-Preston at the "Fancy Fabric and Dazzling Dress Shop" in Abingdon, Virginia.

Of course, many letters were mailed back and forth between Pamela Mae and her mother, Sarah Anne Brewer, concerning the wedding details. Then on December 2nd, she thought affectionately and nostalgically about her dear mamma and wished that she could be with her on her birthday, *Oh Mamma, I love you so much and would love to sing happy birthday to you in person. We had such great times together when I was growing up with my brothers. Lord, please bless Mamma Sarah Anne always and forever more. Amen!*

In addition, Aaron and Martha Hendricks were very helpful in their role as hosts and for planning and providing logistical items and support for the December 21st, 1861, nuptial festivities. Furthermore, both Mario and Pamela Mae were very interested when Aaron Lilburn Hendricks proudly recalled that he had at least seven patriotic ancestors: Grandfather, Great Uncles, and Cousins that served and fought during the Revolutionary War to include support and/or participation in the "Battle of Point Pleasant" in Virginia on October 10th, 1774, and the "Battle of Kings Mountain" in South Carolina on October 7th, 1780. Pamela Mae was indeed delighted to find out about the bravery of the Hendricks, Van Hook, and Van Meter men, respectively.

The Hendricks' Estate, Elk Garden, Virginia
December 7th-14th, 1861

On the morning of Saturday, December 7th, 1861, Pamela Mae received a hand written note from Martha Hendricks inviting her only to attend an afternoon tea party at the mansion at 3:00 p.m. "Our Lovely Virginia Lady" had this overpowering inner feeling that something significant in her life will occur at her ancestral home in the post morning.

Upon arrival at the splendid mansion, Pamela Mae Brewer was escorted into the parlor where she saw her dear cousin, Martha Hendricks, seated on the very ornamental "Louis XV red velvet chaise sofa" with Mrs. Doris Floyd-Preston and her head seamstress Shelby Tyler by her side. Pamela Mae, who loves surprises, was so exhilarated at seeing the ladies from Abingdon and shortly thereafter, noticed two huge white rectangular boxes wrapped with bone white silk ribbons stacked on the table in the corner of the cultivated social room.

She figuratively and literally "jumped for joy" as all three of the other ladies— Martha, Doris, and Shelby— gave her hugs and kisses. Pamela Mae had tears streaming down her delighted cheeks as she expressed her appreciation to all saying in her three fluent languages of English, German, and Spanish, "Thank you, thank you, thank you, *Danke, Danke, Danke, Gracias, Gracias, Gracias* to you wonderful ladies and I can't wait to open up the boxes."

Even though Mrs. Floyd-Preston thought realistically, *Assuming that I know the answer, I better ask Miss Pamela Mae, if she wants to open up the boxes here in the parlor or with permission from Mrs. Hendricks, upstairs in the big dressing room.* Our beautiful "Bride to Be" with an ear to ear smile said, "Let's all go upstairs immediately and open the packages and try on my wedding apparel!"

Upon arrival in the dressing room, Pamela Mae carefully untied the silk ribbons and slowly opened the first box which happened to contain her elaborate white dress. She gasped with bated breath and picked up the pretty garment by the shoulders and exclaimed, "Oh my goodness, this is the most heavenly 'wedding gown' that I have ever laid my eyes upon. Thank you again, Mrs. Floyd-Preston and Miss Tyler. My mamma told me 'Pretty Feathers Makes a Pretty Bird.' *Hallelujah* (Praise the Lord)." The custom handmade "Guipure bobbin lace" made from linen and silk, pleated wedding gown was pure white with a "sweetheart bodice neckline," and long bell flounce sleeves.

Pamela Mae took off her day dress with the assistance of Shelby Tyler and put on, for the first time, her brand new wedding dress/gown and it fit ideally. "Our Lovely Virginia Lady" was dressed "picture and portrait perfect" as she walked across the room and utilized two full length mirrors to see her adorable and unforgettable image.

Thankfully, the temperature was cooler in the dressing room. Pamela Mae tried on her full length matching white woolen cape and cloak with hood. Both outfits were fabricated superbly as she expressed her appreciation and joy physically with more hugs to Doris, Shelby, and Martha and then verbally spoke, "Ladies, I am so blessed to have your love and assistance with our wedding arrangements and plans. Thank you again, and may God bless you for everything you do for Mario and myself. Amen!"

After their time in the dressing room was complete, Martha Hendricks ensured that Pamela Mae's wedding gown and matching cloak would remain secure for the next two weeks. Consequently, the "Lady of the Manor" led Doris Floyd-Preston, Shelby Tyler, and Pamela Mae Brewer downstairs where they all enjoyed the fine teas from India and delicious servings of homemade peanut butter cookies, peach cobbler, and buttermilk pie made by Lydia, their excellent house baker.

When Pamela Mae returned to the Hendricks' guest house, Mario was there to greet her and remarked, "Mia Pamela Bella (My Pretty Pamela) you look so totally joyful. You must have had the best time at the 'Ladies Tea' and experienced something very special, I assume." Pamela Mae wrapped her contented arms around her "Northern Gentleman" and hugged him tenderly and replied, "Yes, I most certainly did *Mio Mario Bello* (My Handsome Mario) and you will find out what was so special on the evening of December 21st, 1861, at the Hendricks Mansion. "

Well, Mario thinks he understands and begins to tell Pamela Mae about his recent time spent with the Master Aaron Lilburn Hendricks. "Mister Hendricks was gracious to me as he explained many things about his family's plantation. He went into detail about having black slaves and white laborers and the many financial and operational difficulties in maintaining all of his holdings during the burdensome travails of the War between the Confederacy and the Union."

"In addition, he confided that he had a lot of anger and hate against 'The Yankees,' but has changed his mind upon meeting and knowing me and his affection for his beautiful and charming cousin Pamela Mae."

"Our Northern Gentleman" paused a few moments and gave his "Southern Belle" a comforting hug and continued saying, "Thanks be to God, Master Hendricks assured me that he consulted with the local government and military authorities and they guaranteed that there would be no problems, only peace and harmony before and during our wedding day and night here on his estate. *Alleluia!*"

The next two weeks were filled with more coordination with the local food, drink, floral, and other commercial establishments. Pamela Mae and Mario continued writing letters and invitations to their families and friends while receiving regrets and confirmations on attending their "Winter Solstice Wedding" on the 21st of December 1861.

"Oh Happy Day" occurred on Saturday December 14th, 1861, when both Pamela Mae and Mario received an invitation to attend a formal dinner party that evening at 7:00 p.m. at the Hendricks Mansion. Pamela Mae had this very warm intuitive feeling and supposition, *Mario and I could be blessed and we need to be ready to encounter a surprise visitor or two or three. Oh Lord, we are in Your loving care. Amen!*

Since Mario LaGrande and Pamela Mae Brewer are known to be "early birds," they arrived by horse and carriage at 6:45 p.m. the evening of December 14th. There were a few torches that provided light outside and Pamela Mae looked briefly to her right and saw a familiar form of a very muscular negro man who was talking to the stable workers. She had a perplexing idea, *The shape of the man reminds me of Will, my friend Gloria Faye's father and the husband of Lizzy. How can that be?*

Well, certain things became obvious when she heard a very familiar voice inside the mansion in the hallway say, "Miss Pamela Mae will surely be pleasantly surprised when she sees her mamma, Sarah Anne and me at the party." Of course, our joy filled Virginia Lady could not contain herself when she called out, "Lizzy and Mamma, I'm here. Come see me right away." It was such an emotional scene that even Mario shed a few tears when he saw his fiancée Pamela Mae greet, hug, and kiss her dear mammy, Lizzy, and then her beloved mamma, Sarah Anne Brewer.

"Our Lovely Virginia Lady" looked so exceptional in her coral rose dress with hoop skirt. Her luxurious and voluminous ebony hair was thick and curly and extended to her waist. Pamela Mae's sparkling smile was accentuated with her adorable ruby lips. Her glowing brown eyes were beaming with cheeriness while she sat between her handsome fiancé, Mario Patrizio, and her dearest mamma, Sarah Anne. Martha and Aaron Lilburn Hendricks sat at the head of the table.

Lizzy had been assisting in the kitchen outside and yes, it was Will who Pamela Mae saw outside earlier and he was helping to serve the dinner also. Each of the happy attendees had a glass of vintage "French Champagne" in their right hand. Master Hendricks began the wondrous occasion, as he stood up and raised his glass and with a strong voice, looked at Pamela Mae, Mario, and

Sarah Anne, and then said in Dutch, *"Proost op de toekomstige knappe bruidegom en lieftallige bruid en op haar mooie moeder* (To the future handsome groom and lovely bride and to her beautiful mother, Cheers)! "

Pamela Mae knew that the Dutch spoken by her cousin Aaron was approximately eighty percent similar to the German language that she understood. She knew that Aaron was saluting her, Mario, and her mother. Our Italian American Vermont Cavalier went along with the gracious toast and replied in Italian, *"Mille Grazie e a la salute di tutti* (Thousand thanks and to health of all)!"

It was such a grand dinner and the Hendricks' cooks with Lizzy's expertise served many of their family's favorite Southern foods to include:

Dutch Potato Salad   Creamed Corn
Honey Glazed Ham   Collard Greens
Fried Chicken   Buttermilk Biscuits

In addition, there were a variety of strong drinks that were enjoyed by all to include hard Virginia apple cider, German beer, Italian wine, and French Cognac.

Mario LaGrande and Aaron Lilburn Hendricks went outside for a while to discuss military history. They were both knowledgeable and agreed that Alexander III of Macedon (Alexander the Great), Hannibal of Carthage, and Julius Caesar of the Roman Empire were three of the greatest Generals from the ancient world between the year 336 Before Christ (B.C.) through the year 45 Before Christ (B.C.). However, they did have a friendly discussion and disagreed about who was the greatest General in Europe between 1796 *Anno Domini* (A.D.) and 1815 Anno Domini (A.D.). Aaron Lilburn Hendricks always admired the Duke of Wellington who was the British General who defeated the French General Napoleon Bonaparte at the Battle of Waterloo. Mario LaGrande, who read and studied Napoleonic Warfare, had to support his fellow Army Officer Napoleon I, who also had Italian and French ancestry like himself.

At the same time back in the mansion, Martha Hendricks and Pamela Mae took her mother, Sarah Anne, and Lizzy upstairs to the dressing room to look at the wedding gown and matching winter cloak. All four ladies were completely ecstatic and overjoyed as they assisted and watched "Our Lovely Virginia Lady" get dressed again. Sarah Anne wept tears of happiness to see her "Baby Girl" so grown up wearing her elaborate and stunning white lace wedding gown. She told her daughter, "Pamela Mae, your father, John Brewer, will be so blessed when he walks you down the aisle one week from today. Praise the Lord!"

At the end of the evening, Aaron Lilburn Hendricks took Pamela Mae and her mother, Sarah Anne, to the side of the parlor on the first floor for a private word. "My dearest cousins, I want to invite you to attend worship service together with Martha and I at the Methodist Episcopal Church tomorrow morning. The old church that was first established in 1788 is located a couple of miles down the road from here. We have a carriage that can seat six comfortably, so of course, Mario LaGrande can go with us."

"In addition, after the service is complete, I feel the need to take you on a trip to a different part of our property so that you may pay your respects to our mutual grandparents together. All five of us may gather together here at our mansion tomorrow at 10:30 a.m in our Sunday best outfits."

December 15th – 20th, 1861
Hendricks Family Estate, Elk Garden, Virginia

Mario and Pamela Mae walked hand in hand up the hill to the "Hendricks Mansion" on that crisp Sunday, December 15, 1861, morning. Will was there to assist with the ladies— Martha Hendricks, Sarah Anne Brewer, and Pamela Mae Brewer— who climbed into the customized Barouche carriage. Mister Hendricks sat near the front of the vehicle.

This would be a novel experience for Mario who was the last to enter the luxurious carriage and he humorously thought, *It appears that the Hendricks and Brewer families are very close in so many ways as I look forward to sitting next to Mia Pamela Bella in la chiesa (My Pretty Pamela in the church).* During the ride to the church, Aaron Lilburn talked about the Elk Garden Fort that was located north of the Methodist Episcopal Church. The fort was built in 1774 so that the European settlers in this area could help defend themselves against the indigenous Cherokee and Shawnee warriors.

The worship service was such a hallowed experience for all and Pamela Mae was especially blessed when the congregation sang one of her father, John Brewer's, favorite German hymns,

*Zein feste Burg ist unser Gott (*A Mighty Fortress is Our God) written by the very faithful and intellectually gifted Martin Luther between 1527 – 1529, *Anno Domini.*

Mario was not familiar with the hymn and yet he appreciated the beliefs and testimony of the faithful lyrics and he also felt it was coincidental and relevant to the recent story about the Elk Garden Fort. The Reverend Matthew Paul Leonard gave a very appropriate and touching sermon about the wedding feast at Cana as recorded in the Gospel of John, Chapter 2. During the message, Mario had his left arm wrapped around the shoulders of Pamela Mae and she remembered this passage well from her biblical studies and previous sermons and thought sacredly, *It is so interesting that Jesus' mother Mary inspires him to change the water into wine after she gives the servants some of the very best religious advise in the holy scriptures, "Do whatever He (Jesus) tells You."*

It was now 12:30 p.m., December 15th, 1861, on that "Lord's Day" afternoon back on the "Hendricks Estate." Mr. and Mrs. Hendricks, Sarah Anne Brewer, Mario LaGrande, and Pamela Mae Brewer were riding once again in the expansive carriage and they were en route to the old "Hendricks Family Cemetery" in Elk

Garden in Russell County, Virginia. Pamela Mae had this remarkable feeling of attachment to her great great grandparents as she could see a few grave sites in a distance. She remembered that her maternal great great grandfather, Thomas Aaron Hendricks, was born on November 1st, 1737, and died on November 21st, 1823 and her maternal great great grandmother, Sarah (Van Hook) Hendricks, was born on August 30th, 1740, and died on October 11th, 1813.

Mario affectionately looked at his wonderful young woman whose ancestors immigrated from the Netherlands in the 17th and 18th centuries to the British Colonies in North America. He helped his darling Pamela Mae out of the carriage and held her close as the entire Hendricks/Brewer family group walked prudently through the iron gates of the family cemetery. Mario LaGrande made the Roman Catholic "*Signum crucis* (sign of the cross) and then prayed in Italian, "*O Signore Gesu, per favore benedici mia Pamela Bella e sua Madre, nel nome del Padre, Figlio, e dello Spirito Santo, Cosi sia* (Oh Lord Jesus, please bless my Pretty Pamela and her mother, in the name of the Father, Son, and Holy Spirit. Amen)."

Pamela Mae was now holding Sarah Anne close as they stood in front of the first gravestone.

Headstone of Thomas Hendricks
Elk Garden, Virginia

Pamela Mae read the inscription and whispered tenderly in her mother's ear, "In Memory of Thomas Hendricks."

Sarah Anne was visibly shaken as Pamela Mae held her even closer, comforting her with the following words," Mamma, we are here today by the 'Grace and Mercy of God' while we 'Praise the Lord' for your great grandfather and American Patriot, my great great grandfather, Thomas Aaron Hendricks, who we both love and cherish."

After a few of minutes of crying, grieving, and praying, Pamela Mae noticed the next marker and then moved with her mother in front of the second gravestone.

Headstone of Sarah Hendricks
Elk Garden, Virginia

Pamela Mae again read the inscription and whispered in a gentle manner, "In Memory of Sarah Hendricks." This time it was Sarah Anne who clung to her daughter in loving support and consoled her with the following words, "My Dearest Daughter, as we are within a week of your own 'wedding ceremony with Mario," we have been so blessed by the Lord to finally pay our respects to my namesake, great grandmother Sarah, as we also honor your great great grandmother who we love dearly. Amen."

During the next five days, Mario LaGrande and Pamela Mae were making the final preparations for their December 21st, 1861, wedding day. More written confirmations of attendance and a few regrets were received from family members and friends. There was good news from the Methodist Episcopal Church in Elk Garden. The Reverend Matthew Paul Leonard made the commitment with the nuptial couple that he would officiate the "wedding ceremony." Furthermore, he agreed to have Mario and Pamela Mae each read a personal scriptural related "love poem" in addition to the official standard church vows.

It was now Friday, December 20th, 1861, and there was a light snow falling from the cloudy skies on the dwellings, fields, and creeks of the Hendricks Family properties in Elk Garden, Virginia. Many of the invited guests to Pamela Mae Brewer's and Mario Patrizio LaGrande's wedding ceremony and reception would arrive on this very active and busy day.

Prior arrangements were made with many of the Hendricks and Garrett families and friends to host the close to fifty attendees. Pamela Mae, who loves to count and keep records, made notes on a "guest book" when each person or family appeared on site or in Lebanon or Abingdon, Virginia.

Mario was so happy to see his father, Louie LaGrande, and his beautiful mother, Anna Rosa, arrive that morning all the way from Burlington, Vermont. They were able to travel by train and horse and carriage with their good friends Jacques Flambeau and his pretty wife Suzanne Marie. They were the parents of his childhood friend and fellow "Vermont Officer" Maurice Flambeau. They all were exceedingly happy to be together and Mario's parents were so impressed with the loveliness and grace of Pamela Mae.

Upon meeting his future daughter-in-law, Mario's French speaking father, Louie LaGrande, bowed and kissed Pamela Mae's pretty right hand.

He then stated in French, "*Je suis enchanté de vous rencontrer ma belle et charmante Mademoiselle* (I am enchanted to meet you my beautiful and charming Young Lady)!"

Mario's Italian speaking mother, Anna Rosa LaGrande, was equally complimentary to Pamela Mae as she hugged and kissed her future daughter-in-law and commented, *"È davvero un piacere conoscerti mia ella e splendida Signorina* (It is indeed a pleasure to meet you my beautiful and splendid Young Lady)!"

It was now the early afternoon of that exciting December 20th, 1861, day in Elk Garden, Virginia. Pamela Mae was in the guest house when she heard a very familiar voice in the front yard call out, "Where is my sweet cousin and the future Mrs. Mario LaGrande?" Lo and behold, her dear relative, Mindy Sue Russell, was outside standing in the front yard and there were two other people, one on each side of the house who were waiting to show themselves.

Pamela Mae was so very happy to see Mindy Sue and yet at the same time she felt that there would be others that would soon appear. She was right of course, as her bilingual cousin Christopher Russell came around the west side of the house and exclaimed in Spanish and English, *"Sorpresa, Sorpresa, Sorpresa* (Surprise, Surprise, Surprise), We finally made it to our ancestors' land and will be here for your wedding tomorrow!"

Mindy Sue and Christopher Russell exchanged many warm embraces and welcoming kisses from Pamela Mae as she said, "Praise the Lord.

We are here together for my wedding. But where is Papa?" Consequently, it was decided to save the best and biggest surprise for last as a strong voice in German could be heard from the east side of the guest house say, *"Dein ist mein ganzes Herz und diese Blumen sind für dich, meine schöne Tochter* (You are my heart's delight and these flowers are for you my lovely daughter)."

Pamela Mae was extremely overjoyed to see her *Liebster Vater* (Dearest Father) walk towards her with a slight limp while he held a gorgeous bouquet of flowers that contained red roses, pink carnations, baby's breath, and violets that were from a "Green House" located in Abingdon, Virginia. "Our Lovely Virginia Lady" replied affectionately, *"Vielen Dank, Papa, ich schätze deine Anwesenheit* (Thank you so much Daddy, I cherish your presence)!" Father and Daughter then held one another in a comforting embrace for the longest time. Pamela Mae had the most tender, faithful thoughts while holding her Papa closely, *Oh Glorious Lord, you have richly blessed me in three ways with a loving Father in heaven, a devoted father on earth, and my Mario will be a wonderful father to our children. I thank You in the name of the Father, Son, and Holy Ghost. Amen!*

The arrivals of the wedding and reception guests continued into the afternoon of December 20th, 1861. Pamela Mae was so very pleased to see her landlady from Alexandria, Madame Brigitte Moreau, with her husband, Julian Moreau, in a very elegant "Landau Carriage" at the "Hendricks Mansion." The conveyance was driven by their trusted stable master Henri.

In addition, an hour went by and another pair of distinguished guests would grace the premises of the "Hendricks Estate." Mario and Pamela Mae were so excited to once again be in the company of Mister John Henry Carter and his charming wife, Victoria Louisa Carter, who traveled all the way from Philippi, Virginia (now West Virginia). The Carter's are maternal relatives of the Hendricks and Garrett families. Pamela Mae fondly remembered that after the June 3rd, 1861 "Battle of Philippi," they opened their home and helped to provide medical care and personal support to her wounded cousin, Captain Christopher Russell.

Mario LaGrande also recalled the generous hospitality of Mr. and Mrs. Carter in June 1861, and knew that Victoria Louisa spoke Italian. Therefore, he greeted her in his mother's tongue saying, "*Buon pomeriggio Signora, che meraviglia per lei e suo marito essere qui per la celebrazione del nostro matrimonio* (Good afternoon, Madam, how wonderful for you and your husband to be here for our wedding celebration)."

Both couples embraced and exchanged affections. Pamela Mae expressed her personal appreciation to Victoria Louisa saying, "Thank you again Mrs. Carter, for you were the first person to tell me about Mario LaGrande, my Vermont Cavalier, when I was at your home in Philippi in June. I will be forever grateful to you. Lord bless you and Mr. Carter, always!"

It was now half past 4:00 p.m. and Mario LaGrande decided to take his gray and white Arabian stallion, *Marengo il Secondo,* on a ride in a mostly southwest direction down Elk Garden Road. He told his remarkable steed in French and English, "*Mon ami magnifique, roulons vers l'horizon occidental* (My magnificent friend, let's ride towards the western horizon)."

The purpose of Mario's ride was to meet up with his best friend and future best man, Maurice Flambeau, and his beautiful fiancée, Gloria Faye Brewer. They were reportedly en route from downtown Lebanon, Virginia, traveling with his other best friend and future best man, Joseph Wei and his attractive fiancée, Marie Louise Yang. Mario LaGrande was able to ride back up the long and twisting road towards the "Tazewell Turnpike" in about fifteen minutes.

It was getting darker by the moment and Mario thought, *Thank You Lord in heaven, it looks like the full moon and the stars will be out tonight to glow and light our way back towards the Hendricks properties.* A few minutes later, Mario LaGrande was able to get a glimpse of two very familiar forms. First, he could initially identify the large silhouette of a gentleman riding an impressive looking Arabian stallion that looked like his fellow Vermont Major, Maurice Flambeau. Second, Mario determined that the smaller figure, who was mounted upon another Arabian stallion, was also his fellow Vermont Major, Joseph Wei. *Alleluia* (Praise the Lord). The riders were followed by Gloria Faye Brewer and Marie Louise Yang who were seated in an open carriage.

Mario was so elated as he hailed the approaching foursome and greeted them in his three fluent languages of English, Italian, and French, "Welcome, my dear friends, *Benvenuti* miei *Cari amici,* et *bienvenue mes chers amis!*"

After a very happy ride towards the "Hendricks Guesthouse," Mario and Pamela Mae enjoyed a very celebratory evening and night with their best friends and family members. The festivities and reunion included an abundant amount of laughter, reminiscing, smiles, savory food, tasty drinks, and plans for the expectant wedding set for tomorrow evening.

December 21st, 1861
Wedding Day of Mario Patrizio
and Pamela Mae
Hendricks Mansion, Elk Garden, Virginia

It was half past five on that monumental Saturday, December 21st, 1861, frosty morning as Pamela Mae held on close to her Mario Patrizio in their comfortable bed. She had just woken up after experiencing the most phenomenal and vivid dream in which "Our Lovely Virginia Lady" was officially Mrs. Mario LaGrande and she was outside on the front portico of the "Hendricks Mansion" in Elk Garden in Russell County, Virginia.

In her dream, Pamela Mae could feel the presence and experience the vision of her great grandmother, great great grandparents, and what appeared to be the image of a "great white Pyrenees dog." She thought, *Oh my goodness, my great grandmother Elizabeth and my great great grandparents, Thomas and Sarah Hendricks, will be with me soulfully and spiritually on my wedding evening, and I will see a mysterious dog too. Lord, have mercy. Amen!*

She told Mario later that morning about the dream, and he was amazed and responded in Italian and English, *"Mia Cara Pamela Bella* (My Dear Pretty Pamela), you are my beautiful woman and beautiful dreamer. I sincerely believe that your dream with a spiritual sign and vision will come true on this Winter Solstice day and night. Of course, Darling, you will always be my ultimate dream come true and I love you, too!"

After a very busy and hectic morning and afternoon of wedding and reception coordination and planning, Pamela Mae was now upstairs in the Dressing Room of the "Hendricks Family Mansion." She looked around the well-decorated room and expressed her heartfelt appreciation to all of the ladies individually who were assisting her at about 3:30 p.m. "Thank you so much Mamma for giving me life and showing me the daily example of faith, hope, and charity and being here with me on this special day. Lizzy, thanks to you also for being my mammy and for caring and loving me as a daughter, and for seeing me go from a little girl to a grown up becoming a bride."

Pamela Mae shed a few tears, paused, and then continued saying, "Gloria Faye, I thank you so much for being my best friend and like a sister through all of my seventeen plus years, and for being a bridesmaid today." The two close friends embraced and then Pamela Mae continued her gratefulness by saying to her dear cousin, "Mindy Sue, I am so filled with happiness that you are with me on my wedding day, and I love you, my dear cousin." Well, at this point the "Ladies in Waiting" are together for one last group embrace before the nuptial ceremony begins.

It was now exactly 4:00 p.m. on that very cold Winter Solstice day of December 21st, 1861. The exceedingly radiant Pamela Mae Brewer descended the long sectional staircase to the first floor. She enjoyed the view of the large fir "Christmas tree" that was decorated with bright red and emerald, green colors with silver bells for the "holiday season" as she thought melodically in German and English, "O Tannenbaum, O Tannenbaum, how ever green your branches. Yes, we will joyously celebrate the birth of Jesus in a few days. Hallelujah!

Her father, John Brewer, was standing on the bottom landing and had the very best view of his exceptionally resplendent daughter. Pamela Mae's "soft as silk," coal black, luxurious hair was adorned with a sparkling diamond and pearl silver tiara imported from Italy. Her adorable and beaming brown eyes illuminated each step as she got closer to her papa who was waiting to escort his Pamela Mae.

Queen Victoria would have been elated to see the image of her beautiful relative, Pamela Mae Brewer, wearing her custom handmade "Guipure bobbin lace wedding gown." The elaborate pleated gown with an intricate floral pattern was made from linen and silk. The formal dress was pure white with a "sweetheart bodice neckline" and "long bell flounce sleeves." Her father, John, gazed at his only daughter who looked heavenly and thought personally and religiously about what was written in the Book of Revelation, Chapter 21, verse 2: *And I, John, saw the holy city, New Jerusalem, coming down from God out of Heaven, prepared as a bride adorned for her husband!*

Pamela Mae was now on the main floor and held a bouquet of pretty flowers as she reached out both arms and gave her father a long loving hug. He whispered to her affectionately in German, "*Mein kostbares Mädchen, du bist mein Schatz und Möge unser Herr Dich segnen und immer beschützen* (My precious girl, you are my treasure and may our Lord bless and keep you safe always)!"

"Our Lovely Virginia Lady" replied back with her tender heart completely filled with love for her father and replied in English and German, "Papa, I love you for being the best father in the world, *und vielen dank für all Ihre Lehren und Weisheit* (and thank you so much for all of your teachings and wisdom)"

Major Mario Patrizio LaGrande was wearing his Union Dress Blue Army Uniform. His noble-looking military outfit was accented by his gold-plated scabbard which contained a 34" saber that was worn on his left side. He was standing in front of the officiating minister and was waiting patiently for his darling Pamela Bella (Pretty Pamela).

Within a couple of minutes, everyone in attendance in the ballroom of the "Hendricks Mansion" in Elk Garden, Virginia arose simultaneously. They all listened to the wonderful melody that is properly named "Bridal Chorus" more commonly known as "Here Comes the Bride." The talented pianist named Mrs. Rose Ann Nash played the famous song beautifully much to the delight of everyone in the gala room. Mario decided that he would sing the words to this traditional song to his angelic Pamela Mae as she strolled towards him. "Here comes the bride, all dressed in white, sweetly serene in the soft glowing light. Lovely to see, marching to thee, sweet love united for eternity."

Historical Note: This traditional wedding song, "Here Comes the Bride" was composed and written by Felix Mendelssohn and later Richard Wagner. It was first played and sung during the wedding ceremony of Princess Victoria Adelaide Mary Louise and Frederick William III of Prussia on January 25th, 1858.

John Brewer escorted Pamela Mae Brewer who was elegantly dressed in her majestic white lace wedding gown. Her devoted Papa gave *seine süße Tochter* (his sweet daughter) one last fatherly hug and kissed both of her rosy cheeks. Pamela Mae had the most glorious thoughts, *"Thank You Dear Lord Jesus for blessing me on my wedding day, and Your Grace will always sustain Your Mario and Pamela Mae. Amen!* Mario immediately reached out his left hand while Pamela Mae extended her right hand as the adoring couple interlocked their fingers in the most romantic way.

Reverend Matthew Paul Leonard began the wedding ceremony of Mario Patrizio and Pamela

Mae by the trinitarian invocation/prayer and in the traditional nuptial manner stating out loud, "In the name of the Father, and of the Son, and of the Holy Ghost. Amen. Dearly Beloved, Families, and Honored Guests, we are gathered here today in the sight of God to join together Mario Patrizio LaGrande and Pamela Mae Brewer in holy matrimony...!"

Pamela Mae continued to hear the solemn words of Reverend Leonard and then took a moment to look at her Mario Bello (Handsome Mario) who was on her right. She had the most affectionate and amorous feelings for her future husband while she smiled lovingly and squeezed his hand slightly. Mario soon responded in kind and looked to the left while admiring his Pamela Bella (Pretty Pamela) and grinned cheerfully as he realized that his precious treasure would soon be his wife forever.

Mario and Pamela Mae listened intently and understood the message completely when Reverend Leonard read out loud from the Book of Genesis, Chapter 2, verse 24 saying, "Therefore shall a man leave his father and his mother, and shall cleave unto his wife and they shall be one flesh." Pamela Mae and Mario then looked at one another at the exact same time and nodded their heads in agreement, and said together as one voice, "Amen."

The wedding ceremony would include one of Pamela Mae's favorite songs. The first musical selection would include Lizzy and Gloria Faye singing an *a cappella* version of *Swing Low, Sweet Chariot* which brought back fond childhood memories and tears to the eyes of Pamela Mae. She decided to sing along during the second stanza, "I looked over Jordan and what did I see, coming for to carry me home. A band of angels coming after me, coming for to carry me home."

The second song was one of Mario's favorite hymns titled *Faith of Our Fathers* since he wanted to honor "Our Father in Heaven" and his father, Louie LaGrande, and Pamela Mae's father, John Brewer. Our soft-hearted "Vermont Cavalier" thought about the U.S. Civil War that his dear America was currently waging and was therefore moved emotionally during a particularly significant part of the song, "Faith of our fathers! We will love both friend and foe in all our strife. And preach thee too, as love knows how, by kindly words and virtuous life."

The wedding ceremony included the recitation of the Lord's Prayer that is based on the words written in the Gospel of Matthew, Chapter 6. This prayer that Jesus gave his disciples during his "Sermon on the Mount" was Mario's favorite prayer that he recited daily. He held on to Pamela Mae's hand securely as they spoke together, "Our Father, who art in heaven, hallowed be Thy Name..."

Before the wedding vows were made by Mario and Pamela Mae, they decided to recite their unique love poem to one another and to everybody who had gathered with them on that evening of December 21st, 1861. Of course, their words were based on and inspired by Saint Paul when he wrote Corinthians, Chapter 13.

Mario's and Pamela Mae's Wedding Love Poem

"Love is patient, love is kind.
It is a gift from our Lord Jesus in heaven, so divine.

Our love for one another is exceedingly fine.
It's from our Redeemer and Savior above, as sweet as the best wine.

Today, we honor our fathers and mothers, our ancestors from The Netherlands, Germany, *Italia,* and *La France.*

We invite all of our dearest family and loyal
friends after the ceremony,
to our wedding reception to eat, drink, laugh,
tell stories, and to dance.

Our prayer and wish for all of our loved ones is
that,
You may be richly blessed with faith, hope, and
charity in abundance!

Hallelujah, (Praise the Lord), and Amen!"

The wedding vows were exchanged by Mario
and Pamela Mae in a very heartwarming manner
as the silver wedding bands were placed on the
ring fingers of "Our Lovely Virginia Lady and Our
Handsome Vermont Cavalier." The Minister
concluded the very splendorous sacramental
service with those most significant words saying,
"I now pronounce you husband and wife and you
may kiss your bride." After a long impassioned
kiss between Mario and Pamela Mae, Reverend
Leonard said with a loud voice, "Ladies and
Gentlemen, I have the honor and privilege to
present to you for the first time ever, Mr. and
Mrs. Mario Patrizio LaGrande."

Well, everybody stood up, applauded, and
shouted out jubilantly to the very happy

newlyweds. Pamela Mae and Mario hugged and kissed each other again and walked through the middle of the crowd and were showered with rice from most of the invited guests.

Afterwards, Mario and Pamela Mae greeted and thanked everyone who came through the reception line. She heard a very eloquent, familiar, and soft voice say, "Pamela Mae, it is snowing outside. Please put on your new winter full length white hooded cloak and go outside on the front portico with your husband. "

Pamela Mae recognized that the woman's voice belonged to her dearly departed great grandmother, Elizabeth Garrett. Her phantasmic dream was about to play out in front of the "Hendricks Mansion." Mario and Pamela Mae walked onto the front portico as they both could feel and see the icy snowflakes coming down.

Pamela Mae LaGrande was now holding on to the right arm of her husband, Mario LaGrande. She could feel her great grandmother Elizabeth on her other side clinging onto Pamela Mae's left arm. She heard her grandma say graciously and spiritually, "My Dearest Granddaughter, I love you with all of my heart and soul. I am so thankful to our Heavenly Father for blessing me and the rest of your ancestors with your wedding ceremony that was conducted in the "Hendricks Family Mansion" this winter day.

At this point, Pamela Mae looked towards the road where she could see the most wonderful apparition and vision of a distinguished looking man dressed in a "Revolutionary War" uniform and he was standing next to a beautifully dressed woman who was smiling and waving in a welcoming manner to Pamela Mae and Mario. The elegant looking couple were standing between the giant oak tree and the large maple tree on the lawn that was about thirty feet from the edge of Elk Garden Road. Mario could not hear or see what Pamela Mae was experiencing but he could sense that his bride was interacting with her deceased loved ones.

Suddenly, a "great white Pyrenees dog" walked near the man and woman and began to bark in a friendly matter as if he knew and recognized Pamela Mae. Soon thereafter, her great grandmother Elizabeth said, "Pamela Mae, look straight ahead. My parents, Thomas and Sarah Hendricks, your great great grandparents are here in honor of your marriage to Mario LaGrande." Pamela Mae was, of course, in awe of who she saw and replied, "Praise the Lord Almighty, thank you Great Grandmother, my dreams have come true this evening. I will name the amazing 'Ghost Dog Tom' and I will cherish every moment of this miraculous time."

In an instant, her great grandmother Elizabeth Garrett and her great great grandparents, Thomas and Sarah Hendricks, and Tom the dog, were no longer heard or seen. Pamela Mae hugged her handsome husband for a very long time as the snow continued to fall on "Our Lovely Virginia Lady and Our Handsome Vermont Cavalier." She told her Mario, "Sweetheart, I just had the most amazing and supernatural episode of existence. Three of my demised grandparents came to visit me on our wedding day. Amazingly, I believe they brought their Pyrenees dog with them from the 'other side' to make me feel loved and precious to them. Amen !"

Mario replied in an understanding manner, "Darling, I believe every word that you said about your loving grandparents appearing to you so mysteriously on our wedding evening. It is surely a heavenly sign and a Godly vision. Now, let's go back inside, dry off, and join our family and friends who have already begun our wedding celebration and reception!"

Pamela Mae was the first to enter back into the mansion and saw her mother, Sarah Anne, and explained to her about the amazing apparition and interaction that she had outside the mansion with three of her grandparents.

Meanwhile in the grand ballroom, there was a formal orchestra that was performing for the first two hours of the festive wedding reception for Mr. and Mrs. Mario LaGrande. The musicians were playing the traditional "European Waltzes" that were popular in the mid-1800s much to the delight of the older guests.

Pamela Mae thought about the dream she had previously in which she was in her white lacy wedding gown and dancing with her husband, Major Mario Patrizio LaGrande. He was wearing his "Union Army Dress Blue Uniform" in the dream also. She told him, "Darling, dance with me now and my prophetic dream will come true." At that point, everyone looked at the bride and groom, Major and Mrs. Mario LaGrande, as they began their first dance as husband and wife. Pamela Mae's fondest desire and dream came true and her joy exceeded expectations as her Mario twirled and whirled his radiant bride in an oval pattern on the "Hendricks Family" ballroom floor. At the conclusion, the honored guests and attendees applauded and cheered that very important event in the newlyweds lives. After a few more dances, Pamela Mae and Mario sat down at the head table where they enjoyed a very delicious wedding dinner of appetizing foods and succulent drinks. Some of the choice foods on the menu included:

Beef Wellington
Green beans with bacon bits
Chicken Cordon Bleu
Creamed corn with chopped basil
Risotto al Chianti
Sweet potatoes with butter

The tasty beverages from America and Europe included:

Hard apple cider from Kentucky
German beer from Pennsylvania
Vino Bianco di Italia
French Champagne
British Port
Spanish Brandy

Major Maurice Flambeau, one of the best men, who was also wearing his "Union Army Dress Blue Uniform" took the initiative and proposed the first toast in French and English, "*Que notre Bon Dieu vous bénisse de richesses et d'une Grande Famille, A votre santé* (May our Good Lord bless you with riches and a big Family. To your health), my good friend Mario and to your lovely wife, Pamela Mae." All the guests in the room joined

Maurice in the toast and raised their glasses, clinked them together, and drank the bubbly French Champagne cheerfully. The very joyful bride and the very happy groom smiled and treasured the moments as they both drank the Champagne and then got up and hugged Maurice thankfully.

It was now the turn for the next "Best Man," Major Joseph Wei, who was also wearing his "Union Army Dress Blue Uniform" to propose a toast to the newlyweds. He decided to start his toast in English and conclude with some words in Mandarin Chinese. Joseph was a little apprehensive and nervous and then stated, "Ladies and Gentlemen, please join me on this very special occasion as I honor my best friend Mario LaGrande and his very pretty bride Pamela Mae in a very special and traditional Chinese way with three wishes. My first wish is for the couple to have a blissful marriage (百年好合 *bai nian hao he*), the second is to wish the couple everlasting eternal love (永浴爱河 *yong yu ai he*), while the final toast is for the couple to have a baby soon (早生贵子 *zao sheng gui zi*). "

Well, Joseph Wei's English and Mandarin Chinese toasts brought numerous smiles and lots of laughter in the ballroom of the "Hendricks

Mansion." Mario took the lead and bowed to Joseph and gave him a big "bear hug" which lifted Major Wei off the floor. Pamela Mae followed her husband and gave Joseph a warm embrace and kissed him on his right cheek. Major Joseph Wei's parents, Zhang and Linda Wei, were also in attendance; as they proudly observed and heard their son give the marital toast perfectly in "Mandarin Chinese."

Last but not least, the third toast of the evening would be the honor of Pamela Mae's benevolent father, John Brewer, who would give his salute in German and English.

"*Meine liebste Tochter Pamela Mae und mein neuer Schwiegersohn Mario, an die Braut und den Bräutigam, ich wünsche Ihnen Gesundheit, ich wünsche Ihnen Glück, ich wünsche Ihnen Reichtum – und alles, was Sie sich sonst noch wünschen können* (My Dearest Daughter Pamela Mae and new son-in-law Mario, to the bride and groom, may I wish you health, may I wish you happiness, may I wish you wealth and everything else you could wish for)! More importantly, may our Dear Lord Jesus bless and keep you both prosperous and safe and may I become a *Großvater* (Grandfather) next year. *Prost* (Cheers)!"

With a lot of joyful tears, Pamela Mae walked towards her father and gave him a long affectionate embrace and told him lovingly and humorously in German and English, *"Ich danke Dir Vater, Von ganzem Herzen* (I thank you, Father, with all my heart)!" She paused momentarily, smiled, and then continued saying, "I promise Mario and myself will do our best to give you a grandchild, starting tonight!" Both father and daughter shared smiles and giggles because of Pamela Mae's witty remarks.

Within fifteen minutes, there was a lively change in the atmosphere and mood when Christopher Russell and his younger sister Mindy Sue Russell got out their guitar, banjo, and fiddle. They began to play the contemporary "country and folk music" that was popular in the "Appalachian Mountains" and other sections of Dixie.

Christopher and Mindy Sue were so talented instrumentally that they could perform many of the well-known parlor and minstrel songs that were written by Stephen Collins Foster. Their music inspired a couple of the Hendricks' servants to join in and accompany the Russell's with a harmonica and a tambourine in a very enthusiastic manner.

The very "celebratory and spirited" music inspired numerous people to clap, dance, and sing along. During a short break, Gloria Faye approached her dear friend Pamela Mae and proposed that they perform a duet of Foster's famous song, "Old Folks at Home/Swanee River" and the gorgeous bride agreed.

After the ten minute break, Pamela Mae LaGrande held the right hand of Gloria Faye Brewer while they sang the complete song with the musicians playing wonderfully. At this point Mario LaGrande, Maurice Flambeau, Joseph Wei, and Marie Louise Yang were arm and arm and were swaying to the melodic music.

Many of the people listening and watching the duet were drawn to tears while Pamela Mae and Gloria Faye beautifully and sweetly sang,

"Way down upon the Swanee River, far, far, away, there's where my heart is turning ever, there's where the old folks stay."

It was now close to 11:00 p.m. on the first night of the winter of 1861, in Elk Garden Virginia. Christopher and Mindy Sue Russell played a new "Love Song Ballad" that they wrote together to commemorate the wedding of their wonderful cousin and bride, Pamela Mae, and her husband, Mario.

The newlyweds held one another close and had a very intimate conversation as Pamela Mae said endearingly, "Oh Darling, what a fabulous wedding day and night that we have had and I will cherish and remember every special moment spent together with you and our guests." Mario responded kindheartedly, "Sweetheart, you are the loveliest bride in the whole world and I will revere every amorous minute of this joyous day."

Pamela Mae responded sweetly, "Oh, my 'Handsome Vermont Cavalier,' I am your woman and wife and I will do everything I can to please you because I love you absolutely, completely, and totally. Amen!" Mario replied warmly, "My Lovely Virginia Lady, I am your man and husband and I will give you as much pleasure as humanly possible because I love you entirely, positively, and everlastingly. Amen!" Pamela Mae and Mario were dancing the last few steps of the final song of the night and they were sharing a very long amorous "French Kiss." They could clearly hear the ending stanza of the song.

Darling, the love I have for you is written in this song,

It is a love that is durable, resolute, and strong!
Honey, it is a love that will last for thousands of days,
An eternal love between Mario Patrizio and Pamela Mae!

At the conclusion of the music, Pamela Mae and Mario personally hugged and kissed individually all of their family members and guests. They expressed their sincere gratitude and gave their fondest regards to each person for honoring them with their presence and presents at their wedding.

Mario thought joyfully for a few moments upon the "Holy Day Christmas" that would be celebrated from December 24th – 25th, 1861, here in Virginia and throughout the world. He recalled the sacred words by Saint Alphonsus Liguori who wrote, *"Tu scendi dalle stelle, O Re del Cielo* (You came down from the stars, O King of Heaven).

Shortly thereafter, Major Mario Patrizio LaGrande escorted his exquisite and graceful wife, Major Pamela Mae LaGrande, and they ascended three steps upon the wide staircase. They both turned around and faced the single girls and women who were assembled near the landing. Pamela Mae then took the bouquet of flowers that was tied with a white ribbon and tossed the pretty blooms into the awaiting crowd. Unsurprisingly, Mindy Sue leaped up high and grabbed the bouquet out of the air as the audience applauded and celebrated the spectacular catch.

Pamela Mae and Mario were again holding hands and then continued their walk up the long stairs to the second floor of the "Hendricks Mansion." Midway down the long hall, Mario told his "pretty as a picture" bride, "My Lovely Virginia Lady, we have just accomplished another exciting and wonderful Mario and Pamela Mae wedding day adventure most happily and what a wonderful world, and I love you so very much!"

Our beautiful young woman smiled broadly from "ear to ear" and said naughtily, "Yes, and all is right with the world as we will have a new beginning, my 'Handsome Vermont Cavalier.' Now, in the next hour or so, we will begin our next exciting, gratifying, and marvelous adventure as we consummate our marriage a few times. Of course, this is necessary in order to procreate a grandchild as Papa proposed in his toast, and I love you so very much, too!"

At this point, Mario and Pamela Mae, our newlyweds, stood in front of the door that was open to the master bedroom. He picked up his cherished wife and held her in his loving and strong arms as they crossed the threshold. Mario carried Pamela Mae to the king-sized bed and laid her down in the middle. Mario looked into her angelic brown eyes and softly said in Italian and English, "Pamela *Bella, La Mia Incantevole Moglie* (Pretty Pamela, My Enchanting Wife), today, all my dreams and hopes have come true, and I adore you."

Pamela Mae looked up into his celestial blue eyes and responded gently in Spanish and English, "Mario Bello, *Mi Marido Encantador* (Handsome Mario, My Charming Husband), tonight, all of my dreams, hopes, and prayers, have come true, and I adore you, too!

The adventures, lives, and times of "Our Lovely Virginia Lady and Our Handsome Vermont Cavalier" and their "Epic Love Story for the Ages" will be continued...!

The End of Book Three

Bibliography/ References/Songs

01.Wikipedia- wikipedia.org, wikimedia.org, and Wikitree.com
02.American Battlefield Trust, Map- battlefields.org
03.Google Translate- translate.google.com
04.Merriam-Webster dictionary
05.King James Version of the Holy Bible
06."The Three Musketeers" by Alexandre Dumas; 1844
07."Napoleon's Art of War" by Napoleon Bonaparte
08."STAND AND FACE THE MORNING" by Helen Owens
09."J.E.B. Stuart's Birthplace" by Thomas D. Perry
10.Washington and Jefferson College, Historic Buildings Web Site
11."Train Song" by Jo Allison
12."Oh Susanna and Camptown Races "by Stephen Collins Foster
13.Carnifex Ferry Battlefield State Park- wvstateparks.com
14."Paul Revere's Ride" by Henry Wadsworth Longfellow
15.Largo Al Factotum, The Barber of Seville, by Gioachino Rossini
16.Henry IV, Part 1, by William Shakespeare
17.Mount Vernon Ladies Association

18. Oxford Dictionary
19. *L'amour est un oiseau rebelle*" by Georges Bizet.
20. "Amazing Grace" by John Newtown.
21. "O for a Thousand Tongues to Sing" by Carl Glaser and Charles Wesley
22. "Rock of Ages" by Augustus Toplady
23. "Aura Lea" by W.W. Fosdick and George R. Poulton
24. "Dixie"by Dan D. Emmett
25. "The Birthplace of Country Music Museum" in Bristol, Virginia
26. "The Tavern" in Abingdon, Virginia
27. "The Martha Washington Inn and Spa" in Abingdon, Virginia
28. Daughters of the American Revolution (DAR)
29. "The Virginia Housewife" by Mary Randolph
30. "Come Thou Font of Every Blessing" by Robert Robinson
31. "Old MacDonald had a Farm", by Frederick Nettingham and Thomas d'Ufrey
32. "Dein ist Mein Ganzes Herz" by Franz Lehár und Fritz Löhner-Beda
33. "Here Comes the Bride" by Felix Mendelssohn and Richard Wagner
34. "Swing Low, Sweet Chariot" Composer and Lyricist Unknown
35. "Faith of Our Fathers" by Frederick William Faber

36. "Old Folks at Home/Swanee River" by
Stephen Collins Foster
37. *"O Tannenbaum"* by Melchior Franck and
Ernst Anschutz
38. *"Tu Scendi dalle Stelle"* by Saint *Alphonsus
Liguori*

The Authors' Intent and Purpose

This novel piece of historical fiction is based on our mutual interest in reading and discussing history, knowledge of, and service in the U.S. Army. In addition, we have toured and visited many United States Civil War national and state battlefields, numerous historical markers, monumental locations, homes, and other properties. We are honoring both sides of the Mason-Dixon line, soldier men and women, free and slave, and family members and friends. The authors take our made-up characters and story based in part on our own experiences and personalities through some actual historical events with authentic people. We emphasize that Pamela Mae Brewer and Mario Patrizio LaGrande are fanciful characters in our books who we identify with intimately and personally and write about imaginatively. In addition, the "Saint Albans' Mountaineer Regiment" of the Vermont (Green Mountain) Infantry Brigade" and the "1st Manassas (Virginia) Infantry Regiment" of the "Virginia (Old Dominion) Infantry Brigade" are purely fictional Army Regiments and Brigades. The units did not participate in the United States Civil War. In addition, the actions and the conversations by the members of the Regiments and Brigades are purely from our mutual creative abilities. All of the individual fictional conversations, dreams, memories, and similar names are fabricated in order to enhance our story. However, in the book, Pamela Mae's great grandmother Elizabeth Garrett and her great great grandparents, Thomas and Sarah (Van Hook) Hendricks, are actually Pamela Bella's authentic real-life ancestral grandparents.

The sequence of actual events and chronological occurrences are based primarily on internet searches of Wikipedia sources. Additional information about the battles is from the American Battlefield Trust. All of the historical people are real, of course, but the additional characters and heroes of this story are fantastical in nature. We enjoyed telling this story in an entertaining novel and personal way, while enhancing the events and people who made history prior to the U.S. Civil War and during the first year of "The War Between the States."

About the Authors

I, Davidé Mario Romano (pen name), from the North, am a retired officer and a graduate of the United States Army Command and General Staff College. I have visited over twenty Civil War battlefields and read numerous historical books while researching countless aspects of military warfare and the exploits of many famous generals. I have been a factual editor, photographer, and writer for over thirty years while this trilogy of books is my first endeavor in historical fiction and novels. In addition, I am fluent and familiar with several languages as reflective in this multilingual story. Furthermore, my geographic expertise and travels throughout the United States and Europe has been influential in the completion of this literary work(s). Once I met Pamela Bella, I wanted to incorporate our romantic love for each other. We desire to transport us back in history, in the medium of a novel, to the Antebellum and Civil War time in America. In our three books, we become Mario Patrizio LaGrande and Pamela Mae Brewer in this novel manner.

I, Pamela Bella, turned my interest in writing an historical novel about romance and love during the tumultuous "Antebellum and Civil War" period. I met "My Handsome Cavalier" in 2018 and fell in love with him as we have traveled together. We have visited numerous Civil War battle sites which has given us the insight, knowledge, and motivation to personally transport us back in history and write these stories in a very personal loving manner. "Our Lovely Virginia Lady," Pamela Bella, is shown on the cover of all of our trilogy books.

Book Four Teaser

Our Lovely Virginia Lady and Our Handsome Vermont Cavalier Love Story Book Four: Photos, Poems, Recipes, and More will be a very unique book supplement to our Trilogy of published works. The talented Co-Authors, Davidé Mario Romano and Pamela Bella, wish to provide our loyal readers with a book they will enjoy as they get to see Pamela Mae in a diverse variety of Southern Belle dresses and gowns. In addition, a collection of the previous and new poems will further describe and detail the intense amorous and passionate love that existed between our two heroic and lead characters, Mario Patrizio LaGrande and Pamela Mae (Brewer) LaGrande. Furthermore, our accomplished writers will provide our devoted readers with delicious recipes and new exciting short stories that will delight one and all.

*Pamela Mae in her white winter cloak
outside on her wedding evening*

Made in the USA
Columbia, SC
07 May 2024